THE

REALM

OF

DARK AND

LIGHT

BOOK ONE:
THE SOURCE OF DARKNESS

The Realm of Dark and Light is a work of fiction;
any similarity regarding characters or incidents is entirely
coincidental.

Published in the United States by Riverhaven Books,
www.RiverhavenBooks.com

ISBN: 978-1-937588-17-5

Printed in the United States of America
by Country Press, Lakeville, Massachusetts

Edited by Edward Young, Riverhaven Books
Designed by Stephanie Lynn Blackman
Whitman, MA

THE
REALM
OF DARK
AND LIGHT
BOOK ONE:
THE SOURCE OF
DARKNESS

PATRICIA PERRY

Riverhaven Books

www.RiverhavenBooks.com

To Pookie:
from the ashes I have risen

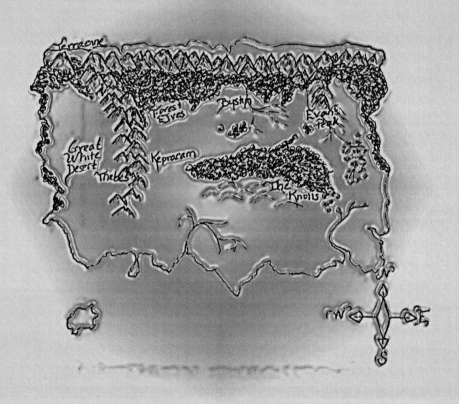

Also written by Patricia Perry

The Black Fairy and Other Fantasy Stories

The Realm of Dark and Light
Book Two: Escape From Caldon Island

Praise for The Realm of Dark and Light

This story grabbed me and held my interest to the very end!
…I decided to give fantasy one more chance. I was relieved when I realized I had made a good choice. There were surprises that got my adrenaline pumping, which is a key ingredient to a good read for me. It didn't take me long to be drawn into several of the complex and interesting characters. Soon, I found myself anxious to see how certain relationships would evolve, and curiosity took over. I had to find out more about their mysterious pasts. The message of the book is very real and relevant to real life, which is another reason why I was pleasantly surprised. The characters, story line, and extremely imaginative writing did not disappoint me!

Thomas Cirignano, Author
The Constant Outsider- Memoirs of a South Boston Mechanic

An excellent and well-told fantasy story
The Realm of Dark and Light is an excellent and well-told story, one which caught my interest on the first page and maintained its grip until the last. The characters are well defined and come to life as the tale progresses… The action-scenes and landscapes are finely detailed, allowing the reader to envision clearly the events taking place. Patricia Perry keeps the reader turning the pages, needing to find out what happens next. A very entertaining fantasy novel, one I thoroughly enjoyed. I believe she has a hit on her hands. I look forward to reading a great deal more of this author's work.

Brian R Hill, Author,
The Shintae and *Shadows From a Time Long Past*

The Realm of Dark and Light has an action fantasy story line with a strong mystery theme and an interesting romantic twist. This is no short novel…you'll be kept entertained for quite a while…the book expertly unfolds little tantalizing bits to the reader at just the right pace. *The Realm of Dark and Light* is a larger sized book that will take the reader on a fantasy adventure for many days.

Lillian Brummet, Book Reviewer, ldbrummet@yahoo.com

"…very well written…truly a great example of the triumph of human spirit over any possible unexpected evil…"

Steven Manchester, author *Twelve Months, Pressed Pennies*

Vivid and intricate…

As a reader and writer of mainly science fiction, I read this fantasy with an open mind. Immediately, I was struck with the colorful and vivid world and characters…The settings are rich and intricate and the characters, strong and compelling. I quickly connected with the central characters and found myself deeply caring for what happened to them. Intertwining with the good against evil central plot, there are a number of sub-plots, including romance and inter-cultural relationships…This is a clever and intricate story with fast-paced action, tragedy and a deep underlying sense of humanity. I recommend *The Realm of Dark and Light* and will look out for more offerings from Patricia Perry with interest.

Rod Glenn (UK), Author,
The King of America, Holiday of the Dead, Sinema 2

…I got drawn into the story to the point that I did not notice how long I had been reading. I not only wanted to know where and how the source of darkness was housed and how the leaders of the kingdoms would manage to overcome the evil forces that darkened the land, I couldn't help but care about the characters. I needed to know who survived and who died, and as the story drew to a close, I cried. I cried for the living and the dead...Whether you like action adventures, fantasies, or character-driven stories, read *The Realm of Dark and Light*.

Betsy Gallup

I found myself compelled to persevere… motivated by the strength of the primary characters and intriguing nature of the land created in *The Realm of Dark and Light*. The author creates absorbing characters that seem to stick with the reader long after the book has been closed.

Pamela Victor, Reviewer, Feathered Quill Reviews

PART I

ONE

She awoke to a deafening peal of thunder. Her heart raced with fright as she bolted upright and scanned the area with her saucer-shaped eyes. She was in an unfamiliar place with a vicious storm raging just beyond the entrance to the cave. Lightning streaked across the inky sky, illuminating rain intent upon beating the earth into submission. The wind shrieked and moaned as it, too, sought to punish the land. She shivered, more from the storm than from the cold seeping into her shelter. She pulled her knees up to her chest, struggling to remember what she was doing in such an inhospitable place during such a ferocious tempest. She stared around the cave.

The brief flashes of lightning lit up an area that was not very large but strewn with boulders, especially near the back. The air was dust free. The thought of the mountain being unstable, however, made her uneasy. Could a deafening clap of thunder loosen up more of the rocks, burying her in this stony crypt? She flinched as the sounds from outside took on a human timbre and slowly realized they were indeed human.

She cautiously approached the entrance, mindful of the driving rain, and cocked her head to the side. For several long minutes, all she heard were the noises caused by the storm. Then a faint cry reached her ears. She crawled forward to the very lip of the cave and squinted downward, staring at the wreckage loosened by the howling winds and rain. Flashes of lightning revealed nothing that could have been the source of that faint cry.

She was about to edge back into her sanctuary when a white-hot bolt exposed a hapless soul desperately clinging to an outcropping of stone several yards away. She immediately headed toward it, her fingers gripping whatever seemed remotely stable as she half-climbed, half-slid down the slope. A large chunk of rock skittered past her, nearly dislodging the desperate figure below. She redoubled her efforts, finally reaching the shape just as it lost its grip and descended a few more yards. She silently cursed to herself, grabbing its wrist before it could disappear into the black nothingness far below.

The touch seemed to bring the figure back from its acceptance of doom. It lifted its head upward. A burst of light illuminated a man's battered face. His eyelids drooped; spittle ran from his mouth as he gasped for air. Blood, diluted by the rain, trickled down his face. She yanked on his hand to catch his attention then pointed her head back up the way she had come. Something registered in his face. He offered her as much help as his exhausted body could give; clawing his way up the viscous side of the mountain. His hands bled from the effort and sharp objects blocking their upward progress tore their clothes.

He began to tire and she realized that if she had misjudged the entrance to the cave, she would not have the strength to help either of them the rest of the way. She glanced upward, forcing her eyes to stay open against the pounding rain long enough to find the cave- it was just a few more yards away. She pulled him with a short-lived energy. Mud oozed down over her, which the torrential rains washed away. A large boulder shifted somewhere overhead and began its descent showering the mortals with small stones and more dirt. She instinctively pressed herself against her exposed charge a mere second before it dropped onto the ledge next to them and splintered in half. Some of the razor sharp pieces bit into their flesh. She groped along the shelf then stared up toward the mouth of the cave; they were almost there. The storm intensified as if it meant to destroy them. Time, she knew, was not on their side. She dragged the benumbed man inside and fell in a heap beside him, instantly succumbing to her fatigue.

~

She woke hours later. It took a second or two for her to remember another being lay in the cave beside her. Flinching with pain, she propped herself up on her elbow. The faint light that managed to trickle into the cave revealed a jagged cut above the man's left eye, along both of his cheeks, and across the lower portion of his jaw. Bruises were widening under his skin, giving him a misshapen appearance. She worked hard to get his wet clothes off then gently examined his injuries. His wounds, to her relief, looked much worse than they were, but they needed attention nonetheless. She sighed then cast about for her belongings, hopeful that she had some items in her pouch that could help them both. She found some dried food, a set of clothes, several small briquettes, a few ointments and bindings, a small pot, and a spoon.

Necessity compelled her to dig a shallow depression in the dirt floor and light a briquette with some tinder from her pouch. She was both surprised and pleased that the small black chunk gave off as much heat as it did. It would take very little time to heat a pot of water. She spread her blanket then rolled the man onto it before cleansing his cuts and applying the balms, satisfied none of the injuries required binding. She placed her warm cloak over him, tucking the edges all along his body to keep him warm before checking herself for any damage. Other than a few lacerations and bruises, she was unscathed. She changed into some dry clothes then walked over to the entranceway to view the storm's destruction. Did anyone else seek shelter from the thunderstorm?

She stared at the uprooted skeletal trees and piles of rocks littering the landscape below. A reddish mud covered everything. She focused on the animals- some partially buried, others ripped apart by the force of the storm- that lay scattered in twisted heaps. She carefully left the cave and maneuvered past the overhanging ledge where she could get a better view but found only more of that same destruction. *No, not quite*, she thought spotting a lizard, its tail caught beneath a boulder. She removed a black knife from its sheath, crawled over to it, and beheaded the creature with one deft movement. She cut off the mangled tail and hefted the dead reptile over her shoulder. The sky darkened in a matter of minutes. She hurried back into the cave, glancing down at her companion before skinning the lizard and placing it on a makeshift spit over the fire.

The deluge began once more. She placed the pot outside to catch some rainwater then sat down beside the man to study him. He was lean yet strong, his hands bearing calluses and his skin tanned by the sun. He had slightly angular features, gracefully arching brows, and elegantly pointed ears. She lightly ran her fingertip over their curves several times wondering what sort of creature he was. He shifted in his sleep then opened his eyes.

"Sleep," she gently advised him.

He drifted off into an uneasy slumber. Fragmented images of the time just before the storm's onslaught filled his mind. He and his companions had been patrolling along the Broken Plain when the first dirty gray clouds blotted out the sun. Caught in the open, the group searched for shelter. They lost sight of one another when the sagging clouds disgorged their contents. He remembered distant shouts and the screaming of horses, but the chaos drowned out his voice. While he slept, every heartbeat marked a different memory. *Thump-thump.* He was climbing the unforgiving mountain, clawing for something, anything that would allow him to ascend to safety. *Thump-thump.* The remnants of a bush tore his flesh as he crawled over it. *Thump-thump.* He could still feel the burning sensation as the rocks cut his face and hands. His mind continued to assault him with the images until he finally drifted off into a fitful sleep.

Unaware of her companion's flood of disjointed memories, she rose and walked over to the entrance, crossing her arms as she leaned against the rock. The rain beat down upon the earth while she sought answers to who she was and why she was here. Had she been traveling to or from somewhere? Was her home nearby or far away? She had some provisions but not enough to last for very long. A change of clothes meant she would be away for a few days at least. Other than the stranger who slept behind her, she had been alone. The desolate plain below was not familiar either. Had she scaled the mountain seeking refuge from the impending storm? Was this a meeting place? If so, whom was she supposed to meet? She shook her head, trying to shake the knowledge loose but it refused to budge. The sizzling lizard broke through her thoughts. She crouched down beside it and poked at it with her knife: it was almost ready.

Her companion roused himself, grimacing in pain as he attempted to roll over onto his side. She helped him sit up, holding him in her arms while he drank a few sips of water.

"Who…who are…you?" he asked in a thick voice.

"A friend," she replied, trying to get as much food into him as possible before he went back to sleep. "What is your name?"

"Danyl…the others…"

"You were alone," she replied.

"Must…find…" He tried to rise but the parts of his body that did not hurt had no strength left.

"No. You must rest. There are no signs of anyone else out there, but that doesn't mean something happened to them."

The thought of his companions out in that storm troubled him greatly, but there was nothing either one of them could do right now. When the weather cleared and he recovered his strength, they could look for survivors. He finished a few more mouthfuls of food before lying down, his bleary gaze aimed toward the entrance.

She filled her stomach after he had eaten, then licked the grease from her fingers. They had supplies for a few days then she would have to hunt for food. If he did not get better before then, she would have to leave him alone and at the mercy of whatever ventured into the cave. The smell of decaying flesh would not long go unheeded by the scavengers. The weather, however, would provide some protection for the time being. She lay down beside him, placed her head upon her arm, and drifted off to sleep.

The next morning began as the previous one had but she was pleased at the progress Danyl was making. He became more active despite his vision problems. He painstakingly dressed himself while she surveyed the plains below.

"Can you see anyone out there?" he asked in a hoarse whisper.

"No."

"Twelve men cannot simply have vanished."

"The storm could have dispersed them."

"What if they are hurt? We have to look for them."

"Not while the storm still rages," she reminded him.

He squinted, willing his eyes to focus long enough to catch any movement below. All he could see were blurry forms devoid of color. It left him feeling disorientated no matter how hard he tried to concentrate. His only reward for his effort was a splitting headache and a queasy stomach. He swayed unsteadily on his feet, one hand gripping her arm while the other rubbed his throbbing forehead. Reason finally took root in his mind. He wanted to look for his companions but his body was not yet strong enough for such an undertaking.

"We need to leave…and soon."

"Why?" he asked.

"Wolves. I could hear them looking for food."

She shuddered. Even though there were plenty of dead animals, the predators preferred fresh meat. The wolves hid during the day and hunted at night. She and Danyl would have to increase their vigilance or become the wolves' next meal. She willed the sun to harden the muddy earth below to give them a chance to escape. Danyl lay down and closed his eyes to conserve as much strength as possible.

That night the wolves did come closer but they had not yet picked up their scent. It was a small consolation for they both knew their luck would not hold out. It finally stopped raining. The waterlogged ground placed them in a dire predicament: attempt to cross that sticky red morass or wait one more night and take their chances with the wolves. She had gauged the distance between the cave and the faint green tinge to the east during the day, judging it was perhaps a day's journey. He had insisted things were safe there, yet who knew how far the wolves would forage for a fresh kill.

Unable to sleep, they sat huddled together awaiting the dawn. Their bodies tensed when they heard the unmistakable sounds of large paws dislodging the loose debris outside the cave. He reached out and tapped her arm; both looked beyond the mouth of the cave. Danyl groped for his short sword, the only object he had not lost, while she unsheathed her blades. She eased closer toward the entrance, keeping in the shadows as best she could and listened for the sounds of death. She heard Danyl shift somewhere behind her as she caught sight of two silhouettes beyond the lip of the long, flat ledge to her right. A pair of wolves was passing by when they suddenly froze. The moon illuminated their outlines. The hair on their backs stood straight up; their ears lay back against their skulls. A low, sinister growl broke the silence. She barely breathed, fearful they would turn from their path but it was too late. The pair altered direction and skulked toward her, their yellow eyes rife with hunger and anticipation. She watched the pair split up and withdraw into the darkness. The hunt was on. The wolves' coarse, gray fur blended perfectly with the scraggly brush and rocks littering the mountainside. The murky night added to their invisibility. She squeezed the hilts of her knives, the feel of the cold metal reassuring. There was a moment of silence, one she recognized as only one thing: attack.

Her heart pounded in her chest as the shadows of death circled in front of the cave. Perspiration trickled down her face and neck as she nervously gripped her knives, all the while straining to hear any sound. She detected scraping claws moving across exposed rock and instinctively knew the wolves were close. Growling sounds preceded the charging pair as they lunged at her in unison, their fangs snapping at the air around her. Their merciless eyes were mere inches from hers. The thought of their jaws clamping down around her throat propelled her to slice at them with a desperate urgency. She sucked air in through clenched teeth as one clawed her thigh, an act she rewarded with a deep gash along its muzzle. Howling in pain, it charged at her with a renewed fury, splattering her with its blood as it thrust itself upon her.

She kept them from entering the cave for as long as she could, but one managed to sneak past, disappearing into the cave behind her. She could hear Danyl grunting while fighting the wolf. She had her hands full with the wolf trying to rip her apart. She buried the blades in its neck then yanked them upward. The beasts' decapitated head dropped next to its still twitching carcass. She kicked the beast once then turned to help her companion, the eerie silence issuing forth from the darkness stealing her breath.

Danyl's keen hearing and the faint light spilling into the cave offered him some hope as the fuzzy shadow surged toward him. The wolf with the gash across its jaw moved purposefully, yet unsteadily forward, the need to feed outweighing the pain. Although injured, the wolf sorely tested Danyl's weakened condition. Every time he dodged the beast, its fetid breath threatened to overwhelm him. He hacked at the creature until he finally brought the blade down into its skull. He dropped to his knees, gulping in air as the remainder of his strength dripped off his body along with his sweat. He could barely hear the woman calling to him from the front of the cave.

"Danyl?" she cried out tentatively at first, then with a sense of panic. "Danyl!"

"I'm fine: the wolf is dead."

She found him on his knees before the wolf, breathing hard as the tip of his sword rested in a pool of blood on the ground. She dropped down beside him, placing her arms around his shoulders.

The thought of being alone again was too much to bear. Danyl let the hilt slip from his hands and gripped her tightly. His keen hearing had helped him win the battle, but the amount of energy it had cost him was very unsettling. Other wolves would undoubtedly come and he would not have the ability to fight them. As soon as the sun came up, they would have no choice but to leave. Would he be able to cross the plains? She certainly would not be able to carry him nor would he be able to outrun the wolves if the creatures pursued them.

"We are out of choices, Danyl," she began in hushed tones, fearful of attracting another unwanted visitor. "We must leave at daybreak or we will die here when night comes. Do you have the strength to get across the plains?"

"Yes," he lied.

They ate out of need, ignoring the dead wolves she had dragged into the far corner of the cave. She packed up her few belongings as they waited for the sun to rise. The hours seemed like days, and they often started at the imaginary sounds of paws dislodging rocks outside the cave. They managed to find comfort in each other as the night slowly gave way to daybreak.

"You never told me your name," he whispered into her ear.

"If we survive then I will tell it to you," she said, wishing she knew what it was and wondering if she would ever remember it.

"Why not now? After all, you did save my life."

"I have only prolonged it, Danyl. We must still cross the plains. How is your vision?"

"Blurry. The rest of me is strong enough, I suppose. By the way," a hint of mischievousness laced his words, "did you peek?"

"What?"

"When you took my clothes off."

"I took no unwarranted liberties, if that's what you mean." She couldn't help but smile. "You shouldn't talk, Danyl. Save all your strength for the crossing."

They both silently begged for the sun to hasten into the sky where it would dry the land and give them a chance to live another day. It did indeed rise but in a way neither one could have imagined. The sun began to bake the earth with such intensity that steam rose from the abused land. They felt the heat even in the relative coolness of the cave and dreaded having to face it once they left their shelter.

It was finally time to leave and so began the difficult descent down the mountain. The storm had spared nothing. The pair crawled over debris or scampered downhill on their backsides. She held Danyl's hand, guiding him down the rough terrain. By the time they reached the bottom of the mountain, it was already mid-morning. This left them with precious little time to make the crossing to the greenish haven miles away.

Beads of perspiration ran down their faces as the sun baked the earth. Rifts great and small spread out along the plain making for treacherous footing. Both stumbled as the brittle ground beneath their feet gave way. She ripped her extra tunic into sections, covering their heads for protection. They could do nothing against the nasty black flies, which appeared out of nowhere once they reached level ground. The insects had been feasting on the rotting carcasses but they, like the wolves, preferred to suck the blood from the living. The pests swarmed around them, invading every moist part of their bodies where they landed and bit at will. It became almost impossible to shoo them away. They adjusted their head coverings to deal with the constant annoyance as best they could.

Within an hour, a reddish dust rose from the parched earth, intensifying with every step and puff of wind. The flies hated it and left to harry some other creature. Their relief was soon short lived. The dust infiltrated everything and they could not speak without coughing. She kept a careful eye on Danyl, touching his hand as it rested on her arm to confirm he was still able to continue.

The sun began its descent, elongating their shadows until the silhouettes stretched grotesquely ahead of them. They did not stop, even when she handed him the canteen. He rinsed out his mouth before taking a deep swallow, an act she repeated. They managed to plod on and, as evening approached, reached the line of scraggly trees. There was a change in the air as they stepped off the rust-colored plains and entered the greenery. It was much cooler and fresher beneath the branches, the sound of running water reaching their ears. They both glanced over their shoulders at the nightmare they had left behind and, for the first time, felt as if they had a chance to survive.

"Do you want to stop and rest, Danyl?"

"No, not here...by the water," was his raspy reply.

They were both exhausted, ready to plunge into the cool water, but they needed to make sure the region was safe. She settled him onto a fallen log then made a quick search of the area. Satisfied that they were safe, she returned and helped him to the stream. They splashed water on their faces and necks, the refreshing liquid reviving them. She filled her canteen and shared the last of her food with him. Fish surfaced to feed on the flies; with any luck, one would fry in her pan later on.

"How well do you know this area?"

"Fairly well." His voice sounded hoarse. "There are villages to the north and east...patrols use this area to water their horses."

"What kind of patrols?"

"Elves."

"Like you?" she asked after a long pause, her gaze drawn to his ears.

"Yes...I thought you knew?" He strained to see her features

but could only distinguish vague shapes and little color. He couldn't think of any race that didn't know about the elves.

"I'll look for a safe place for us to spend the night while you catch your breath." With that, she turned and searched for an easily defensible location, the wolves never far from her thoughts.

She found a suitable place about a hundred yards up a little hill. Hemmed in by pine trees, its sides were steep enough to deter an invader. She went back and led him up to their shelter. She broke several boughs, placing them on the ground for cushioning, the makeshift bed a vast improvement over the unyielding rock of the cave.

"Here... you are already half asleep."

She smiled, his eyes closing the moment he lay down. She pulled the blanket over him and watched his chest steadily rise and fall. Sleep eluded her until her mind and body gave in to her exhaustion. She curled up against his slumbering form for warmth; his nearness offered her some measure of comfort. He shifted in his sleep and placed his hand upon her arm.

She rested her hand within his, her mind grappling with the fact that even though she had no clue about her past, her presence in the cave had preserved their future. They were not meant to die on that mountain or while they crossed the plains. What fate had in mind for them down the road was unknown, but she hoped it would not end within this piney hollow.

She awoke at dawn, more tired than refreshed. Danyl, too, began to stir and gave her a little smile of encouragement before rising stiffly. He stretched out his cramped muscles, squinting to take in his surroundings. She stared at his face, noting that his cuts had formed scabs. The swelling from the fly bites was beginning to shrink and his eyesight, she surmised, would improve in a few days.

"I'll try to find something to eat," she said while brushing the leaves and dirt off her clothes.

"You'll find a root growing beneath low bushes with long slender leaves...they have frilly tops and a deep reddish color. They require a bit of digging but are quite good."

"I promise I'll return with something," she replied.

She began to search the area for the shrubs, keeping alert for any woodland animal she might be able to catch while staying within sight of the shelter. The patrols he spoke about would have been a welcome sight, but as the day passed, she realized they might not be so fortunate. He wanted to be with his people and she needed to learn about herself. *Which direction should she travel? Where was her home? What if she had come from beyond the Broken Plain?* She noticed the bush Danyl had described, the leafy tufts clustered beneath droopy branches. It took a lot of effort to dig up the slender tubers but she managed to extract a few. Meat would be a welcome bonus.

She hid behind some bushes and waited. A rabbit appeared to her right, its nervous little nose testing the air before nibbling on the grass. She withdrew her blade, estimated the distance between them and then threw the dagger. Her aim was true, the weapon pinning the startled hare to the ground. She pulled the knife from the creature, slit its throat and picked up her prize.

The unmistakable sounds of hooves thudded hollowly just beyond the stand of trees ahead of her. She squatted amid the bushes, unsure of who approached or what to expect. The undergrowth blocked her view. She peered over at the shelter, silently pleading for Danyl to remain hidden. The seconds ticked by; the roots and rabbit forgotten as she waited for the strangers to break through the hardwoods. They rode cautiously around the area. She absorbed every detail as they came closer, remaining motionless as they dismounted.

They were dressed in greens and browns. Their sleek horses had reins of braided leather and well-oiled saddles atop plain brown blankets. Bows, arrows, short swords, and numerous small daggers strapped to their legs and arms marked them as a formidable group. She noted their arched brows and pointed ears: they were elves. They had come to search for Danyl to take him back home. One elf in particular stood out from the rest. His sturdy frame and uncompromising demeanor commanded a great deal of respect. His piercing dark eyes scrutinized everything leaving her with the impression that little, if anything, escaped

12

his attention.

A part of her wanted to break out from her concealment and lead them to Danyl, but she resisted. She watched as they split up, each pair searching the area for any danger while calling out Danyl's name; their routine was precise and well practiced. The leader moved toward the hill, attracted by the broken twigs and flattened grass. His hand rested on his weapon as he peered into the semi-darkness. He shouted an unfamiliar word then waited for a response. The reply was immediate. She spotted Danyl as he stumbled down from the hill, smiling as he greeted his companions. She was grateful he was with his own folk but saddened, too. She would now be alone. She watched as two of his companions stayed with him while the others began to look for her. She remained hidden, unwilling to expose herself. She should have met with them, told them what had happened, and then gone her own way. She could see Danyl arguing with his comrades, gesturing back toward the shelter while they tried to urge him onto a horse. The disagreement finally ended with Danyl mounting the steed and reluctantly following his companions through the trees and out of her line of sight.

She waited until they were gone, emerging with roots in one hand and the rabbit in the other. Her eyes never left the point where the riders had disappeared from view.

"Most people would welcome a chance to leave this place…why not you?" A voice called out to her from behind.

She jumped in shock; dumbfounded that she had failed to see one of the elves sneak around behind her. She dropped her dinner and drew her knives in response. She stared at the stocky brown elf with the expressionless face then slipped the daggers back into their scabbards. She scooped up her meal, her eyes locked with his dark ones as they studied her from top to bottom.

"You startled me."

"Answer my question."

"I must go my own way," she replied.

"You have done a great service to my kin by saving Danyl and must be rewarded."

"I need no reward…all I care about is that he is alive."

13

"I am called Lance. You will be welcomed if you ever travel to Bystyn." He turned to leave but she stopped him.

"Lance? I ask that you keep this between us."

"Why?"

"I don't really know. I just need to take care of a few things first," she stated as candidly as she could.

"If we meet again in Bystyn that might change. What are you called?"

"That's one of the things I need to find out," she said quietly before heading back to the shelter.

Lance stared after her for some time. There was nothing in her demeanor to alarm him but he did have several questions he wanted to ask her. *Why was she here? What was she doing along this cursed plain? Did she know whom she had saved? Why did she refuse any sort of recognition for her act?* Perhaps Danyl had answers to some of these questions or maybe she would reveal them if they ever met again. Lance whistled for his horse, mounted it in a single fluid motion, and rode after his men.

She watched him ride away through the trees, feeling completely alone for the first time. The hare and roots dangled from her hands. The afternoon light began to lengthen her shadow while she stared at the now abandoned area. She should have gone with them. Her stomach began to growl, diverting her attention to the details at hand. She made a small depression in the ground, placed a briquette into it, and then erected a spit for the rabbit. She watched it cook, absently munching on one of the vegetables, its flavor tangy and sweet. She ate the entire animal then climbed up the hill to sleep. She was about to roll herself up in the blanket when she spotted a pouch a few feet away. Curious, she opened it and smiled: the elves had left enough food to last many days. She pulled the generous gift up to her body and drifted off into a restless sleep.

TWO

She awoke as the sun poked over the horizon, ate, then packed up her things. She headed down to the stream, washing the sleep from her eyes before heading east. She walked through the trees and low brush until the land opened up, offering her a spectacular view. To the north and many leagues away was a dark forest line. It extended to the northern borders of the plains in the west and as far to the east as she could see. Behind them were the majestic snow covered peaks that even from this distance seemed to touch the sky. The southern section of the land sloped away behind a series of rolling hills. The eastern portion lured her with its wide expanse and clusters of budding hardwood trees. The earth was beginning to awaken from its long winter slumber. There would still be crisp nights and chilly mornings but spring reclaimed the land. She smiled, hiked her provisions over her shoulders, and headed east. She would have plenty of time to think along the way and maybe, just maybe, she would run into Danyl again.

The road to Bystyn took longer than she had anticipated even though the journey itself was pleasant enough. The farther east she traveled, the more people she encountered. Many swept out the dust and gloom of winter from their homes while others prepared their fields for planting. She inhaled the aroma of freshly turned earth and reached out to touch the tiny leaves on the branches, their velvety feel a balm to her travel-weary soul. She slept beneath their protective boughs and hunted among them for fresh food. She hadn't been able to recall anything from her past, but the beauty and serenity of the land compensated for her disappointment. She greeted a farmer and his wife as they crossed in front of her, politely declining their invitation to join them for a meal. The farmer's wife dug into her basket and handed her a loaf of bread and a block of cheese. She gratefully accepted them and placed them into her empty pouch. She waved to the couple as they continued on their way.

It had been more than two weeks since she had left the plains. The land before her spread out, undulating in gentle green waves as the wind blew over knee-high grasses. The stands of ash, oak, and maple trees were alive with birdsong and small animals scurrying along the branches. Many patrols had been traveling the road making her wonder if such vigilance was a normal occurrence. Their faces, like those of the group that rescued Danyl, were firmly set.

She crested a small line of hills a few hours later, stopping at the top to gaze down below. Less than a mile away stood a sight she that left her speechless. An expansive and impregnable yet wholly inviting structure rose from the middle of the verdant plain. Its walls were built of gray stone blocks; its massive front gates thrown open wide. A myriad of wagons, people, and horsemen entered and exited. Four monumental towers stood at the corner of the solid walls; a series of buttresses leaned out from the battlement at intervals between them. Sentinels walked along the ramparts keeping watch over the steady stream of people coming and going; their weapons glinted in the sunlight. A series of low trees covered in pink and white blossoms extended from the eastern wall to a copse of pine trees to the east. A silver current wound its way near the pines, flowing slightly south then west before resuming its easterly course. The abundant vegetation growing along the banks of this river was visible even from her vantage point. Farmlands beyond the river were collections of deep browns separated by low rock walls. The snow covered peaks she had seen from the edge of the Broken Plain towered over the city in the north, their precipitous sides a deterrent to anyone who sought to scale them. *Was this Bystyn?* She looked up and noticed the sun already beginning to descend. The initial excitement at finding the city gave way to reality. Her aching body and growling stomach demanded appeasement. She needed to find a place to eat, sleep, and bathe but had nothing with which to pay for any of those amenities. She decided to take a chance and headed toward the vast complex nestled amid the grassy plain.

16

The sun hung midway in the late afternoon sky as she entered the gate. She felt overwhelmed by its width and depth as she walked beneath it. Shadows swallowed her up mid-way through the gate's corridor; the permanent chill seeped out of the stones making her shiver. Two wagons and four horsemen riding abreast passed by each other and still there was plenty of room for at least another cart. A second wall stood just inside the outer one where barracks and stables were located. The area in between the walls was bustling with activity. Elves worked at several large stones, busily sharpening swords, lances, and other weapons. Blacksmiths banged away on their anvils, the clanging reverberating off the thick walls. Elves groomed their horses; cartloads of provisions were unloaded, the heavy sacks forcing the bearers to walk at odd angles. She finally entered the city proper, following the main avenue as it ran straight ahead.

Shops claimed the prime spots along this road; an occasional inn or tavern was situated between them. The cobblestone streets were clean and well maintained, even with the constant traffic. The elves took great pride in their homes and city. She passed a bakery and inhaled the aromas wafting out into the street, the distinct fragrance of honey-drizzled baked goods somehow eliciting one tiny memory: her name. It came to her as a voiceless whisper from deep within her mind, leaving her grateful that at least she now had something to call her own. She lingered in front of the shop for so long, the proprietor waddled out and placed one of the delicacies into her dirty hand.

"The first batch is always the best," he said with a smile.

"I can't pay you for this."

The baker winked at her then retreated into his sweet realm. She stared at the pastry covering her entire hand, her stomach imploring her to devour it. It gurgled with anticipation as she brought it up to her lips. The treat was still warm, the sugary coating soft to the touch and the cake still springy. It was her first bite of food since the previous morning.

She nibbled on the cake, scanning the street for inns. She went to all of the inns in the city yet none could offer her a room. She had nothing to pay for the lodging and, considering there were plenty of helping hands, she realized her luck had run out. The late afternoon turned to early evening. She burped up the treat; it was all she had eaten. The provisions the elves had left for her were long gone. A chilly breeze drifted through the streets as the sun descended. It was time to abandon the city and seek refuge along the riverbank.

Standing in the middle of the city where the two main streets intersected, she looked around one last time for a place of lodging. No signs greeted her tired eyes. An inviting set of steps urged her to sit for just a few moments before heading out into the night. She sat down on the broad stair, ignoring the trellis and bright green shutters flanking the windows. Her body ached; she leaned her forearms on her knees. She rested her head on her arms. The street sounds diminished; the hardness of the stone stair no longer bothered her. The distant whisperings in her mind became muffled.

"Excuse me," a voice called out from somewhere beyond the haze of exhaustion, "may I help you?"

Was someone speaking to her? Who would address her? She was a stranger here…looking for shelter and a hot meal…sitting on a step. She was so tired…couldn't she just rest for a few more minutes?

"Young woman," the voice gently persisted.

Sophie looked down upon the dirty bundle of rags with pity, for the woman who wore them was too weary to lift her head. Sleeping on her front steps, however, was out of the question. She watched the woman slowly rouse herself and glance up, the dark circles under her puffy eyes noticeable even through the dust clinging to her skin.

"I'm very sorry, good woman," she managed to say. "I was just resting for a moment."

She struggled to stand then headed down the avenue. Sophie watched her leave, the prospect of finding any lodging in the city nonexistent. People poured into the city this time of year to be with friends and family and to participate in the spring festival. This girl needed a break.

"Wait," she called out to her. "You may stay here for a night

18

or two."

"I have no money but I will gladly lend my services to you in payment."

"I do have a few things that need attending to around here. I am Sophie. And you?"

"Ramira."

"Good: first a bath then a change of clothes, some food, and sleep. When was the last time you ate or slept in a bed?"

Ramira's appearance was dull: shades of brown, gray, and red covered her from head to toe. Sophie's kindness rejuvenated her a little, the thought of food and a bath chasing away some of her fatigue.

"A treat from the baker a few hours ago and I cannot remember the last time I slept in a bed," replied Ramira following Sophie into the kitchen at the back of the house.

It was cozy here, the smell of freshly baked bread and a simmering stew making her mouth water. She pulled off her cloak, placing it and her things beside the fireplace. Sophie disappeared into a chamber behind the large stone hearth. The sound of running water brought a smile to Ramira's face. Sophie reappeared briefly, nodding for her to sit while she fetched a clean set of clothes from upstairs. Sophie walked back into the kitchen and handed Ramira the clothes. She ushered her into the bath chamber.

"There's plenty of hot water, Ramira," she called through the door. "By the looks of you, I figure you'd need a bit more than one tubful."

Sophie had been correct in her assessment. Ramira ended up filling the tub twice more, the dirt she had accumulated over the past few weeks stubbornly refusing to yield to the washcloth. The infrequent washings in a river or stream had done little to keep her clean. Her clothes stank and needed mending, too, but she would leave those chores for tomorrow. She remained in the tub for as long as she could, then left the tepid waters and dressed. Her appetite was next on the list. She combed out her long hair letting it hang loosely down her back. She accepted a mug of tea from Sophie, and drank the dark liquid with great relish.

Sophie placed her hands on her hips and studied the girl, amazed at what the absence of filth revealed. She scrutinized Ramira's subtle bronze-hued skin, amethyst eyes, and long red-gold hair. Her brows arched elegantly upward like the elves, but her ears were rounded. Ramira had entered Sophie's home a dirty stray, emerging from the bath a polished young woman.

"You are beautiful, Ramira."

"I am clean, Sophie, and that is far better."

"Sit." Sophie invited her to the table where bread, cheese, and a bowl of stew awaited her.

Ramira ate until she thought she would burst, her embarrassment quickly erased by Sophie's words.

"Don't worry, child, you'll have worked that off and more by the time you finish with my list of chores!"

"You are too kind, Sophie."

"Repeat that to me tomorrow," she said with a gentle chuckle, pouring them both a glass of wine. "What brings you to Bystyn?"

Ramira gazed into the ruby red contents of the goblet, the bath and food beginning to sap the last of her strength. Sophie needed reassurance that she had not let a dangerous stranger into her home. Unfortunately, Ramira had little information to offer her.

"I'm afraid I cannot tell you much about myself," began Ramira quietly. "I came from the west but can't remember exactly who I am or where I came from. As to why I ended up in Bystyn…well…it was a destination as good as any other place. I was hoping I would be able to recall some things along the way but the only thing I could recollect was my name."

"Did you have an accident?" asked Sophie.

"I don't know," she replied honestly.

There were no apparent lies or deceptions in her words or tone of voice. Ramira sat quietly at the table waiting for Sophie's judgment. Her hands lay folded in her lap while she fought to keep her eyelids from closing. Sophie's gaze shifted from Ramira to the darkness gathering outside beyond the patio.

"How long have you been traveling, Ramira?"

"A little more than two weeks." She drained her glass,

straining to keep her eyes open.

Sophie decided any further questions could wait and suggested Ramira get some rest. Sophie began to lead her up the stairs when Ramira caught her sleeve.

"If you feel uncomfortable with me here…"

"Nonsense, girl. If I thought that I would never have let you into my house." She led her to a room at the end of the narrow hallway and opened the door. "There's a basin, a dresser, and a chest with extra blankets. I'll look in on you in the morning. Sleep well, Ramira."

"Thank you, Sophie," she replied as the woman left the room. She walked over to the balcony, peering through the curtains at the garden below. Ramira wondered why she kept such a delightful room for guests instead of for herself. She headed over to the bed and slipped between the warm quilt and fresh linens, immediately falling into a deep sleep.

Sophie did not waken Ramira, letting her sleep out her exhaustion. She washed her clothes and blanket, hanging them out in the fresh spring air then decided to launder her pouch as well. She was surprised to see it was of elven handiwork. Ramira had mentioned she had been on the road for more than two weeks, approximately the time it would take to reach Bystyn on foot from the Broken Plains. There had been bits of caked-on reddish mud in her blanket and cloak. It wasn't a significant amount but the only place to find that type of soil was along the Broken Plain. Danyl had traces of it on his person as well. Did she meet up with Danyl and the scouts somewhere along the way? They would have shared supplies with anyone who needed them, especially in that unpleasant land. Ramira would have encountered dozens of homesteads, villages, and patrols along the way, any one of which could have furnished her with provisions.

Sophie believed Ramira when she confessed she had no memory of her past, but she evidently remembered the last few weeks. Perhaps she should invite Danyl and Lance to her home, pitting their reactions – or lack thereof – against her theory. Sophie suddenly chided herself for meddling in things that were none of her business. Her days were full enough of things requiring her attention without investigating this little mystery. She stared at the pouch in her hands then out to the things dangling from the line and back again. She sighed and finished her task, her mind on the mysterious creature sleeping in her house.

Ramira entered the kitchen in the late morning feeling refreshed, but upset because she had slept so long. She accepted the strong cup of tea Sophie handed to her, uncomfortable when she spotted her belongings draped on the clothesline.

"I would have done that, Sophie," she protested.

"It is done, besides, they were borderline foul," she said with a little laugh.

"I noticed that after I left the bath last night," she confessed, her nose wrinkling up in distaste.

"My daughter, Anci, will be back this afternoon and will take care of her chores but," she handed Ramira a pair of leather gloves, "you get to clean out the woodshed. The broom is behind the door and don't waste any time, more wood will be delivered early this afternoon."

Ramira nodded, eager to begin repaying Sophie for her kindness. She walked to the side of the house, unlatched the rough-hewn door, and entered the little hut. Sunlight squeezed through the cracks, illuminating the dust launched into the air by her entry. The cloud of dirt made her eyes water. She opened the windows, propping them up with slats of wood to get a better view. Most of the wood was gone leaving her to contend with a few pieces toward the back and piles of bark. She finished the task then pulled out enough slivers from her arms to start a roaring fire.

She went into the kitchen and poured herself a glass of water, drinking down the refreshing liquid in just a few gulps before refilling her glass. Sophie's kitchen was cozy with plants and herbs on the windowsills; bright copper pots and pans hung from hooks on the wall. A rocking chair rested on a braided rug in front of the hearth; its back bowed slightly outward and the finish on its arms was worn away.

Sophie appeared laden with baskets of food and other items,

bunching the plaid tablecloth as she pushed the container toward the middle of the table.

"You seem too content, Ramira, I think you need more work to do!"

"I am at your service," replied Ramira. She helped unload the purchases, wondering how long her good fortune was going to last before Sophie asked her leave.

"You'll have a busy day tomorrow," began Sophie as she put away the stores. "I am sending you to an elderly couple beyond the orchards who need a few things done for them. Jack and Ida will appreciate the help for their sons are currently out on patrol to the west." *Your absence will also give me a chance to do some snooping*, she thought.

"When do I leave?" asked Ramira with some measure of comfort. The extra work was a hopeful sign that she would be able to stay a while.

"At sunrise, no lounging in bed until most of the day has already passed by," she playfully chided her.

"I'll try," she joked.

"Ah...hello Anci."

Anci entered the kitchen, her glance lingering on the stranger helping her mother. Anci's slim form seemed to get lost within her mother's ample embrace. She brushed back her auburn hair and smiled as Sophie introduced her to Ramira. Anci studied Ramira, her brown eyes glancing questionably at her mother without any hint of discourtesy to their guest. Ramira noted the slightly pointed ears yet Sophie's were as rounded as hers were. Anci's elven blood flowed more strongly through her veins.

They chatted while finishing the last of the chores, Anci talking amiably about her day. She was young and spoke of innocent delights, her exuberance bringing smiles to the women's faces. Sophie mended some clothes after supper, keeping a watchful eye on Anci as she worked on her studies. Ramira poured a cup of tea and sat on the terrace behind the kitchen, a wrought iron fence covered in climbing rose vines providing privacy from the neighbors. Clay pots of varying sizes stood against the wall, the seedlings poking up over the rims.

As night descended, the city quieted as its inhabitants settled into their homes. Ramira noticed dark shadows slowly undulating in the gentle breeze and remembered her things were still hanging outside. She drained her mug and retrieved them, folding the items on the way back to the kitchen. She stifled a yawn, nodded sleepily at Sophie and Anci and then went upstairs to bed.

"It's not like you to take in strangers, Mother," Anci stated in a matter of fact tone, wondering why Sophie had taken Ramira in.

"She was worn out and I couldn't see her spending all those nights in the woods."

"It's odd that she can't remember much about herself."

"Things happen, Anci. I don't believe she is a bad person or I would never have let her stay, besides, we could really use an extra pair of hands around here."

"True."

"Anyway, I am really looking forward to the spring festival; it's been such a long and dreary winter. It'll be nice to meet up with friends we haven't seen in a while." Sophie leaned back in the rocking chair, her sewing forgotten. The frigid days and icy nights became distant memories, replaced with balmy winds and sun warmed skin. Flowers, not icicles, adorned homes and birdsong, not silence, greeted them at dawn and dusk.

"It'll be a great way for Ramira to learn more about the city and its people, too," said Anci.

"Perhaps." Her daughter's voice pulled her from her reverie. "Will you be done with your studies before the festival?" Sophie eyed Anci, then her books.

Sophie put away her mending, her thoughts on the woman sleeping above them. Maybe the festival would invoke a memory or two but even if it didn't, she was sure Ramira would thoroughly enjoy the celebration. She rose from her chair and pulled a few dead leaves off the plants over the fireplace, closing her eyes as she inhaled the fragrant aroma.

~

Ramira walked down the main avenue at sunrise the next morning, laden with a knapsack full of things for Jack and Ida. She was eager to explore more of this wonderful place. The only open shop belonged to the baker. Lights shone through many of the curtained windows as the elves began to prepare for the day. She reached the gate, the guards acknowledging her as she passed by. Ramira was about to step upon the plain when a group of riders exited behind her. Shadows clung to the gray stonework of the tunnel-like gate, yet she could still make out the profile of one of the riders. She had spent hours studying it in the semi-darkness, tracing the lines and curves with her fingers while he slept. The empty feeling she had experienced when he rode away with the scouts began to disappear, replaced with contentment and relief. She paused, the subconscious purpose of her trek to Bystyn fulfilled. She dropped her gaze as he started to turn toward her, but the horses exited the gate before he could get a good look at her. Ramira stared after him for a few moments, remembering the cave and the urgent trek across the Broken Plain. She shivered involuntarily as her mind replayed the death duel with the wolves, the flies, and dust. Watching Danyl's shadowy form pass by made all of those terrible things worthwhile.

~

She headed east, the low-lying silhouettes in front of her becoming more distinct as the sun burned the fog from the land. The river began to sparkle with life as the first rays of the sun ignited the water until it appeared composed of molten silver. Birds and small, furry creatures, freed from the long winter, chirped and scurried beneath the growing light, their cacophonous enthusiasm greeting the promising day. Her eyes absorbed every nuance around her; her spirit reveled in the rebirth of the land. The landscape offered her a measure of calm and serenity. Her pack may have been heavy but it certainly could not weigh down her eagerness. The sun chased away the shadows and mist, exposing a vast orchard to her left and the tree-lined river to her right. The bright green grass felt soft beneath her boots, the spring flowers dotting the land adding color to the rich meadow. She spotted the house as she broke through the orchard. The diminutive couple greeted her warmly as she stepped up onto the porch, grateful for Sophie's gifts and Ramira's eagerness to help.

~

Danyl glanced briefly over his shoulder at the silhouette walking away from the city; a peculiar sensation washed over him. He shrugged, the indistinct impression fading away the farther he and his companions traveled west. He recalled the words spoken at last night's meeting. The strange set of circumstances taking place in the west prompted the elves to increase their vigilance. Cooper, King of the Race of Man, kept a tepid relationship with Bystyn, usually sending an emissary to feign a connection with the elves. His ambassador was four weeks overdue. Elven patrols scouting the land abutting Cooper's city, Kepracarn, had seen no activity. This was an oddity considering his people should be preparing their fields and homes this time of year. Herkahs, the feared desert nomads who had been man's sworn enemy for hundreds of years, were rarely seen. Their sudden appearance coupled with the absence of men initially drew a grave picture. The Herkahs, however, avoided the Kepracarnians as much as possible. The probability of the nomads having eradicated the Kepracarnians was nonexistent. He pursed his lips, wondering if a Herkah had saved his life that terrible night on the mountain. He wished he could remember more of what had transpired, often trying to will any images to form in his mind. The only things he could recall were the hungry creatures and the flight over the wretched plains. That and the fact his rescuer was a woman. He owed her a great debt and would forever rue the fact he could not repay her.

He kept his thoughts to himself as they continued to ride on, his preoccupation keeping him silent during most of the journey. They met up with another group of scouts around mid-morning, listening to their brief report before sending them on to the city. Everything was now strangely quiet in the west, the elusive black garbed desert dwellers vanishing without a trace.

"They come and go with purpose," stated Lance.

"Yes, but why? What do they want?" asked Danyl of no one in particular.

"They are not a group of people eager to share such information," replied Lance. "Perhaps Nyk will have learned more."

Danyl nodded, hoping his older brother, who had traveled to the northwestern corner of the plains, would bring back more information. He had departed the previous week, following the vast forest that ran along the foothills of the mountain range to the north. Nyk and his men had to be cautious as they passed by the farthest section of forests for the Khadry, a distantly related group of elves, inhabited that land. There had been little contact with them over the course of the millennium. When they did cross paths, it usually ended in an uncomfortable standoff and even bloodshed. Time had blurred the focal point of their disagreement. Danyl thought it had something to do with the king's refusal to allow the Lords of the Houses to build their own domains. Alyxandyr, the first elven king, wanted to construct one city for them all. The Khadry, afraid of losing their influence, chose to set out on their own rather than accept a ruler not of their choosing. Danyl believed such a split and the ensuing ill will served no purpose whatsoever, especially since the first king had no intentions of stripping the Khadry of their prestige.

They rode on throughout the morning receiving the same reports from different patrols. One group had obtained information from one of Nyk's scouts: the prince and his men had safely progressed past the Khadry without any confrontations. Danyl stared westward after hearing the last bit of news, his mind trying to make sense of the reports. There was no imminent threat looming on the horizon, just a collection of irregularities requiring the elves' attention. It was probably nothing more than a new twist in the Herkah/Man conflict, one that the elves would eventually find out. They always did, especially if Cooper sought the elves' interference with the people he had insulted. Danyl ordered his men to return to the city, knowing as much as he did when they left at dawn. It had been, in his opinion, a wasted trip. They arrived near sunset, grateful to be home as they neared the gate. Danyl glanced down at a passerby, the woman with the long braid illuminated by the torches lining the dark opening. Lance, too, noticed the woman, studying her intently as he rode by.

Ramira looked up at Danyl and nodded a greeting then glanced over at the captain. Lance's eyes narrowed, his mouth opening as if he were about to speak. He remained silent as she tilted her head ever so slightly; his stoic expression promised nothing. She nodded ever so faintly at the captain before heading up the avenue to a hot bath and a warm meal.

~

Nearly a week had gone by and Ramira was still welcome in Sophie's house. The woman never tired of giving Ramira things to do. When there was a lull in chores, Sophie sent her to the old couple's house. The three women finished up the last of their tasks then retired to the terrace. They breathed in the fresh evening air, sipped wine, and chatted amiably with one another. The topic of conversation turned to the festival. Anci's eyes were sparkling, her hands gesturing in the semi-darkness while she described the spectacle to Ramira.

"Everything is brightly decorated and there are tables of food and drink in front of almost every home," she pushed back a lock of hair that had fallen across her forehead. "There's music, dancing, jugglers and acrobats and…well, you'll see!"

The young girls enthusiasm was contagious, her breathless account making Ramira wish the celebration would start that very second. Sophie gave Anci a warm hug then winked over at Ramira. How different would her life be had she found a room at an inn? *Everything happens for a reason,* she thought. Gravel crunched along the side of the house announcing an unexpected visitor. He walked out of the dark, the lamplight illuminating first his boots then the rest of his body, until the soft glow revealed his face. It was Danyl.

"Well, well, well," Sophie playfully chided him as he embraced her, "I thought you forgot about us!"

"Hardly," he accepted a hug from Anci then nodded to Ramira. "There's been quite a bit to keep me busy of late."

"Ramira, this is Danyl, the king's third son." She introduced them, watching Ramira's reaction as she rose to bow to him.

"Please do not do that. Didn't I see you at the gate today?"

"Yes," she replied. A prince? She now realized the true meaning of Lance's words when he spoke to her near the Broken Plains.

Danyl studied Ramira's face, noting the slight flushing in her cheeks and the subtle shifting in her eyes. She pushed a section of her long hair back over her shoulder then met his gaze. He thought he saw a glimmer of satisfaction in her eyes but the contact was too brief for him to be sure. Sophie was quick to help others in need but she was not known for taking in strangers. Ramira did not seem to worry either Sophie or Anci, the two women acting as if their guest had lived with them for a long time. He glanced over at Sophie who waved him to one of the seats before disappearing into the kitchen for more refreshments.

"Tell me, Ramira, from where do you hail?"

His innocent question evoked a hint of sadness as she focused on her hands clasped in her lap. She remained silent for several moments then took a deep breath. He was about to retract his question when she quietly responded to his query.

"I'm not quite sure, Prince Danyl."

"Just Danyl," he corrected her.

"I wish I could tell you but that information seems to have tucked itself away into the far corners of my mind."

"If her mind could extricate as much memory as the dirt I washed away from her clothing, she'd be overwhelmed!" said Sophie.

"A long and dirty journey?" he asked.

"Long and dirty…" she replied as if from far away. The storm on the mountain and the flight across the plains replayed itself in the air in front of her. The memories of their struggles were as potent now as when they occurred. She closed her eyes to erase the scene but not before he saw the dread flicker within them.

"Sometimes life's most treacherous roads lead to the greatest of sanctuaries, Ramira," stated Sophie.

"Fortune has smiled down upon me by bringing me to your door, Sophie."

Ramira listened to them speak, the amiable conversation more akin to a family meeting rather than just friends. A sense of warmth and contentment flowed from one to the other even when Danyl teased Anci about her latest beau. Ramira smiled as Anci rolled her eyes in mock indignation, claiming he was just a friend. Ramira glanced over at the elf and remembered how he had appeared weeks ago. The bruises, scrapes and distortions were now gone revealing his true features. They were strong and tempered by pride but not arrogance. His eyes sparkled when he laughed and, she recalled, had glittered with cold determination when faced with death. He looked over at her and she immediately turned away. It was time for her to escape while she could.

Pretending to be tired, Ramira excused herself and disappeared up to her room. Anci followed suit not long after, leaving Danyl and Sophie alone on the terrace. She refilled their goblets and stared at the prince, waiting for the inevitable questions.

"Why did you to take Ramira in?" he asked keeping his voice low.

"She was exhausted, filthy and very hungry. Besides," she took a sip before continuing, "There is something about her that intrigues me."

"I know what you mean," he replied glancing up at the little balcony overlooking the garden.

"No, you don't." Sophie's tone of voice took on a sterner timbre, one forcing Danyl to pay attention.

"Tell me then."

"Her clothes had reddish dust on them and she carried an elven provisions pouch with her. She also confessed it took over two weeks to travel from the west."

"What are you implying, Sophie?"

"Perhaps she saw you and your rescuer at some point." She watched his features abruptly change, metamorphosing from playful to hopeful in a matter of seconds. His green eyes widened then narrowed at the thought of someone being able to help him fill in the gaps that had plagued him for so long.

"Have you asked her about that?"

"No, for some reason I don't think that's a good idea. I would advise against you prodding her for answers…not yet, anyway. Give her a chance to find herself and I believe she will tell you what, if anything, she might know."

"Everything is still so blurry…" he exhaled, his eyes becoming unfocused as the faint memories taunted him again.

"What do you remember?"

"Hands reaching out and snatching me from certain death and then tending to me even though I was a stranger. That woman had placed her own life in peril for me, yet she chose not to accompany us back to Bystyn. What if Ramira was my rescuer, Sophie? How can I ever repay her?"

"Perhaps by honoring her desire to remain anonymous, *if* she was the one who saved you."

"I wish I could recall what she looked like."

"What *do* you recollect about her?"

"That she was fearless and caring."

"Everything will sort itself out in the end, Danyl. It always does."

He did not reply. Staring out into the night, his mind showed him the fuzzy images and muted sounds from the cave, crossing the plains, and collapsing in the leafy bower upon the hill. He faintly remembered her burrowing up against him, a reaction to the chill in the air. The unfamiliarity of their surroundings or the wolves could also have forced her to seek contact. It could have been a combination of all of those things or of something else. Nevertheless, he had welcomed the connection and it remained with him to this day.

Danyl nodded in agreement then bade her a good night. He walked down the avenue greeting the few passersby's still about; his attention was focused on Ramira. How fortunate would he be if she were his rescuer? If she wanted to remain anonymous, he would keep her achievement a secret. All he wanted was to know what happened and, more importantly, to thank her. He was so engrossed in his thoughts that he had passed by the small park and the homes of the nobles abutting the castle without ever seeing them.

"Good evening, Lord Danyl." The sentry acknowledged the prince as he walked up to the gate, the oil lamps dangling from their supports casting wide pools of light.

Danyl waved at him while following the wide walk to the steps leading into his home. An attendant opened the huge oaken door for him, the massive iron hinges creaking as they strained to hold the portal. He headed for the broad staircase in the center of the vast reception hall that led to the royal family's private chambers. He undressed and lay down in bed; his last thoughts before drifting off to sleep were of Ramira.

~

Ramira tossed and turned, trying to shut out the voiceless whispers invading her sleep. They were as elusive as a wind blowing down from a snow-encrusted mountain…and just as cold. Their dismal vibrations thrummed into her, chafing at her nerves until they could take no more. She rose and stepped out onto the balcony, breathing in the fresh air while lost in the inky nothingness of the moonless predawn hour. The darkness began to shift before her eyes; for a moment, she thought sleep still clouded her vision as the images formed before her. They flashed briefly, vanishing before she had time to make sense of them. They were chaotic and the insidious whispers accompanying them made her hair stand on end. She shivered and went inside, closing the door as if trying to lock them out. Ramira sought the comfort of the kitchen. She sat in front of the fire, staring into the flames as they danced on the logs and elicited another memory. This one seemed to assuage her apprehensions for her mind and body began to relax. She must have been a child for she lay curled up in a lap, a pair of hands holding her while rocking back and forth. A soft humming filled her ears, the gentle breath of the singer caressing her cheek. The love emanating from that embrace chased away the bad dreams, leaving her feeling less

32

troubled but still confused. That image faded away until the flames filled her sight once more. She became aware of Sophie watching her from the doorway.

"You're up early," she stated pouring a mug of tea for herself. A tinge of concern flashed in her brown eyes.

"Couldn't sleep," replied Ramira as she rocked in the chair by the hearth.

"That is quite apparent. Anything wrong?"

"No. What needs to be done today?" she asked.

"Nothing that can't wait until tomorrow. Today, therefore, is yours to do with as you please."

"Thank you." Ramira decided to explore the land near the river, eager to get as far away from her nightmares as possible. She packed a bit of food, put on her light cloak, and headed out into the dawn.

~

She left the stirring city behind and headed south. The walk to the Ahltyn River was a pleasant one even if the morning mists concealed the waters flowing between the trees. The rising sun burned the haze away revealing the emerald cocoon enfolding the river. Her short boots were damp with dew as she trod over fallen logs and spongy soil into the stand of trees. It was peaceful here; the sights and sounds of the city kept at bay by something even older than the elves. She made her way to the edge of the river, dropped her light pack, and inhaled the fresh air.

Ramira sat down beside the river and leaned against a willow tree, its long fronds forming a curtain of pale green around her. She purged her mind of the nightmares, letting the soothing sounds of the water and calming lushness of the trees permeate her being. She felt the disquiet seep away, absorbed by the frilly mosses beneath her. She could understand why the elves chose this place: the fertile land provided them with bountiful food; the river supplied them with fresh water. There was beauty in the landscape and the elves honored that splendor without competing with it. Bystyn was immense but it stood humbly upon the land in deference to the majestic peaks in the north and the proud stands of trees to the south.

She reached for her water bottle, drinking deeply while gazing around the emerald enclosure. Deep purple and bright yellow irises crowded beneath flowering bushes along the riverbank. A red and black ringed snake sunned itself on a rock, ignoring the iridescent insects flitting around it. A small waterfall spilled into a pool surrounded by sturdy, velvety reeds and tall grasses with plumed tops. The sun poked through the growing leaves, dropping little puddles of light onto the ground, which shifted as a slight breeze stirred the boughs. She sighed and lay back upon the soft grass, seduced by the natural rhythms surrounding her. The setting reminded her of Danyl. The newly unfurled leaves reflected the green of his eyes and the warm, earthy tones mirrored his unassuming nature. He shunned the titles of his highborn status yet took on the responsibilities demanded of him with true devotion. What of her station in life? Who was she? Ramira closed her eyes and slowly drifted off to sleep, the nagging questions drowned out by the silver river flowing beside her.

Nyk and his men gave the Khadry's realm a wide berth, but he knew they watched nonetheless. The Forest Elves had been nervous of late. Nyk refused to provoke any kind of confrontation by riding too close to their land. The woods began to thin out, the terrain changing to broken ground dotted with boulders, thorny shrubs, and gangly trees. He scanned the area to their west and north. The division between healthy land and the reddish brown soil of the Broken Plain was stark.

"We're too far north," his captain reminded him.

Nyk nodded but his gaze never wavered from the far-off plains. The mountains separating the desert from their current position were a combination of flattened plateaus and spiky peaks. The horizontal then vertical sequence began somewhere up in the far north and continued down, out of sight, to the sea in the south. There were gaps in the foothills close to Kepracarn where the Herkahs could slip unseen past their enemies, including passes west of the Khadry's lands. Nyk wiped away the perspiration on his face with his sleeve. Khadry, Herkahs, and no communication with Cooper: were they all somehow connected or pure coincidence? Nyk hated this part of the land. It offered no cover and what did exist here reminded him of death. The soil was the color of dried blood; the trees and brush appeared skeletal. The hues that did exist seemed pale and sickly; the land never bloomed, not even in spring.

"Nyk," the elf motioned toward the north where six riders atop their black horses watched them.

"I never thought I'd live to see the day..." muttered Nyk in fearful fascination as he beheld the most dreaded of all the races. The elusive and deadly nomads had had no contact with the elves for hundreds of years. Their skill with weapons and their penchant for living in the harsh desert had evoked a host of myths and legends. These legends continued to grow, even to this day, especially in light of their fierce skirmishes with men. Nyk knew Cooper and his ilk usually instigated the conflicts but what eluded him was why the king would pursue the nomads.

"They appear to be interested in us. What are the chances of having a little chat with them?" asked the guard

Nyk stared at the Herkahs, their mystique holding him captive. Rumor had it that they were brutal killers who drank the blood of their enemies. Nyk found rather farfetched but something many believed. The prince slowly exhaled, gripping his reins more tightly as his father's orders to find and communicate with the nomads echoed in his mind. Nyk was on the cusp of fulfilling that obligation. Would the Herkahs receive the elves?

"There's only one way to find out."

He was about to kick the sides of his horse when the Herkahs, as one, turned their attention from the elves to something to the patrols' left. Nyk and the others followed their line of focus. They detected nothing at first then, the earth began to shake and tremble. A deep fissure split the land apart. A noxious, sooty mist issued forth from the crack, spreading outward over the jagged lip and onto the plains. The nervous horses tugged on their reins as the nightmare took on another threat. The Herkahs suddenly sprang into action, riding toward the patrol upon steeds whose hooves barely seemed to touch the ground. Confusion set in as Nyk's mind went blank. What to do? Were the nomads attacking them? His blood ran cold as an unearthly sound rose from within the fissure. He slowly turned his head, peering over his shoulder at the things surging out of the enlarging fracture in the ground.

Man-like in shape but spindly and twisted in form, their clawed limbs bristled with razor sharp talons. Fangs gnashed at the air. Ghastly shrieks preceded them as they raced toward the elves. The Herkahs closed the distance with incredible speed, but whether they were in league with these monsters or coming to the elves' aid was unknown. The demon-like things launched themselves upon the elves with a hateful glee, slashing at the elves and their horses. Wherever their swords cut into the things a noxious black liquid oozed out, burning wherever it splattered. The horses panicked, trying to buck off both rider and attacker as the claws of the things dug into their flesh. One of the creatures launched itself at Nyk. Both fell to the ground, the impact knocking the wind out of the elf. He tried to get up but the unmistakable pain in his side and difficulty in breathing stole his strength. He stared at the carnage occurring all around and realized that of twelve men only three were still atop their horses. His eyes glazed over with agony as he struggled to stand and go to the aid of the nearest elf fighting against two demons. One of the misshapen things lunged at him and hooked the prince along his side and back. The immediate, searing pain from the wounds was so intense he forgot about his cracked ribs. Nyk's teeth clamped together as he brought his sword down upon the monster; the disgust for the still-twitching thing etched on his face. He could hear his men screaming for help. The effort of facing the loathsome creature took its toll on him, leaving him swaying unsteadily on his feet. The wounds burned as if someone was jamming torches into his body. The world spun crazily around him; he fell to the ground in a heap. Flashes of black hurtled past him as the nomads systematically destroyed the demons. Their faces were apathetic yet the savage glitter in their

36

eyes made even the seasoned elf cringe.

He gritted his teeth to endure the stabbing pain in his side while attempting to roll away from a pair of charging demons. Legs draped in black blocked his escape. A Herkah towered over him. Nyk silently accepted his fate as everything around him began to blur. The Herkah pulled out a pair of wicked looking knives and quickly dispatched the monsters trying to destroy him. The other Herkahs were inflicting the same damage for the howls of the demons changed from hatred to pain and anger. They fled back to their foul fissure; those slain by the nomads reduced to viscous black pools.

Nyk watched as one of the Herkahs nodded toward the two surviving elves and, to his complete horror, witnessed their execution. He stared in shock as the nomads stabbed all of the dead men; the elves' dead faces twisted in anguish. His strength and stamina gone, he could only glare at the leader hovering over him with his knife poised over Nyk's throat. He gazed unafraid into the black, merciless eyes peering intently at him from within the face covering. Nyk opened his mouth to speak but nothing came out except a wheezing sound. The prince began to lose consciousness and knew his mortality was about to seep out of his throat. Time ticked by and still the Herkah had not dispatched him. He was completely at the Herkahs mercy yet the blade did not slice into him. The eternal wait began to abrade his nerves; the searing agony consumed his body. Death continued to hang motionless over him. A few moments later white hot flashes of pain rushed through his mind and body as darkness descended into the center of his being.

THREE

Danyl studied the map spread out over Karolauren's massive desk. He traced the route he had taken to the Broken Plain then back to Bystyn. He estimated where the cave was located by where he and his rescuer had ended up. He followed the edges of the plains to the fringes of the Khadry's domain. Elven patrols had detected Herkahs west and north of the Forest Elves' lands and south near Kepracarn. Cooper, ever the opportunist, might have rankled the desert dwellers by finding something of value on or near their lands. Such an intrusion might be the reason why they were so uncharacteristically visible of late, but it did not explain why they ventured so far north of Kepracarn. Danyl absently drummed his fingers on the map; his attention focused on the parchment. He looked up as the door opened and greeted the Historian, an ancient collection of bones and unruly white hair seemingly lost inside his black robe.

"What are you doing?" Karolauren asked in a voice as clear as his bright blue eyes.

"I might have known when I started but not anymore. Karol, what do you know about the Herkahs?"

"Not very much. Why?" He picked a book off a pile teetering on the edge of collapse.

"I'm not sure…it just seems rather odd that they would venture so far from the desert."

"They've been coming and going for generations; people are now paying attention to them," was Karolauren's crisp reply.

"Or perhaps they want or need to be seen. Do you think they have anything to do with Cooper's silence?"

Karolauren shrugged his bony shoulders, cocking his head at the prince who immediately vacated the Historian's chair. He leafed through his book then peered over it. The prince sat patiently waiting for Karolauren to answer his question.

"Herkahs live near the eastern edge of the Great White Desert," he began. "They have been there for a very long time. They despise man, are expert horsemen, unparalleled warriors and have not had any contact with elves for hundreds of years. They leave virtually no evidence of their passing. If you happen to meet up with one, chances are you'll never even know, unless, of course, you are the subject of their interest. That would negate meeting one because you'd probably be dead."

"I already knew those things, Karol."

"Then you are also aware they have no written language, passing their knowledge on orally from one generation to the next?"

Danyl nodded.

"Did you also know they banish their annoying children when they ask too many questions?"

"Your subtlety never ceases to amaze me, Karol. I will leave you alone." Danyl left with an armful of information, the wry smile on his face eliciting a chuckle out of the Historian who resumed his reading.

Danyl returned to his room where he intended to study the books he had borrowed, but he soon became distracted by his thoughts of Ramira. The mystery surrounding her only intensified for if she had been his rescuer, what had she been doing in such a dangerous place? Obviously, he was thankful she was there; he certainly would not have survived had he been alone. She had faced the dangers they had encountered with great courage and kept him alive during their short journey together. *If* she were the one who saved him.

He tried to concentrate on the papers scattered on his desk but the faint recollections persisted. He wanted to believe Ramira was his link to those terrible days. The only thing keeping him from confronting her was the promise he made to Sophie. He would leave his queries for another day and allow Ramira the chance to become accustomed to her new life in Bystyn. The prince sighed heavily and began to sort through the pages before him, even though his interest in her persisted. He forced himself to pay attention to the books, hoping it would distract him.

The Herkahs had always fascinated him. He had often wondered what an encounter with one of the elusive nomads would be like. Their harsh environment demanded they be resilient or perish. Karolauren was correct in saying the elves, even with their keen hearing and sight, would never notice a Herkah standing a few yards away. Hiding in the forest was easy; concealing yourself in a sea of ever-changing sand was much more of a challenge. Their horsemanship was legendary. They preferred short swords and knives; they had no interest in bows and arrows. They were, in essence, warriors rarely seen at close quarters.

"'Like ghosts at midnight beneath moonless night skies, with blades forged of silver and death in their eyes'," he whispered.

The words he spoke came from an ancient account with the mysterious nomads a few hundred years earlier. A patrol had ventured too far onto the Broken Plain in the northern section and chanced upon a group of Herkahs. Although there was no confrontation, the elves were close enough to see the nomads' faces. One of the scouts had been struck by the fearsome power the Herkahs exuded, shivering with awe and respect despite the blazing sun overhead. The Herkahs had scrutinized the elves then simply turned and ridden away. The prince gazed out the balcony window into the darkness, his imagination conjuring up their departure. *Long legged stallions; muscles rippling beneath their black hides as they carried their masters back to the desert. The Herkahs leaned across their great necks until they nearly become one creature. The sun glinted off the daggers shoved in their belts, but even these imposing weapons paled beside the dangerous glittering of their eyes. Elusive. Deadly. Legendary.*

He shook his head and then rubbed his eyes, wondering when he would lose this childish intrigue. The answer made him smile.

~

Nyk slowly emerged from oblivion. The first thing he discerned was the throbbing in his head. It took on a louder and more persistent tempo the closer to consciousness he came. He opened up his senses and probed the darkness around him. The sounds of muffled voices and neighing filtered in; a dry heat touched his overheated skin. He gingerly rolled onto his side, breathing sharply through clenched teeth. His wounds burned as if he had rolled onto an open fire. He gasped, waiting for the wave of nausea to pass; the noises he made extending beyond his confines. He heard silvery jingling sounds then sensed someone crouching down beside him, but when he tried to open his eyes the queasiness returned.

"Lie still," a gentle voice quietly commanded him. "You will undo the sutures if you move around."

She helped him sit up, letting him drink some water before easing him back down.

"I'm still alive," he managed to say, surprised that the Herkah blade did not slice into his throat. His men! They had butchered his men! The woman managed to calm him down enough to explain what had happened.

"Just barely," the woman affirmed, pulling back the blanket to check on the ugly gashes crisscrossing his side and back. "You and your men were attacked by Kreetch, demons in your language, and were poisoned when they clawed you. You would have become like them had we not interfered."

"They...you killed my men but not me...why?" he demanded.

"Your men had no protection against their abominable blackness: we saved their souls from a fate worse than death by slaying them."

"Why let me live?"

"Rest now."

The spice infused compress she placed across his forehead helped ease his unsettled stomach; its cool touch relieved the throbbing in his head. Helpless to do anything else, he drifted off to sleep.

~

He awoke hours later to the chilly air seeping into his shelter. His body was incredibly sore; the fiery sensation still clung to his flesh but the nausea had gone away. Food became a priority. He opened his eyes, allowing them a few moments to get accustomed to the near darkness before looking around the room. No, not a room…a tent. A pole supported a dark canopy overhead; the night winds stirring the material, making them ripple ever so slightly. He turned his head to the side and saw large pillows, a few small wooden boxes, and other items within the deeper shadows he could not identify.

The memory of the battle and the ensuing slaughter of his men flooded back. The thought of those same killers now tending to him filled him with a simmering anger. Then he remembered the woman's words. Nyk would never have believed such abominations existed in the land had he not seen them with his own eyes. Their mindless ferocity had no equal yet the Herkahs fought them with a stoic attitude. The Kreetch feared and loathed the nomads; they had scattered before their blades; their howls of hatred the only defiance they could muster. The elves were not the recipients of such unwilling respect. Nyk shivered, the thought of those demons running rampant throughout the land left him feeling cold inside. He had to return to Bystyn as soon as possible. He groped for his clothes in the dimness while trying to ignore his aching body.

"You are in no condition to travel, elven prince," the woman reminded him.

"I must tell my people about those things."

"In due time," she replied. "The Kreetch are limited to the plains for now."

"You seem to know quite a bit about them," he said, barely hiding the suspicion in his voice.

"We know enough."

"And you know who I am."

"Yes, we do. I am Zada of the Herkahs."

Nyk stared at her indistinct shape for a long time. The discomfort of his wounds, swirling emotions, and horrible memories gradually abated as he realized where he was. He abandoned the search for his clothes, his gaze never leaving the woman lost in the shadows of the tent. *I am Zada of the Herkahs'*, her voice echoed in his mind. She leaned forward, the lamplight illuminating her elegantly refined face, which was framed by thick, brown hair. Dozens of finely crafted silver bracelets graced her slender arms, the dainty tinkling repeating as she shifted her legs.

Wisdom emanated from her dark eyes and patience marked her calm demeanor. The prince lowered his gaze then his head in deference to the stately woman sitting across from him.

"Tell me about those evil things," he asked after a long silence.

"Kreetch are the lowest form of demons," she explained in quiet tones. "They possess no intelligence, existing only to destroy anything composed of flesh and blood. The poison running through their bodies is steeped in an ancient evil; one that corrupts the spirit then transforms it into one of the demons. There is no viable antidote."

"Why did you not kill me as well?" he asked, his fingers gingerly touching his wounds.

"That would incite a war with your people, wouldn't it?"

"Who would know?"

"We would. Now, please rest and we'll speak later." She rose to her feet in one fluid motion and exited the tent.

The soft light visible through the tent flap made him squint. How long had he been here? Exactly where was he: on the desert or somewhere along the Broken Plain?

Nyk could not sleep. Demons? It had been a long time since anything forged of darkness walked the land. He would not have believed Zada had he not seen them for himself. Nyk was a soldier, fighting things of flesh and blood that succumbed to blade or arrow, but only the Herkah knives killed the Kreetch. Was there something special about the blades? Did the nomads know exactly where to strike the demons to slay them? Did he believe Zada when she told him the Herkahs saved his companions' souls by shedding their blood? The vivid memory of the Kreetch's ferocity and mindless need to slaughter gave credence to her statement, but did nothing to assuage the guilt he felt. He dropped his head into his hands lamenting the high cost of accomplishing his mission. He struggled to his feet- careful not to break the stitches- and took a few steps forward. The effort made him perspire, the sweat trickling over his wounds making them burn. He gritted his teeth, his sharp breathing aggravating his cracked ribs; the pain brought tears to his eyes. Nyk swayed unsteadily, grabbing the pole for support as he painstakingly inched back to the blankets. He eased himself down, feeling the sutures stretch to their limit. He hoped he had not ripped any of them open.

He lay still, concentrating on the sounds outside the tent: a horse nickered; a spoon clanked against the side of a pot, and a bird screeched far off in the distance. The noises drifted into the tent along with the dry heat and the aroma of marinated meat. A simple life for a complicated people...or were they? The Herkahs had incited fear in the Kreetch and with good reason. The desert dwellers had systematically slain his men yet tended to him as if he belonged to the tribe. Zada was right about one thing: if they had murdered him, the elves would seek retribution. *That can't be the only reason I was spared. I was poisoned, just like my men and am now a liability.* Nyk began to tire, his eyelids drooping no matter how hard he tried to remain awake. His mind wanted to continue analyzing these strange circumstances, but his body demanded rest. He finally acquiesced and drifted off to sleep.

~

The days began to lengthen as late spring claimed the land. Leaves covered branches; flowers sprouted everywhere as the earth reveled beneath the warm sunshine. The smell of freshly turned sod lifted into the air as farmers prepared the fertile land for sowing; heavily muscled plow horses strained to pull the blades through the ground. Everything was as it should be yet the elven king sensed the barely perceptible ripples of conflict at the edge of his kingdom.

Alyxandyr, named after the first elven king, rubbed his temples after tossing the latest report onto his carved wooden desk. The tall, lanky man standing beside him focused his gray eyes on the map hanging behind the king. His steely features held his emotions in check. Mason, the kings First Advisor, glanced briefly at the report then returned his attention to the map.

"How can Nyk and his men have simply vanished?" asked the king. "Not one body, no signs of a struggle - nothing."

"Taken by Herkahs?" inquired Mason, his deep voice like rumbling thunder.

"Or Khadry. We know what the Khadry might do to them but the Herkahs? That is another issue."

Alyxandyr stared at his lifelong friend. They had met at Terracine, the great learning hall in the far northwest corner of the land, as children and educated by the Masters of Knowledge. Mason's brother, Cooper, already had his sights set on ruling Kepracarn and was elated when Mason voluntarily left, leaving him free reign over the city. Alyxandyr and Mason went to Terracine as boys, emerging as learned and highly skilled young men. Their shared ideals, beliefs, and goals cemented their friendship. These were the very things that Mason and Cooper disagreed with. Alyxandyr asked Mason to come to Bystyn with him. Mason and his sister, Sophie, accepted Alyxandyr's offer and started their new life in the elven city. When Alyxandyr was crowned king, many were suspicious of Mason's influence over him, never forgetting his roots in Kepracarn. This intensified when Alyxandyr announced Mason would be his confidant. It had taken years for Mason and Sophie to gain the confidence of the elves: Mason with his unwavering loyalty to the king and Sophie with her steady yet unobtrusive commitment to the city. A few still grumbled about Mason's background, their discontent mired in their inability to prove themselves worthy of obtaining such a high status. In any case, he felt satisfied and very fortunate they were both in his city.

"So much unconnected activity all within the span of about a month…"

"And still no word from Kepracarn," Mason quietly reminded him. "The scouts report no movement of any kind: not on the grounds nor the surrounding villages. If they plan to eat this winter they should at the very least be tending to their fields."

"You think something happened over the course of the winter, don't you?"

"Yes, but not pertaining to the possibility of Cooper's capitulation. Besides, who else could stir the Herkahs into action quicker than Cooper?"

"Why would he consistently poke a stick into that hornets' nest?" asked Alyxandyr.

"They have something he wants," stated Mason, a distracted expression in his gray eyes. "Rumor has it that an ancient city abounding with treasure is on or near the Herkah's lands. As a child, I heard some of the tales and dismissed them as just that- tales. Cooper became obsessed with finding the fortune. Apparently it is real enough for him to accost the desert dwellers."

"Do you think the nomads are protecting this supposed city?" asked Alyxandyr, intrigued by the story.

"I believe they are simply safeguarding their home, Alyx."

"So many questions could be answered if we could speak to just one Herkah," said the king as he leaned back in his chair.

"Perhaps. The difficulty lies in locating one."

"What of that supposed city, Mason?" Alyxandyr asked after a while.

"That city remains a mystery to this day. It ceased to exist long ago, so it is difficult to ascertain what it may or may not hold. In any event, if my brother thinks there is something to dig up from within its ancient foundations, I must believe his objective is not without merit."

"You expect there is something beneath those sands?"

"Something, yes. The problem is the Herkahs do not want Cooper to retrieve it."

"Can you blame them?"

"I think they don't want anyone to take whatever lies beneath the desert, be it gold, jewels or something else."

"Cooper's situation indicates a problem I don't think we want to get involved in but, I'm sure, eventually we will."

The king knew all too well that Coopers scheming ways had a habit of rebounding on them. He remembered early on in his reign when Cooper decided to harass a city far to the south of Kepracarn. Coopers dogged pursuit for tribute ended when a group from that city sneaked onto Cooper's lands and burned all of his crops. Cooper came to Bystyn seeking food and, fortunately for him, the elves had enough to share during that mild winter. There were other such incidents over the years but the thought of having to contend with the Herkahs was another matter: Alyxandyr did not intend to confront the nomads.

"The messengers should be arriving soon, Alyx," said Mason. "I'll attend to them and send the reports up to you."

The king did not acknowledge him. He stared past the walls toward the west; hands clasped behind his rigid back. *Where are you, Nyk?*

~

Sophie had been busy baking and cooking for the spring celebration. She took inventory of the platters full of food and jars of refreshments, worrying she had forgotten something.

People had streamed into the city to be with friends and family. They wanted to catch up on the news or just escape the four walls that had imprisoned for so many months. Traditions such as setting out food and drink in front of homes and exchanging little trinkets crafted during the winter kept the elves connected with each other. The land had not always been bountiful and the elves had depended on each other for survival, facing starvation on more than one occasion. The gifts harkened back to those times, promising no one would ever be deprived of sustenance again.

Ramira reached out and helped herself to a little cake before Sophie could turn around. The guilty look on her face did not fool Sophie for a moment.

"You keep eating those things and the only man who'll have you is the baker. Don't bother speaking - you'll only choke."

"You don't miss much, do you?" Ramira was finally able to say, after swallowing the treat.

"Not when your cheeks are the envy of every chipmunk in the land!"

Danyl entered the kitchen just as Sophie disappeared into the pantry, his finger up against his lips before shoving two cakes into his mouth. Sophie re-emerged from the pantry and looked down at the plate, bursting out in laughter as both raised a finger to implicate the other. She shook her head, and then reached into the larder for another plate of cakes.

"I always leave a few for the mice," she said smiling at the two of them, "or I would have none for my guests." She headed out the front door, quietly chuckling to herself as she greeted a neighbor.

Ramira busied herself with the food, the prince studying her as he leaned against the counter with crossed arms. Her long braid fell to the small of her back. It swung gracefully back and forth as she moved about, the simple leather tie binding it somehow inappropriate. The plain tunic and trousers she wore over her supple frame accentuated her beauty, even if they were a size too big for her. Her fluid movements brought her closer to the back door; her quick, lateral glances made him grin.

"Are you done staring?" she asked in a slightly annoyed tone of voice, inching closer to the door.

"Almost."

He approached her, turning her around until she faced him. He watched her search his face, hesitating where his injuries had been, until her amethyst eyes met his emerald ones. The room began to dissolve, taking with it all sounds and smells. She stared deeply into his green eyes, for although she could not identify what lay within their verdant depths she sensed its presence. She pulled away from him and the unfamiliar sensation.

"You seem to be rather interested in how my face healed." His need to know what happened pushed aside the strange feeling that passed between them. For now, anyway.

"I heard you recently suffered some bad luck," she replied trying to avoid the subject she sensed he was trying to breach. Perhaps she should have been more reserved in her contact with the elf. The budding familiarity between them was becoming more difficult to ignore.

"My brother recently disappeared in the area near where my misfortune occurred. I thought you might know something since you traveled here from that part of the land."

"I'm sorry but I don't," she said rather unconvincingly. "Ramira, I…"

Danyl was about to pursue the matter when he heard Sophie and her guests entering the house. He decided to continue the topic another time when there would be no interruptions. Ramira straightened her tunic then repositioned the plates for the fourth time, her attention focused on anything but the elf. He noticed the slight flushing in her cheeks as he lifted her chin, the determined expression on his face promising another such encounter. He offered her a slight nod then headed out the back door.

She slowly exhaled but the tightness in her chest would not go away. His convictions had given him the strength to survive and were now on display once more. He suspected her and for good reason. Sophie noticed the dirt and pouch, and she had told her from which direction she had traveled. The woman's loyalty to him had prompted her to reveal this information, hoping to ease his confusion. She brought her fingers up, massaging the tense muscles in her arms until the memory of that odd feeling resurfaced. Her hands immediately dropped to her sides.

She tried to shake those thoughts from her head but her guilt would not relinquish them. She needed a distraction, finding it on the front step where Anci chatted with a few neighbors. Ramira intrigued them for they often asked Anci and Sophie about her. They had graciously declined to discuss their guest with anyone, which only increased the neighbors' nosiness. Ramira caught Anci looking over at a young elf sitting on a stoop a few houses down, and the shy gaze he sent her way. Their admiration, it seemed, was mutual and it would not be long before he came to the house to court the young girl. A subtle smile crossed her face as she imagined Sophie scrutinizing Anci's nervous suitor.

~

Ramira left the house to find a place where she could be alone with her thoughts for a while. She went down the avenue toward the gate, one of only a few that were leaving instead of coming into the city. She headed for the river. She was halfway there when the sound of hooves caught her attention. She turned to watch a group of riders advancing toward the city and wondered if they bore any news concerning the prince. Ramira hoped they did for the family's sake.

She continued and soon found herself beneath the bright green canopy of trees hugging the river. She picked her way over the exposed roots until she reached an isolated area next to the river. She removed her short boots, rolled up her trouser legs, and rested her feet on the soft grass. She lay back and stared up into the branches, her mind wrestling with the information that Danyl wanted to know. She could help Danyl but not his brother, a sad reality that made her frown. She had grown fond of her new life, the quiet yet busy days and nights giving her a purpose. Wouldn't her preferred anonymity change once it was known she saved the prince's life? Would he agree to keep that information quiet? She thought of her own murky past, the longing to know tempered by the dread of finding out. Who exactly was she and why did her memory refuse to open up? She closed her eyes, willing everything from her mind and hoping it would fill with something from her past. She could not remember anything before the cave. She rolled over and leaned toward the water, her fingers absently drawing circles in the silvery blue liquid when an image slowly formed in its shallow depths…

Stars glittered overhead in an indigo sky; a chill breeze blew across her body. She shivered as she stared at a dark line of low-lying hills that shifted with every puff of wind. Silent whispers pulsed from those mounds as they sought to seduce her with soundless promises. She thought she saw the knolls waver then reform into faint human forms. She watched in fascination, as they appeared to drift slowly toward her. They were familiar yet completely unknown at the same time, a feeling that did not change the closer they came. She was unafraid of them, their reassuring undertones beguiling her until she fell under their enchanting spell. She exhaled like an expectant lover, opening her mind to receive it but another presence begged for her attention. Ramira tried to look beyond the intruder whose closeness began to fragment then shred the scene…

Ramira bolted upright blinking several times, the light blinding her. She had somehow become accustomed to the darkness in the vision and, as she spotted the gooseflesh on her skin, the cold as well. Ramira scanned the area for whoever had broken the connection but she was alone. She splashed some water on her face, slipped her boots back on, and headed back to the city. She emerged from the trees, surprised at the long shadows stretching to the east. The vision faded away and she managed to recover her composure while walking beneath the gate. The inexplicable sensations, however, continued to clog her mind. She heard people speaking and laughing as she walked up the main avenue, but their voices were nothing more than distant echoes. Ramira stumbled on the uneven cobblestones; an elf grabbed her arm to keep her from falling. She smiled in appreciation, ignoring his raised brow as she gathered her senses together. Ramira finally reached the comfort of the kitchen, the peculiar hallucination now a distant memory.

She fixed a plate of food and ate it on the terrace; the sounds from the street more muffled now that the leaves had sprouted. Ramira stared out into the garden, its rebirth a joy to behold. The bright spring blooms along the fence gave way to the herbs and other perennials; the vegetable patch along the shed was already germinating. She finished her meal and went inside, poured a glass of wine then took it back out onto the patio.

"Ramira," Sophie walked out onto the terrace smoothing down her dress, "Anci and I will be dining at the castle this evening."

"You look lovely, Sophie. Enjoy your dinner."

"Thank you. I'll bring a few sweets home for you."

Ramira smiled and leaned back into the chair, the women's voices silenced when the front door closed. She looked up at the trellis laden with climbing roses, anticipating their sweet fragrance during the hot summer months. That is, if she were still here then.

Things change quickly. She clung to the present with a renewed appreciation for the good fortune she now enjoyed. The day would come when she would remember her past, yet she doubted it could be more pleasant than her current life.

~

Sophie joined Danyl on the balcony after the meal, the two of them gazing silently over the castle gardens. The long-dead queen had created a refuge where one could read, think, converse, and court. Fountains and benches sat neatly tucked beneath roses, wisteria, and other climbing plants; there were rows of finely manicured hedges and flagstone paths throughout the garden. The queen had especially loved the white roses growing in the far corner. She had often sat there during the early evening hours when the breeze lifted their delightful aroma up toward the star-encrusted heavens.

Danyl's mother had died a year after his sister Alyssa had been born, the epidemic spreading throughout the city claiming many lives. It had been a terribly cold and damp winter with few escaping the deadly chill. Many to this day still thought about that awful time for everyone had lost friends and family. Her death had devastated Danyl's father. Danyl and his siblings were very young then but they remembered her nonetheless. Sophie was determined they should never forget her and helped rear the royal children. She had formed the strongest bond with Danyl.

"There is beauty here even in the dead of winter," Sophie said in soft tones.

"She is always here," he replied tenderly.

"You have something else on your mind though, don't you? Ramira, perhaps?"

"Yes."

"Did you speak to her about the plains?"

"I started to but between her being evasive and your untimely return, I didn't get very far. She did, however, give me the impression she was hiding something."

"Perhaps tonight might be a good time to continue that conversation," she suggested then sipped from her glass.

Sophie disliked the idea of prodding the girl into disclosing something she obviously did not want to divulge. He had a right to know. Besides, Danyl would honor the privacy she coveted. He offered her a slight smile then slipped away into the darkness. The queen had imparted a great deal of empathy to her children; Sophie fervently hoped she had been successful in perpetuating that attribute. She had help, of course: Karolauren, Mason, and Alyxandyr had taught them with both their strengths and weaknesses. All of them firmly believed you must teach with failure as well as victory. Danyl was about to learn a valuable lesson. Ramira would require not tact but honesty in his search for the truth. If he failed then Ramira, Sophie was sure, would be on her way. If he succeeded, then a close friendship might develop. Sophie sighed and rejoined her dinner companions, Danyl and his endeavor never far from her mind.

~

Ramira began to nod off beneath the trellis and decided to head upstairs. She rose and stretched, jumping as Danyl materialized out of the darkness. The light from the kitchen illuminated his set jaw and the resolute look in his eyes. He was intent on pursuing their earlier discussion.

"I hope I didn't startle you," he apologized.

"I was just heading to bed," she muttered.

"Perhaps you'd like to join me for a glass of wine before you do?" He promptly retrieved a glass and bottle before she could protest.

"You should be with your guests, not wasting your time here," she stated lamely.

He grinned and wondered what tactics she would use to wiggle her way out of this predicament.

"Most of them have already retired," he replied, the sudden light in her eyes steeped in the hope that Sophie and Anci would soon be home. He decided to let her believe the women would return even though they would not be back for at least another hour.

"You've had a long day so shouldn't you?"

"I am not tired, Ramira, but I am in need of some information which, I believe, you may possess."

There was no point in trying to sidestep it any longer. She motioned him into the kitchen, then described what had happened from the moment she pulled him from his imminent death to how she came to Bystyn. A dark, un-approving look crossed his features when she recounted her conversation with Lance, but he remained silent until she was through. He studied her face while she spoke; his scrutiny made her uncomfortable but she did not waver from her story.

"I owe you a great debt," he began after some time had passed, then raised his hand to silence her protests. "It's obvious you do not want anything for saving my life. I will respect that for as long as I can. Someday it may be necessary to reveal what you have done, do you understand?"

"Yes," she sighed, relieved that he now knew the truth.

"Now," he asked, "what were you doing in the cave?"

"I don't know. I woke up when the storm hit and that was the first recollection I had."

"Are you a Herkah?" The quizzical expression on her face answered that question. "Not elf; not man, then what?"

"Just lost, I guess." Sadness and a tinge of fear laced her response.

"We all become 'lost' at some point in our lives, but there are always those who help us find our way…like you aiding me in my hour of need. If you had not been 'lost', then I would now be dead."

Danyl read her face and saw no deception within it. He wanted to continue questioning her, but not at the expense of stirring up her private torment. He cringed at the thought of facing Sophie if Ramira left because of his persistent intrusion. Sophie had taken to this woman from the onset. Danyl realized that he found her uniqueness attractive. The elf was not one to surrender to beauty; he needed more than a beautiful façade to make him notice a woman. He disliked the phony attempts at seduction that were so prevalent in the court, finding Ramira's restrained demeanor refreshing. He reached over and cupped her chin in his hand, raising it until her amethyst eyes met his. Her skin was warm and soft to the touch; a faint blush rose in her cheeks.

"You did peek!" He smiled as she averted her eyes, her cheeks darkening with the memory.

"I tried not to," she confessed, rising from the table in an attempt to busy herself. She heard him approach and a moment later felt his arms encircling her from behind. The contact eased her embarrassment until she sighed inwardly.

That peculiar sensation began to arise again, originating from a place deep within them. It was faint, rising upward with an ethereal quality not unlike smoke curling up from a fire. The impression was both deeply sensuous and frightening at the same time.

"You should be upset with me for keeping what I knew hidden."

She placed her hands over his and reluctantly extricated herself from his embrace. He initially resisted until her growing uneasiness warned him to let her go.

"That would not be beneficial to either one of us." The brief, inexplicable flare in the core of his being left him feeling confused and exhilarated. He noted the same emotions on Ramira's face as she, too, fought to make sense of them.

"I'm sorry, Danyl. Why is it so important that I tell you about that night?"

"My brother and his patrol were sent back to the plains to try and contact the Herkahs. We haven't heard from them in quite some time and are getting worried. I was wondering if you might be able to tell me anything that might help."

"I wish I could, Danyl, but I know nothing more than what I have already told you."

"Ramira, did you see anyone else during the time we were together?"

Ramira thought back, remembering she had spent most of her time caring for him. If there had been others, they certainly had taken little interest in the rag tag pair scrambling to safety. She shook her head.

"Why did you risk your life for me?" he asked.

"I was confused and scared," she began in a small voice, "and didn't want to be alone."

Danyl stared into her eyes, the fear from that experience clearly reflected within their depths. It had been a difficult decision, one that would have been even worse for her had she chosen to ignore his cries and remain in the shelter of the cave. She could have left him to fend for himself once the wolves came, but again she endangered her life to defend him. The need to protect seemed to be ingrained in her, even if she could not recall her past. Danyl reached out and touched her cheek, the innocent contact stirring that odd sensation back to life. He could sense its unfamiliarity bewildering them both and decided to leave well enough alone.

"I should go," he stated bluntly and disappeared out into the night.

She watched him leave. She stood in the middle of the kitchen for a long time trying to make sense of what had just occurred. The attraction, if that's what it was, must not be allowed to grow. He was a prince and she an unknown outsider with an unrevealed past. The only way to make sure it would not progress was to avoid any contact with him, unless it was necessary. She felt better after having confessed her part in his rescue, but not about her decision to dodge him. *You cannot allow that particular sensation to reoccur,* she thought while climbing the steps to her room.

~

She managed to be absent for most of the day and well into the evening for nearly a week. Sophie had had enough. She kept an unhappy Ramira busy with chores around the house. Sophie noted her tense reaction every time the bell sounded, relief flooding Ramira's features when she spotted a neighbor or other acquaintance. Ramira's distancing began the day after the conversation she had with Danyl. She always feigned an errand or a task the few times he had paid them a visit. Sophie had seen his reaction, his quiet disappointment spoke volumes about his feelings. His inner struggle rippled subtly across his handsome features. Sophie watched Ramira work in the garden from the kitchen doorway, her far-off gaze staring well beyond the weeds poking up through the soil. Sophie realized Ramira avoided the elf because she had feelings for him. Sophie shook her head, wanting to go up to Ramira and tell her it was perfectly acceptable to be with Danyl. The young woman's private apprehensions, however, would continue to keep her at bay. She had to deal with them on her own terms, but Sophie wondered how much might be lost before she reached that conclusion.

"Mind your own business, woman," Sophie chided herself, "you've already stuck your nose in too far."

~

Nyk grew stronger every day. He could no longer abide lying still within the tent. His wounds smarted if he moved too quickly, but he managed to rise and dress without too much difficulty. He slipped through the flap of the tent and squinted into the late afternoon sun. When his eyes had adapted to the light he realized he was somewhere on the edge of the Great White Desert. Some Herkahs tended to their magnificent horses; others approached the camp from several directions. The prince watched the black garbed man advance toward him, his cat-like movements closing the distance in moments. The Herkah stopped in front of him. Nyk looked into his eyes.

"I am Allad," the man said while removing his face cover. Allad's hawkish features, browned by the sun, were as keen and sharp as his blades. "You are most welcome in our tribe."

"Thank you," replied Nyk, unsure how he should react. Allad had come within inches of killing him. He was successful in the assignment his father had given to him...a small consolation given the sacrifices his men made.

"You'll need to change clothes, young elf, for the nights here get very cold and the days will burn the flesh off your bones. Zada has set aside some things for you in the tent."

Nyk nodded. The sun was still hot enough even in the late afternoon to make him perspire; the sweat trickled down and irritated his wounds. Allad motioned toward the shady spot in front of the tent, inviting him to sit cross-legged upon a red woven rug and share in some refreshments. The prince noted the Herkahs glancing at him every now and then, their curiosity as great as his own. Nyk noticed the Herkahs did not burden themselves with useless luxuries, but what they did own would have made any king envious. The thick rug on which they sat was plush and comfortable. Stylized horses and rolling dunes contrasted starkly against the rich red background. The plates and cups were forged from a light and sturdy metal. The pillows were soft; the blankets light yet warm. Everything was easily transportable; an absolute must for their nomadic way of life. Zada's melodic tinkling caught his attention. He accepted a plate of food from her, the meat marinated in unknown spices made his mouth water. She handed him a flattened piece of bread and a mug of strong tea then prepared the same for Allad and herself.

"When may I leave?" he asked after swallowing a mouthful of food. The tender morsels melted in his mouth.

"In a few days," replied Allad. "First you must heal more."

"I feel fine," lied Nyk. A few minutes on a horse would open up more than one of the stitches on his body.

"There are some injuries you do not want to aggravate," Zada reminded him.

"Zada, why has no one from Kepracarn been heard from yet?" He hoped they would be able to supply an answer, news of their bitter confrontations running rampant through his mind.

"You think we destroyed them all, don't you?" Allad grinned as the prince sat up straight and opened his mouth to reply. "No, we don't know what they are doing but we prefer the conflict over this peculiar silence. It is better to face your enemies and know where they are rather than guess at their absence. Especially Cooper."

"You think they are regrouping and attempting some other plan?"

"Kepracarn is shrouded in utter stillness…no one goes in or out, young prince," Zada informed him.

"What could have happened?" he asked, watching the Herkahs exchange a secretive glance. "You know, don't you? Does it have something to do with those Kreetch?"

"Partly." she replied. "There are other things at work that go beyond the Kreetch, Nyk, things that have yet to materialize."

"I mean no disrespect, but your words explain nothing. I must inform my people of what has transpired here yet, except for the Kreetch, I know nothing." He glanced from one to the other, his set expression demanding some sort of an explanation.

"There are three levels of demons," Zada began after a long pause. "Each is bound to an ancient evil for a particular purpose. They are Kreetch, Radir, and Vox. You have already encountered the Kreetch. The Radir are just as ferocious but they have a viable intelligence. This ancient evil uses them to 'see' what is going on in the land and if they are spotted, we become nervous. Their arrival indicates that the evil is gaining strength and intends to infiltrate the land once more."

"What 'evil'? You mean it has surfaced before?" asked Nyk, his brow furrowed in concentration.

"Yes, elven prince. It seeks a powerful magic called the 'Source of Darkness'. If the evil senses this magic, it will send the Radir out to find it."

"How is it that you know so much about this evil and its ilk?"

"We have been living with it for nearly a thousand years. We do not know, for example, how this evil originated or what this Source of Darkness looks like. Legend states if the evil succeeds in acquiring this dark magic, every living thing will suffer. The land will become so desolate the Broken Plain will appear like a lush garden in comparison."

Nyk's mind wrestled with the information. He placed little confidence in the mysterious arts although he knew they had at one time dwelled within his own people. The Herkahs had no reason to lie to him. If the Kreetch were a harbinger of this evil, then the elves could be forced to confront the demons on their own lands. He needed more information.

"I know what the Kreetch look like but what about the Radir?" he asked, wondering what misshapen form they would have.

"Therein is the problem," Allad spoke holding his mug in both hands. "They steal and eat the souls of others, existing within their bodies while living amongst the possessed individual's family and friends. The Kreetch blindly attack from without; the Radir poison from within."

"So they could be about anyone," Nyk said. "Is there no way to identify them at all?"

"Sometimes, young prince, the Radir act contrary to their host," Zada explained. "But unless you have the right weapons to defeat it, you will become its next victim."

"And the Vox?"

"Ah…the Vox." She exhaled sharply before continuing. "Their place in the scheme of things should be left for another day as should the evil."

"You think this evil is near, don't you?" Nyk asked.

"We aren't sure, elven prince, but I would be surprised if it wasn't trying to get back into the land."

"You keep saying 'getting back into the land'… where does it originate from?"

Zada's brown eyes gazed through Nyk and out onto the desert. The elf glanced at Allad; the Herkahs' intense focus on Zada like a coiled snake ready to strike. The prince swallowed several times, ignoring the dryness in his throat as the motionless drama persisted. Allad began to lean closer to her, his gaze never leaving her perspiring face. Nyk could have sworn the Herkah floated toward the woman, the dry heat wavering behind Allad distorting his form. Then, without any forewarning, Allad barked out her name.

"Zada!"

Nyk jumped. His watched Allad catch Zada as she slumped forward, cradling her in his arms while she sluggishly regained her composure. The Vox clearly concerned Zada and Allad, a fact that gave him a sickening feeling in the pit of his stomach. What sort of monsters were they that frightened the mighty Herkahs? He hoped he would never find out. The elf needed to pass on what he knew even if it was all just conjecture at this point. He tried to ignore the healing claw marks but the itching begged for relief. He would have to tolerate them and get back to Bystyn as soon as possible.

A Herkah signaled for Allad who, after casting one more look at Zada, walked over to him. Zada invited Nyk to join her as she walked to the crest of a nearby dune. The sand shifted beneath his feet; the white sand changing color as the sun began to set. It glittered with shades of red, lavender, and finally silver.

"It's quite dazzling to behold," he murmured.

"And extremely dangerous. The wind is changing direction… a storm is brewing out there," she pointed toward the heart of the desert. "It will follow the air currents from the west striking here sometime late tomorrow morning. We will leave at dawn and head north along the mountains to escape it."

"What lies out in the desert and how do you manage to survive there, Zada?"

"The power to test your soul," she replied, subconsciously fingering her bracelets. "The challenge to endure in any place- whether desert or mountain- is to know your limitations, young prince. The desert is a vast and uncompromising place. There are places where water flows close enough to the surface, allowing broad-leaved trees and waxy bushes to grow. These places, oases, permit us to exist. They can disappear very quickly, too. A single storm can devastate them in an instant."

"Have you ever gone to one of these sites only to find it gone?"

"Indeed we have, Nyk, and yes," she anticipated his next question, "the hardships we endured on the way to the next oasis were severe."

The elf scooped up a handful of sand, letting the grains flow through his fingers. They were still warm to the touch, unaffected by the cold breeze beginning to blow over the dunes. He had been with the Herkahs long enough to dispel the myths surrounding them and gained a growing respect for them as a people. He brushed away the last of the sand then looked over at Zada. She had remained quiescent, rising now that he was paying attention.

"Follow the same path back to the camp or the sand will swallow you."

Nyk sat down on the dune, his arms resting on top of his knees as he stared out into the night. The sun had set fire to the sands earlier; the moon and stars now turned them into a sea of silver sparkles. The cold air began to flow over the dunes until it made him shiver. The elf rose to his feet and turned only to find an older woman a few feet away. She wore a simple brown dress; her mahogany features radiated compassion. She offered him a slight smile in greeting.

"Good evening, Grandmother," he said in respectful tones.

You have come a long way… that is a good sign.

"What do you mean, Grandmother?" Nyk's brow furrowed for he had clearly heard her speak yet her lips never moved.

It means not all is lost.

"What hasn't been lost?" He felt the hair on his arms begin to stand on end.

Hope.

"I don't understand…" he began, but the brown woman lifted her hand to turn aside any more questions.

Hope will light the way even during your darkest hours, child. Take care not to let the foul winds that are blowing extinguish the flame burning in your breast. Look closely upon the Children of the Sands and gaze past their black concealment to see the light blazing in their hearts.

Nyk was about to question her further but she disappeared. Had he seen a ghost? Her words echoed within his mind. Her aura of kindness clung to his body like a warm blanket on a cold winter's night. He headed back to camp where he kept the encounter with the woman to himself. Her unspoken words, though, haunted him.

~

The small band of Herkahs rode northwest toward the base camp, their last perimeter check just completed. They had left at dawn and would meet up with the tribe before sunset. They crested a dune when two, unmoving blotches of black appeared up ahead. Haban, the leader of the party, reined in his horse and scrutinized the silhouettes. The steeds pranced nervously causing the tassels on their blankets and bridles to jerk. Satisfied the two shapes were the only oddities, Haban and another Herkah approached them, their eyes narrowing with alarm as they recognized what they were. Haban dismounted, cautiously advancing upon the dead horse and rider. He drew his blades from their sheaths squatting between them. The dead Herkah had stabbed the horse in the neck then ended his own life, the dried blood indicating this had occurred many hours ago. Haban nodded to his comrade, the two of them proceeding to bury their blades into the hearts of the dead nomad and horse.

"Just in case," muttered Haban.

"This does not bode well, Haban," stated his companion. He eyed every square inch of the dune while nervously fingering the small dagger hanging from his neck.

"No, it does not," Haban replied. The sun slipped down the sky, flooding the dunes with vivid reds and oranges making the scene even more grotesque. Shivers of alarm ran up and down their spines as they hurriedly buried the dead. The remaining Herkahs joined them, their shared silence during the uneasy task hastening the process. Haban offered a quick prayer for their souls from atop their fidgety horses, and then the party galloped back to camp. They arrived just as the sun disappeared below the horizon. Haban headed straight for Zada's tent where he passed on the news. Zada's lips formed a tight line; her skin grew paler with every word he spoke. She reached for Allad's hand. Haban left the subdued couple alone.

"They are here."

"It is time to leave, Zada, *before* the sun rises tomorrow morning."

~

Nyk kept out of Zada's way as she packed away everything but their bedrolls, surprised at how few boxes held the contents of the tent. Her tight features and rapid movements alarmed him; Allad's brisk orders from somewhere outside only confirmed his apprehension. He quickly sidestepped the Herkah as she brushed past him to retrieve a pouch hanging on the pole. He finally could not stand the tense silence any longer.

"What's going on?"

"We'll be leaving soon."

"I can see that, but why?"

"Because of the storm and…"

"And what?"

"Vox. I'd prefer that you not ask any questions about them right now."

"Why did you let me live yet take the lives of my men?" asked the prince after a while.

"Because the poison did not affect you the same way it did them."

"That is a vague answer, Zada."

"Allad noted a certain strength running through you and decided to take a chance by letting you live. We will, however, kill you if you show any signs of being tainted."

"Then you are taking a grave risk by keeping me in your tent."

"On the contrary, young prince. Allad and I are your worst adversaries if you have been poisoned by the Kreetch."

Nyk locked eyes with her and realized that for all of her gentleness she was still a Herkah. Generations of nomads had fought the demons and the bodies the abominations occupied meant nothing to the Herkahs. Their only choice was to eliminate the threat regardless of whose face they wore or risk the same fate. The nomads would not hesitate to slay him despite the resulting strife that would occur with the elves. The spread of the Kreetch to Bystyn through Nyk was unacceptable to the Herkahs. It was not a pleasant situation but if they did not protect the rest of the unsuspecting races, and themselves, who would? The elf marveled at their resolve, but he did not envy their position in the scheme of things.

"I am both terrified and grateful at the same time," he stated, suddenly aware of his mortality and the delicate balance upon which it hung.

"You should be," she replied in tones devoid of arrogance or danger, but resonant with a certainty that made him drop his gaze.

Nyk gingerly touched his wounds, remembering the great care with which Zada had tended to him. He found it difficult to imagine her wielding a dagger against his neck, unlike the very real image of Allad out on the plains. *Look closely upon the Children of the Sands*...the ghost had told him. The Herkahs ferocity against the demons allowed the other races to survive. This 'strength' had saved him. Allad would not hesitate to carry out his deed if Nyk showed any signs of turning into a demon, a sobering truth indeed.

"Rest, Nyk, for tomorrow will be a long day."

~

The prince awoke the next morning as the Herkahs hastily broke camp. He helped as best as he could, the uneasy feeling in growing the closer the ominous wall of sand gyrated toward them. It was still recognizable even in the semi-darkness; a vast blackness bent on devouring the world and it was heading straight for them. The elf glanced over at the Herkahs who silently packed their remaining belongings without ever looking at the monster. The nearer it came the faster they worked and, less than fifteen minutes later, they were ready to ride. The elf tucked the flaps of his head covering more tightly into the folds as the wind began to whip them against his face. A deep rumbling sound reverberated in the distance, increasing as the sandstorm grew in height and breadth.

"Stay beside me, Nyk, and do not tarry." Allad commanded as he stared past the elf at the sandstorm, his demeanor dark and forbidding.

They started out at a brisk pace, heading north in the direction of the mountains separating the desert from the Broken Plain. Nyk could feel the leading edge of the storm push against his left side, forcing them all to ride at a slight angle. He sniffed the air, and then repositioned the folds of his face covering. The blasting air began to drive into them from a more northerly route, pounding into them from the front. Nyk began to believe the massive sandstorm was shifting direction, and one look at Allad confirmed his thoughts. The Herkahs' grim facial cast made the elf grip his reins more tightly. The hard ground allowed the horses to run at full speed. They squinted as they fled the gigantic mass of swirling sand. The Herkahs followed the undulating foothills of the mountains. Nyk's anxiety intensified as their escape route became blurred and lost within the whirling sand. The wind became so loud he could no longer hear anything and it took a great deal of effort to keep his horse from bolting. It strained at the bit; ears laid back and snorting nervously. Trapped between the annihilating storm and the rock, they kept riding on as panic began to build in Nyk's stomach. He had no choice but to place his trust in the Herkahs' ability to survive and kept pace with Allad. The lead group rounded a bend up ahead but when Nyk and the others reached that spot, the riders had disappeared. Allad edged his horse into Nyk's mount pushing the elf into a deep crack within the rocks.

"Keep your head down and do not stop!" Allad shouted as they sped up the rocky slope and into the darkness.

Visions of striking a low hanging ledge or vanishing with his mount into a chasm filled Nyk's mind as the darkness swallowed them up. He instinctively dropped low over the horse's neck. The elf jolted upright as a tremendous roar followed them into the stony darkness. The storm, deprived of its victims, lashed out at the mountain with a fury that seemed surreal. He swore he heard it shriek. Sweat poured down his body and into his wounds, but he was too engrossed in the dangers at hand to notice the discomfort.

They proceeded on into the bowels of the mountain, the Herkahs forward progress never wavering. He could discern the outlines of numerous tunnels branching in different directions by the torchlight, but the nomads moved ahead without hesitation. The elf could still hear the angry howling behind him, the sound echoing with ferocity as it streamed into the tunnel. The sound took on an almost human tone; Nyk fought the temptation to dismount and cower in the gloom. The well-trained Herkah steed kept pace with the others. He had no choice but to hang on and pray that he might live to see another day. The air became heavy; there were no sounds except for the hooves striking the rocky ground and the creaking of leather. When all of the Herkahs were finally within the mountain, they slowed their pace and stopped.

Allad rode down the line checking to make sure everyone was safe.

Nyk stayed behind Allad and Zada, often looking back but seeing nothing more than an occasional torch and vague silhouettes. He recoiled from the outcroppings appearing out of nowhere, then silently chastised himself for dodging something that was not there. Time seemed to stand still, becoming disproportionate and vague. The lack of any landmarks disorientated the elf. For a few brief moments, Nyk believed he was in a procession of the dead as they made their way into the underworld. He half expected the searing flames of hell rise up from the abyss and burn them all. He shook his head to dislodge the disturbing images, collecting his thoughts to keep himself from panicking. They stopped for a while, resting their horses and making sure everyone was still in line. Except for a whispered word here and there, everyone remained silent. If there was something skulking about in the darkness, the elf preferred knowing about it ahead of time. He approached Allad to find out.

"Do we remain quiet for a specific reason?" he asked in hushed tones.

"The mountain can be quite unstable."

Allad's succinct reply left Nyk feeling even more anxious than before. The elf glanced up, the thought of tons of rock collapsing down on top of them making him yearn for the grasslands even more. He banished the question 'has it ever happened before?' from his mind.

The time for resting was over. They remounted their horses and resumed their trek through the mountain. Nyk strained his eyes, searching for that pinpoint of light indicating their journey was over. All he noticed was an endless blackness. The torch held by the lead rider began to flicker, prompting the Herkah to light another before it went out. The thought of being in total darkness within this oppressive place made Nyk shudder. He was used to a wide expanse covered in green, not this inky vault threatening to crush him to dust. His keen hearing picked up sounds reverberating faintly through the vast network of tunnels. He heard crackling and skittering noises as bits of the mountain broke loose somewhere in the blackness. Wind rushed through the passageways off to his right, moaning weakly like some injured animal. He detected the sound of water in the distance and visualized an icy black river carving its way through the mountain. If a creature managed to exist within this forbidding environment, he was positive he did not want meet up with it. The bowels of the mountain may have been desolate but they were certainly not devoid of activity.

The elf did not lose his apprehension as the mighty weight continued to press down on him. The nomads were cautious yet showed no fear or confusion as they wound their way through the silent labyrinth. It suddenly dawned on Nyk how much he had learned about the Herkahs. He grinned wryly. The elves would be astonished when they saw the dreaded nomads. He assumed Zada and Allad would accompany him to Bystyn while the nomads camped beyond the Broken Plain, but not too close to the Khadry. The Forest Elves would certainly take note of the Herkahs but avoid any conflicts with them. Nyk brought his horse alongside Allad.

"How long before we are through the tunnel?"

"It will be well after dawn," Allad whispered.

Dawn. It would take an entire day to ride through the mountain. He resumed his place in line, Allad's shadowy form his only link to the direction they were traveling. He had plenty of time to think, but his dismal surroundings consumed his thoughts. He gave up trying, deciding it was easier to concentrate on nothing.

The darkness and rhythmic swaying began to lull him to sleep and soon his chin rested against his chest. He dreamt of cloudless blue skies and brilliant sunshine. He closed his eyes against the glare, smiling as the warmth penetrated into his very core. A cloud obscured the sun then spread outward to encompass the whole sky; a chill suddenly replaced the heat. He watched with horror as the wall of sand devoured everything in its path, grinding up trees and buildings as if they were made of paper. He turned to run but his feet were stuck in the ground, holding him in place as the monster bore down on him. He opened his mouth to yell but the storm filled it with sand; his upraised arms a futile last gesture… He awoke with a start, sweat pouring down his face as he gulped in huge draughts of stale air. He was still within the mountain but something was wrong. There were no torches, no fellow riders anywhere; even his horse was missing. Nyk blinked several times yet they beheld the same thing every time: he was alone. How could he possibly have managed to veer away from the line? He could not have been asleep for too long. Completely blind, he groped at the empty air around him. His breathing increased, the sharp intakes spreading the stitches and aggravating his ribs. Hysteria began to build in his stomach, extending up into his chest until it reached his throat. Nyk shouted at the top of his lungs then fell to the ground as something crashed into his head.

~

Ramira sat beneath the shade of a maple tree, wiping the sweat from her face. Ida approached with a pitcher of cool water. She had spent quite a bit of time here, the couple's warmth making all the work worthwhile. She had managed to chop and stack enough wood for a week, but there were some tasks requiring the help of others. She had attempted to tackle them on her own, the efforts leaving her bruised and frustrated. Jack tried to assist her, but his gnarled hands weren't strong enough to hold anything heavy. It was disconcerting for them both but neither one complained.

She heard the horses before they rounded the lower part of the orchard, catching sight of Danyl, Lance, and two other elves. She returned their greeting as they dismounted in front of the house. The couple welcomed them and, after a brief conversation, began to work on the projects she could not handle. She finished weeding the garden, gazing at Danyl now and then. The elves repaired a section of fence, straightened out the sagging shed, and replaced the posts holding up the porch roof. Ramira wandered over to the stables, the unenviable chore the last on her list. The earthy odor of manure clung to her skin and clothes; the flies bit her. Ramira glanced sideways at Danyl as he used his tunic to wipe away the perspiration running down his face. She could not help but admire his lean yet strong upper body, smiling despite herself until he looked her way. She turned her head, hoping he hadn't seen her stare at him. Danyl did not miss very much. She felt the flush rise up in her cheeks. She increased her exertions, hoping they would distract her from her thoughts. The hours passed and Ida forced them to stop and eat. She ushered them to the garden behind the house, where a cool breeze stirred the clematis growing on the arbor. Ramira washed up as best as she could. She sat apart from the others, claiming she did not want to ruin anyone's appetite. She grinned at the playful jabs. Danyl smiled but the short-lived flicker in his eyes was anything but amiable. Her avoiding him chafed at his normally easygoing nature, turning his disappointment into frustration.

She finished eating and, beginning to wilt under Danyl's quiet ire, headed over to gather up a pile of kindling. She looked up and felt her stomach tighten as Danyl purposefully strode toward her. She outwardly pretended that nothing was wrong as she placed the wood into the wheelbarrow. Inwardly, however, was a different story.

"You've been scarce."

"Sophie has been keeping my days full," she replied without looking at him.

"She has a knack for doing that," he agreed then gently took her by the arm and sat her down across from him. "Although it can't all fall onto her shoulders, now can it?"

"No," she quietly admitted, "it can't."

"Then perhaps you would be so kind as to explain it to me?"

What could she say? That she had reveled in the embrace and found herself attracted to him? That she believed she had no right to harbor such feelings for someone of his stature? That her unknown past could bring shame, or worse, upon him? He needn't be friendly with her simply because she had saved his life. She looked into his eyes and realized that he would not think that at all. It would upset him if she told him what was really on her mind. Danyl deserved better. She pushed aside a soggy strand of hair, flinching as she bumped her finger. She turned her hand over and saw the splinter buried in her finger. The elf took her hand, trying to work out the sliver from her stiff forefinger with the tip of his knife.

"Let it relax, Ramira."

"I still feel guilty for keeping the rescue from you."

His attention remained on his task. He dug out the piece of wood then kissed her finger, the tangle of emotions stealing her voice.

"Perhaps…but I think there is something else, isn't there? That sensation maybe?" He watched her squirm.

"That could have been rooted in a lot of things, Danyl," she stated a bit too harshly.

"Tell me."

"I'm very confused about what happened that night, Danyl, and it scared me."

"So your solution was to avoid me?"

She remained silent.

"Perhaps there is something more between us."

"No," she shook her head. "There can't be."

"Why not?"

"You are a prince and I am…I don't know what I am…" her voice trailed off into silence.

"I see," he said quietly. "You don't think you're good enough for me. What you fail to see is there are more important qualities to a person than their position in life. My feelings for you are real, Ramira, but I won't force them on you."

The prince stood up, looked down at her for a moment and then rejoined his men. She stared after him; his honest words making her feel foolish.

She maintained a discreet distance from the elves. She could sense Danyl glancing over at her every now and then. Danyl didn't care about her past or that she wasn't highborn; it mattered only how he felt about her. Ramira thought back to those days in the cave when he was simply 'Danyl', a person in dire need of help. She had no right to change her perspective of him once she found out his highborn status. She applied her rules onto Danyl, then expected him to comply with them. She now faced not only his disappointment but also her own. She watched Danyl working by the barn then hung her head in embarrassment. The afternoon slipped away, the shadows lengthening across the land. Ramira waited for the elves to ride out of sight then gathered her things. Ida fretted about her taking so long. She missed the opportunity to have a horse carry the heavy basket. Ramira smiled at her, heaving the load over her shoulders.

"It's not that heavy, Ida."

"Then why are you straining?"

"I'm...I'll be fine," she stated, leaning forward to give Ida a kiss on the cheek. She walked down the front steps, the straps pressing her flesh against her bones. Ramira could barely maintain her balance. It didn't take long for blood to stain her tunic. Ramira broke through the trees and stopped in her tracks, chagrined when she spotted Danyl. He stood with crossed arms in front of his horse. He shook his head at the red blotches on her tunic. The elf attached the basket to the saddle then pulled her up in front of him before she could protest.

"You are the most stubborn person I know! Honestly, Ramira, ask someone for help every once in a while."

They rode in silence for a while, Ramira's discomfort stilling her tongue. Danyl enjoyed the fact that she could not run and hide from him. Ramira began to relax; she avoided prolonged contact with him fearing that the peculiar sensation would arise once more. Besides, the sweat and pungency she had acquired while cleaning out the stables lingered on her clothes and body. She wrinkled her nose and wondered how he was able to tolerate her stench.

"I stink," she said apologetically.

"Yes, you do," he agreed and began to laugh, the joyful sound quickly spreading to her own throat.

"That would be your repayment for lurking behind the apple trees," she said in a playfully vindicated tone.

"Elves don't 'lurk'," stated Danyl with mock indignation.

"What do they do then?"

"They set themselves upon smelly, obstinate women."

"Lurk," she corrected.

Danyl smiled; she could call it anything she wanted to. Her dour demeanor melted away taking with it her rigidity and silence. He slid his arm around her waist, subtly leaning forward until he could see her face. She turned and looked at him. The tentative acceptance in her eyes and her hand resting on his forearm was a promising beginning. He wished the ride to the city took hours instead of minutes, the gray walls looming larger with every beat of his heart. They passed beneath the gate, the understated contentment radiating from their faces drawing more than one look from the passersby. They were in front of Sophie's house before either one was ready to end the contact.

"Thank you for the ride."

"My pleasure. Why don't you let me carry that in for you?"

"Because it's not as burdensome anymore." She offered him a shy smile then disappeared around the corner of the house. Danyl patted the horse's neck, heading up the avenue no longer feeling tired.

~

"Nyk? Come on son, wake up."

Allad gently shook the elf, ignoring the bruise visible even in the faint torchlight. Nyk returned to consciousness, suddenly upright as he remembered what had happened. He grabbed the front of Allad's tunic with both hands, the fistfuls of cloth anchoring him to the present. The prince glanced around and saw Zada and the others staring down at him. The snorting horses and occasional coughing eased his panic. He gradually loosened his grip; his breathing returned to normal as Allad helped him to his feet.

"What...?"

"You dozed off then fell from your horse," Zada explained to him. "You were fumbling around, still in a daze, and began to yell. Allad was forced to..."

"I apologize for the blow to your head, Nyk, but your screaming could have been disastrous."

The elf reached up and carefully touched his hot cheek, flinching as his gloved fingers probed the sore area. He nodded in understanding, his embarrassment flooding his face. He should have been more alert and not allowed himself to drift. He mounted his horse and waited for his companions. They noticed the tight line along his jaw and clenched fists.

"The mountain seduced you, Nyk. That has befallen all of us." Zada patted his arm, her confession only slightly alleviating his lapse in judgment.

They moved on again, the elf determined not to fall under any more spells. The hours they had spent within the mountain seemed like days; Nyk was sure they would never reach the other side. A rumble then the sound of something large bouncing until it splashed into a body of water echoed from somewhere to their right. Nyk tensed up immediately, relaxing only when he heard Allad's voice.

"The lake…good; we are almost on the other side."

Nyk squinted into the darkness to his right. A bizarre forest of rock hung from the ceiling and reached upward from the ground. Some appeared dull while others shimmered with luminous hues. The pale blue, pink, and green shades gleamed wetly in the torchlight. The elf strained to see into the gloom beyond them, and caught the briefest of flickers of light far below. A chill rose up from the depth compelling him to ride nearer to the uneven wall on his left.

The Herkahs finally emerged from the darkness of the caves and into the early morning light. They shielded their eyes until they became accustomed to the brightness. Nyk heard more than one sigh of relief from his comrades. The warm sun chased away the shadows of the trek through the mountain. The elf glanced over at Zada, her smile confirming they were indeed safe. The nomads urged their mounts on even though they were tired from their all-night journey. None of them wanted to be on the Broken Plain after dark. They headed northeast, angling toward the edge of the forest. The group hoped to reach it by noon and rest beneath their branches. The prince analyzed what had so far transpired. He looked over at Zada, her ashen face and unfocused eyes staring into a place he instinctively knew he did not want to see.

The Herkahs were now far from their homes, heading for Bystyn and the shock that would undoubtedly await them there. He had more than fulfilled his father's order by contacting and bringing back the elusive desert dwellers. Nyk grinned, thinking how his brothers could not possibly surpass this assignment. They reached the edge of the forest, concealing themselves as best as they could within the vegetation. The nomads were not used to the closeness of the trees or the unyielding ground beneath their feet. They were too tired to notice the difference, preferring to rest instead. Sentries protected the perimeter of the camp. The Herkahs tended to their horses in utter silence, a feat that never failed to amaze the elf.

"How far to your home?" asked Zada in hushed tones, the color seeping back into her face.

"About a week," he said scanning the area south and east of the camp. "If we travel a bit farther south we'll run into patrols from my city. It might be prudent to be seen by them and minimize the...." He wanted to say their dumbfounded expressions but no amount of advanced notice could avert that.

"The what?" she asked.

"The commotion our approach will make."

He could picture the open-mouthed stares and hear the sharply inhaled breaths as the Herkahs advanced upon the plain. Many would rub their eyes to make the nightmare go away while others would usher their children indoors. The elves normally welcomed anyone seeking shelter, but those who came were anything but typical travelers.

"We must have quite the reputation in your city," she said without malice.

"Yes, well, it's amazing how the lack of knowledge, coupled with an intense imagination, can turn an ordinary person into something completely different."

"How *are* we perceived within your city?" she asked, curious to know what sort of welcome they could expect.

"Dangerous, brutal...perfect killing machines," he stated uncomfortably. He had witnessed those very things firsthand.

"That we are, young prince, that and more," she added

cryptically.

"Zada, tell me about the storm. It was sent, wasn't it?"

"Yes, Nyk, it was. Evidently the evil has managed to gain enough power to exist in the land once more."

"What do we do now?"

"Whatever we can," she replied and closed her eyes.

Nyk stared hard at her for those three little words did not fill him with comfort. The nomads were visibly uneasy with the events that had just transpired, but were undaunted with what awaited them. If these great warriors fretted over the demons they had fought over the years, how would the elves react? Had Cooper encountered them on his forays onto Herkah lands? Had the demons infiltrated Kepracarn and killed everyone within its walls? He picked up a water skin and took a long drink from it, wiping away the rivulets running down his chin with his sleeve. He ripped off a piece of his tunic, saturated it with water then placed it on his cheek. The bruise had spread upward, giving him a partial black eye. He dabbed at it a few times then lay back on the grass.

They moved on a few hours later. Nyk led the procession, mindful since they were now in Khadry territory. They made camp after dark, posting sentries along the perimeter as they spent one of many unsettled nights on their journey east. Nyk knew the Khadry watched them; he could sense their movements within the trees. Various farmers and travelers spotted them; the former running into their homes, the latter sprinting onto Khadry land. They preferred facing the wrath of the Forest Elves rather than spending another second on the plains with the Herkahs. They scattered like rabbits darting away from an approaching fox, seeking their burrows where the hunter could not get to them. Allad shook his head; Zada raised a brow in amusement. The elf pushed back the hair from his face and rubbed the back of his neck. The effort did not ease a single muscle.

They made good time over the course of the week, covering more distance than Nyk had anticipated. A patrol spotted the group three days out from the city, their flabbergasted expressions eliciting several chuckles from the tribe. One of the riders managed to regain his composure. He immediately peeled away from the group and sped back to Bystyn as fast as his horse could gallop.

"Here we go," Nyk said to no one in particular. He kicked his horse and rode forward, hands up and palms facing the patrol.

The elves waited until he was within shouting distance before ordering him to stop. The prince heeded their command and removed his head covering. The elves stared hard at him, unsure of whether they were seeing a ghost or if this were some sort of trick. They fingered their weapons with one hand. Tightly clenching the reins with the other, they waited for the Herkah to make the next move.

"It's Nyk," he shouted.

The leader of the patrol urged his mount a little closer. He scrutinized the Herkah, noting the swarthy face marred by an ugly bruise extending past his eye. The elf glanced over at the other Herkahs then back to Nyk again.

"Drand! It's me…Nyk!"

"Nyk? Is it really you?"

They rode forward in unison; Nyk with a sense of urgency and Drand filled with disbelief. The prince had been gone a long time and, although no one doubted he would return, none thought he would come back with all of these Herkahs.

They dismounted and embraced, the patrols wary stares focused on the line of black garbed riders. Nyk hastily scribbled a message to his father, dispatching an elf who hastened to catch up with the first rider.

"It's good to see you unharmed, my Lord," the captain stated looking at the bruise. "We thought, well, we didn't know what to think."

"How are things in the city?" asked Nyk, eager to hear any news.

"There is nothing out of the ordinary happening there," he glanced over at the Herkahs then added, "not yet, anyway. There is still no news from Kepracarn, but your return will thrill the entire city."

The prince nodded but said nothing. He had been absent for

many weeks, and was puzzled that the only news to be had was of the tribe following him. Zada had been right about the evil being restricted to the desert area, a momentary bit of good fortune. What would happen when it had the power to sustain itself beyond the range? The Herkahs had some sort of skill when fighting the Kreetch, an ability the well-trained elves apparently did not possess. What was that capability and would the nomads be able to teach the elves if the demons came to their gates? He looked over at Zada and saw that same wan and unfocused appearance. Who exactly was she? She and Allad were indistinguishable from the other Herkahs yet were revered by the nomads. The couple led the tribe without any visible trappings of power. Nyk watched as perspiration began to appear on her forehead, the concern for her visible on Allad's face. The Herkah narrowed his eyes, calling out her name and pulling her back from wherever she had gone. Where did that inner sight keep taking her?

"My Lord," the captain interrupted his thoughts. "How will you explain the Herkahs to our people, not to mention anyone else who happens upon Bystyn?"

"I'm not quite sure yet."

Nyk tried to visualize the sequence of events. After the initial shock wore off, the elves would demand an explanation. What could he tell them? That there were demons loose in the desert forcing the Herkahs to seek sanctuary with the elves? Many believed the nomads *were* demons, and to see nearly two hundred at their gates would surely overwhelm them. Would the nervous elven guards accidentally initiate an incident that might become very ugly very quickly? Allad informed his people that under no condition were they to unsheathe their weapons against any elf, an order Nyk would give to his people as well. What would happen if the myths were too deeply ingrained? He exhaled slowly and prayed everything would somehow fall into place before they reached the city.

They rode for a while longer, setting up camp as the sun began to dip below the horizon. Drand sent the remainder of the patrol off, staying with the tribe and keeping close to Nyk. The captain watched the prince interact with the nomads as if he had been with them forever. The Herkah garb seemed to better suit the prince than did the green and brown elven attire. His mannerisms, too, represented more tribe characteristics rather than elven ones. Nyk waved him over to eat, sitting down cross-legged in front of the fire in one easy motion as the captain joined him. The prince handed him a plate of food; the aroma of spices tantalizing yet foreign to him. Drand remained respectful of his hosts, keeping his emotions in check. He consumed his meal in silence, every bite tastier than the previous one.

"More, Drand?" Zada held up a large spoonful of marinated meat and vegetables, smiling as he stuck his plate out to her.

"Thank you, Zada. It's delicious." The captain finished his second helping then stood to help with guard duty.

"That won't be necessary, Drand," Nyk said.

Drand shrugged and retrieved his bedroll, placing it on the ground next to the prince. Nyk grinned, for the captain was determined to safeguard him regardless of the highly skilled Herkahs surrounding them. The captain was quiet for so long Nyk thought he had fallen asleep.

"My Lord?"

"Yes, Drand?"

"You've done well."

Nyk interlaced his fingers behind his head and stared up at the stars and quarter moon. Crickets chirped and a gentle breeze played with an unruly lock of his hair. These were perfect rewards for surviving the trek through the mountain. He fell asleep within minutes, the smell of grass and dirt the last thing he remembered.

~

Alyxandyr glanced over at Nyk's chair, and then took a sip from his glass. Had his son somehow survived? If so, why hadn't there been any news? He looked over at his remaining children, grateful they were here. He watched his daughter, Alyssa, roll her blue eyes with disapproval as the serving girl made an insignificant error while holding a tray of food. He could not grasp why she fretted over such little things. She straightened out an errant curl, her impeccably coifed auburn hair held in place with bejeweled hairpins. Alyxandyr sighed, for the only thing more annoying than her pursuit of perfection was her attempts at finding suitable mates for her brothers. The king had lost count of how many arguments he had to end because Alyssa would not relent to her brothers.

She ran the daily functions of the castle with an iron will and few living within its gray walls outranked her. She gave Mason and Karolauren a wide berth: the former too serious for her and the latter too cantankerous. The king admired his daughter. Although she could be difficult and demanding, she ran the household well, keeping everything in perfect order. Danyl, he noted, was rather subdued this evening while Styph, the crown prince, playfully engaged the Historian in conversation. He met Mason's gray eyes; the First Advisor knew the king pined for his son. They were doing everything they could to find him, all to no avail.

Alyxandyr's attention strayed to the door where a dirty and exhausted guard demanded to see him. He exchanged tense words with the guard at the door then came forward when the king nodded to him. The guard bowed and handed him a letter. The king read it. He slowly looked up, stunned as the words in the message began to register. Alyxandyr suddenly shot upright, grabbing the startled guard by the front of his tunic and dragging him to the far corner of the room.

"Where did you get this?" demanded the king.

"The prince handed it to me two days ago, my Lord."

"Is it true? Are there Herkahs with him?"

"Yes, my Lord, nearly two hundred."

The king released him and scanned the message once more. "Go clean up and rest, son, you have done well."

The guard nodded and left; the king dropped into a chair by the hearth. His friends and family gathered around him, eager to hear the news contained within the letter. The king remained motionless for a long time, the crumpled note in his hand.

"What does the message say?" everyone asked in unison.

"It says Nyk is on his way home," the king replied, the relief in his voice shared by the others.

"What else does it say, Alyx?" Mason inquired in his deep voice.

"That he is not alone."

Alyxandyr handed the piece of paper to Mason, whose usually veiled thoughts and emotions crowded onto his gaunt face.

"Two days, Alyx? Two *years* wouldn't be enough to prepare the city!"

"For what!" demanded Styph.

"What is said here is not to leave this room tonight, understood? Nyk is scheduled to arrive in two days' time and is accompanied by nearly two hundred Herkahs."

His words were so incomprehensible he might just as well have spoken in a different tongue. The same thoughts ran through everyone's mind. Two hundred Herkahs were coming to Bystyn? Why bring them all here? What would prompt the nomads to travel all this way? How in the Four Corners of the land were they to explain their black garbed guests to the elves?

"He couldn't have brought back one or two," muttered the crown prince. "What are we going to do with two hundred Herkahs?"

"Well," began the king as he took the letter back from Mason, "for one thing, we are not going to turn them away."

"What if they are using Nyk to get into the city?" asked Alyssa, the idea of so many Herkahs on elven lands making her nervous.

"The scout spoke with Nyk and indicated he never noticed anything out of the ordinary. Well, save for the Herkahs themselves. He said Nyk was dressed like the nomads and seemed quite relaxed."

"Why would they leave the desert and come here?" asked the princess.

"Why indeed?" asked Mason. He surmised their departure had been out of necessity rather than a visit to satisfy their curiosity.

"What happens after they arrive?" asked the king.

"Learn from them," stated the Historian.

Karolauren's bright blue eyes sparkled with delight at the prospect of being able to spend time questioning the Herkahs. He was already thinking about what he would ask them and only half listening to the conversation around him.

"First we have to come up with a plan to keep chaos out of the streets," the king reminded them. "Then we have to decide where they can make camp and steel ourselves for the news of whatever brought them to our door."

They worked well into the night, catching a few hours of sleep as dawn painted the sky in pastel shades. Danyl would inform the elves living within the city; Styph would meet with the guards and patrols, and the king would meet with the court. No conflicts would be tolerated, the king vowing to punish anyone, regardless of station, himself.

~

The news traveled through the city like wildfire. The elves congregated on stoops, in shops, and on the street talking about the legendary nomads converging on their city. They kept glancing nervously toward the gate as if the Herkahs were about to enter. They held their breath whenever a group of riders emerged from the shadowy portal. Sophie navigated her way through the crowds, nodding politely to people who wanted her to join in on conversations. She refused to stop and add her opinions. Sophie had seen the nomads before when she was a child living in Kepracarn. They did not frighten her then nor did they now, a fact she was unwilling to share with her friends and neighbors. Not yet, anyway. She snaked her way past the last throng in front of her home and escaped with her bags into the house.

"What's all the excitement about?" asked Ramira. She had been watching the commotion from the front window. She noticed the fingers pointing toward the main gate and dismayed faces but could not figure out what was going on.

"The elves are concerned about Herkahs coming to the city."

"Herkahs? Coming to Bystyn?" Ramira's eyes went wide with excitement.

"You haven't heard?" A slight smile played on Sophie's face.

"You don't seem to be afraid of them," remarked Ramira.

"Well, I'm not."

"Why do the elves fear the Herkahs?"

"Their reputation, fueled by rumor and imagination, has turned them into things they are not."

"You sound very sure of yourself."

"When I lived in Kepracarn, I would go out riding alone, Ramira. The nomads would occasionally roam the edges of Cooper's land immediately following one of my brother's raids. They never accosted me. They had every right to, you know, for the terrible things he used to try do to them, but chose not to. Afraid of them? Hardly. I will welcome them into my home."

Sophie studied Ramira as the young woman leaned back in the rocking chair and placed her hands behind her head. She stared up at the rafters with an introspective look on her face. There was a glimmer of hope in her eyes, hope of possibly encountering her kin.

There is nothing wrong with having the Herkahs as your kinfolk, thought Sophie.

~

Ramira found sleep difficult that night, and not just because of the expected arrival of the Herkahs. She tossed and turned as vicious nightmares tormented her, leaving her drenched in sweat and overly anxious. Her dreams revolved around voiceless phantoms pointing their fingers at her as if she were the bane of the land. She finally managed to shut them out but their wordless insinuations continued to echo within her mind. She rose well before dawn, ate a few bites of food then headed down the avenue. The cool air refreshed her skin. There were quite a few elves out on the plains, their curiosity concerning the nomads exceeding their fear. Was that the reason she now ventured forth? She had told Danyl 'no' when he had asked if she was a Herkah, but could they indeed be her kin?

Daylight began to warm the land, the soft morning rays chasing away the shadows lurking amid the stones and brush. She heard the sounds of hooves behind her, the hollow echoing marking their course through the gate. She turned and recognized Danyl, who motioned his men on before riding over to her. He dismounted and stood before her.

"Are you all right?" he asked. His hand reached up touched her warm cheek.

"I had a sleepless night."

"Anything I can do to help?" The sun had yet to flush the phantoms from her features, leaving her face pale and drawn.

"No, nothing. Your men are waiting for you."

The concern on his face embarrassed her- she was the least important thing to worry about.

Danyl stared at her for one more moment, silently vowing to speak with her later. He jumped into the saddle and raced after the others.

Ramira decided coming onto the plains wasn't a good idea after all and turned to go home. There were an increased number of guards patrolling the streets and stationed along the parapets. The king was determined that no incidents were going to take place. She shrugged and walked up the path alongside the house, joining Sophie and Anci sipping their tea on the terrace. Ramira poured herself a mug and sat down beside them.

Sophie noticed not just her fatigue but also the restlessness in her behavior. Ramira lifted her cup to her lips, the slight trembling in her hand prompting her to steady the mug with her other. She blinked several times then rubbed at her eyes and the back of her neck.

"They must be close by," said Sophie. "I saw Danyl leave a little while ago."

"I passed him on my way back into the city."

Sophie nodded but remained silent.

~

Danyl and his men rode west, locating the undulating black line near mid-morning. The nomads awed the prince; a thrill ran up his spine as three of the black garbed riders made their way toward them. The rest of the Herkahs waited off in the distance. The prince held his breath as the trio approached, their fluid movements and elegant carriage remarkable to behold. Their horses' manes and tails shimmered and fluttered like black silk threads; their glossy black bodies were adorned with tasseled bridles and blankets. The Herkahs trotted toward Danyl, who shrugged off the elves forming a protective circle around him. The Herkahs wore loose fitting attire concealing everything except for their eyes. There was something frightening about someone who exposed the most vulnerable part of the body. For all of Danyl's respect and admiration for the Herkahs, even he felt a pang of fear when they halted before him. One of the horsemen pulled back his face covering. It took Danyl several seconds to realize it was Nyk. The younger prince stared at his brothers' deeply tanned face, the black clothing, and the ease with which he interacted with the nomads. Nyk grinned at his brother. They dismounted and heartily embraced each other, Nyk ruffling Danyl's hair then slapping him on the shoulder. Danyl's complete attention was riveted on the Herkahs who joined them.

"Danyl, this is Zada and her mate, Allad."

Danyl stuck out his hand after wiping the perspiration on his trousers, his eyes sparkling with excitement at the couple before him. Allad's hawkish features and piercing black eyes commanded Danyl's respect; the nomad firmly gripped his hand. Zada studied the prince with soft brown eyes, which were equally as intense as her mates' were. The subtle tinkling her bracelets made as she lifted her hand to Danyl elicited a smile; the dainty sound so contradictory with their perceived myth.

"It is an honor to meet you both."

"You and your brother share a great many good qualities," remarked Zada. "Your father must be very proud."

"Thank you, Zada."

They jumped back on their horses; the princes kept the Herkah pair between them while Danyl's men rode along behind. The guards paid extra attention, fearful that the Herkahs would suddenly strike out and kill the princes. Allad informed Danyl that the Herkahs would remain camped outside the city, but he and Zada would accept the invitation to stay in the castle. They had much to discuss and both races wanted to learn more about the other.

Nyk began to relax as they wound their way past the last line of trees and espied the city. It had been a long two months and the sight of his home sent a wave of relief over him. Allad motioned for the Herkahs to set up camp; Danyl ordered the elves to stay with them. The guards hesitated and exchanged wary glances, unsure if they were more afraid of leaving the princes or of being in the midst of the nomads. The guards, however, obeyed and watched their charges continue on to the city.

They rode up to the mighty edifice, straining their necks as they gaped up at the ancient elven stronghold. Nyk could see many heads sprouting up along the walls, hair and clothing draping over the gray stone as they glimpsed the nomads. The elves whispered to one another. Nyk looked up and scanned the rampart, first confused then disturbed by the odd expressions looking back at him. He had not foreseen the wariness directed at him. The murmuring accompanied them under the gate and up the avenue, passed on by the bystanders staring with disbelief at the fabled desert dwellers.

The couple removed their head covers; Allad's black hair and Zada's shoulder length tresses stirring in the breeze. The Herkahs absorbed the sights, smells, and sounds of the city, nodding approvingly at what they beheld. Zada smiled at a little girl holding a pale pink rose then leaned from her saddle as the girl rushed forward to hand it to her. The nomad inhaled the scent then tucked it into a fold in her tunic. Zada hesitated when they reached the main intersection, the sensation precipitating the indecision disappearing before she could identify it. She attributed it to the unfamiliarity of her surroundings.

"She's a lovely woman," observed Sophie while standing on the front steps with Anci and Ramira.

"One head, two eyes, the correct number of arms and legs." Ramira's sarcastic reply made her smile for some of the elves had exaggerated the Herkahs appearance to the point of ridiculousness.

"It shouldn't take the elves too long to see that the Herkahs are composed of flesh and blood," Anci stated, her eyes wide with wonder.

Ramira watched them go by, disappointed that her vivid cast did not match the swarthy nomads. Perhaps they knew of her people. She sighed, her attention wandering over to Danyl. He was at ease with his guests, pointing to the layout of the city as they wound their way to the castle. The elves, she noted, huddled amongst each other once the riders passed by, talking but not daring to point at the nomads. There would be plenty of conversations and opinions as the days wore on. Ramira retreated into the house after the group progressed beyond her line of sight, her list of chores awaiting her.

~

The king greeted Zada and Allad as they dismounted in front of the main entrance under the sharp eyes of his guard. The Herkah pair followed Alyxandyr to a room at the end of the corridor where they could refresh themselves. They dined together, and then listened to Nyk recount what had transpired since he left the city weeks earlier. He spoke of the meeting with the Herkahs, his time amongst them, and the horrifying fight with the Kreetch. More than one elf recoiled when Nyk described his men's terrible fate. The elves noticed that although the Herkahs were regretful about having to slay Nyk's men, they showed no guilt for their actions. They understood and accepted their lot in life, and would make no excuses for carrying out that unenviable duty.

The elves and nomads studied each other without appearing disrespectful: the curiosity was mutual. Alyxandyr's fascination for the nomads intensified as he sat in their presence. His children, except for Alyssa, seemed to share that intrigue. Finished with his report, Nyk glanced over at Zada who began to tell them of the demons.

Zada described the first two levels of demons, then took a deep breath and spoke of the Vox. Nyk listened intently as the

87

words he had been waiting to hear for a long time filled the air.

"Vox are almost as dangerous as Mahn," she began. "They were at one time Herkahs, taken by the evil and twisted until they became a direct extension of the evil. The Herkahs know how to prevent themselves from becoming a Vox, but are on rare occasions caught off guard and taken by the evil. Once Mahn manages to acquire one, he treats them with the utmost care because they are so difficult to replace. It will only dispatch them with the most urgent of tasks. Anyone getting into a Vox's way will meet an end no one living can describe."

"How do you protect yourselves from becoming one of these Vox?" asked Danyl, Zada's words keeping the room completely silent.

"Every Herkah has a small dagger dipped in my blood; they will use it to end their life if confronted by a Vox."

"Your blood is an anathema to them?" inquired Mason.

"Evidently. That was something we found out by accident. We were missing one of our tribe who happened to return a few days later, apparently well but there was something odd about him. Allad had taken one of my knives from me when it nicked my hand. When the Vox saw the blood, it flinched involuntarily motivating Allad to slash it. We were stunned as we watched it writhe in pain then die. The wound Allad had inflicted was hardly fatal and could not have caused the agony."

"Is there magic flowing through your veins?" Karolauren stopped writing long enough to ask his question; his messy script was an enigma to them all.

"I wield no magic, Historian, but the elves do, which is why we have undertaken this journey."

"What do you mean, Zada?"

"We have fought the Kreetch and the Radir, King Alyxandyr. Shortly before we left we found one of our tribe with his coated knife thrust deep into his chest. The Vox are seeking new recruits and that means the evil is active in the land once more. It searches for the Source of Darkness that would allow it to annihilate every living thing in this land."

"Where is this Source of Darkness located and what does it

look like?" asked Alyxandyr.

"We don't know the answer to either question; all we know is it is somewhere in the land and the evil has ventured forth to find it."

"Does Mahn know what its appearance is?" inquired Styph, the strangeness of their predicament ballooning before them.

"No, I don't believe so or it would already have possession of it."

"You seem to know quite a bit about this Mahn and its ilk," stated Mason. "Why?"

"The evil, First Advisor, originates from the desert and our history, what little remains, tells us that it destroyed a city on the edge of the desert about a thousand years ago. We do not know why. The evil has been silent for almost a thousand years, even though we have battled its minions over that same expanse of time."

"Kepracarn is silent." The king looked her in the eye. "Could the evil and its subordinates have caused them harm…or worse?"

Zada shrugged, the reasons for Cooper's silence a mystery to her.

Her words hovered before them with the promise of horror and death. The Herkahs had come to Bystyn to offer the elves their swords and to ask the elves to use their magic against the demons. The darkness swelling in the west was going to sweep across the land, and weapons of steel would not be sufficient to fight it. The elves' powerful magic, long dormant, had to be awakened. They glanced at each other, wanting to disbelieve the Herkah yet knowing the nomads would not proceed to Bystyn without a valid reason.

"How much time do you suppose we have before Mahn comes to our gates?" asked Styph.

"It will grow in strength but will not venture from the desert until it is time to take possession of what it so desperately covets."

"What if we go to the desert- find and destroy it before it has a chance to become a threat?" suggested the king.

"We barely escaped from the sandstorm, Father," Nyk

reminded him. "It apparently can defend itself from such an assault."

The long afternoon shadows chased the sunlight from the city. Those gathered within the chamber remained silent; each lost in the words spoken by Nyk and Zada. Alyxandyr gazed down upon his clasped hands, the unbidden vision of a sword tightly clenched in them surfacing in his mind. Styph stared out the long window, striving to imagine the abominations growing steadily in the west. Karolauren shuffled through his notes, his uneven white brows forming one continuous line across his forehead. Danyl absently scratched at his arm, his attention repeatedly drawn to the Herkahs seated diagonally across from him.

"It is getting late and you have had a long journey," stated Alyxandyr. "We should adjourn and meet again tomorrow."

~

Danyl headed for Sophie's house, Zada's words sending chills through him despite the warm early summer evening. He increased his pace, relying on his feet to help him escape their dire situation… for a little while, anyway. Sophie and Anci were out visiting but Ramira sat at the kitchen table reading from one of Anci's books. The shadows obscured him as he watched her labor over the elven script. He smiled as she followed each symbol with her index finger. One in particular was difficult for her to decipher; her forefinger remained poised underneath it for quite some time. He silently slipped up behind her, her concentration so intense she didn't even notice him enter the kitchen. He leaned over her shoulder and read aloud the word that puzzled her.

"'Shast' means to 'explain something that has no physical substance'."

"Sweet mercy, Danyl!" she cried out.

"I didn't mean to scare you."

She looked up at him, his anxiety making his features appear tense and tired. She poured them both a glass of wine then patiently waited for him to tell her what was on his mind. He straddled the bench, studying her face by the flickering lamplight while running his fingers along her soft cheek. Something deep down inside him flared to life, gently urging him to trust her. He revealed what he had learned at the meeting and then watched her reaction. He was pleased that, although the words alarmed her there was no sign of panic in her eyes.

"What will you do now?" she asked after a few moments.

"We don't know, Ramira."

"And your magic?"

"It slumbers somewhere within these lands," he replied, rubbing the tension in his temples. "The first king and his people were all imbued with this power. The farther they ventured from their land of birth, however, the more the magic began to coalesce into only a few individuals. The king retained all of the power by the time they reached the future site of Bystyn. It disappeared when he died. It did, however, surface a few times when we battled other races wielding their own particular arts. Other than that it has been absent."

"When was the last time it was used?"

"A few hundred years ago, Queen Sathra battled the witch Envia from the city of Daimoryia in the east. Sathra ended up dying from the poison Envia had exposed her to but not before defeating the witch."

"Perhaps the other power roused it from wherever it went and maybe that's how it will awaken this time?"

"Maybe, but from what Zada said this evil makes the other confrontations seem insignificant. I remember reading about how potent our power was but I'm not sure if it is strong enough to defeat this enemy. Especially if it manages to acquire this Source of Darkness."

"Do the Herkahs have any magic?"

"Zada says no, but I have a feeling there is something they are not telling us. Nyk told me about this unfocused look in her eyes, one so intense that Allad becomes very concerned for her."

"An inner eye?"

"Possibly," he replied. "She also mentioned the evil covets Vox, meaning Herkahs taken, then transformed into high demons

91

that even Mahn is wary of."

"You don't believe they are responsible for this evil, do you?"

"No, but they are somehow linked with it."

Ramira looked into his eyes and saw no criticism of the Herkahs. The nomads were as vulnerable to the evil as the elves, but at least the desert dwellers were willing to face it with the Bystynians. She took a sip from her glass and closed her eyes, the ruby colored liquid warming her stomach. Danyl toyed with his glass, his fingers absently turning the stem, his head supported by his other hand. There were dark circles under his eyes and his normally tanned face had lost some of its color. His hand reached behind his neck, rubbing at the tension that had been building up for several days. Ramira got up and sat behind him. She leaned into his back and wrapped her arms protectively around him. He took her hands into his, welcoming the contact.

"You need to rest."

She led him to her room, made him lie down, and took off his short boots. The prince was fast asleep before she tucked the blanket under his chin. The moment took her back to the cave months ago. She had urged him to sleep then, too, watching over him as she wrestled with her own confusion. Ramira somehow knew she would always watch over him. She smiled at him, pushed aside an unruly section of his hair then left, closing the door softly behind her.

FOUR

Gard watched the nomads pass by his forest, disbelief radiating from his bright gray eyes. They were heading for Bystyn. The reasons that prompted them east were possibly tied to the oddities occurring in his own land. Game had disappeared from the far western fringes of the forest; the vegetation appeared scorched. Guards patrolling that area went out but never came back. Some unknown force kept pushing them farther east until they halted in the hollows. This was the unmarked boundary between the Khadrys' and the Bystynian elves' domains. The tribe's exodus underscored the unsettling feelings in his chest. He contemplated his options while studying the hastily erected camp. Makeshift lean-tos and unpacked bundles reminded him of how often they had to flee on a moment's notice. The Khadry's nervousness increased every time the foul winds blew from the west. If this continued, the Khadry would end up at the gates of Bystyn before the summer reached its zenith. He was their leader; a descendant of royalty. He was unafraid to face any obstacle but could not fight an invisible enemy. He stuck his hands in his pockets and rested one foot on a decaying tree trunk. He glanced to his right toward their abandoned lands, then to his left where he knew the city stood. A young woman approached him, her strained features adding years to her face as she held out a water skin to him. He reached out and cupped her chin, she smiled tiredly back at him. Gard didn't like his options. The split between the Khadry and the city elves was bitter and centuries old. That had to change if he were to keep his people safe. The Khadry were a fiercely proud people but the whispered fears that arose from the strange happenings gave them only one logical choice.

Gard pushed his black hair from his forehead, revealing the lightning bolt zigzagging through an oak branch brand. He respected the nomads, but not the irksome Kepracarnians. Gard could not imagine what they possessed that would motivate Cooper to instigate those endless attacks. Had Cooper finally driven them off the desert? Gard didn't think so. He had to find out what was happening and that meant going to Bystyn. He chose five companions and rode south then east toward the main road. With any luck, they would meet up with an elven patrol and send word to Bystyn requesting a meeting between the elves.

~

Danyl, Allad, Lance, and Ramira reined in their horses beneath a copse of trees and dismounted. They stretched their legs while viewing the area. This patrol had left Bystyn to conduct a widespread search just short of the borders. The principal route passing from west to east and back again was little more than a well-worn dirt road. A few inns and an occasional farm stood along its edges.

Allad, dressed in elven garb, was growing used to the greenery. He told the elves about the roots, berries, and wild-growing vegetables the nomads gathered during the course of the seasons. The precious spices they used were located at only one oasis; the journey to it was hazardous even for the hardy nomads. Danyl asked what perils lay concealed within the sands.

"The dunes are not stable, and if you are not careful the sands will suck you down before you even realize what is happening. Scorpions and snakes are rare but lethal; the storms cropping up unexpectedly change the landscape. We only travel at night and use the stars to guide us; to try during the burning heat of day is sheer folly."

"And I thought nothing could survive in the desert," stated the prince.

"Quite the contrary, Danyl, for although the sands may seem barren there are areas where things grow. The scorpions and snakes thrive around the oasis and it is there where the greatest danger lies."

"An oasis must be a welcome sight even with those perils," said Ramira.

"Indeed it is, but when you are thirsty or in need of sustenance the danger is worth the risk."

Lance looked up toward the northwest sky: a long low line of clouds hugged the horizon. Sheets of rain pouring out from their gray underbellies blotted out everything beneath them; lightning streaked randomly throughout. The leading edge of the wind stirred their hair. Danyl urged them onto their horses, leading them to an inn a couple of miles farther south. They arrived moments before the thunderstorm. Two of the guards saw to the horses; the rest entered the inn and made themselves comfortable at a corner table. They could see the innkeeper mentally counting his profits. He approached the table and gave them a hearty welcome. They ordered bowls of stew and mugs of ale, which the innkeeper promptly brought. He placed the bowls in front of his guests. The strange elf's expressionless features compelled the innkeeper to stretch out his arms to serve him.

"Is it always this quiet?" asked Allad.

"There should be more movement along this road but word of the Herkahs on elven lands might have dampened some travel plans." Danyl quickly added, "No offense meant."

"None taken."

"It hasn't hindered the innkeeper's mood," remarked Lance.

"We're probably one of the few customers he has gotten in a while," replied the prince.

The innkeeper brought them another loaf of bread and refilled their glasses.

"We'll undoubtedly make up the difference when we pay for this," stated the captain, cutting the bread into slabs.

The captain glanced at the innkeeper who immediately amended his assessment of the patrons sitting at the table. He absently scratched his left palm while re-estimating the cost of the meals he had served them.

"Captain Lance's unspoken convictions may leave us with a couple of extra coins jingling in our pouches," Allad stated wryly.

Danyl was about to speak when the door opened. To his amazement, a half dozen elves dressed in brown walked in from the rain. Danyl's men immediately drew their swords and surrounded the prince, a confused Allad and Ramira following suit.

A pair of bright gray eyes studied each member of the group sitting at the table. The innkeeper dropped a glass and backed up against the wall.

Ramira felt every nerve in her body becoming tauter as the seconds ticked by. They were elves like the ones she was with, yet the smoldering energy passing between them vibrated in the air. She watched one of the elves stride forward, his upturned hands facing outward. Danyl gave a quick order, the sound of weapons sliding into their scabbards relieving some of the tension. The prince met the other elf in the middle of the room, the unabashed scrutiny lasting for several long moments.

"I am Gard, leader of the Khadry. You are Prince Danyl?"

"Yes," replied the prince, wondering what the Forest Elf wanted. He watched the emotions ripple across Gard's weathered features, indecision and displeasure the most prominent ones. Danyl invited Gard to join him at a table away from the others, a sinking feeling growing in the pit of his stomach. Both sets of elves watched intently, their hands on their swords as their leaders moved away from their protection.

"You travel with a Herkah and an outsider," remarked Gard.

"I don't think my choice of companions is what brought you here," Danyl crisply replied.

"Actually it is. You see, we observed the nomads heading to your city."

"I'm sure they avoided trespassing upon your lands."

"That they did, but such a trek is highly unusual, don't you think?"

"What do you want, Gard?"

Gard studied Danyl in silence, attempting to gauge his character. He had to make a choice whether or not to unburden his problems for his people's sake.

Danyl's patience was wearing thin, but he waited for Gard to continue speaking.

"Strange things have been happening in our forest. The nomads abandoning the desert for your city made me wonder if they were, possibly, related."

When Danyl asked what these peculiarities were, Gard told him.

"We are slowly being pushed into the eastern half of the forest and do not expect to be left alone there either. I want you to know we are there in case there are any unexpected encounters."

Danyl nodded in understanding. A brilliant flash of lightning and an immediate rumble of thunder punctuated the dire circumstances of which Gard spoke.

"There is an evil entity that has awakened in the west, and it threatening all of us. You and your kin will find sanctuary within the gray walls of Bystyn. That I promise you."

Gard stood, hesitating for a moment before sticking his hand out to the prince. Danyl took it and shook to the temporary truce. The two elves returned to their respective tables; the innkeeper closed his eyes and slid down into a chair. Profits or not, he wanted the storm to end.

Danyl ate his meal, ignoring the others as they engaged in small talk, all the while burning to know what had been said. Gard carried his goblet to a chair in front of the fireplace, mulling over what Danyl had revealed. The Khadry had much to think about, not the least of which was the day they would face Bystyn's walls. His meeting with the city elf went better than he had anticipated. Gard believed the ill tiding sweeping across the land had already prepared the Bystynian elves for any possibility, including the Khadrys' presence. What would occur once the Khadry knocked on Bystyn's gate was another matter. He hoped Danyl would keep his word.

The storm intensified then drifted away only to be replaced by another one. Thunderstorms this time of year followed each other in succession across the land. The fields depended upon them; many innkeepers made a lot of money from individuals seeking shelter. This host, however, prayed for the rains to cease so the two enemies would leave. Danyl joined the Khadry after he had eaten his fill.

"The Herkahs were forced out of their lands for the same

reason you now face," stated Danyl.

"I thought as much," he said glancing over at Allad. "The nomads do not easily abandon the white sands. Don't tell me Cooper has gotten the upper hand on them?"

"No. We haven't heard a word from him nor have the Herkahs, for that matter."

"We have not spotted any of his raiders…I mean, patrols, either," confessed Gard. The thought of Cooper being quiet and leaving the nomads alone was yet another piece of the puzzle.

"By the way," added Danyl, "I would avoid any confrontation with whatever is lurking in your forest. Your skills are no match for whatever hunts you and will not be felled by your blades."

"Why are you telling me all of this?" The suspicion was clear in his voice and in his glittering gray eyes. The few words he and Danyl had spoken were more than had been exchanged over the past several generations.

"I don't know, but the problem growing in the west is better met with friend than with foe."

"Are you asking me for help, city elf?" Gard stared hard at Danyl.

"I am saying that you will not be turned away if and when you come to our gates."

"What would your king say to such an unabashed invitation?"

There was a hint of sarcasm in Gard's voice as the remnants of the bitterness between the two elves resurfaced. Danyl ignored it. There was no logical reason for him to argue with the Khadry; there was too much at stake to resort to petty emotions. The king had witnessed the arrival of an entire tribe of Herkahs: would another unexpected group make any difference?

"He would say you are welcome." Danyl left, the Khadry watching him as he walked back to the table.

~

The weather refused to break as the afternoon turned into evening. It became clear they would have to spend the night. The innkeeper assigned the elves rooms at opposite ends of the building, just in case their reprieve was short lived. The city elves made their way upstairs after dinner, nodding to the guard posted in the hallway outside their rooms.

Allad and Danyl sat in front of the fire, the elf telling the nomad about the conversations with the Khadry. Ramira sat in front of the window staring out into the stormy night. The tempest reminded her of the cliffs far to the west by the Broken Plain. She glanced over at Danyl, the friendship developing between him and the Herkah quickly taking root. She liked and respected the nomads: there were no flowery pretenses to their ways. They kept to the desert, avoiding contact with others. The repercussions against those who harassed them were swift and deadly. She was relieved they had befriended the elves.

She yawned and stretched then lay down upon the bed, her eyes closing while listening to the elf and the Herkah. She drifted off to sleep; there were no bad dreams that night. Ramira awoke briefly during the night and realized she was not alone. Danyl slept beside her; she placed her hand over his as it lay by his side. His fingers caressed hers; her head rolled against his shoulder as sleep whisked her away.

~

They rose to a milky dawn and went downstairs to eat. The innkeeper gave both parties heaping plates of food and pots of tea, hoping they would fill their bellies and leave. The rains had been relentless, leaving puddles of mud the size of small ponds everywhere.

"I don't think I'll be riding behind anyone," muttered Allad as he surveyed the slushy earth.

Both groups of elves congregated under the porch in front of the inn as they waited to depart. Danyl walked over to Gard and handed him a letter.

"If you need to get to Bystyn, deliver this to the first patrol you see. It will grant you safe passage into the city. Word will already be spread that you are not to be harmed."

Gard took the message, the resigned expression on his face tinged with bitterness. The Khadry knew time was against them. Allad joined Danyl on the porch as Gard mounted his horse and sped off toward the line of trees to the north. They stood there for a while before they resumed their journey home.

"The evil is tainting their homes," said Allad. "The Kreetch have been busy."

Allad absently tugged on his ear thinking how unfortunate- and unprepared- the Khadry were to deal with those nasty fiends. Mahn was forcing them into the forest and Kreetch hated being in enclosed places.

"Why? What are they hoping to accomplish?"

"The evil must eat, and the souls of the good are just as easily digestible as those of the bad."

"Can those spirits ever be set free, Allad? I mean after they have been 'eaten'. Are they still alive while being inhabited by those...things?"

"The hosts are, in fact, alive, but it is more merciful to kill them rather than to try and revitalize them. They are never the same afterward. Defeating the evil, young prince, would break the connection, but in the meantime it will consume many more."

Danyl contemplated the legendary Herkahs encamped outside the gates, the Khadry, and the ancient evil intent on destroying them all. All of this was precipitated by the emergence of a dark power that Mahn coveted. Flesh and blood alone would be unable to fend it off, yet the elven magic remained dormant. He glanced over at Ramira. She offered him a slight smile, one that he returned. The news they were bringing back affirmed that what was developing in the west was moving steadily toward them.

~

A vast hall chronicling the lives of the elven rulers stood adjacent to the castle garden. A series of floor to ceiling windows ran the length of the wall; plants, trees, and shrubs were visible beyond the thick panes. The elves sought to bring in the peaceful outdoors, filling the wall space between the windows with well-manicured birches and flowering bushes. Careful pruning kept the ancient birches as supple and delicate as saplings. Mahogany pedestals held a variety of ancient artifacts once owned by the great kings and queens of the past. Weapons, jewelry, and personal items lay upon beds of velvet, as if awaiting their long dead masters to pick them up and use them once more. A narrow and thickly woven red rug ran the length of the chamber and led to the altars. All of the shrines were of equal size, including the one belonging to the first king of Bystyn. A large tapestry hung on the wall at the end of the hall depicting the elves crossing the land on their way to the future site of Bystyn. Annal, the first king's queen, wove the tapestry with great skill and infinite patience. The endeavor took years to complete.

The foreground consisted of a small knoll covered in sparse brush; the background a line of majestic peaks and a dense forest line located at their feet. A string of shorter mountains tapered off to the left of the picture, the land at their bases lush and plentiful. Danyl knew that land all too well and how very different it was today. The Broken Plain had undergone a cataclysmic change since the elves passed by it a thousand years ago. He concentrated on the piece; his eyes were focused on the elf standing apart from the travelers milling around campfires to the right. The image of the dead king looked squarely up at the knoll and right into Danyl's eyes regardless from which direction the prince stood. Alyxandyr's stare was so intense it made the hair on his arms stand up.

~

The table beneath the tapestry held the king's sword and Annal's silver circlet: simple items for such esteemed people. Their foresight and courage brought the elves untold leagues to their present location, where they had thrived ever since. Alyxandyr had never fully revealed the reasoning behind the trek east. Faded references mentioned strife within the elven community he had abandoned. The split between the Bystynian elves and the Khadry could have been rooted in the same conflict. The king's decision to alter the method of ruling might have exacerbated the separation. He had opted for a monarchy, foregoing the council that had governed the other society. He wondered, not for the first time, if their kin still lived somewhere far in the west.

He cocked his head to the side, remembering what Zada had told him about the evil. Alyxandyr and his people had crossed the Broken Plain prior to the cataclysmic destruction. The king had sent back a patrol a year after establishing the city. He was aware of the devastation yet chose to write very little about it in the historical records. A peculiarity considering Alyxandyr kept meticulous accounts. The prince glanced back to the king. He stared so long and hard at him that the branches and brush in the foreground began to fill up his vision. An unseen wind stirred them to life and blew a strand of his hair across his forehead. He heard insects and felt the floor beneath his feet become soft and yielding. The smell of earth drifted up into his nose.

"What are you looking at?"

"A true mystery," stated Karolauren, chuckling at the startled prince.

"Do you know?" he asked, throwing the bemused Historian a dark look.

"I've scoured every written word but he never mentions a thing."

"So you think there is something there, too, don't you?"

"Absolutely, now, I have some work for you to do if you can spare a few moments."

The Historian turned and left the hall. Danyl gazed at the scene for a few more moments then followed him to the expansive library around the corner.

~

Karolauren handed Danyl a list just as an attendant informed him that he had a visitor. The prince smiled as Ramira walked in, her jaw dropping as she took in the shelves filled with maps, books, and other documents. Danyl introduced her to Karolauren, who nodded then pointed at the inventory in his hand.

"What a pleasant surprise," said Danyl.

"Sophie asked me to give this to you."

She passed him a letter, her eyes trying to absorb the marvels all around her.

Danyl unsealed it and stared at the blank sheet of paper, grinning at Sophie's ingenuity. He folded the note and put it into his pocket, making a mental note to thank the meddling woman the next time he visited her.

"Why don't you stay for a while?"

"I'd get in the way," she replied.

"Unlikely, for Karol despises idle hands."

The Historian gave him a crusty look.

"I'll show you around."

He motioned for her to follow him, and then proceeded to give her a quick tour of the maze that seemed to go on forever. He pointed to the different sections where everything from birth and death records, yearly harvest tallies, and the chronology of the city had been stored. She accompanied him to the far corner of the room where a set of massive oaken doors stood. He opened the doors with ease, grabbing a couple of lamps before inviting her inside. She walked into the center of the chamber and stared at the priceless artifacts occupying the shelves. There were busts of people, small jars carved out of pink stone, and burnished shields bearing family crests. Chests of oak, maple, and cherry wood sporting fine brass hardware were stacked along one wall; a folding screen in need of repair leaned across from them.

She spotted an item partially concealed within a bed of velvet that was set far back from the edge of the counter. She picked up the small perfume bottle fabricated out of pale blue glass; its delicately carved stopper formed an undulating point. She held it to the light and swirled its contents, then deftly plucked the top free. The Historian walked into the room, the strangled cry of panic remained stuck in his ancient throat. She never noticed him. Ramira was overwhelmed by the fragrance emanating from the bottle. The intoxicating combination of spices, incense, and essences of exotic flowers transported her far away from the library. She imagined herself along the banks of a far off river, beneath a full moon that bathed everything in a silver hue. She could hear a waterfall from somewhere nearby and feel the gentle caress of a cool evening breeze. Anticipation and seduction floated in the air; she shivered with pleasure as she dabbed a drop behind her ears. One word came unbidden to her mind: Nephret.

"You could have broken that!"

The agitated historian sputtered his disapproval, the string of old elvish words bringing her back to the present.

"It's a perfume bottle…just a slight twist of the stopper opens it."

Ramira handed it to him, the relief on his face replaced with displeasure. He took the bottle from her, unsure if he should be angry or thank her.

"That girl is your responsibility, boy!" He shot the prince a look of warning then huffed back toward his book-strewn desk.

Danyl shrugged his shoulders. A small stone box situated near the perfume bottle caught his attention. The prince had spent countless hours within this chamber, handling every item many times but never this box. His curiosity got the best of him. He opened the lid and lifted out a delicate bracelet, its clasp broken but still intact as he held it up for Ramira to see. The little blue beads caught the light; Danyl thought they resembled sapphires.

"Very lovely," she said taking it from him. The beads felt warm, even though they had been within the confines of the stone box in a cool room. He returned it to the box and slipped it into his pocket, determined to get a better view of the beads in the daylight.

The Historian was absent when they emerged from the rear of the library, giving Danyl a few moments to examine the piece of jewelry. It was not elven for the blue glass was foreign; the method used to string the beads along a fine filament of gold unknown to their craftsmen.

"You seem rather fascinated with that," remarked Ramira.

He squinted while trying to bend the end back into shape but the delicate piece took on the consistency of iron. It was not going to comply with his wishes.

"I was just wondering whose skilled hands made it and why it was in the first king's possession."

"Perhaps someone placed it in there to keep it from being lost or further damaged," she suggested.

"Maybe." He searched for a piece of cloth and carefully

wrapped the bracelet before placing it in his pocket.

"The Historian will undoubtedly be angry," she playfully warned him.

"He won't know, will he?"

"It would be my duty to report any kind of thievery, wouldn't it?"

Ramira grinned at him, which elicited a playful pout before he returned his attention to the list. During the ensuing silence, her thoughts drifted to the Khadry. Their bitterness toward the Bystynians bothered her the most. Both elves belonged to the same group once and, in essence, still did. What kind of mistrust had arisen between them to warrant such a reaction?

"How did your father take the news concerning the Khadry?" she asked, unwilling to wallow in the silence any longer.

"He was mildly astonished, but I think recent events told him that was inevitable. If they do end up in the city, the shock the elves received by the Herkahs' presence would surely blunt the commotion the Khadry would bring."

"What will happen if all three peoples were to end up in the city for the winter?"

That thought had not occurred to the prince, since he believed any confrontation from the west would happen prior to winter. Distrust of each other, limited food supplies, and a host of other problems could arise and send the city into chaos. If the conflict were to transpire while the groups were at odds with each other, the evil would already have won.

"I hadn't thought of that, but it is something we will have to address if need be."

"Well," she stood and faced him, "I must leave. Sophie told me to return before noon so I can take some things to Jack and Ida."

"I'd like to go with you if you don't mind. I think I've had enough of these walls for a while."

"What about your list?"

"What list?" he asked innocently, sliding the piece of paper in amongst the pile on Karolauren's desk.

~

Danyl, Ramira, and the ever-present Lance rode to the house beneath a brilliant blue sky. The warm sun chased away the shadows and doubts. Allad spotted them as they passed under the gates and accepted the prince's invitation to join them. They chatted amiably as they rode toward the orchards, avoiding any discussion concerning what lurked in the west. They rounded the lower section of the trees and spotted the house. The couple sat beneath the shade of the porch, their attention on the Herkah as the group dismounted.

"It's a pleasure to meet you," Allad stated, his hand extended to the couple.

They hesitantly accepted the nomad's handshake. Allad's friendly grip eased their apprehensions; the couple visibly relaxed before the contact was broken. Ida offered them refreshments. They sat together for a bit; the old couple studied the nomad.

Danyl noticed the sagging barn doors; the ramp leading up to it had begun to splinter. Much to the dismay of Jack and Ida, their guests headed over to repair them. Ramira and Ida watched as the nomad and the young elves removed their tunics, noting the myriad of scars running across Allad's back, shoulders, and chest. He had seen- and survived- many battles. When and if it came time to fight, it was clear he would not back away from any conflict.

"Kreetch, Danyl," explained Allad in response to the elf glancing at his scars. "They tend to leave a lasting impression, don't they?"

"I didn't mean to stare, Allad," said Danyl. His curiosity got the better of him. "Allad...when the demons attacked Nyk and his men, you killed them to keep their souls from being taken yet you are not affected?"

"The Kreetch despise and find us 'distasteful'. They can and have killed Herkahs, but we are somehow immune to their poison."

"But the Vox..." began the prince.

"The Radir, on the other hand, have the ability to inflict their venom into us; the Vox are a demon unto themselves. They exist independently of the evil, choosing to tie themselves to it to further their own plans. They can survive without the evil, understand?"

"So any other creatures slashed by Kreetch are not immune to them?" asked Lance.

"None that we know of, Lance." He grunted with effort as the weight of the unhinged doors taxed his strength.

"Is there a way to tell if someone hasn't been overcome by their poison?" asked Danyl, removing the metal mounts from the door.

"I don't know," replied the nomad. "If there is we haven't been able to determine that yet."

"Then why was Nyk spared?" asked Danyl, needing to know that answer.

"Your brother, young elf, wasn't killed because without him we wouldn't be here."

"That was quite a risk. What would happen if he showed any signs of being possessed, Allad?"

"There is a strength that runs through his veins, Danyl, one that would cease to flow if our worst fears came to light." The Herkah spoke diplomatically, yet Nyk's death was imminent if he showed signs of being possessed by the demons.

"You would slay my brother and jeopardize a confrontation with the elves?"

"Son, I would execute anyone if it meant deterring the evil. May I suggest you speak with Nyk…he of all people understands, even if he doesn't agree with our reasoning."

"I think I will, Allad, even though I do not gainsay what you have told me."

"Good, now, let's get to work on these doors."

～

They worked on through the afternoon while Ramira helped Ida in the house. She stared out the kitchen window as the elves and the nomad labored on. A wry smile touched her lips for titles and stations in life meant nothing if you removed yourself from life. Was she separating herself because she feared that her past might affect those she cared about? The Herkahs accepted their lot in life even if it meant killing good men defiled by the evil. That made them pragmatic and, to some extent, honest. Her eyes strayed to Danyl. Did she have the courage to follow her heart? She crossed her arms further denying the ember of emotion glowing within her.

~

Ramira went back into the house to help Ida pack some items to take to Sophie. By the time the women had filled the baskets, the others had washed and joined them. Jack placed a small bundle into Ramira's hand and watched as she unfolded the cloth, smiling at the silver hair clip he had created. She held up the silver hair clip and gazed upon a tiny engraved songbird nestled within the boughs of a blooming apple tree. He must have spent hours polishing it for it shone and sparkled like the joy emanating from her eyes. She kissed him on the cheek in gratitude. They mounted their horses and looked at the couple.

"We can't thank you enough for your help, especially you, Allad," the old man said.

"I have thoroughly enjoyed the afternoon, Jack, and I hope I will be invited back."

"Wait! I almost forgot!"

Ida disappeared into the house then came back out carrying a sack, which she handed to Danyl. He lifted it to his nose and inhaled the scent of the spicy cakes.

"Those won't make it past the orchards," Jack teased as the prince plucked out four of the little treats and tossed one to each of his companions.

"Thank you," he said around a mouthful of cake.

~

They entered the city as the sun began to sink, feeling tired yet content at the same time. Allad watched the vermilion orb float over the land until the gate blocked out the image. They had accomplished much during the day; the elf and Allad would now attend to their own duties. Danyl glanced at the expressions on the elves' faces, noting the variety of responses the nomad elicited as they rode by. Their eyes reflected everything from uncertainty to a lingering fear; the one thing they all shared was respect for the Herkah. It was difficult not to admire him. Allad and his people chipped away at the myths surrounding them in indirect ways. They helped where they could and remained at arm's length where they could not. Their constant presence with the prince also eased some of their apprehensions for if the family trusted them, then so should they. The prince studied the nomads' profile, noticing the proud bearing of his head and the fierce determination in the set of his jaw. The wisdom shining from his black eyes did not come from reading tomes in a comfortable library but from the harsh realities that made up his world. The burning sun, vicious sandstorms, and confrontations with the demons were forces he and his people resisted on a constant basis. Nyk had had a brief taste of those conditions and barely survived. Were the elves beginning to realize the nomads' dark demeanor was rooted in their harsh setting? He certainly hoped so. They stopped in front of Sophie's house where Ramira dismounted, grabbed her baskets, and wished them a good evening. She expertly caught the cake Danyl tossed to her without dropping a crumb, finishing the treat before she walked the few paces to the front steps. Danyl stared after her for a few seconds before Allad interrupted his thoughts.

"She reminds me of a Koro flower."

"What is that?" asked the prince.

"It's a snow white flower composed of layers of petals the size of a plate with a scent you would give an entire kingdom for," began Allad. "It's also highly poisonous. Nestled amongst those velvety petals is a single thorn, and more than one has pricked their nose on it as they inhaled its perfume."

"Are you saying she is venomous, Allad?" asked Danyl, who failed to see Lance's interest in the conversation.

"I'm simply advising you to find the whereabouts of that thorn, young prince."

Allad noted the attraction between Danyl and Ramira. She was physically beautiful and her intentions, those he could identify, were honorable. She was not an elf nor did she belong to the tribe; Kepracarn was not her home, either. This left few other possibilities. For the time being, she was an enigma to him and, from what he had seen, to herself, as well.

~

Bathed and fed, Danyl retreated to his room and poured himself a glass of wine. He sat in front of the fire to catch up on the day's events. The bit of cloth lying on his desk caught his attention. He held it up to the light and thought he saw something swirling within the beads. He rubbed his eyes then looked again but the results were the same. He used the tip of his knife to try to isolate one of the beads when his hand slipped breaking one of them. Before he could curse his awkwardness, a strange thing happened…

He was no longer in his chambers but walking down a side street beneath a full moon; a cool breeze stirred the pure white sand on which he walked. Thick walls painted silver by the moonlight flanked him; the scent of spices and simmering meat tantalized him from a nearby open window…

The image lasted for no more than a few seconds, but he could not figure out why it had appeared to him in the first place. The details had been so sharp that his senses responded to what he had experienced. No. That was impossible. He was just tired. Danyl looked down and saw the remnants of the bead, the tip of his knife tapping closer to the bracelet. Karolauren wouldn't notice two missing beads, now would he? Danyl shattered another blue sphere…

A small, skinny man with a shaven head and piercing black eyes sat cross-legged across from him. His mahogany-colored skin was clad in a crisp white kilt on which a pile of scrolls rested. He wore an earring in one ear and a broad necklace studded with blue, white, and green stones. They were in a courtyard. Water splashed from somewhere behind him; wide leaves hung from slim trunks that provided shelter from the unbearable heat. The man sat as if waiting for him to speak…

Danyl snapped back to his room and put the bracelet down, the visions as alarming as they were exciting. A part of him wanted to keep on breaking the tiny blue globes, for the remarkable scenes fascinated him. Something stayed his hand, however, as if warning him that some of the images would not be quite so innocent. One more couldn't hurt, could it? Danyl picked up the knife and, after hesitating for a second, brought the point down…

He was leaning on a boulder for support. His legs burned with exertion; he gulped in air to fill his heaving lungs. Perspiration poured down his face and into his eyes; he wiped it away while the suns merciless rays baked the back of his head. Everything became blurry. The dizziness and nausea forced him to his knees; he struggled to get back onto his feet and on his way…

His room slowly materialized around him, but that offered no measure of comfort. Whatever he had experienced had felt so incredibly real. What were these beads? They were almost like repositories for memories, but such a thing could not exist. He quickly wrapped the bracelet in its cloth and placed it in his drawer. Danyl refilled his goblet and walked out onto the balcony. He was shocked to see the golds and lavenders staining the night sky to the east. He realized that what he thought had taken only a few moments had actually taken all night. The bracelet beckoned to him from its hiding place, but Danyl ignored its tempting summons.

~

Ramira lay wide-awake. Her nightmares crouched on the edge of sleep, waiting for her to close her cycs. She got out of bed, denying them the chance to further torment her. Ramira was about to go downstairs when she sensed something just beyond the edges of her senses. She grabbed her knives and cautiously moved out into the hallway. The only sound was Sophies' distinct snoring. Ramira could not shake the feeling that someone was inside the house. She slipped downstairs but found nothing. Ramira eased her way onto the terrace and stopped as a malevolent sensation washed over her. It seemed to be everywhere yet nowhere at the same time. It probed her with cold fingers; no part of her being escaped its contemptuous transgressions. She felt overwhelmed then it suddenly vanished with such abruptness she sank onto her heels as if it had taken her strength with it. The unnerving dreams invading her tired mind were understandable, but now she was imaging things while awake. The echoes of that strange sensation lingered on suppressing her desire to go back to bed. She walked into the kitchen and lit the fire just as Sophie came down the stairs. She saw the fatigue in Ramira's face and vowed to do something about her sleeplessness.

"Ramira, why don't you let me brew you some tea to help you sleep?"

"No, Sophie, I'd rather be able to waken and escape."

"What kinds of nightmares haunt you?" asked Sophie.

Ramira shook her head then placed the kettle over the fire.

"Why the knives?" she asked, the wicked looking blades stark against the smooth tabletop.

"I thought I heard something downstairs, but I was mistaken," Ramira filled two mugs with tea and handed one to Sophie. "Apparently my nighttime delusions are spilling over into the day. Don't worry, Sophie: I won't mistake you or Anci for an intruder."

"I wasn't even thinking that, girl, but I am worried about you," she stated and touched Ramira's cheek.

Sophie sipped her tea, her mind on Ramira's nightmares and the inky black knives that lay upon the table. She had never seen anything like them before. She squinted and was barely able to make out some mysterious symbols engraved on them. The craftsmanship was extraordinary but the daggers did not appear to be for everyday use. Sophie wondered how Ramira had acquired such enigmatic items. Ramira finished her tea and picked up the daggers, stowing them within their sheaths. She offered Sophie a tired smile before heading out into the early morning.

~

Zada strolled through the fragrant garden, opening her mind to the peace that thrived within it. Laughter and love floated amid the flowers; tears and sorrow clung to the leaves. She saw the faint shadows of children hiding around the shrubbery and the silhouettes of lovers holding hands while walking upon the flagstones. She felt a sensation touch her. It gently propelled her to a corner of the garden toward a rosebush with radiant white flowers. She sat upon the pink granite bench beside it and waited. Soon, the ethereal figure of a woman approached her and joined her on the bench. She was exceedingly lovely; kindness radiated from her glowing form. Zada's inner sight held no specific powers but it did allow her to sense things from a place she could only go to one time.

There are those of us who have planted the seeds that will, we hope, bear fruit when the time comes. We can no longer nurture them like the living. Your presence tells us that, so far, we have not failed. The road is fraught with indecision and doubt, and that is when we will truly see if we have been successful. Remember: things are not always what they seem to be, Zada.

"Who needs to be guided, Lady?"

They must make their decisions on their own, Zada, but they must do so armed with as much information as possible.

"What can I do to help?"

You are already helping...

Zada opened her eyes and found herself alone on the bench. The woman exuded a sense of power. It gave her an immense feeling of comfort to know that those who had passed on long ago continued to watch over those that now lived. The hopes and dreams they had instilled in their scions would survive, but it was now up to the living to carry out that legacy.

Zada looked up at the façade of the castle. The elves had managed to thrive for a thousand years, yet they like everyone else, were now in jeopardy. She was the leader of the Herkahs and had gone through extensive and painful training to determine if she was truly worthy of the role. She had prevailed through it all. Zada learned the lore and exercised her mind until it was receptive to what others abhorred; she strengthened her body through the art of combat. It was only then that she could walk to the center of the desert to meet her final test. She had offered her heart, mind, and body to the Horii, who scrutinized every aspect of her existence. Silver bracelets covered the scars but they could not conceal the memory of the agonizing initiation. She pushed the bracelets back and gazed at the numerous small slashes crossing her wrists.

She had voluntarily placed her arms out to them, invoking their presence with a series of chants. She had watched with a mixture of dread and horror as the tiny snake-like creatures thrust their black bodies upon her skin. Their razor sharp teeth sliced their way through flesh and bone as they tunneled toward her soul. They had become one with her spirit where they saw all of her strengths and weaknesses. The pain their presence created was unimaginably intense.

She had endured the rite and passed their unyielding scrutiny before they slipped back into the sands of the Great White Desert. A harsh and cruel death would come to the imposter, the unprepared or the unsuited. The leader was not privy to the origin of the Herkahs, something she had never been able to understand. The Horii had deemed her deserving; the nomads believed in her and now they had befriended the elves. All would need to depend on her to expose her mind to what they would need to defeat. She, like all the others, could not afford to fail: failure meant a fate worse than death. She exhaled slowly, her gaze returning to the bench beneath the roses. The dead woman seemed to know more about their predicament than she did and expected the living to prevail using more than sword and bow. Those who walked beneath the sun would also need to wield their deep-set convictions if they wanted a chance to succeed.

"Zada?" the king quietly called her name. "May I join you?"

"The garden is yours… you needn't ask me for permission."

"The garden might be mine but the solace you seek within belongs to you," he stated offering her his arm.

The two of them walked through the garden, the king telling her about his people. Passion for his home resonated in Alyxandyr's voice, yet there was a hint of sadness, too.

"What was your queen's name, Alyxandyr?"

"Anjya," he replied as if from a distance. "It means 'summers day' in the old elvish tongue. Ironically she died on midwinter night."

Zada did not wish to cause him further pain, offering him her quiet presence while the memories flooded back into his heart and mind.

They walked in silence for a little while longer, each lost in their own thoughts. Zada suspected that the shade by the roses had been Anjya, the dead queen as concerned for her family and friends in death as she had been in life. The fact that the dead were disquieted only added to her anxiety. The evil was sending ripples of horror across the land and the dead were not immune to his foulness. Zada glanced over at the king and noted that the lines of worry added years to his face. The garden eased some of those furrows but it could not alleviate the danger growing in the west. They left the solitude of the garden, returning to the castle and the unending tasks awaiting them. The memories of the dead would have to wait or there would be none to remember them.

~

On a dreary and dismal evening two weeks later, the Khadry sent Danyl's letter back to Bystyn. The prince, Allad, and a few others rode out to meet them. The rain soaked through their cloaks before they reached the intersection in the city; the wind picked up once they left the protection of the high walls. The implications of the Khadrys' arrival dampened Danyl's spirit. The evil had forced them out of their home and that meant the search for the Source of Darkness was steadily moving east. The power it sought was not in or near the desert; the evil suspected that the dark magic had moved eastward. Why not? Everyone else was outside of Bystyn's walls. It was quite possible that someone might have inadvertently picked it up, the finder unaware of its significance. He chuckled over this last thought, for if the Source of Darkness was some sort of talisman, then who wouldn't pick up a lost sword or charm? Was it nothing more than a fine mist carried away by the wind?

Danyl took a sharp breath: if Mahn were edging eastwards then its minions would certainly be in the forefront in its search for the magic. He shuddered, remembering Allad and Nyk recounting the Kreetch's mindless rage and destruction. The only redeeming factors were that the Herkahs were capable of fighting these demons.

Lance interrupted his thoughts as he pointed in the direction of a line of drenched figures waiting for them to approach. They stopped and stood slightly apart from the Khadry, Allad determining if they were demons or not. He nodded; Danyl urged his mount forward.

"We meet again under difficult circumstances," Gard greeted the prince.

Gard glanced south, noting the Herkah tents that occupied that section of the plains before turning his attention back to the prince. The road ahead was more threatening than he had first thought, for the nomads were indeed camped outside the city far from their lands. He wondered who else would seek refuge from the ill wind blowing from the west.

"You are welcome here. What provisions do you need?"

"None, for now. We would like permission to set up our camp along the western edge of the woods," said Gard.

"Agreed, but I must ask you to pass on whatever information you have to my father."

Gard assigned duties to his men then joined Danyl for the ride back to the city. Gard glanced silently at the impressive fortification as they rode up the main avenue. The rain forced most of the elves to remain indoors but that did not keep the news of the latest visitors from spreading. Gard did not care what they thought for the alliance with the city elves would end once this matter was concluded. He glanced from left to right as they wound their way up the roadway, absorbing the details of the city. Even he had to admit that the Bystynians had planned the layout very well and maintained it over the centuries. The castle became visible from behind the trees in the park. Gard noted the extra guards standing upon the balconies and surrounding the First Advisor. The Khadry and Mason locked eyes long before the group halted at the gate, each studying the other with an intensity that was palpable. Gard understood the no-nonsense look in Mason's steely gaze for he, too, wore the same expression. Gard was well aware of Mason's fierce loyalty to the elven king, but that did not diminish the fact that he was Cooper's brother. Anyone hailing from Kepracarn was suspect. The Khadry had to be careful not to let his suspicion show or allow his feelings to jeopardize this truce.

They dismounted in front of the castle, Danyl urging Gard to change into dry clothes before meeting with the king. He disliked the soggy clothes clinging to him; the additional time would allow him to collect his thoughts. An attendant showed him to a spare room; Danyl waited for him in the hallway.

The king, princes, Mason, Karolauren, Allad, and Zada waited for them in the study. The sounds of thunder reverberated across the city, the ominous booms shaking the gray walls. After the introductions, Gard filled them in on what had compelled the Khadry to the city gates.

"Danyl, I'm sure, informed you of our previous meeting. The reason for our presence is that there has been something even more sinister happening in the forest. Foul winds have been blowing ever deeper into our home, leaving the trees and brush singed and withered. A few of my people have been 'touched' by this loathsome thing and the results have been particularly gruesome. Their bodies are found contorted; the agony and shock on their faces hideous to look upon. Whether our coming here only delays the inevitable or not, I cannot say. I will not run and hide and lose more of my people along the way."

117

"How far into the forest is this wind blowing, Gard?"

The king studied the elf, Gard's frustration clear on his face; the need to appeal to the city elves had not been an easy choice for him.

"It has reached the hollows," he replied.

Karolauren's brows shot skyward, for the hollows were halfway through the forest and well past Khadry territory.

"What do the patrols say of the borders south and west?" the king asked Nyk.

"Most towns and villages have been abandoned and there is still no sign of anyone in Kepracarn."

"Cooper has still not been heard from?" asked Gard.

The Khadry despised King Cooper and his people. There were rare encounters along the far western edge of the forest. The Kepracarnians learned quickly to avoid the Khadry. Those from Cooper's patrols who foolishly ventured into the woods never saw the light of day again. The distance and lack of fortune prompted Cooper to circumvent the forest and its denizens. Gard, however, preferred to deal with his annoying enemy rather than being in the dark about his absence. He could see the same opinion etched on the faces of those gathered in the room.

"No, Gard, and neither have the emissaries I sent to him."

The thunderstorm intensified making it difficult to hear or speak. The king ended the meeting, promising to hold another one within the next few days. Danyl escorted Gard back out the gates then stopped at the house on the corner to escape the disconcerting news, even if it was only for a little while.

He was drenched. Sophie fussed over him until he dried off and changed, sitting him down in front of the fire with a cup of tea. Ramira joined them. Sophie smiled for her appearance seemed to lift some of the worry from his face. Anci lost all interest in her lessons and suggested they play cards. The storm lasted for several hours; the prince and Ramira exchanged more than one glance as the memories of the Broken Plain surfaced in their minds. Unlike then, however, they were safe within the confines of the city and friends. Anci yawned and bid them a good night as she headed for bed.

"She cheats as badly as you do," Sophie teased him.

"Me? Cheat? How dare you woman!" he cried in mock indignation.

"I dare!" she emphatically stated bringing her hands to her hips. "You had more cards lying at your feet than Alyssa has attendants!"

"They slipped out of my hands!"

He winked at Ramira who rose and placed another log on the fire.

"Yes, I'm sure they did," she patronized him then wished them a pleasant night.

Ramira cleared off the table. She stared out the window at the rain, dreading the demons awaiting her upstairs. Danyl's reflection filled the window as he came up behind her and encircled her with his arms. She accepted his embrace. They remained that way for several long minutes, and then she slowly turned and faced him. That peculiar sensation began to rise again, sending ripples of energy from one to the other. The elf closed the distance between them until his lips brushed against hers; the tender kiss was filled with emotions neither had ever encountered. It lasted for only a few seconds but that was long enough for them to realize that it was futile to fight what strained to be freed. Something deep inside both of them responded, but it was more than just their physical nearness that stimulated it. Whatever it was allowed the bond to grow unchallenged between them. He rested his face against her neck and smiled with pleasure. He could detect the perfume she had applied in Karolauren's library, its subtle fragrance eliciting a number of thoughts and desires. The latter compelled him to break away, for neither of them was prepared to deal with that aspect of their budding relationship.

"It's getting late."

His fingers lingered on her warm cheek; his body was reluctant to pull away from hers. He could have stayed this way forever. He kissed the tip of her nose then disappeared into the soggy night, the memory of her touch and perfume accompanying him home.

Ramira stood rooted in place, welcoming the calm he left in his wake. She blew out the lamps and went upstairs, falling into a restful sleep moments after she lay her head on the pillow.

One of the stewards handed Danyl a note when he entered his home. He nodded to the attendant then walked up the wide staircase to his father's rooms. The king was sitting at his desk when his son walked in and sat down across from him. Danyl noted how tired his father looked; Alyxandyr probably stayed up well into the night contemplating how to deal with their dilemma. The king looked into his sons face then exhaled heavily.

"I need you to ride to Evans Peak, Danyl," began the king. "I think it would be wise for Seven to know what is happening."

"Have you sent a messenger?" asked Danyl.

"No. I want this information to come from this house personally. I have offered Allad the opportunity to accompany you and he has accepted."

"I can think of no better traveling companion."

The nomad would be welcome, especially considering his ability to discern and kill any demons that might have slipped beyond Bystyn. Besides, he greatly admired the hawkish man and wished to further his friendship with him.

"Explain to Seven that it might be wise for him to join us for a while. I would rather have the dwarves here and not needed rather than have them come too late when they are."

"You anticipate a conflict, don't you, Father?" asked Danyl in worried tones.

"Yes, son, I do. Everything we have so far learned points in that direction. I, for one, do not intend to sit idly by thinking that it won't. Zada and even Gard are under the same impression or they would not be outside our gates."

"When do I leave?"

"Tomorrow morning. Everything has already been prepared for the journey, but do not tarry once you have arrived, Danyl, understand?"

The king knew all too well how easy it was to lose oneself

within Seven's charming and entertaining hall. The carousing usually lasted two days; the recovery period three days after that. Alyxandyr grinned; his son nodded in response to his father's unspoken memories. The prince had experienced more than one banquet at Evans Peak.

"Understood, Father."

Danyl embraced him and returned to his own rooms, the journey east already settling into his mind. They would be gone for at least three weeks. He undressed and slipped into bed, wondering if Ramira would make the trip with him. Perhaps they could build on their growing relationship along the way. He doubted his father would care and Sophie would surely set her free for a while. The problem was convincing Ramira to go; she would undoubtedly feel obligated to stay and not shirk her duties.

"I just won't give you a chance to say 'no'," he whispered to himself.

FIVE

The riders stopped in front of Sophie's home, their horses laden with blankets, provisions, and extra weapons for the long journey. Danyl dismounted and walked around to the back of the house. He was looking forward to the reunion with the dwarves, whom he had not seen in a couple of years. He greeted Sophie as he walked in the door, but declined the mug of tea she held up to him.

"Can you spare Ramira for a while? We are heading out to see the dwarves," he explained.

"I don't see why not."

She noted the restrained excitement on his face then watched it change into something else as Ramira walked into the kitchen. Tenderness and desire filled his eyes for a fleeting moment, which he quickly concealed.

"You're up early," she stated taking the cup intended for the elf.

"We are on our way to pay Seven a visit and I was wondering if you would like to go with us?"

Sophie nodded; she knew Danyl was going to the dwarf king to ask for help. That meant things had changed dramatically over the past few days. She began to collect supplies for Ramira but Danyl stopped her.

"Who's Seven? Where are we going?" she asked even when Danyl brought his hand up to still her questions.

"We have enough, Sophie; you need to bring a few changes of clothes and personal items. I'll explain along the way."

"Send Seven and Clare our love," Sophie said as they walked out the door.

Ramira was ready in no time and they were off before the sun lifted over the horizon. They headed east, swinging around the orchards and past Jack and Ida's home then toward the swiftly flowing Ahltyn River. They forded it at its lowest point, lifting their legs and supplies to keep them from getting wet. They reached the lush meadows on the other side before mid-morning where they stopped to rest. Ramira sat down beside Danyl.

"Who is Seven?" she asked accepting a slice of bread.

"Seven is the dwarf king living in the foothills of those mountains," he pointed to a low line of purplish stains in the east. "He and his kin have been our friends and allies for a very long time, and what affects one eventually concerns the other."

"What's he like?

"Seven is…well…he must be seen and heard to be appreciated," replied the elf with a lop-sided grin and a twinkle in his eyes.

"You're going to ask for his help, aren't you?" she asked, noting the instantaneous change in his demeanor. She immediately regretted her question.

"Yes. Things have progressed far enough to warrant such a request," he responded in a subdued tone of voice.

She didn't need to ask what he was alluding to and nibbled on her food in silence. They resumed their trek east, making camp just before dark. The guards placed along the camp's perimeter melted into the shadows.

The evening was chilly; they clustered around the fire while they ate and chatted amongst themselves. The broad canopy of oak, maple, and pine trees blocked out most of the stars. They glittered in harmony with the sounds of the insects rasping all around them. Night birds chirped overhead; small animals moved furtively about in the underbrush.

"How will the dwarves react when they see who rides by your side?" asked Allad.

"Seven will study you from top to bottom then offer you some of his homemade poison. His queen, Clare, will reprimand him for being rude, then attempt to remove that burning liquid from the table with very limited success!" replied the elf with a laugh.

"There is great love and admiration in your eyes when you speak of them."

"They are indeed some of the best people in the land, Allad, and I would lay my life down for them without hesitation."

"Your words convey more than you know," said the Herkah smiling at the prince's enthusiasm.

"And you, Ramira? Have you ever met a dwarf?" asked the nomad.

"I don't believe so, Allad," she replied quietly, enjoying the lighthearted attitude Danyl sported for his friends. It was beginning to infect her, too. The joy the dwarves derived out of life had taken root in the elves as well. Queen Clare, it seemed, had her hands full with Seven.

"I must warn you that Seven is outspoken and boisterous but his antics and words are meant to entertain and not to offend. And you, Ramira, will be scrutinized as well ...just be prepared," he warned good-naturedly. Ramira knew what he meant and stared into her nearly empty mug.

"We should get some sleep," suggested the nomad as he walked over and rolled himself up in his blankets.

He was asleep within moments yet Danyl and Ramira knew his senses were as keen now as they were when he was awake.

She lay down a few feet away from the elf and pulled the blanket up over her shoulders. She tried to envision what the dwarves, especially Seven, looked like. She failed to get a physical impression but thought he must be a bundle of energy.

~

Their routine never varied and, fortunately for them, the weather remained fair. There were easily crossed rivers and streams in this part of the land, presenting them with a continuous supply of fresh water. The broad canopy of leaves shaded them from the summer sun beating down from a cloudless blue sky as they traveled on. They met few travelers in these parts because, other than a few isolated villages, those who did inhabit the area were outlaws. The thieves preyed on wealthy travelers and chose to keep their distance from patrols and well-armed groups of riders. The prince knew a vast network of tunnels in the mountains to the north was their main outpost. The bases exact location was unknown for the land around it cleverly concealed the entrances to it. The area they now traveled in was a no-man's land. They would reach Seven's realm by late morning the following day. The reunion would be brief before he placed their dilemma firmly in the king's lap.

"I'm worried that I am beginning to like the proximity of the trees too much," Allad said as he sat down beside the prince. They stopped for the night after enduring an unbearably hot day. The companions sat beneath the cool confines of the trees, their bodies and clothes soaked with sweat.

"A big change from the vastness of the desert, I'll wager."

"Somewhat. I just think of them as big brown and green dunes that can be walked through instead of over," he said, evoking a quiet laugh from the elf.

"I wish our predicament was as easy to deal with."

"Sometimes things that appear daunting because we make them so," said Allad glancing over at Ramira. "She furrows her brow too much."

Danyl nodded and told him about her inability to remember her past but left out the part she had had in his rescue.

Allad found Ramira beautiful and peculiar at the same time; he was unable to determine what race she belonged. There were elements about her that had not yet surfaced, and these characteristics might offer an insight as to her origin. Allad got to his feet and left the prince to his musings; he walked over to his blankets and lay down to rest.

Danyl smiled to himself. Ramira and her blankets had moved closer to his every night until she now slept a scant few inches from him. She was overcoming her own doubts and worries and that, he was sure, would bode well for them in the future. He felt her hand on his shoulder, the subtle touch as important to him as it was to her. Danyl faced her.

"You'll not find a more comfortable bed than in Seven's house," he whispered to her.

"It isn't so bad out here," she replied in hushed tones. The natural tranquility flowing from the ground to the sky one of the reasons, she believed, that kept the nightmares at bay.

"The dwarves will spoil you even if we only stay for a few

125

days," he said moving a strand of hair from her face.

"Perhaps," she answered with a little laugh.

He smiled then brushed his fingertips across her cheek. Her presence somehow eased the burden he carried. He rolled onto his side and fell fast asleep, Ramira's hand rested on his shoulder.

~

Shouting and metal striking metal woke them several hours later. As one, they rolled free from their blankets with swords drawn, prepared to confront their attackers who clashed with the sentries beyond the firelight. Danyl signaled for Ramira to stay put as he and the others disappeared into the darkness. The clamor increased immediately as the elves found and repelled their assailants. Ramira t scanned the area around her for any intruders. She did not have long to wait. Two burly men dressed in mended homespun clothing emerged from the shadows, swords in their hands and sneers on their dirty faces. They pulled back their lips exposing teeth that reminded her of dried ears of corn. They approached, mocking her as she pulled out her blades.

"What are you going to do with those, wench?" growled one of the men.

"Come closer and find out."

"I say we just tie her up and take her along before her friends come back...those who are left, anyway," suggested the other thief.

Ramira waited for them to come within a few feet of her then cut one down with ease. He fell in a silent heap at her feet, his throat neatly sliced under his jaw. The other man raised his sword, hoping that its length would keep her weapons at bay. The sounds outside the circle of light lessened. Ramira noted the perspiration trickling down his forehead; she remained cool and steady. A sense of preparedness surged through her; her body relaxed and assumed a fighters stance. She twirled her blades then gripped the black hafts, her unwavering gaze fixed on the rugged man clutching his weapon with both hands.

The thief glared at her then furtively glanced toward the clanging of metal and occasional shout. The conflict was almost over. Was she worth the risk? He moved his foot and tightened his grip on his hilt, his eyes watchful of the woman who stared at him from a few yards away. To Ramira's relief, she identified several of the voices and knew her companions- not her adversaries- had survived.

"What are you going to do, thief?"

"I'm going to kill you," he hissed lunging forward.

Danyl and Lance, followed closely by Allad, rushed toward the horses, the first things that the thieves would try to seize. The thieves quickly learned that elven mounts answered only to their masters. The harder the outlaws pulled on their reins, the more dangerous they became. One man lay on the ground with half of his skull crushed; another released a bridle and ducked behind a tree to avoid a similar fate. Danyl raised his sword to deflect an attack from the side as the thieves began their charge. The horses, freed by the intruders, galloped away from the fighting. The darkness concealed the fighters' identities making the possibility of killing one of their own a deadly reality. The elves forced the riffraff out onto the plains where the moon gave off a feeble light. Danyl could hear Allad sparring in the woods, his foes resistant to exposing themselves in the open. He heard an abrupt scream from the general vicinity of the camp and hoped it wasn't Ramira. He cursed himself for leaving her alone. Fear for her safety forced him to finish off his attacker. The elf sprinted back to the camp. The sick feeling that began in his stomach reached upward and gripped his heart. Danyl broke through the trees and skidded to a halt. A figure squatted beside a body just beyond the firelight. Lance and Allad flanked him, their swords drawn in readiness.

"Stand up slowly and turn around." Danyl's tight voice gripped the area like a giants' hand.

The figure rose obediently and turned around. It pushed back the hood that had slipped over its head while leaning over the corpse. Another body lay several paces away, his eyes staring unseeingly at the embers of the fire. The elves and the Herkah breathed a sigh of relief as they beheld Ramira, then they saw the look on her face. Her expression was hard and menacing; blood dripped from her knives. All three stared at her for several long seconds.

"Are you hurt?" asked Danyl.

"No," she replied, the darkness ebbing from her features.

The rest of the group joined them, most suffered only a few minor cuts. They packed up their belongings and broke camp even though sunrise was still a couple of hours away. They knew the thieves who escaped would return with more of their companions. The outcome of any future confrontation would not end as favorably as this one. They rode out onto the plains, more than one pair of eyes glancing at the woman riding in their midst.

~

Smoke curled up over the treetops about a mile away- they were close to Evans Peak. A valley opened up in front of them as they passed through the last line of trees. Cradled in an immense crevasse along the mountainside, was the city. Its stone buildings, constructed of the surrounding rocks, were nearly indistinguishable from the mountain. Only the open windows gave any indication that they were homes. Gardens cascaded down the undulating slopes, the bright red and flowers were visible even from this distance. A deep and wide river, fed by the melting snows to the north, meandered along the base of the mountain. It swung farther south where it branched out into dozens of tributaries that crisscrossed the farmlands. There were caves and recesses within the split where the dwarves could seek refuge if the river could not hold back any attackers. It was also where they stored their goods and supplies. A group of dwarves rode toward them. As soon as they recognized the new arrivals, one of them sped back to the city. Before the elves covered half the distance to the river, dwarves poured over the two bridges to welcome them.

Allad and Ramira peered from face to face, the dwarves' enthusiasm at their arrival punctuated with greetings and questions. They guided them over the bridge and toward a weathered dwarf with crossed arms and a glowering expression. He shot one look at Ramira, then the Herkah before focusing on Danyl's sheepish countenance. The prince dismounted and walked up to the dwarf, bowing deeply from several steps away.

"Lord King Seven...."

The dwarf rushed forward and picked the elf up, hugging him as if he were a long lost son. The prince heartily returned the embrace, ignoring the auburn braid dancing maniacally along the king's broad back. The dwarves clapped and began to sing, knowing there would be a feast tonight to welcome the elves and their fellow travelers. When the joyous mayhem finally calmed down, Seven invited his guests to join him in his home. Clare's moss green eyes gazed kindly from her demure face; her light brown braid snaked around her neck and rested on her chest.

"It's good to see you again, boy," Seven boomed as he slapped the elf on the back. "Who'd you bring? Other than the dour Lance, I mean."

The captain nodded respectfully, unmoved by Sevens jab.

"This is Allad of the Herkahs."

The nomad offered Seven his hand. The king took it after studying the Herkah for several long moments.

"Hmm. Not at all what I expected."

"It is an honor to meet you, King Seven," Allad said, his piercing black eyes glittering with admiration.

"Please, just call me Seven." He was already scrutinizing the apprehensive woman at the prince's side.

"And Ramira."

"Neither are you," he said, a broad grin spreading across his face.

"I am Clare and you are all most welcome here. If you need anything, ask me, not him," she added with a playful nudge to the kings' side. She noted the torn garments and patches of blood.

"We had a little run-in with some of your neighbors."

"They love your horses, boy. Can't say that I blame them," stated Seven. "Are you all accounted for?"

"We were fortunate," replied the elf.

"Good, now come inside and refresh yourselves," commanded the queen as she led them into her home.

~

The companions were ushered into the hall where food and drink covered a long wooden table. Ramira and the nomad craned their necks as they took in the room. Huge fireplaces lined three of the walls; a long hallway led to the sleeping quarters. Drums, flutes, and stringed instruments were stored on shelves against one wall; dishware and condiments filled the ledges next to the closest fireplace. The area behind Sevens chair was reserved for a large cask of ale that rested upon a v-shaped cradle. One of the dwarves was busily filling tankards that another dwarf placed on the table. Covering the smooth, hand hewn stone floors were thick, brightly colored woolen rugs. Blankets and small pillows covered the chairs surrounding the massive wooden table. The table itself was laden with so much food the visitors thought it would surely collapse. Bowls of fresh fruit, platters of meat, and piles of bread and cheese were everywhere. They suddenly realized how hungry they really were. Their meals during the trek had become rather mundane. They had eaten dried meats and hardening bread for nearly a week and looked forward to the sumptuous meal before them. The food stilled their tongues as they ate heartily while listening to Seven and his stories.

"Before you fill my ears with bad news tell me something good. How is everyone? Is that old bundle of sticks still skittering around the castle? I'd ask about Alyssa finding a mate for you but somehow I doubt she'd pick Ramira...no insult meant, girl."

"Seven," Clare growled at him.

"What? I just meant that whomever Alyssa chose, Danyl would not care for and...."

"No offense taken, Seven," said Ramira, a little smile playing on her face.

More than one voice snickered at Seven, who decided, for the time being, to listen to the elf fill him in on the goings on within the castle.

"Karolauren is as lively and cantankerous as ever and no, Alyssa had no hand in Ramira."

"Let the boy eat, Seven! Honestly, Danyl, I don't know where he stores his manners sometimes!" interrupted Clare who nodded for another plate of bread.

"I doubt he would keep them on the table or he would have eaten them long ago," muttered the prince good-naturedly.

"Insulting me in my own house will be countered with forcing everyone to listen to my stories," said a smug Seven.

"Sweet mercy, not that!" Clare cried in mock horror, making everyone, including Lance laugh.

They finished their meal while Seven brought them up-to-date on what had transpired at Evans Peak over the past couple of years. Things had been relatively quiet but those gathered knew their visitors were about to change all of that.

Danyl gave them a brief summary of the past few months. He told them why he had come and watched their faces cloud over with worry. Seven's personality took on a new demeanor; those who had never met him now understood why he was king. A cold, calculating intelligence shone from within his dark eyes replacing the playfulness that marked their meeting. He scrutinized Allad as the prince recounted what the Herkahs had revealed to the elves regarding the demons. When the prince was through, the room remained silent for a long time.

"If you are asking for our support you know you have that," Seven finally said, "but it sounds as though that will only delay, not avert the problem. Do you have any idea when you expect that dark troop to knock on your door?"

"We really do not know, Seven," confessed the prince. "We must assume that it will."

"The convergence of the different races upon your city is a hopeful sign, Danyl," added Clare.

"In that we are somewhat heartened," replied the elf.

Seven glanced at a silent Ramira, who sat looking down at her clasped hands. She seemed undaunted by the news and that intrigued him. She was unafraid of things that should frighten her. The Herkah, too, sat with a determined nonchalance but then again he and his people had fought these demons before. How would everyone else react if the elves and dwarves fought those creatures? Seven noted the wearied expressions on their faces and decided they needed to relax.

"You've had a long journey. Go and rest for a while and I

will speak with my kin. We'll meet again later on."

The queen led them down the hall and opened the door for each of her guests. Clare raised a brow at Ramira as they neared her room but the prince subtly shook his head. The queen shrugged her shoulders and led him to the next chamber, a bit wiser about their relationship. She did not know Ramira but he must have noticed something special in the girl.

Ramira entered the room, shutting the door and immediately heading for the bath. She stripped off her clothes and sighed as she eased her road weary body into the steaming tub. The hot water soaked away the stiffness from spending too many days upon horseback and too many nights upon the ground. The bath, coupled with the bed, would be a welcome treat. Danyl was right: she would recant her words.

She found the dwarves to be a delight, their effervescence contagious and their love of life a true joy to behold. She surmised that when they gathered this evening there would be little, if any, discussions about the evil. She looked forward to such a night; hearing the dwarves sing and laugh would chase away the impending shadows from the west. For a few hours, anyway. The water began to cool so she rose and dried herself off before slipping into a set of fresh clothes. She felt her eyelids droop and decided to lie down for a few moments before heading out to the hall…

~

She awoke and smiled at Danyl gazing down upon her. Her attention shifted to the window. Rich oranges and vivid lavenders pulsed across the sky. She had slept much longer than she had anticipated but felt refreshed and ready to undertake anything. She reached over and laced her fingers with his, welcoming his kiss.

"Clare wasn't sure if she should put us in the same room." He smiled as a slight blush crept onto her cheeks. "Dinner and entertainment are minutes away. Would you allow me to escort you to the hall?"

"I would be honored."

She stood up and combed out her hair; he stopped her from braiding it. She left it loose and took his arm, the pair making their way to the hall under the watchful eyes of those already gathered there. Seven could barely contain his delight; Allad's black eyes focused on the couple as they sat at the table across from him.

The dwarves began to celebrate old friendships and new ones; music filled the air and food overflowed on plates. Their vim and vigor took the breath away from those that watched and participated. Laughter and song were side dishes from which all took huge helpings.

Danyl saw the glow on Ramira's face and wondered how much more vitality lay hidden within her being. He was determined to find out.

"Whatever you do, Ramira, do not drink from the goatskin he will surely pass to you later on," warned Danyl, even though his eyes sparkled with joy.

"What's in it?"

"I don't think even Seven knows! It will, however, remove all the air from your lungs and leave you with a terrible headache in the morning."

"Sounds as though you are speaking from experience," she teased, then laughed as he rolled his eyes.

They ate until they thought their stomachs would burst; the dwarves mercifully removed the food and concentrated on the merriment. A group of musicians set up in the middle of the hall, the stringed instruments, low toned drums, and high-pitched flutes making even the normally reticent Lance tap his fingers to the beat. It was not long before Seven grabbed Ramira's hands and dragged her to an open space in the hall. Clare nearly fell off her chair as Ramira tried to keep time with him. He finally gave up and hauled her over his shoulder, performing the dance while Ramira held on for dear life. He brought her back to the elf, who helped a dizzy Ramira find her seat before seeking out his next victim. Allad immediately held up his hands in playful warning. The king shrugged then grabbed Clare; the pair danced in perfect unison across the floor.

"Danyl, I think I need some fresh air," she whispered into his ear. "Please stay...I'll be back in a few minutes. Which door leads outside?" He pointed to a door in the far corner. She slipped outside and walked down near the river, the night air steadying her head and her stomach. She had eaten too much, was very tired, and her head still reeled from being spun about by the dwarf king. She inhaled deeply and closed her eyes, grateful that Danyl had revealed another wonder in the land.

"Are you feeling ill?" a voice spoke from the darkness behind her.

"No, Clare, just very warm. The king gave me quite a ride."

"Seven never tires...I should know."

Clare laughed then her attitude became more serious while she studied Ramira by the light of the full moon. Ramira fascinated her. Seven, of course, was thrilled. He thought he would die before Danyl chose a mate. Initially Clare had shushed him, telling him to mind his own business and behave. Nevertheless, he was right. Whether these two recognized it or not, there was something between them and Clare hoped they would be better because of it.

"It is beautiful here."

The cool breeze caressed Ramira's skin. The full moon ignited the river until it shone liked molten silver and the sounds of crickets and birds instilled a sense of calmness into her being. The energy the dwarves possessed came from the land and it seemed as if the land thrived off the dwarves as well.

"It is home and we like it," agreed Clare. "What's your home like?"

"I'm not sure," replied Ramira quietly, "I can't remember and I don't know why."

"An injury, perhaps?"

"Maybe."

"I didn't mean to temper your enthusiasm," Clare apologized, hearing the sadness in Ramira's voice.

"You haven't, Clare. Besides, I've found enough happiness in Bystyn and here to last a lifetime."

"And in Danyl?"

"I don't know what I'll find there."

"Perhaps you'll find what you're missing."

Ramira heard the muffled celebration as the evening breeze carried it from the mountain to where she stood. Was Clare right? Would she find what she was missing in Danyl? She inhaled deeply several more times, letting the cool night air wash over and through her. She stared in wonder at the fireflies that briefly illuminated the area around them. They were oblivious to the worries of the world, leaving that dubious chore to those without wings. Danyl was right about this place: it was a paradise in a sea of uncertainty.

Ramira stayed for a little while longer then made her way back into the hall. She gave the elf a slight touch of reassurance on his shoulder as she sat down beside him. Seven engaged the Herkah in conversation, asking him questions about his people. The two of them began to form a friendship, one that was based on respect and admiration. Danyl subtly nodded at the progress they were making. For all of their differences, the nomad and the dwarf were very much alike.

The hall began to empty as the night progressed until only a handful of people remained. Danyl, Ramira, Allad, the king, and queen sat close together and chatted as if it was still early evening.

"Everything was absolutely delicious and delightful," Ramira said leaning back into her chair.

"You caught us off guard...we had to throw all of this together at the last minute," Seven grinned. "Here, try this."

Danyl and Clare lifted a brow in warning; Seven filled their glasses with a small amount of clear liquid and handed one to everyone at the table.

"Good, yes?" laughed Seven.

The first sip made her shudder, her face scrunched up as the potent liquid assaulted her mouth and tongue. "Peppermint." muttered Ramira, the refreshing aftertaste almost worth the fire it caused as it went down her throat.

"I think there is some of that in there, too," replied Seven.

"I told you the ingredients were a mystery even to him,"

135

Danyl teased them both.

"Allad?" The king turned his attention to the nomad; his anticipatory expression eliciting a muffled chuckle from more than one person.

"Refreshing...crisp...not too bad, Seven," replied the Herkah as he held out his glass for more.

"You just made a lifelong friend," muttered Danyl good-naturedly.

"I think we should let them get some rest, Seven." Clare's suggestion was more of an order, for the king would keep them up until daybreak. "Escape while you can," she pleasantly told them.

They bid the couple a goodnight before heading down the hallway to their rooms. Allad nodded to them then entered his chamber, leaving the elf and Ramira alone in front of her door.

"Thank you for inviting me along," she said. "Even under these dire circumstances."

"I thought you'd enjoy it here," he replied. He touched her cheek before disappearing to his own room, the feelings growing within him overwhelming him. She watched him for a second then went inside, undressed, and slipped into bed. She fell asleep almost immediately.

~

Danyl did the same but he remained awake for a while, his mind alive with a host of thoughts. They swirled around inside his head, demanding his attention. The demons menaced while the absent Kepracarnians stared hollowly from within shadowy recesses. The elven magic flitted somewhere just outside of his sight and hearing, daring him to discover its secret. It took quite some doing but he finally quelled their incessant demands for attention and drifted off to sleep...

~

He strode through an endless stone corridor where heavy oaken doors appeared to his left and right. He tried to open them but they were locked. He looked ahead and realized he would walk forever so he turned around to go back the way he had come. Danyl realized that both distances were equal. Was he lost in a maze that was nothing more than a straight line? That was not possible. He cocked his head and listened, but heard nothing more than the far-off drip dripping of water. He was underground, therefore there must be a stairway leading back up. Should he continue on or turn back to find it? Was he heading back when he stopped or moving forward? He immediately lost his bearings. Danyl tried the doors again but they would not open; no reference points appeared in either direction. Frustrated but unafraid, he chose one route. He would eventually reach the end of the corridor since everything had a beginning and an end. Which destination would he reach and what would he find there? Beginning or end?

It dawned on him that his senses had no place here; the elf would have to rely on something else that could penetrate the semi-darkness around him. What that could be was a mystery. The stone corridor irked him with its secretiveness, which only increased his determination to find his way out of the maze consisting of a straight line…

~

Danyl awoke, the labyrinth still fresh in his mind as he swung his legs over the side of the bed. He stretched and yawned while trying to make sense of the dream. The oaken doors had no keyholes yet he had been unable to push them open. What secrets did they hold? He shook his head hoping to dislodge the dream as he walked to the hall. The table was already laden with food and drink. He was still full from the previous evening so he helped himself to a mug of tea and carried it to the wide stone steps leading down from the city. Danyl smiled while watching the dwarves involved in their daily chores, their enthusiasm now focused on their work. He looked over his shoulder and nodded a greeting to Allad, who also carried a cup of tea.

"It is good to share the land with such people. It makes fighting the evil so much more important."

"Yes, I agree, Allad." *So many good people and so many of*

them will die.

They had been gone from Bystyn for more than a week; nearly three would pass before they returned to the city. What, if anything, was happening not just there but everywhere else? Had the evil pinpointed the Source of Darkness yet? Hopefully not. The inability of the evil to find the Source of Darkness gave them the hope to endure.

"Danyl...the elven magic...how is it used?"

"Well," the question took him off guard for a moment until the elf remembered Karolauren's teachings. "It manifests itself into a suitable bearer and he or she wields it...or so we think."

"Would this powerful transformation not destroy the bearer?"

Danyl never thought of it quite in that way. His ancestors each carried a part of the magic with them; all of the elven magic eventually filtered into the first king. Allad had a point, though. The shock of such a sudden transfer into a mortal could be overwhelming. He was about to respond when Ramira joined them while sipping her tea.

"You look well rested," Danyl said to her.

"It was that clear liquid, I think," she chuckled. "No headache, though."

"You didn't have enough."

"Yes, I did," she corrected him.

"Seven!" bellowed Danyl.

The ailing king shuffled over to them, his hand rubbing his aching head. He gave the elf a sour look. "Clare 'suggested' that I give you a tour."

"That was very thoughtful of her," the elf said with a smirk.

The others laughed, for they knew it was Clare's way of teaching him a lesson. The king had had more than his share of food and drink last night; the cask behind his chair had coughed up the last of its ale before they had gone to bed. The king motioned toward the stables; he accepted Danyl's cup, swallowing the strong liquid in one gulp. He drained Ramira's mug next. Seven regained some of his old spark when the horses arrived.

They mounted the horses then followed Seven as he headed

out over the main bridge, then turned left toward the farmlands. The area stretched south and east, its flat terrain and numerous streams ending in the far distance. Once clear of the mountains, they could see a blurry line of trees far to the east; low, rolling hills fronted them. The day was warm and sunny; great birds of prey spiraled lazily within the updrafts.

Danyl glanced westward, contemplating what might be occurring in Bystyn. Anxiety clouded his features. He felt a gentle touch on his arm, Ramira's smile of encouragement easing his troubled mind. Seven held up his hand and they reined in their mounts, stopping on the plains a few miles from the end of the range.

"More of our land is in the north and ends where that river flows," he explained, pointing to a silver ribbon running in the south.

It was one of the last tributaries of the Ahltyn River and disappeared as it wound its way to the northeast. A section of the river meandered north and hugged the base of the mountains. Seven told them the river was deep everywhere; the loop that ran north provided the dwarves with a natural line of defense. The river was swift and wild and cut off any attacks from that direction.

"I didn't realize that the river ran so far east," said Ramira.

"It ends along the border with the wild people living within the outskirts of the trees," added Danyl.

"That bothersome ilk likes to raid us on occasion. We'll have to keep an eye out for them," said Seven.

"With any luck we won't run into any," said Lance as he scanned the area.

The friends rode for about an hour when they spotted a group of riders off in the distance. Seven spat on the ground and watched as the horses headed straight in their direction.

"Barbarians," muttered Seven. "Seems like we'll get a bit of exercise this morning."

He withdrew his sword and waited, knowing Clare was going to give him an earful about riding so far without enough guards. In truth, he worried more about that than the unruly group racing toward them.

Ramira couldn't help but smirk, for the king apparently enjoyed these confrontations. He calmly sat on his horse, checking the edge on his blade and looking up at the riders every so often. This time, however, he recognized the leader of the barbarians. Worried for her safety, he glanced over at Ramira. His fears dissipated when he saw the intense look on her face.

"Rock Lords," he explained. "We should have gone back."

They could see the tall, muscular men with short-cropped hair barreling in their direction at a full gallop. Their bare chests were marked with swirling black tattoos; gold bands covered their upper arms. Animal hide blankets flapped around their legs as they sped on; their drawn weapons glinted in the morning sun.

They nearly crashed into the small party, their eyes focused on Ramira as the fight ensued. The Rock Lords quickly managed to isolate her. Much to the dismay of her companions, one Rock Lord forced her off her horse. He smiled, already anticipating having his way with her while she unsheathed her knives and assumed a combative stance. He laughed at her then mockingly withdrew his own short swords. The man feinted to her right, yet she did not move. He slashed at her a little closer from the other direction with the same results. Danyl and the others tried to make their way over to her, but the other Rock Lords kept them at bay. She was on her own for a little while. Ramira's friends were about to witness how she had defeated the two outlaws.

The barbarian was no longer amused and charged at her. He swung his blades at her mid-section; she deftly sidestepped him and blocked his strikes with her black blades. He growled at her then proceeded to push her back. His knives moved quickly; Ramira warded them off with ease. She was much smaller than the brawny man was yet she kept pace with his attacks. The man rushed forward trying to crush her with his strength. He grinned as she tripped over a rock and fell flat on her back. The barbarian pounced on her, but she rolled to the side and up onto her feet before he had the chance to attack again. He tired of the game and hated her for making him look ineffectual in front of his men and enemies. He assaulted her with a renewed fury. Ramira knew death would come to one of them and vowed it would not be her. She braced herself and waited for the man to come at her. She did not have long to wait. He lunged at her with all his might, cutting her flesh as he bore down on her. Ramira evaded him but began to tire. She pretended to twist to one side and, as he fell for the ploy, rotated the other way and slashed his throat. Surprise and anger registered on his face as he grabbed at his windpipe then fell into a lifeless heap. Her head snapped up as one of the Rock Lords lifted his sword over the back of Lance's head. She let fly one of the blades, watching as it buried itself up to the haft in his chest. The captain nodded his thanks then turned to take on a new opponent.

Her technique awed Allad, for they were very similar to his as he dispatched two of the Rock Lords and severely wounded two more. A quick glance to see how his comrades fared told him that they, too, had noted her fighting capabilities. They could hear hooves in the distance and knew help was on the way. The men pressed on, determined to fight until the last possible moment. Ramira was about to be challenged by another man when he and his men decided to escape. They left their dead but took their horses with them.

"Any serious injuries?" bellowed the king as he watched the barbarians disappear behind clouds of dust.

"Nothing a suture or two won't fix," replied Danyl spreading the rips in his tunic.

The prince glanced over at Ramira and noted that she wore the same dark look after the battle with the outlaws. This side of her personality confused him but did nothing to dampen his feelings for her.

"Ramira?"

"The same," she replied quietly. She stared at the blades then down at the lifeless man at her feet.

Allad studied her but kept his thoughts to himself. She bore elements of Herkah training and mannerisms yet had fought like an assassin rather than a fighter. *Your traits are slowly coming to the surface, Ramira.*

The friends remained silent while they rode back to the city.

"Honestly, Seven, you should have known better than to ride so close to their lands," she chastised him. "You are all lucky it was a small party of Rock Lords or you'd be dead or taken prisoner!"

"Well, we aren't," he grumbled, inwardly pleased with himself. "You and Allad were quite impressive, Ramira."

"I'm curious to know what master taught you how to use those knives...may I see them?"

Ramira unsheathed one and handed it over, wincing as Clare began to sew up her cuts. He marveled at the craftsmanship; there wasn't one nick or scratch on them. He stared at the jet-black surface but was unable to determine what type of metal it was nor could he decipher the picture-like images etched onto the blades. The images seemed to shift as he turned them in the light. They felt heavy in his hands and elicited an eerie sensation. This perception sent a shiver up his spine and urged him to give it back.

"I'm not sure but I am grateful to whoever trained me."

"So you should be," stated the dwarf king.

He had watched both Allad and Ramira wield their weapons with an almost refined cunning. Each precise stroke blocked their opponent and dictated how the men would fight. In the end, the expert swordsmen fought like novices by comparison.

"What of the Rock Lords, Seven? Are they always so aggressive?" asked Allad.

"Ah, skirmishes between us are normal. They are an ill-natured, ill-tempered bunch whose only pleasure in life comes from fighting. The man that Ramira killed was Dross. His father will be beside himself when he finds out a woman got him." Seven chuckled as he imagined the old man spitting at the indignity of a woman besting any Rock Lord, especially his son.

"Will they retaliate?"

"Absolutely, Allad. I can't wait, either."

Clare suggested they clean up and rest for a while. The medicines she gave them, she explained, would make them sleepy. They agreed and returned to their rooms, already becoming drowsy when they lay upon their beds.

Ramira closed her eyes but sleep would not come so easily. Her mind replayed the moves and techniques she used during the conflict. She slowed down her movements until they moved a mere fraction of a second at a time...

He reached around her and grabbed her wrists. A pair of large hands attached to deeply tanned and muscular arms guided her. The hands turned her wrists; the fingers twisted her hands to increase her flexibility while she held onto the wooden knives. She focused on the images of the snakes tattooed between the finger and thumb on both hands and swore the creatures moved. Their exposed fangs dripped venom; their hooded heads shifted back and forth. She felt a tall and powerful presence behind her. She watched his hands conduct her arms so she could cross the blades under and over her arms without slashing herself. The movement was awkward and slow at first then, as her timing and confidence increased, the blades whirled and bisected each other at an amazing speed. She was shocked at her ability and her momentary hesitation was enough to break the rhythm. She lost control of the blades. Ramira cut herself; one incision drew blood on her upper right shoulder while the other left a mark on her left thigh. She felt the presence move away from her as if the lesson was over...

Ramira bolted upright, ran over to the lamp on the table and pulled her tunic down over her shoulder. A faint scar. She excitedly checked her thigh and saw another faded mark. She acquired the scars by someone with tattooed hands who had trained her. For what exact purpose she might never know yet the exercises had served her well. Ramira silently thanked the unknown man and lay back down on the bed. Her fingers absently traced the long ago acquired scars as if they would reveal more of her past life. They didn't, but that did not discourage her from trying to remember more. How many other unforeseen circumstances would release more of her memories? The probability of that occurring both frightened and thrilled her as she closed her eyes and drifted off to sleep.

~

Zada walked onto the balcony and looked up at the moon, its silver face calmly gazed down upon her. The night was warm; she inhaled the fragrances lifting upward from the dark garden below. She sighed, closed her eyes, and relaxed her mind. There was nothing for a long time. The nomad was about to exit the in-between place when she sensed a far off stirring. The Herkah tried to focus on it but it remained elusive, evading her attempts but never quite disappearing. The standoff continued for some time; the effort drained the Herkahs energy forcing her to break the contact. Bystyn disappeared when she turned to enter her room…

She found herself in the middle of the Great White Desert standing upon the crumbling platform where she had endured the Horii. The broken columns that stood on each corner of the square dais rose to their full height, the spectacular images carved into them alive with color. Banners snapped in the wind, their elongated forms ending in silk tassels. Clay bowls filled with incense, fresh fruit, flowers, and precious spices lined the areas between the columns; an elegant basin filled with water stood in the center. This is what it had originally looked like all those years ago. It had been a place of offering. She felt the sun beating down on her and the dry breeze drifting across the endless white sands. Then she noticed the changes around her. The wind became colder; the sky darkened. The ground began to shake; the clay bowls exploded sending their contents out across the desert. Fear began to gnaw at her but she was powerless to do anything until the vision passed.

The columns began to crack; all but one toppled onto the sands. The last one fell across the middle of the dais shattering the basin and fracturing the platform. The black sky erupted with vivid flashes of lightning and bone-jarring thunder. The sand swirling around her nose and mouth kept her from screaming. The wind tore at her garments; the grains of sand abraded her skin. The shrieking wind forced her to cover her ears. She begged for the vision to be over then, mercifully, it was…

Zada gulped in huge draughts of air as she picked herself off the balcony floor. She had had potent visions before but never one so real. Why had she been shown the altar's destruction? This storm was eerily reminiscent of the one that had driven them off the desert and to the elven city. Had she glimpsed their future? Would the same whirlwind bear down on Bystyn? The Horii still existed beneath the dais, continuing to choose the leaders of the Herkahs as they had for a thousand years. Did that far-off stirring have anything to do with her vision or was its presence merely coincidental? The sensation she had felt prior to the vision did not feel evil. Was it a message from whoever had chosen her? Zada sorely missed Allad's comforting embrace.

~

The time for merriment and exploration was over. The dwarves, elves, and Allad gathered in the main hall to make plans against the evil. Ramira stayed for a while then left, heading out into the sunshine and fresh air. She followed the edge of the mountain as it wound its way northward. It ran in a straight line for miles until it curved westward, running past Bystyn and over to the Broken Plain. The sheer vastness of the range overwhelmed her. She imagined that the mountains were thrust up from the earth to keep the mortals from finding out what dwelled on the other side...or was it the other way around? She decided to concentrate on more pleasant things, glancing instead up the side of Evans Peak. Faces peered down at her from rectangular windows carved out of the mountain. The dwarves had hollowed out the outer section of the mountain where a network of tunnels connected the homes and halls. The openings along the highest points were for the sentries, who could see for many miles in three directions. There were observation posts on the other side of the mountain, too, in case the Rock Lords planned to visit.

Ramira found a shady spot beneath a cluster of oak trees near the river. She sat down, removed her boots then dipped her feet in the cool water. Ramira moved too quickly and winced, fearful of having torn one of the stitches. She lifted her tunic and moved the bandage: the sutures remained intact. She did not want to endure another round with the needle and thread. Ramira lay back, placed her arms under her head, and gazed up into the canopy. She caught sight of a squirrel studying her with unblinking eyes, its tail flicking back and forth. It scrambled over to another branch, evicting a bird that scolded it from its new perch. The scene made her laugh. She felt truly relaxed and leaned over to splash some water on her face. Somewhere out there was the key to her past; she hoped it was not as awful as her nightmares indicated. There had to have been an equal measure of good in her life.

She looked down at her folded hands, which had given her a glimpse into her past. They had not forgotten how to wield the knives nor had her body failed to remember the lessons that the faceless man had taught her. What other incident would arise that would further prod her memory out of the darkness? She dabbed at her cuts and hoped it wouldn't take another injury. She watched as a figure approached: Danyl was making his way to her and that meant the meeting was over.

He greeted her with a smile and sat down on the grass beside her, pulling off his boots and placing his feet into the refreshing water. He leaned back on his elbows, staring pensively ahead.

"We'll be leaving tomorrow."

"I'm going to miss this place," she stated, reaching over and slipping her hand into his.

Danyl appreciated her gentle touch then repositioned himself so she could lean against his chest. The two of them sat in silence for a while each lost in their own thoughts. Neither one noticed the suns descent in the west. They were content just to share the physical contact, a connection allowing the strength of one to flow into the other.

"Clare and a handful of dwarves will accompany us back to Bystyn," he stated after a long silence, his fingers absently twirling a silken strand of her hair. "Seven and the rest will follow in a few days. He wants to make sure there are enough dwarves left to confront the Rock Lords when they come back to seek retribution for their slain kin."

"Perhaps I should just have injured him."

"That was not an option, Ramira, and you know it."

"I know, Danyl, but I did not come here with the intention of making the dwarves' situation worse."

"It already was, besides, you did Seven and the others a favor by getting rid of him. The others will come once or twice to show the dwarves they aren't afraid."

"Why do they fight them?" she asked.

"The Rock Lords take great pleasure in combat."

"That's it?"

"Well, that and the spoils they acquire after they have bested their foe."

"What do their homes look like?"

"They live in mud brick houses nearly indistinguishable from their surroundings. I've heard their homes are an odd collection of things taken from a variety of people, including furniture, fabrics, and wares. They prefer gold, silver, and bronze items. They melt the metals and fashion them into marvelous pieces of jewelry. They don't have too much use for the gems, though: they pry them off and toss them into the waterways surrounding their land. The gemstones occasionally wash up along the riverbanks where the dwarves put them to good use. Their hospitality leaves a lot to be desired, as you may have deduced for yourself."

"Why is the city called 'Evans Peak', Danyl?"

She had been curious about the name from the moment she had heard it. She could feel him take a long, deep breath before speaking.

"Evan was a great warrior who lived a long time ago, even before the elves established Bystyn. He found out that Earl, his king and closest friend, was secretly making deals with their enemies. The treachery resulted in the deaths of many good people. It fell to Evan, the highest-ranking warrior, to rectify the situation. He tried to reason with the king and nearly lost his life for doing so. Left with no other option, Evan slew Earl and the few who followed the king. The deed was for the greater good of the dwarves but Evan could never forgive himself. The dwarves wanted him to rule but Evan abhorred that thought for the blood of his lifelong friend stained more than just his hands. His guilt destroyed his confidence then his heart. One day he climbed to the top of that mountain," he pointed to the peak directly over the main entrance, "and jumped to his death."

"How very sad," she said softly.

"And 'Bystyn' means 'dawn' in the elvish tongue, for the spot it would be built on was first seen by the rays of the morning light," he said anticipating her next question.

She lowered her head and thought about both cities, their names reflecting the hopes of their respective people. Evan killed his own king so the dwarves could survive; Alyxandyr's folk followed him onto unknown lands to start anew. Perhaps the bad things that happened in the past served as an effectual deterrent against repeating the same mistakes.

"Thank you for bringing me along."

"I'm glad you came," he replied, hugging her tenderly. He caressed her neck with the side of his face, the softness of her skin and the lingering perfume arousing his senses.

"I wish I could take you to a place as special as this."

"You can."

He felt her shift in his arms and regretted speaking those two little words. She was readying to bolt and all he could do was release her. To his surprise, she twisted around to face him, awkwardly bracing herself to keep her weight off him. He held his breath while her beautiful amethyst eyes studied his features.

"I can't take you to a place I've never been to," she quietly admitted.

"I didn't mean...."

She silenced him with a kiss. "Yes, you did."

"Yes, I did."

He felt a slight chill in the air and realized they had been sitting under the oaks for some time. He nudged her and the two of them walked back to the main entrance hand-in-hand. They entered the hall and passed by the table piled with food and drink.

~

They freshened up and joined their companions for the

evening meal, a sumptuous feast with everything from roast duck to fresh berries. They were so full afterward that even Seven was unable to leave the table to dance. They decided to sit and listen to the musicians playing while enjoying their last night together. At least until all the dwarves could converge upon Bystyn and spread their mirth there.

"I hope your brief stay here was satisfactory," Seven said to them lighting up his pipe. The tobacco filled the room with a woodsy aroma.

"Your kindness and hospitality could not have been better, thank you," replied Ramira.

"Indeed it has, Seven," Allad exhaled as he patted his protruding midsection. "Zada will undoubtedly repay your kindness but I doubt she'll so much as throw me a crumb until I lose this!" They laughed. All of them would carry the dwarves' generosity back to Bystyn with them.

Seven insisted they drink to the upcoming trek; glasses sprouted up in front of them all. Clare said nothing for the only thing worse than waking up with a headache from the liquid was to ride while its aftereffects still coursed through the veins. Danyl warned both Allad and Ramira to avoid drinking too much or the ride back would be most unpleasant.

"When you come back to visit we'll show you what a real dwarven banquet is like," chuckled the king.

"What do you call what we've been eating over the past few days?" asked Allad.

"Those weren't proper meals, my friend. No, hardly worthy of guests at all!" cracked Seven.

"Seven firmly believes that a 'meal' should consist of at least a dozen courses, a minimum of three casks of ale, and should last no less than two days and nights."

"Followed by several skins of my potion, since it does help settle your stomach, you know," added Seven, wearing a huge smirk across his seasoned face.

"It's true," agreed Clare. She could tell by their expressions they were having a hard time imagining such an evening. They eventually gave up and silently swore to satisfy their curiosity when all of this was over.

~

The night went by quicker than they wished; they needed to get some rest before the long journey home. They dispersed to their rooms, Danyl bidding Ramira a good night before entering his room. Sleep would not come for a long time. His mind was preoccupied with what might happen over the next few weeks, and with the woman slumbering on the other side of the wall. He could still feel her body against his and smell her perfume. It would have been a simple thing to abandon his bed for hers; he ignored that temptation and forced himself to sleep.

~

Seven and Clare remained in the hall after everyone had gone to bed. They sat quietly for a while, Seven brooding over his nearly empty tankard while Clare stared off into the shadows.

"It's going to get mighty ugly, Clare."

"I know."

The queen knew there was a good chance that some of those with whom they had dined would not visit in the future. It was a sobering fact. The dwarves, like the elves, believed everyone had a part in the greater scheme of things. Individuals composed the fabric of life whether they were good, bad or indifferent and right now, that textile was fraying at the edges. She slipped her hand into Seven's and led him to their chambers.

~

They gathered their things the next morning and made their way to the bridge where their horses awaited them. The mounts were eager to return home; their riders wished they could stay for one more day. They bade each other farewell and mounted up, following the winding path back into the forest overlooking the river.

Seven would leave for Bystyn soon but at least they had Clare and a few dwarves to make the trip back less mundane. Clare blew Seven a kiss; the others waved farewell.

Seven remained rooted in place for a long time while

watching them disappear into the woods. He had learned much in the past few days about events that loomed upon the horizon. Herkahs had dined at his table; he had danced with the mysterious woman who would become the prince's mate. The king had believed he would die of old age before experiencing any of those things. Seven shook his head and chuckled while heading back into the hall.

~

Faint sounds woke Ramira on their third night out from Evans Peak. She glanced at Danyl then at the other members of the party: everyone was asleep. The night breeze stirred the leaves and, other than the chirping insects and soft warbling of a night bird, all was still. The sensation, however, would not go away. She slipped from her blankets and disappeared into the darkness, emerging from the woods to stand at the edge of the plains. Stars and a quarter-moon illuminated the land. She strained her senses, trying to pinpoint what had awakened her but nothing stirred on the dark plains. She sighed and was about to return to her bedroll when the wind carried with it the sounds of creaking leather and muffled hooves. Somewhere out on the plains a group of riders was passing by, unaware of the party sleeping behind her. Were they friend or foe? Should she waken the others or wait until morning to tell them about the strangers? She heard footsteps behind her, their deliberate strides announcing their owner.

"Vagabonds," stated Lance quietly. "They travel along these plains in search of people to steal from."

"I thought I was hearing things."

"You fought well against the Rock Lords. I am indebted to you once again."

Ramira could barely make out his features; the tone of his voice had softened, taking on emotions she did not expect. The captain was not a conversationalist nor did he allow his feelings to show, yet there had to be another side to him. He had voluntarily forsaken his personal life to serve the prince. That dedication was both noble and poignant.

"You would have done the same, Lance," she said as pity for

him touched her heart.

"Nonetheless I am grateful that you fight on our side."

"Lance?"

"Yes?"

"How were you…how are captains chosen to protect the royal family?"

"Those who guard the family have none of their own, Ramira," he began in a quiet voice. "We are given the chance to learn everything our charges do and are, in a way, absorbed into the family. We understand our primary goal is to keep our charges safe, even at the expense of our own lives. This responsibility begins at a very young age."

"You grew up with Danyl, then."

"Yes."

"What would happen if you were to…."

"If I were to die then I would, of course, be replaced by another member of his personal guard."

His response was so matter-of-fact that all she could do was stare at him. Then the captain did the unexpected: he smiled. Ramira did not think such a serious topic warranted that kind of response.

"It is a privilege to serve the family, Ramira, and an even greater honor to die for them. I consider myself fortunate to be in this position and, although you apparently think otherwise, am not deprived of anything."

Lance left her standing alone, her embarrassment cloaked by the night. He had answered her unspoken question, an inquiry she had no right to ask in the first place. Ramira returned to her blankets and rolled over on her side. She studied Danyl's profile as he slept and understood how Lance could dedicate his life to him. Her last thoughts as she drifted off to sleep were of how she was beginning to feel the same way.

~

The message arrived while they were eating breakfast. Alyxandyr glanced over and smiled at Zada. She accompanied the king as they made their way onto the broad balcony that fronted the second floor of the castle.

Alyxandyr warmly greeted his friends and family. They freshened up then gathered in the king's private rooms where everyone exchanged the most recent news. The Khadry preferred to keep to the edge of the forest while the Herkahs interacted with the elves on a more frequent basis. Danyl nodded, for there would come a day when one would have to fight beside the other, and it was better to do so on friendly terms. Allad whispered a few words into Zada's ear; she raised her brows in surprise. Danyl knew what he told her. Ramira stirred uncomfortably in her seat when Zada's gaze focused on her.

"We had a little skirmish with the Rock Lords, Father."

"No one was severely hurt or killed, were they?" asked the king.

"They suffered both of those fates," replied Clare. "It seems as though Ramira was able to slay one of the High Lords' sons."

Ramira looked at the floor, the unwelcome attention making her fidgety.

"Really? You must be either very lucky or highly skilled," stated the king while studying her more closely.

"Highly skilled would better approximate her talents," explained Allad.

"Well," Danyl tried to change the subject, "I'm starved. Did you leave us any breakfast?"

Ramira was aware of the stares and, although invited to stay and eat, declined and left. She headed down the hall but Danyl caught up to her just as she reached the door. He pulled her out of earshot; more than one pair of eyes watched the interaction between them.

"He had to be told."

"I understand."

"Sophie will be glad to see you again. I'm sure she's saved up plenty of chores for you to do."

"She'll have to wait until after I've bathed and slept for a few hours."

"I'll look in on you later," he promised then walked her to the door. The gossip, he knew, was already beginning. He would have to deal with Alyssa before the day was over.

~

'Later' ended up being several days. Between catching up on his duties and helping Clare prepare for the dwarves arrival, Danyl's days were extra busy. Alyssa was already asking questions. Her prying was beginning to grate on his nerves until he told her to mind her own business. This did not sit well with the princess, who was now determined to find the answers her brother would not give her.

The princess visited Sophie's house but the object of her curiosity was not home. She devised another way to force a meeting. Alyssa sent a dinner invitation for all three women. Her brother would be furious.

~

It was dusk when an exhausted Ramira entered the kitchen. She was relieved that Sophie and Anci were dressed to attend some function at the castle. All she wanted was a bite of food, a long bath, and sleep.

"All three of us will be dining with the king tonight," Sophie said smoothing a wrinkle on her dress.

Too tired to argue and knowing she would not win anyway, Ramira bathed and started slipping into the dress Sophie held out for her.

"Princess Alyssa expects us within the hour."

"Sophie...no," she nearly moaned.

"Yes. Just go and let Alyssa take a look at you." She was about to pull the gown up over Ramira's waist when she saw the scars. "What are these?"

"A token from my visit to the dwarves. We had a little conflict with Rock Lords and, well, now I have these to remind me."

Sophie eyed her for a few seconds then buttoned the back of the dress.

"As I was saying, you'll get to see Danyl and Clare and meet Zada, so it won't be such a bad evening after all. Let me look at you."

Sophie made Ramira turn around. Pleased with the deep lavender gown, Sophie made a few minor adjustments then ushered her out the door.

The evening breeze chased away the heat of the day as the carriage brought them to the castle. Ramira would rather face the Rock Lords than endure the princess's scrutiny. Alyssa's resolve knew no bounds and she would face any consequence to satisfy her nosiness. Danyl would be furious, a fact that Alyssa was willing to accept. Ramira gazed up at the gray stones forming the castle façade and the lights escaping from the windows as the carriage stopped. She took a deep breath, accepted Sophie's smile of encouragement headed for the entrance to the castle.

They were escorted to the dining hall where most of the guests, including Gard, were already gathered. The prince was puzzled yet pleased when Ramira entered the room. Her simple gown and single braid only enhanced her beauty. Those gathered noticed his reaction. He introduced her to Zada and Nyk.

"I am honored to meet you." Ramira offered them both respectful nods.

The king entered the room with Alyssa on his arm. The princess glanced at Ramira then over to Danyl, who immediately understood what was going on. The brief look he gave his sister promised he would deal with her later. He smirked because as much as Alyssa wanted to corner Ramira, the king and Zada managed to intervene. Danyl whispered into Styph's ear, his older brother grinning in anticipation of thwarting his sister's plans. When the dinner bell rang, Danyl led Ramira to the seat beside him while Styph sat next to his fuming sister.

The king watched the conflict between his children and offered them a stern look of warning. Fully-grown or not, they knew he would express his annoyance with them when the night ended. Alyxandyr understood his sons would never concede to Alyssa's prying. She held herself erect for a moment then wilted under his glare, leaving her brothers victorious for at least this night. The elven king wondered what relationship was brewing between his son and the woman beside him. Alyssa's keen interest in the woman hinted at something more than just friendship. Alyxandyr watched Danyl raise his goblet and salute his sister; she acknowledged him with narrowed eyes.

Dinner was pleasant for everyone but Alyssa, although her outward demeanor could not have been more gracious. They retired to the balcony where lamps gave off a soft and cozy light, the fragrant oil meshing perfectly with the scents floating upward from the garden. They sat together realizing good had come from the darkness slowly rolling eastward, for the friendships and alliances would sustain them in the end.

Gard had been silent through most of dinner, but was beginning to relax as the evening wore on. He appreciated the fact that his treatment was equal to everyone else. The bitterness handed down through the generations was no different from drinking from an empty cup, and he began to wonder why he still held onto that vessel. The Bystynian elves had absolutely no intention of taking away what the Khadry had built over the years; therefore, there was no need to feel threatened or to hate. Indeed, none of the races gathered in the comfortable darkness had their sights set on anything but surviving, giving up much to unite with one another. The Herkahs had, for the time being, lost their home, as had his own people. The dwarf queen was a reminder that her folk would also abandon their city for Bystyn and stand beside those gathered here. Gard's eyes strayed to a quiet Ramira, who watched and listened from her seat beside the prince. The moon and duskiness only enhanced her beauty giving her a nearly ethereal quality. It was easy to see why Danyl found her so alluring. Gard remembered the fairness and respect the prince had bestowed upon him when he had confronted him at the inn weeks ago.

The nomads, although quite fierce and proud, also radiated those same characteristics. He glanced over at Zada whose soft voice and tinkling bracelets brought calm over their gathering. Her elegance and grace disguised her brutal capabilities. He wondered what expressions would drift across her tanned features as she wielded her knives. Allad's features, he was sure, would be devoid of anything but a glacial resolve as he smote his enemy. He was renowned for his notable skills, proficiencies that pulsated even here where no real threat existed. The Khadry had seen the Herkahs from a distance and now shared drink and conversation with them. The one thing he was sure of was that he did not want to be their foe.

"I would like to propose a toast to those gathered here," the king raised his glass. "May we face the future side by side and let the faith and honor that has grown between us continue."

They clinked their glasses then sat down in chairs or leaned up against the balustrade.

"I understand you have developed a deep admiration for the dwarves, Ramira," the king smiled as her face lit up.

"A most delightful people," she began, offering a beaming Clare a little nod. "I hope that I am invited back."

"You most certainly are welcome any time…there will always be a bed open to you."

"When Seven comes here you know he will be laden with his poison, Father," chuckled Styph.

"Yes, I know. Thank goodness Clare will also be here to temper his enthusiasm."

"I will have to bring our version of that drink," Allad stated with a knowing little smile. "I believe he will find it equally refreshing."

"Yours is as potent as his?" asked Mason leaning against the rail beside his sister and niece.

"Let's just say the glass from which it is sipped is only this high," he replied, his thumb and index finger indicating about an inch.

"Seven will call a vessel that small a waste of clay," laughed Danyl.

"How are your mementos, Ramira? All healed?" asked Clare.

"Yes, and I must say your stitching will leave virtually no scars." She remembered her dream and the ghostly perception of the man who had taught her to wield the knives. The fight was on the mind of Zada, too, for she had been studying her for most of the evening.

"I hear you are most adept at handling knives, Ramira. Allad tells me he was most impressed."

"I was fortunate to have been able to defeat the Rock Lord, Zada. It could have easily gone the other way," she humbly replied.

"Perhaps, but I think Captain Lance would beg to differ. He is alive today because of you," she said.

Ramira, thought Zada, might not be such an enigma after all. It was just a matter of certain situations -dire or otherwise- that would prompt her to revert to things she had learned in her past. The skirmish on the plain, for example, awoke her skill and training with her knives. Perhaps a certain food or something as simple as stroking a cat would elicit some other response. People lose their memories but their bodies never forget.

"I was thinking that when Seven arrives we might have a little festival," began the king. "Nothing too elaborate, just some food and drink and maybe a few contests out on the plain. It might help relieve some of the nervousness and strain of the past few weeks."

"I agree," replied Clare.

"Alyssa," the king looked over at his daughter, "you will make the arrangements."

"Well," Danyl offered Ramira his arm, "care to stretch your legs with a walk in the garden?"

They strolled toward the far corner of the garden where a stone bench stood beside a fountain. A carved fish spouted water from its open mouth while ivy completely hid the gray stones below. A circle of shrubs with tiny wax-like leaves provided plenty of privacy. Hooded yellow flowers at the base of the fountain exuded a soft fragrance.

"Your sister has quite a stubborn streak."

"Alyssa means well but her methods are truly annoying," he said. "When our mother died, she took on many of her responsibilities. Alyssa has this strange notion that my brothers and I are incapable of finding a suitable companion, while she ignores the stirrings in her own heart."

"That is sad, Danyl."

"It doesn't have to be," he replied then lifted her chin and kissed her lips.

He straddled the bench and pulled her up against his chest. That peculiar sensation began to vibrate deep within them again. Danyl inhaled her perfume and wondered if she had placed another drop on her neck. He asked her but she said she had not touched the bottle since that day.

"When will the dwarves arrive?"

"I'm guessing tomorrow." The thought of their exuberance elicited a quiet laugh.

"What's so amusing?"

"Seven loves tormenting Karolauren, and I do believe the Historian revels in getting back at the king. You'll see what I mean. Come," he began leading her away from the corner, "I want to show you something."

They walked along the flagstone path to the opposite corner where a magnificent rosebush bloomed; its snow-white flowers radiant even in the darkness. Ramira lifted one of the fragrant blooms to her nose and inhaled deeply.

"My mother planted this when she wed my father, a sort of token of their love and new life together. She has been gone many years yet it flourishes as if she still tended to it."

Ramira closed her eyes; her fingers lingered on the velvety petals…

She was a little girl sitting on a lap, the woman holding her rocking and humming in her ear. The room in which she sat was sparse and lit by a single lamp on the table before her. The arms holding her were warm with love; gentle kisses landed on the top of her head. She squirmed deeper into the embrace.

"I want to be big," she sleepily told the woman.

"You will be someday," she replied.

"Tomorrow?"

"Maybe…or the next day."

"Will I still fit in your lap?"

"You will always fit into my lap, my sweet…"

"Ramira? Are you all right?"

159

"What?"

"It's almost as if you went somewhere else for a moment."

"I guess I did," she replied, the memory increasing the yearning for the woman who had so loved her. She smiled at him and told him what she had seen.

"Not everything in your past life has been unpleasant, has it?"

"Nor much in my present one, either," she said caressing his cheek. "It has been a long day, Danyl, and I need to rest."

He wanted to escort her home but she refused, reminding him that he still had guests. She thanked the princess for the invitation and bid them all a good night. Ramira walked down the avenue and neared the intersection when everything changed around her. The shops and homes became hulking shadows; the yellow globs of light shining from the windows reminded her of wolves' eyes. She thought she heard low growls; the sounds making her skin crawl. Her hands instinctively reached for the knives but they lay upon her dresser in the house. Ramira blinked and Bystyn returned, but she could not shake the uneasiness coursing through her. She took a deep breath and crossed the street in front of her home, her scanning the darkness around her. She entered the house and froze. Ramira bolted upstairs, retrieved her knives and searched the house. She found nothing and began to wonder if she were imagining things. She exhaled and poured herself a glass of wine, careful not to spill any on her dress. Satisfied that no one was in the house, she went to bed.

~

Laden with packages, Ramira and Anci were heading back home when a group of riders came down the avenue. They could see Clare among the nomads and princes: Seven was coming and they were riding out to meet him. The riders stopped in front of them; Danyl held out his hand, his bright green eyes sparkling invitingly. Styph was already helping Anci up into his saddle; their parcels ended up in the arms of a guard while Ramira jumped up behind Danyl. She looked up at the walls and smiled for many had gathered to watch the dwarves' arrival. They trotted beneath the gates and out onto the plain; the Herkahs advanced toward the walls to greet the dwarves. Groups of elves had joined them, talking and pointing as if they had been friends for years.

Ramira could hear them long before they broke through the orchard. She turned toward Clare whose face radiated pride and love for her folk. The dwarves sang in their own tongue, the cheerful rhythm and booming chorus energizing all who waited. She peeked over Danyl's shoulder; the prince gave her a sideways glance while his free hand lay flat against hers. The first wagons entered into view, the king rode beside the cart laden with casks of ale.

"Very protective, isn't he?" chuckled Ramira.

"An army couldn't pry that dray from his fingers!" Clare said shaking her head back and forth.

The bulk of the band passed beyond the orchards, the sun glinting off weapons hauled in three of the wagons. Ramira felt Danyl tensed as his sudden apprehension threatened to extinguish his enthusiasm. She patted his hand, pulling him back from the dark brink he was about to step into. The queen suddenly kicked the sides of her horse and raced forward, the elves not far behind. Styph reined in his mount and jumped off before it came to a complete stop. The crown prince stood at least a head higher than Seven but that did not stop the dwarf from hoisting him way up in the air. Danyl and Ramira grinned at them.

Seven came prepared for there were many wagons filled with provisions and one cart sagging with the weight of ale barrels. Ramira laughed because the king had brought the most essential of supplies and was determined, she was sure, to bring them home empty. She kept off to one side allowing the princes and the others the chance to greet Seven. A loud cheer erupted from those gathered on the parapets as they passed beneath the gate, the dwarves waving back while eyeing the black tents with curiosity. They made their way up the avenue, smiling at the elves lining the street. Ramira peeled away from the group as they passed Sophie's house. She joined the woman on the front steps, watching Danyl crane his neck to look for her. He winked at her before the crowd swallowed him up.

Ramira glanced over at Sophie, the adoration for the dwarves visible on her features. The dwarves' awareness of their own mortality urged them to enjoy the time they had with each other, an idea the elves heartily embraced. From what Ramira had seen so far, some of that exuberance was already rubbing off on the Herkahs, especially Allad, who had taken to the dwarf king almost immediately. Sophie tapped Ramira on the arm, her gaze never leaving the vanishing figures heading up the avenue.

"You had better grab a few hours of sleep because it's going to be a long and raucous night."

Sophie went into the house; Ramira followed her a few moments later.

~

Ramira smiled at the animated dwarf king as she walked into the main reception hall: she watched Sophie brace herself for his bear hug. Seven picked her up in one arm and Anci in the other, warmly embracing them as if they were no heavier than a pair of dolls. It took some doing but Sophie was finally able to disentangle herself and straighten out her dress. She sat down near the fireplace. It was the perfect time to exchange stories and further cement their friendships.

"I still think Styph and I bested you," laughed Danyl, his brother-in-crime nearly spitting his wine across the room.

"Yes, that incident nearly caused a war between the dwarves and the elves," Seven scowled good-naturedly. "When those two were no higher than my knees, they decided to go bear hunting. The little imps went into the woods, mistook me for one and each let an arrow fly! I came out of the brush with an arrow embedded in each cheek. All I wanted to do was get my hands around their little necks. When their father ultimately stopped laughing," he threw the bemused elven king a sour look, "he managed to discipline them. I still have marks...."

"No, Seven!" Clare stopped him before he could show everyone the scars. She glanced over at Allad who approached the king with a glass bottle filled with an amber liquid.

"Do you remember when I proposed you try our version of your concoction?"

162

The Herkah poured a small amount into a glass. Seven swirled the contents under his nose then drank it down in one gulp. Zada placed her hand over her mouth as the dwarf king began to sweat, the tears running down his cheeks indistinguishable from his perspiration. He opened his mouth but the fire burning in his throat incinerated his words. After a few very long moments, he wiped his face, and nodded his head in approval.

"You and I are going to become good friends, Allad," he finally managed to say in a raspy voice.

The nomad smiled and slapped the dwarf on the back in agreement.

"It isn't enough that Seven has tainted the elves," Clare quipped. "He won't be happy unless he does the same to the Herkahs."

"The Herkahs are not innocent bystanders, Clare," said Zada watching Seven shudder after drinking another glass of Allad's potion.

Zada felt her inner sight. She rose and headed out onto the balcony, an ever-vigilant Allad trailing but not crowding her. She stood with her hands on the balustrade, closed her eyes, and opened her mind.

There was a rustling sensation; nervous whispers followed. She faced west, a foul wind curled and twisted as it searched for the Source of Darkness. Everything it touched wilted then died, unable to survive its horrific contact. She gripped the banister more tightly for even at this distance the evil was almost overwhelming. She gasped as she recognized the solid shadows lurking within its fetid haze: Radir. Zada knew that the Vox would not be far behind. Time was growing short. She withdrew her inner sight fearful of being seen by what skulked in the west.

Allad caught her as she fell, grateful they were alone while she returned to her surroundings. The trepidation in her eyes did not bode well for them. He saw a figure emerge onto the balcony. Ramira knelt beside them as if summoned by some unheard call. Her eyes were wide, staring at the prone woman with awe then bewilderment. She reached out and touched Zada's shoulder before Allad could stop her. The contact yanked her into the vision. Then, the unexpected happened: the nomad's sight flared up again...

They stood hand in hand upon a sliver of rock that stretched high into the cloudless orange sky. They dared to look down at a thread-like river meandering its way through barren canyons. Its silver waters turned crimson, as did the mist slowly wending its way up the sides of the bedrock. A loathsome wind preceded it, swirling around them and threatening to push them into the chasm. Zada tightened her grip but Ramira began to move toward the edge, heeding the voice that had suddenly erupted from within the fog. Ramira's expression began to change from horror to ecstasy, spurred on by the sensual murmurs rising upward. The Herkah grabbed her with both hands, silently screaming for her to stop. Ramira moved closer to the brink. Bits of stone and dirt gave way beneath her feet as she reached out to touch the mist...

Allad forcibly wrenched Ramira away from Zada, the brief contact making him suck in air through clenched teeth. Ramira sat against the wall breathing heavily, her gaze never leaving Zada. Allad helped Zada to a nearby bench, holding her as she fought off the dizziness and nausea.

"Help...Ramira."

Allad hesitated then walked over to Ramira. His face pulsated with anger; his rigid body was more terrifying than anything she had ever seen. She pushed herself against the wall, struggling to contain the whimper lodged in her throat. She trembled more from his wrath than from the vision she had shared with Zada.

Pity for the frightened woman chased away the rage and released his locked limbs, allowing him to kneel beside her. "Foolish girl," he muttered.

"I'm sorry, Allad...I didn't mean to..."

"Of course you didn't but don't ever do that again!"

"Leave us," said Zada, placing her hand reassuringly on his arm.

Allad paused then went inside, closing the door after him. He

164

persuaded the others that everything was fine. Danyl glanced over to the balcony then back to the Herkah who stood in front of it. Seven and Alyxandyr exchanged perplexed looks; Gard kept his thoughts to himself.

~

"Come and sit, Ramira." Zada held her hand out to her.

"No…" she replied in a raspy voice.

"The trance is over …there will be no more images."

They sat together in silence for a long time; the Herkah scrutinized Ramira's profile. Others had touched Zada while her inner sight controlled her but they had recoiled from the power, not been absorbed into her mystic state.

"Where were we?" Ramira finally asked.

"A place between the land of the living and the dead." Zada watched her stiffen.

"I…I wanted to jump, Zada. What would have happened if I…"

"You'd be dead. That fate would have befallen me, too, which is why Allad is at my side when the visions come. He is my link to the present. The images usually play themselves out before it gets to that point but this one was different. You obeyed its call." *And that concerns me a great deal.*

"I didn't want to, Zada."

"I know, child. Are you feeling better now?"

"Yes," Ramira lied. The seductive whispers adhered to the last vestiges of her nightmares.

Their friends became silent as the ashen-faced women entered the room. Danyl started forward but Allad held him back; Zada and Ramira seated themselves in front of the fire. The nomad took a deep breath and told them what she had seen. She did not divulge the conversation she had with Ramira.

"Zada," asked the elven king with a hint of trepidation in his voice, "did your vision tell you if the evil has found the Source of Darkness?"

"He still searches for it, Alyx."

"First Kreetch then Radir…how soon will the Vox come?"

asked Styph.

Zada shrugged. The Source of Darkness was still out of the evil's grasp. This meant that the evil would head westward to continue its hunt. Zada knew the days of merriment were gone and there would be no festival on the plains. She suggested they hold the celebration in the city and, after hesitating for a moment, the elven king agreed. It would be better than nothing would.

SIX

Ramira approached the orchards a few days later, the brilliant blue sky and hot sun not enough to chase away the chill of the shared vision. She shifted the heavy basket and realized how quiet it had become. Nothing moved, crawled or chirped anywhere. Even the breeze had ceased to blow over the grasses. She strained to hear any sound but the only thing she heard was the beating of her heart. It reminded her of the sensation she had when she chased the phantom intruder in Sophie's house. She reached down toward her knives, the cold feel of their hilts reassuring to the touch.

~

Zada lifted her cup to her lips but never drank from it, the sudden and overpowering second sight freezing her into place. The danger was so near that she was unable to prepare herself for the thrust into the black void. Allad warned everyone back, and then stationed himself near Zada as he kept watch with the others.

The darkness turned gray; she could make out the image of a house by the orchard. A figure stood nearby: Ramira. Her hands hovered over her knives; she scrutinized her surroundings. There was something wrong in the old couple's house, the very place Ramira was heading. Ramira advanced a few paces, hesitated then moved forward once more. She slipped the straps off her shoulders, the heavily laden basket spilling its contents onto the grass.

Ramira disappeared from her inner sight, replaced by a black haze she could not penetrate. Zada did not need to 'see' to know what lurked within the mist. The Kreetch's foul presence invaded her mind and forced her to bear witness to their vileness. Zada shuddered with disgust at the smell of blood and the feel of tattered flesh. They fought amongst each other for the body parts then tore apart and ate their mortally wounded kin. Their gnarling and high-pitched screeches wrenched her nerves until she thought she would scream. Ramira headed straight for them.

"No...don't..." Zada could barely breathe the words.

The tension pressed down upon them like the oppressive air right before a severe thunderstorm.

Ramira let the basket fall, ignoring the thump it made as it hit the ground. The specters she had chased in her home were here and their presence ignited something within her. It responded to the menace, forcing every thought and emotion from her. All that mattered was eradicating the threat waiting for her inside the house. She moved forward with purpose, fearless in her intent and eager for the encounter. Her foot reached the first step. Claws instantly scrabbled across the wooden floor. Ramira tiptoed up the stairs; her muscles tensed as the things inside abruptly fell silent. She stared at the door for a second, then pushed the handle down and went inside.

~

Zada snapped out of her trance, her face bloodless and her hands shaking with fear. She spoke to Allad in their native tongue; her mate's features took on a dangerous cast. She gazed at Danyl, the sadness and fright etched on her countenance stealing his breath away.

"Where is she?" he demanded.

"Come with me," Allad commanded then nodded to Lance and Nyk. He would need their brawn to keep Danyl from interfering with what was taking place on the plain.

They mounted their horses, Nyk calling for two more elven guards to join them before speeding from the city. Allad signaled for more Herkahs as they passed under the gates. Four more horses joined the group as they raced toward Jack's and Ida's house. They were riding so swiftly that speech was impossible; the dark looks on the Herkahs faces indicated it was bad news. The horses raced across the plain at a full gallop and still their riders urged them faster. The fruit trees loomed up ahead then the chimney poked over their tops. They hastened past the basket then finally arrived at the house.

A terrible silence met them. They dismounted and it took all of Lance's and the elves' power to keep Danyl away from the house. The prince repeatedly called out her name.

"Do not, I repeat do not, under any circumstances go near that house. If you approach it we will be forced to kill you, understand?"

Nyk understood perfectly because he had seen this before. There were Kreetch inside and the Herkahs were the only ones prepared to confront them. Nyk shifted over to stand beside his brother then motioned Lance to the other side with a jerk of his head.

~

Ramira stood in front of the closed door searching for the demons; her hands grasped her knives. A movement to her right and scrambling sounds near the kitchen caught her attention. Shadowy forms darted around the main room vying for the best spot from which to attack. She counted at least four of the things, each with teeth and claws capable of shredding her flesh. Nothing moved for several long minutes, the creatures choosing to watch her in the semi-darkness. Suddenly one of the demons launched itself from across the room, its twisted black body intent upon ripping her to pieces. Her hands came up, the knives blurs of motion as she slashed the fiends' midsection. It shrieked in pain once, and then dropped lifeless to the floor. Its foul blood spread outward from its mortal wound.

She turned as two others attacked her from opposite sides, their assault more difficult to defend as they closed the distance. They catapulted past her, tearing their claws along her side and shoulder. She inhaled sharply through clenched teeth as the burning pain coursed through her body. Her blood excited the Kreetch; they anticipated her death with glee. One of the Kreetch miscalculated its pounce to her back, paying for the mistake with its life. Another tried to rake its claws across her chest but it, too, was a second too slow to escape her blades. That left one more. Ramira hoped it would show itself soon because the poison was beginning to steal her strength away. She became weak and sick to her stomach; the perspiration running down her face stung her eyes. Her loose tunic was so shredded it fell off on its own accord, baring her bloodstained undershirt.

It crept out from the kitchen, its head covered in blood; pieces of flesh hung from its jaws. Ramira hated it even more for what it had done to the old couple. It emitted a low growling sound; its mangy hackles lifted upward as it stalked into the main room. She raised the blades, its hunger for her death the only reason for its existence. It lunged at her, forcing her to spiral to the side and slip on the blood-soaked floor. She dropped to the floorboards with a thud, rolling away just as the demon launched itself on top of her. The demon raked her in the same gash made by one of its wicked brethren, the pain so intense she screamed in agony. The Kreetch jumped up and down, maniacally howling with delight at the anguish it had caused. She surged forward, her rage energized and cut the unprepared Kreetch in half. She gasped for air, fighting the fire claiming her mind and body, staggering in search of more demons. There were none. Bleeding and in pain, she went into the kitchen where the bloody remains of the gentle couple lay.

Ramira had one more task to perform and, crouching between them stabbed them with her daggers. She would not let the demons use these bodies. She stared at the corpses for several long moments, the thought of being bereft of their compassion gripping her heart. They had done nothing to deserve such savagery. Their tragic deaths summoned the grief within her soul; tears and silent sobs wracked her pain-filled body. She forced her leaden limbs toward the front of the house, each step a monumental challenge. Her burning muscles and ragged breathing made the short trek to the front door seem an eternity. Ramira left the horror behind her.

~

The sun beat down on those waiting to see what or who might come out of the house. The Herkahs did not move; their eyes remained focused on the door. They heard unsteady footsteps within the house. Weapons scraped their scabbards as the men prepared to confront whatever was inside the house. Lance tightened his grip on Danyl, the knots on the prince's shoulders growing beneath his hand. The latch clicked and the door opened sluggishly, the shade beneath the porch obscuring the figure emerging from the house. For a moment, they could see nothing then a bloodied Ramira shuffled out and down the stairs. She staggered into the sunlight. Her head hung down and her bloodshot eyes were framed by deep purple stains. She was unable to catch her breath. Danyl glanced at her wounds and cringed at the blood flowing freely from the rents in her garment.

"Ramira!" His voice startled his companions but not Ramira.

Allad swallowed hard, the duty at hand the hardest he had ever to perform. He grasped his daggers with sweaty palms; his determination remained undaunted.

Nyk exhaled slowly, the dying screams of another necessary slaughter echoing in his mind. He remembered the sorrow and anger he felt and wished Allad had left Danyl behind. It was not fair to his younger brother, whose affection for Ramira would not die with her. Pity began to seep into Nyk's heart.

Ramira could barely remain erect, the blistering heat robbing all of her strength. She struggled to make sense of the dark smudges and, for a brief moment, was able to identify Allad. Her constricted throat imprisoned her cry for help and soon her mind forgot how to ask for it. Allad became a blur again while she swayed unsteadily on her feet. Her perspiration trickled down her neck and chest, following the curves of her arms to her hands. The blades slid from her nerveless fingers and buried themselves to the hafts in the hard ground at her feet.

The nomad stepped forward fully expecting the demon-possessed woman to strike yet she did nothing. The Herkah moved toward her, his blades glinting in the light heedless of Danyl's cries behind him. He hesitated, the poison not provoking the usual reaction. Was this some sort of trick? Had Mahn contrived a new way of ensnaring Herkahs?

He focused his gaze on the rivulet of sweat dripping from the corner of her unresponsive eye then realized it was a tear. Ramira had been marked but she wasn't a demon. Not yet anyway. Allad squeezed the hilts, uncomfortable with the decision before him. He had mere seconds to respond. Ramira began to collapse; he instinctively lunged forward regardless of Danyl's outcry. The only thing anyone saw was the flash of Allad's knives as she fell into his arms. No one moved or even breathed for many long moments, rooted in place by the scene before them. Ramira's head lay on his shoulder; her body sagged against his. Allad's knives were out of sight. The nomad had fulfilled his somber obligation. The stillness was finally broken when Allad shouted at one of the other nomads, who hastened to retrieve a blanket. Allad wrapped it around her, a raging Danyl breaking free of the arms holding him. He launched himself at the Herkah but Lance tackled the prince just before the prince made contact with him.

"She has been corrupted by the demons, Danyl. Her tears give me hope that she might be able to beat the poison, but if she cannot, then I will bury my blades into her flesh. Until we are sure of what may or may not thrive within her, she will remain under Herkah guard, understood?"

Allad mounted his horse, took the unconscious woman in his arms, and headed back to the city. Danyl rode alongside Allad; his attention riveted on the lifeless form cradled in the nomads arms. He tried not to think of what would happen if the Herkah judged her a demon. The ride back to the city took forever.

Allad continued to hold her as he raced into the castle and toward a room in the back with barred windows. He wanted her to be well contained in case his judgment turned out to be wrong. Zada waited for him; her eyes still wide with the memory of what she had seen. He gently placed Ramira's body on the bed and began to undress her. Zada stopped him. Some of the blood had dried the shreds of cloth into her wounds; a steady hand was needed to loosen them without further injuring her. Allad's hands shook with a myriad of emotions. He relinquished the task but refused to leave. Zada positioned herself between those in the chamber and Ramira to offer her some measure of modesty. She washed away the blood then frowned with concern at the wounds inflicted by the Kreetch. She was going to need a lot more help, and called for the healer and Clare.

They worked on her for a long time yet Ramira never flinched. She seemed dead to them, or worse. She began to sweat more profusely as the poison coursed through her body, its heat burning her from the inside out. Zada ordered towels soaked in cold water to help relieve the fire, but Ramira worsened with each passing hour. They forced as much water down her throat as possible without drowning her. Nothing seemed to help. Three Herkahs stationed themselves at her bedside, their attentive stares never leaving the recumbent woman.

"Are there no medicines she could take?" asked Danyl.

"No, son, there aren't. She is either strong enough to live or she will die," replied Zada, unwilling to tell him the truth.

"So she'll just die of thirst?"

"That is not what is happening, Danyl." She placed her hand on his chest and looked him straight in the eye. "For some reason the demons venom did not take her right away, but it is in her body and thereby connected to them."

"What does that mean?" he demanded.

"It means the toxin is a thread to Mahn and through it he could manipulate her to do his deeds."

"What can be done?"

"The link to us must be stronger."

Suspicion began to set into Danyl's heart. Allad had taken an enormous chance in bringing her back to the city. The Herkahs killed those who housed the venom, yet something had stayed his hand. He was eternally grateful for that but knew she was still vulnerable to the nomads' blades. How could they possibly form some sort of connection if she was unconscious? He gazed helplessly down at her pale and sweaty face, strands of hair darkened by her perspiration stuck to her skin. He reached over to push them away, feeling her clammy flesh beneath his touch. Danyl wondered what else lay in store for her. He looked over at the Herkah couple who kept their lips sealed.

~

She floated in the blackness and endured the agony until all she wanted was to die. She was without direction and all she had known was far beyond her reach. She was so very alone, so very scared. She hated this stifling place and strained to hear a sound, any sound that could offer her a way out of this hell. All she heard, however, were insidious whispers arising from somewhere far below. They were identical to the ones from her visions, beseeching her to join them. This time, however, she could not wake up. The fire burned into her being, the suffering so intense it began to sear away all she had been and known. Her mind and body were drifting away from each other, forever lost in an endless sea of black and tormented by things just beyond her reach...

~

"How is she?" Allad asked Zada.

"I will be surprised if she lives through the night."

He had recounted what had transpired outside Jack's and Ida's home, and then confessed his uncertainty about bringing Ramira back to the city. His decision could very well have placed them all in great danger, if not now then perhaps later on. He sincerely hoped his instincts had not failed him. Her road, if she even survived, would be arduous to say the least.

"Did you tell him about the convulsions and the slow suffocation?"

"No, Allad," she said and squeezed her eyes shut.

Zada reopened them then looked over at Danyl, who sat by Ramira's side and held her hand. Lines of worry aged him. He was willing to do anything to help her. A blade across her throat was the most merciful thing to do. She sighed and accepted Allad's arms around her, his nearness her only comfort.

~

The spasms began late that night, the ragged breathing shortly thereafter. Low moaning slipped from between her cracked lips; her furrowed brows nearly disappeared into her saturated hairline. Her body jerked violently; blood flowed from reopened wounds. Zada removed Ramira's twisted dressing gown. Clare,

Zada, and the Healer were unable to restrain her and called for more help. Allad and Clare grappled with her legs while Danyl straddled her and pinned down her arms Zada and the Healer worked on her injuries. It became senseless to sew the wounds again while in the throes of the venom.

Danyl could do nothing but watch her breathing come in sharp gasps and raspy exhalations. She had saved his life all those months ago; her had presence touched his spirit like no other. What could he do? How could he help her? How was he supposed to initiate that 'connection' of which Zada spoke? He looked upon her contorted features, the agony transforming her beautiful face into something pitiful to look upon. It was then that the peculiar sensation began to swirl deep within him. It grew in intensity, snaking upward as if seeking its freedom. He could not control the force surging upward, enveloping him from within in a glittering shade of green. It scorched him, threatening to burn him to ash then abruptly dissipated, leaving him in a vast blackness as cold and forlorn as a tomb. The change was so sudden it took several moments for him to adjust to this desolate and frightful place. He finally understood and took a deep breath before thrusting himself through the corridor connecting him to her...

He entered a cold darkness that reminded him of the family crypt deep within the bowels of the castle. He was hurtling downward in an endless spiral, past cobweb-like things and far-off shrieks of glee. This place reeked of death and suffering, the unseen things waiting in the blackness for the chance to snatch him into their foul lairs. He would not stay long enough for that to happen and he was not leaving without Ramira. He called her name repeatedly but received no response. How far had she traveled in this black morass?

Then, amid the disgusting odors swarming around him, he detected one offering him some hope: perfume. It was faint but present nonetheless. He was close. He reached out in every direction for her but his hands felt only the gummy air that surrounded him. She had to be near! Those things shrieking all around him could not possibly have taken her! Panic began to set in; his arms flailed about yet they still came up empty. Finally, his hand brushed against hers. He closed his fingers around it and stopped the downward motion. The howls intensified, the hateful sounds echoing everywhere as he pulled away their prize. The struggle back to the world of the living was fierce; he wondered if he had passed the point of no return. The exertion upon his will began to take its toll. He refused to yield and accept defeat. From somewhere deep inside he found the strength and courage to go on and he pulled her out of that frightful chasm...

~

Weak with his exertions, Danyl slowly opened his eyes and gazed down upon Ramira then over to Zada. He was exhausted, the effort sapping him of every ounce of strength. The look of astonishment on her face was the last thing he remembered. He slipped into a deep sleep, his arms placed protectively over Ramira.

Zada stood as if rooted in place, not so much because of what he had accomplished but what that incredible feat had revealed about him. She glanced over at Ramira who breathed much more easily and whose convulsions had lessened into twitches. The elf's eyes burned brighter than the purest of emeralds. The prince unknowingly housed his people's legacy and used it to steal Ramira back from Mahn. The Herkah slumped down into a nearby chair, her eyes never wavering from the sleeping elf. Her mind grappled with the implications of his act.

"Why now?"

~

Cooper loathed the things that had taken everything from him and hated himself even more for falling into their trap. The stranger who came to him bearing stories of buried treasure in the desert had played his part well; he had portrayed himself as a stupid man with great expectations. Cooper smugly thought he could easily cheat him then effortlessly cast the stranger aside or kill him. This man, however, should have set off every alarm in his mind. The idea that the Herkahs guarded a vast treasure overrode his instincts. Instead of sitting on a pile of gold, he found himself a prisoner in his own city, confined to his rooms. He spat on the floor for the thousandth time.

His people lived on stale bread and stagnant water, walking skeletons with sunken eyes and no hope. He didn't care that they lacked hope; he wanted them fed so they could serve him, a little detail allowing him to rule all these years. And Antama! She could not wait to ally herself with that hulking monstrosity! She had spent countless hours reading every book, studying every map she could find, and listened in on all of his decisions. Antama was smart and he had allowed her to get even more resourceful, a mistake he swore he would resolve. That is if he got out of this situation. He vowed the first time he got his hands around her neck he would choke the life out of her. He grinned as he imagined his hands pressing down on her throat, her arms reaching up to stop him.

The door swung open. One of the Herkah things summoned him to his own throne room, an act still making him simmer. He absently scratched the back of his neck as they led him down the long hallway. The neglect of the past year could be seen everywhere, from the debris and dust strewn about to the huge spider webs draped in every corner. The grime coating the windows blocked out the world and filled the castle with a grayish light. Cooper had forgotten what color the sky was or how soft grass felt beneath his feet. The damp air upon which the fetid odors floated infiltrated every corner of the city. Cooper believed they could clean for months and never remove that awful stench. The demons opened the door at the end of the corridor and, chained at the ankles, he stood before the master devil: Mahn. Cooper glared at the black clad man-shape reaching nearly nine feet in height; animosity and pride surging through his body kept him from groveling at Mahn's feet.

"You will go to Bystyn."

Mahn's voice reverberated throughout the room, scattering the Kreetch and other vile minions that had taken up residence in his expansive mansion.

"What for?"

"You will soften them for me."

"I'll do nothing for you," he began then felt the giants hand as it reached into his body and squeezed every organ. Cooper's face turned purple. Every vein and tendon stood out on his face and neck; tears poured down his face.

"You will go to Bystyn," Mahn repeated, relinquishing his hold on the king who dropped to the floor and threw up.

Cooper gulped in air, his innards throbbing from Mahn's assault. The king loathed everything in the land as he rested on all fours and stared down at his vomit. He would seek revenge on everyone, even if it killed him. Nobody was going to do this to him and get away with it. The Vox yanked him to his feet and hauled the unsteady king out of the throne room. He could feel eyes watching him even after the doors closed behind him.

~

Cooper stared at the Vox as he rode behind them. Their presence made his skin crawl. He hadn't quite figured them out yet for, although they looked like the desert insects, they acted very strangely. They ignored his insults, for one. He had once tried to see how far he could antagonize them before they reacted, receiving only a hiss when he kicked an empty bottle into one of their legs. He lived because Mahn needed him for some plan or they would have killed him long ago. The Vox obeyed Mahn yet seemed to have their own purpose. Cooper focused his attention on his escape, not an easy task considering his sinister escort.

He could head south, the secluded villages providing ample places to hide in. When things quieted down he could ransack his city or the elven one, take whatever remained, and start over again. His number one priority was to get away from these things. The only thing Mahn was going to give him was a slow and agonizing death, something he was already receiving in his city. The king intended to survive and continue to indulge himself in every earthly delight. He grinned as the image of the elf princess appeared in his mind. Now there was an enjoyment well worth seeking out. She would be about the right age by now. And feisty. The pointy-eared ones had everything he wanted, like fertile plains, plenty of riches, and many beautiful women. All he had to do was defeat them, the Vox, and Mahn and all of those things could be his.

Cooper sighed. His anger sustained his determination to run and hide until the perfect opportunity arose. The prospect of scrounging around like an animal did not appeal to him and neither did his only other option: begging the elves for help. They had never trusted him and, he freely admitted, had every right not to. Undermining the elves was his second favorite pastime. This, however, was different. If he could get them to listen to him, they might grant him asylum. It certainly would be easier to work his plans from within their walls.

Cooper studied the Vox as they continued to lead him along his lands just south of the Broken Plain. He didn't think the Herkahs could become more menacing, but, here he was riding with things that made the nomads look like children. The desert insects were brutal in battle but they fought with emotions. The Vox did not fight to kill but to feed off the energies of living souls. No one could stand up to one of the Vox and survive. This sobering thought brought him back to his only route to staying alive, barring any miracles occurring between here and Bystyn.

What did Mahn expect him to do in the city? 'Soften them up'? Was he supposed to instill a sense of hopelessness into them by revealing how all-powerful Mahn was? Despair was a wonderful weapon, one he had used on many occasions. The elves, however, would not fall for that ploy. If, however, the right ingredients were to present themselves and chaos ensued then…well, that tactic might work. What didn't 'work' was his abrupt release - a freedom, he surmised, that wasn't quite as free as he was led to believe.

A sharp hiss invaded his thoughts, the Vox's face inches from his. Cooper recoiled instinctively. He sneered at it while obeying its order to dismount. The Vox stared dispassionately down at him then left him standing alone at the edge of his lands. Amazement, relief, and confusion roiled through his tall frame while he watched them return to Kepracarn. The king inhaled deeply several times, the smell of green grass and clean air cleansing the stench that had infused itself into him. He purged more of those foul odors with every exhalation, until he felt refreshed for the first time in a year. He was finally ready.

"I guess I will pay you, dear brother and sister, a visit, for we have much catching up to do."

Cooper rode for many miles. The sun began to slip beneath the horizon behind him when he spotted a suitable place to spend the night. He dismounted and peered at his horse. The beast had ceased being a mere animal quite some time ago after Mahn had turned it into something else. He regretted that transformation because he used to dote on that horse like some overwhelmed lover, allowing no one but himself to groom and feed it. He ignored it now, letting it graze as it chose without even bothering to remove the saddle and bridle. He knew it would remain where it stood, watching over him with its vacant eyes. He ate a cold meal then rolled himself into his blankets. Although the ground was hard and the night chilly, he was somewhat free and that was enough for him. For now, anyway.

~

Zada placed a cool cloth on Ramira's forehead then lifted the covers to check on her wounds. The Herkah was careful not to disturb the sleeping elf sleeping beside her. She clucked her tongue for even all of Clare's skill would not keep the scars from turning ugly. Ramira had ripped them open too often during her convulsions. That she lived was amazing enough but what had the poison done to her? And why did she enter that house with such conviction? Zada had watched the confrontation with her inner sight and shuddered at the ferocity with which she had destroyed the Kreetch. Her expertise with the knives had stunned Zada, too, for none but the nomads wielded them in that manner. Where had the girl learned that? Zada picked up Ramira's knives and studied them under the light. The metal - if that's what they were cast from - was unfamiliar as were the strange symbols that appeared and disappeared all along the blades. The vague outline of a hawk-like bird came into view then withdrew or did it change into something akin to a feather? The figures surfaced on the entire exterior of the daggers, and the more she turned the knives the more images emerged. She was almost tempted to say they were ceremonial in nature, but what would Ramira be doing with such knives? Zada's inner sight turned on and warned her to put the blades down. She put them away then looked up as Allad silently entered the room.

"What did Danyl do?" he asked her quietly.

"He plucked her from the jaws of hell."

"But how? How can he simply delve into that vast darkness?"

Zada's mind flashed back to the moment when he 'returned' from within Ramira. His glowing eyes frightened her with their significance. The Elven Might, awakened by the desperate act of the unaware prince, flourished in the land once more. She would keep this information to herself for the time being. Danyl would need time to adjust to the magic and the tremendous responsibility it represented. Wielding it unprepared would be catastrophic.

Danyl opened his eyes and immediately checked on Ramira. Satisfied she was doing well, he rose from the bed to stretch his sore muscles. He gazed over at the ever-vigilant Zada. She smiled and then offered him a 'she's going to be fine' look. He rubbed at his tired eyes; his stomach growled in protest. The faint light filtering through the drapes announced a new day.

"Why don't you go and clean up? Eat something, Danyl, I'll watch over her."

He caressed Ramira's cheek then withdrew to his own room where he bathed and changed into a fresh set of clothes. He headed downstairs to the kitchen and fixed a plate of food, taking it into the garden where he ate without tasting a single bite. Danyl stared off into the distance.

"How is she?" asked a concerned Seven sitting down beside the prince.

"Resting," he replied. "Why would she deliberately go into that house, Seven?"

"She sensed danger and wanted to protect the couple inside,

I assume. Zada 'saw' what happened, Danyl, perhaps you should ask her. Either that or wait until Ramira is able to tell you," he suggested.

Danyl nodded. First, he would speak to the Herkah and then with Ramira when she regained her strength. He accepted the glass Seven offered him then shuddered as the clear liquid burned his throat. He breathed deeply then looked over at his friend who was almost like a father to him. The dwarf king had held Danyl in his arms when he was an infant; reprimanded him when he was a young boy then watched him grow into a man. The love in the king's eyes never faltered for one instant. Seven reached up and touched the elf's cheek, a simple gesture of encouragement that the prince greatly appreciated.

"That was very underhanded of you," Danyl said lifting the empty glass.

"Yes it was, but don't tell Clare." He rose and left Danyl alone with his thoughts.

The elf did not stay much longer, his concern for Ramira urging him to return to her room. He watched Allad place the sleeping woman back on a freshly changed bed, her body discreetly covered in a sheet. Zada had bathed her as best she could; she had brushed out her hair and re-braided it. The spasms had left her body drenched in perspiration and her hair knotted and wild. Danyl pulled back the blanket by her side and frowned, for the edges of the wounds were bright red and hot to the touch.

"Infection?" he asked, his face lined with worry.

"No," she replied, dabbing at the jagged lines with a thick spicy mixture. "Her body is expelling the last of the poison…in a day or two this will look normal."

"Zada, how many people have survived the Kreetch?"

"Just Allad, Nyk, and a couple of others. Some of them were beyond my talents."

"The marks across his body…" he muttered remembering the day Allad helped them repair the barn.

"Yes, Danyl. Does it trouble you to look upon her scarred body?"

"What bothers me is how she will feel every time she sees

them."

"The marks heighten Allad's awareness and his need to fight the demons to spare others of this fate."

"What will it make her?" He took her limp hand into his.

"Time will tell," was her cryptic reply. If she didn't know better, Zada would have sworn Herkah blood ran through her veins.

~

The brothers sat atop their horses and, along with Gard, Allad, and Seven watched their men practice side by side. They instilled the need for cooperation into them, a necessary component if they were to be successful in battling the evil's army. The men exchanged techniques and methods; the result was a more competent fighting unit. Almost all of those upon the plain were veterans of many skirmishes, but nothing they had faced before could match what awaited them.

Autumn was still over a month away but the elves already began to stock up on supplies. The extra mouths and the uncertainty of what to expect in the future prompted them to err on the side of caution. The dwarves had brought many items with them; the highly skilled Khadry hunted in the surrounding woods for meat, which was dried and stored away. The city had nearly twice as many people living in or around it and the last thing they needed was for hunger to create dissent amongst the citizens. Seven glanced over at Danyl, his features more relaxed now that Ramira was out of bed and recovering from her encounter with the Kreetch. Zada and the prince made sure she remained in the castle under their watchful eyes. It had been nearly two weeks since the incident. Zada had not sensed any other demons since then. The Khadry and most of the dwarves had elected to remain on the plains surrounding the city until the weather changed or the evil arrived. The Herkahs divided themselves up, staying with the others for their protection in case any demons attacked. They had no idea how the Kreetch that slaughtered the couple were able to approach undetected, compelling Zada to be more vigilant with her inner sight. She kept herself in a semi-trance, hovering at the edge of that nebulous darkness. There was a great deal of disquiet emanating from that in-between world, and the noise issuing forth almost overwhelmed her. The souls begging for release from the evil sensed her and clamored for attention, filling her mind with a cacophony of rustlings. She learned to ignore the whispers, concentrating instead on the feelings of dread preceding the arrival of the demons. The strain forced her to close that 'door' and rest occasionally, leaving them all vulnerable. She was, after all, only human and could only endure so much. They tried to address practically every possibility they might encounter, fully aware that unforeseen events could leave them defenseless. They would have to cope with those unexpected situations when they arose.

~

Ramira left her bed, slipping on her robe before heading out the door and into the kitchen. Her hunger would not wait until morning and she was not about to wake anyone up to take care of such a simple need. After a few wrong turns within the quiet hallways, she finally found the door to the kitchen. She opened the cupboard with one hand while gingerly touching her side with the other, searching for a snack when she heard the voices. She turned around thinking someone had walked in but the large room was empty save for her. Then the room dissolved into darkness...

Her bare feet recoiled with each step as they moved over the frigid stone floor. The walls were perfectly set and aligned but unadorned. Torches were jammed into brackets along the corridor but the magnitude of the hall made their light appear feeble and dim. She passed many corridors, their shadowy fronts the only evidence of their existence. She ignored them, her objective ahead of her. The farther she moved into the stone void the stronger the aromas became. Their fragrance clung to her as she moved through the faint haze, her purpose nearby. She stopped before a monumental set of doors, the iron rings used to open and close them big enough to fit her body through, and listened. From within came the sound of a woman chanting words in a language she could not understand; the eerie tones made the hair on her body stand up.

She opened the doors with surprising ease, and saw a thin woman clad in a red material that floated about with the slightest of movements. Her eyes were as pale as her skin and glittered with fear and loathing. She glanced from Ramira to a pair of black knives that were placed on an altar of gold in the center of the vast chamber. The woman hurriedly began to pour a mixture over the altar, her hands shaking with impatience while keeping an eye on Ramira. Ramira watched the viscous liquid flow down the narrow channels of the altar toward the knives; the channels displayed the same symbols as on the blades. The closer the liquid oozed to the knives the more it began to hiss and boil. Steam rose from the altar. Ramira ignored the red woman's unintelligible mantra, her attention riveted on the coagulated mixture seeping along the channels.

Her fingers twitched involuntarily at her sides, the sudden desire to lunge forward and grab the weapons before the fluid reached them unbearable. Ramira gave in and plucked them from the sacrificial stone just as the solution was about to envelop them. The woman shrieked with fury and continued to scream as Ramira headed for the door. She turned as the red woman ran after her and rammed both blades down into the red woman's chest. Ramira felt no remorse. She stared with contempt at the dying figure then felt a low and ominous vibration begin from even deeper within the stone enclosure. A frigid wind flowed from beneath the altar and spread outward until it hit her feet. It gradually increased, obscuring her ankles then her knees. Ramira shivered and then bolted back the way she had come. The torches went out one by one, leaving Ramira in total darkness. She did not waver or give in to the disorientating effect, maintaining her flight from this unsettling place…

Ramira snapped out of the vision. She grasped the counter for support; her feet ached as they stood on the cold stone floor. Thoughts of food no longer interested her as she hurried back to her room. She massaged the life back into her feet in front of the fire. Ramira thought about the deadly encounter in the stone chamber and wondered what she had interrupted. Her strides to the vaulted room had been purposeful...but why? Who was that woman and why did she feel no regret in slaying her? What was she attempting to do to the knives? Ramira retrieved the blades and held them up to the light, their feel as familiar as they were foreign. The knives were a perfect extension of her fighting capabilities, the results at Evans Peak and at the house by the orchard a testament to that fact.

"Well," she whispered to the daggers, "at least I know how you came into my possession."

Ramira lay on her bed but did not fall asleep. She thought about the snippets from her past. There were both good and bad people in her life, and each in their own way was influencing the decisions she now made. One person had taught her how to fight, and the gentle woman had demonstrated love and kindness. The red woman, however, puzzled her. Their shared hatred flowed freely between them. Ramira could not shake the feeling that the red woman had been preparing the knives for her demise. Ramira fell into a fitful sleep

~

Cooper woke up, his cramped muscles and filthy body putting him in a dark mood. He pulled out his provisions pouch and then flipped the cover back over. He had spent nearly two weeks on the road without one break or idea. He was sick of eating dried food and sleeping on a hard ground. Cooper stomped over to the stream and stuck his entire head in the cool water, holding it there for several seconds before lifting it out. Rivulets of water ran down his chest and back as he sat there with his arms resting on his knees; his eyes were focused on his unseen destination.

"Face it, Coop, you are going to your death and there's nothing you can do about it."

He watched the day unfold, the dark line of clouds indicating rain. He remained rooted in place as if the only sure thing in his life was the grass beneath him. He knew he was not the one who had unleashed Mahn upon the land. The king also understood there was nothing he could have done to stop what had happened to his city. As to his forced trek to the elves? He was Mahn's pawn just as the elves were going to be. Then again, maybe not. Why couldn't Mahn do to them what he had done to him? Why did he need his bizarre army to attack them? Why did he send Cooper east when Mahn knew that he of all people would be the least welcome in Bystyn? What was there that prevented Mahn from just taking it?

Mahn radiated power. The only race he knew of that had any form of magic was the elves. Did their power protect them and prevent Mahn from swooping down like some bird of prey and taking the city? Why amass an army? Why not wield his magic and take the elves' power? No, he would already have done so. He has power but won't or can't use it? The 'won't' would be easy enough to figure out but the 'can't'? He had been debating these thoughts ever since leaving Kepracarn; the answers eluded him. Cooper knew he was not stupid, so why couldn't he figure this out?

He finally got up and collected his things then kicked at the ashes of his campfire. Instead of mounting his demon steed, he stared at the pile of gray, his mind trying to tell him something. Fire. Sticks are rubbed together producing flames. He cocked his head. A slow smile crossed his features as the answer manifested itself. Magic. An unearthly element ignited by the wielder and used to destroy. Mahn had the power but he did not have the device necessary to make it work! He was like a fully prepared fire without the flint essential to create the flames. He burst out laughing and slapped his thigh while imagining the mighty Mahn searching his pockets for some flint. He roared so hard the demon possessed thing stared at him, and that only made him guffaw even harder.

He hopped on the beast's back, the revelation giving him a sense of satisfaction and a completely new outlook. Cooper wondered if he was supposed to figure that out then pass it on to the elves. He wondered what this thing was that Mahn searched for, and if he could possibly find it first. Maybe he could use it to get his city back or anything else he fancied. The king would be near Bystyn soon. Once he assessed the goings-on he would further his own plans. That thought gave him some measure of hope.

~

Danyl reached into the top drawer of his desk where the bracelet was stored. He had forgotten about it and now, as it dangled from his index finger, decided to pay Zada a visit. It was time to find out what this little trinket was all about and who better to tell him than the nomad. He found her resting in her room. The elf wanted to respect her privacy but Zada insisted he join her.

"What brings you?" she asked handing him a glass of wine.

"This," he replied pulling the bracelet out of his pocket and handing it to her.

She lifted it up to the light; the deep blue beads glowed as she spun it around. Danyl recounted how he had discovered it in Karolauren's chambers and that breaking a bead transported him elsewhere.

"I experienced everything that occurred within the vision, Zada."

"How is that possible?"

"I don't know, that's why I brought it to you. Shall I?"

She took a deep breath and nodded, watching the point of his knife crush the bead. Nothing happened. Danyl looked at the remnants of glass, puzzlement etched on his face. He waited a few moments then crunched another one with the same results.

"I swear that what I told you was the truth," he stammered.

"Then where did the images materialize?"

"Perhaps those were…well empty," he suggested. He raised his knife once more but she stopped him.

She looked into his eyes, the memory of him pulling Ramira back from the brink of the abyss still fresh in her mind. She took the piece of jewelry from him and placed it in her pocket, intending to give it back to the Historian.

"Zada," he spoke in an uncertain voice, "will Ramira fully recover?"

"She seems to be doing well, Danyl, but we may never know what the poison has done to her. Listen, to this day I am still very watchful over Allad and, as much as I love him, would not hesitate to deny the evil a chance to use him for his foul purposes."

"Are you saying that I could be forced to do the same?"

"If you love her, then, yes," was her honest reply.

"That is a heavy burden."

"Indeed it is, young prince, and it does not get lighter with time."

"I still don't like the idea of her returning to Sophie's house."

Ramira had left earlier in the day and no amount of cajoling could get her to stay. What would happen if the poison did necessitate her demise? Was he to assign a guard to be with her every hour of the day or would the Herkahs take over such a duty?

"If Ramira believed she was a threat to Sophie and Anci she would never have gone, Danyl."

"Allad isn't convinced he isn't a threat or you wouldn't have told me about killing him."

"That is true, Danyl, but...." How could she tell him about the Elven Might? The magic, she was sure, would have negated the poison running rampant through her system or she would already be dead. Allad did not have that luxury. Zada dropped her gaze.

"But what?"

"I'm convinced she is no danger to anyone."

"What if she is?" he quietly asked her.

Was he strong enough to slay Ramira? He nodded then left. Zada took the bracelet back out and dangled it from her fingers; the tiny beads seduced her. They appeared innocent enough. Whoever made it had an incredible talent and a mountain of patience to thread the minute holes with the single filament of gold.

The Herkah tried to imagine what kind of woman had worn

such jewelry, deciding she was not ostentatious or vain. The bracelets delicate pattern marked a simple woman who appreciated fine workmanship. She bit her lip, the desire to break a bead contrary to what she had just told the elf. The bracelet, however, haunted her. She gave in to the urge, breaking the bead closest to the twisted clasp...

Zada found herself in a small, stone home lit only by a single lamp set upon a table. A fire burned in the hearth. A pot hung from an arm inside it, the aroma of spiced meat filling the room. She heard someone enter and turned around. Zada stared at the stocky woman who wore her graying hair in a bun. Her simple tunic was worn but clean. The surprise on her face melted away as she waved to a cushioned bench. Zada was speechless. Danyl had not mentioned just how real the images were.

"Good evening, good woman," greeted the nomad, "I did not mean to startle you."

"That's all right, child. I see you, too, have found the bracelet."

"Yes. Do you know who it belongs to?"

"Yes, it was a very special gift."

Zada could see lines of worry on her brown features and, although she paid attention to her guest, the woman seemed overly guarded.

"Are you expecting someone?" asked Zada.

"Hopefully not," she replied, "but I think you had better leave or the moment will pass and you will be forced to stay. This is not your place, child."

She rose to her feet and held out her hands to the nomad. Zada took them. She felt the warmth pulse through the work-hardened palms and fingers as the woman began to fade away into mist...

Zada stared into the empty air, knowing that the brown woman had turned to dust centuries ago. Zada realized the visions were more defined because of her inner sight, and therefore more dangerous. The woman warned her not to stay too long or she would be unable to return. Where had the trinket taken her? She sensed no power from it, yet it exuded a kind of connection…a link to the past where everyday activities and people made up the future. The story was a haphazard collection of circumstances that were more important than the logical progression of outcomes. The unforeseen was more potent than the expected; a lesson they had best take to heart.

Danyl's description of the brown man indicated the wearer was being educated. The house he passed may well have belonged to the woman she 'visited'. This last image, however, troubled her. The bracelet seemed innocent enough but it had the power to imprison her in a different time. What had frightened her? Where had those two images gone after Danyl broke the beads? Were they indeed 'empty' as he had suggested? She sighed heavily while staring at the delicate item suspended from her finger.

"Tiny bits of glass revealing their extraordinary secrets…"

~

Ramira left the castle bound for Sophie's house, much to the consternation of those who watched her leave. She wanted her own bed and the less hectic pace the house offered. Danyl had been the most vocal. She had assured him she would not depart the city without at least one guard. Ramira walked into the kitchen, the aroma of freshly baked cakes greeting her.

"Sweet Mercy, girl, it is good to have you back!" greeted Sophie while touching her cheek.

"It felt strange not being given a long list of things to do," she chuckled.

"You weren't exactly in any condition to do them or I would have handed you one. Here," she handed Ramira a plate of still steaming treats, "you're too skinny."

Ramira knew she had lost quite a bit of weight since the battle with the Kreetch. She had been unconscious, then unable to eat much of anything for nearly a week. She suddenly felt tired. The short walk from the castle to the house drained her energy. Ramira went upstairs to lie down for a while, listening to Sophie bustle about in the kitchen as she fell asleep.

She opened her eyes and swung her legs over the side of the bed. The dingy gray light filtering through the window indicated it was either dusk or the weather was changing. An orange glow on the western horizon answered her question. She patted her itchy side, careful not to aggravate her wounds while heading to the kitchen. It was very quiet; Sophie and Anci must have gone out for a while …

She stood in darkness; insidious whispers brushed against her skin. They promised to fulfill their evil intentions …

Dazed by the sudden appearance of the malicious vision, she grabbed the back of a chair to steady herself from the appalling onslaught. It reappeared a few seconds later…

She stood beneath the blistering sun, its rays burning her body as things bumped against her legs. She looked down and gaped in horror at the faces on the rotting corpses stared up at her. Skeletal hands reached up, their fingers flexing and gripping at her until she thought she would go mad…

Ramira collapsed onto her knees, the jarring effect sending waves of pain and nausea through her. She wanted to scream and wail at the awful vision but her throat would not release a sound. She he dropped her face into her hands, the unanticipated and life-like scene slowly dissipating from her sight. People that she knew and had never met before had glared at her with an accusation so horrible she could barely contain her sanity.

When her hands finally stopped shaking, she poured herself a cup of strong tea and walked out onto the terrace. Ramira sat down beneath the roses, but even their soothing fragrance could not erase her nightmare. It took all of her will to stop trembling when Sophie and Anci stepped onto the terrace. The shadows hid the dread on her face; her voice remained strangled in her throat. Anci spoke of the day's events, the joy of her innocence a balm to her tortured soul.

"You're rather quiet," Sophie said after a while.

"It's been a long few weeks," Ramira managed to say while staring into the night.

There was a slight chill in the air and not just from the changing season. It might have been a mistake to leave the protection of the castle. If the images were going to happen, the last place she wanted to be was where they could fulfill their awful threat. Wouldn't being in this house…no, this city, bring that same fate? She shivered as she contemplated that terrible possibility.

Cooper waited patiently for the elven patrol to approach him. He discerned Herkahs, dwarves, and Khadry riding with them. The king raised a brow as the information sank into his mind; the Bystynians had been very busy of late. He silently congratulated the elven king for such a remarkable feat then wondered what other surprises awaited him. Alyxandyr had overcome fear and bitterness to win the support of the nomads and the Khadry. The elves were also preparing for a long war as wagonloads of goods poured in from the east. He noticed soldiers practicing along the western plains. No, the elves were no fools, and neither was he.

"King Cooper?"

Nyk stared at Cooper; the elf prince sensed a trap and treated the situation exactly in that manner. He glanced over at Allad who shook his head: Cooper was not demon infested.

"Yes, good day to you, too, Prince Nyk," replied the king with his usual arrogance.

Cooper offered Allad a slight nod. Allad unnerved him, for he exuded power and tenacity. The Herkah would slay a king as quickly as a thief and regret neither death. If Allad were here then Zada would be, too. Mahn would love to add those two nomads in his stable! Nyk's voice interrupted his musings.

"What brings you to Bystyn?"

"I bear a message for you."

"From whom?" The hint of sarcasm in his voice elicited a slight smile from the king. Nyk couldn't help but notice how similar in appearance Cooper and Mason were, but how vastly different in their dispositions and goals.

Cooper ignored the question for the time being, intent on the demon steeds destruction. He gathered up his courage and locked eyes with Allad, then hinted at his mount. The king needed to get rid of the beast to further his own ambitions.

Allad studied the animal, its docile appearance deceiving. Cooper's willing betrayal of it was another issue. The nomad had no choice in the matter. He caught Nyk's eye and indicated the horse.

"Dismount," Nyk ordered.

The king complied and backed away from it. The animal thing sensed something was wrong but it failed to react in time. Allad pounced onto the saddle, bringing his blades up under its great neck. He rolled away effortlessly when it fell in a shrieking heap. Everyone, even Cooper, shuddered. Allad's black eyes ensnared Cooper.

"Is there anything else you'd like to divulge?"

Cooper kept his composure and shook his head. The Herkah turned away from the king after several long moments.

Nyk sent a messenger to the city. A sense of foreboding rippled through the prince, one that demanded extreme caution. Was Cooper's abrupt arrival his choice or the orders of whatever sent the king east? He knew Cooper would sacrifice anything or anyone to further his own cause, but he trifled with something well beyond his capabilities. They waited for nearly an hour, Cooper never once complaining or speaking. The messenger returned and whispered into the prince's ear. Nyk glared down at the king then ordered them to move toward the gate. Cooper walked in the middle of the well-armed and watchful group.

~

Alyxandyr stared out the window, his hands clasped behind his back as he contemplated their present situation. He was looking for a common thread that bound them all together, because finding it meant being able to trace it back to the truth. This was a difficult task, for the variety of individuals currently involved in this dilemma had no known bonds. The only clear fact was that the races were gathering at his doorstep where the evil intended to annihilate them. He could not shake the feeling that this evil had a personal quarrel with the elves. What that could be he could not even guess. Nothing in the elven archives ever mentioned anything remotely linked to Mahn. Alyxandyr was at a loss as to why this thought persisted in his mind. Cooper would be here shortly. The other leaders already waited for him in the main hall their curiosity mirroring his own. The elven king questioned Cooper's reliability, yet he was bound to say something that would shed some light on this matter. The evil had sent him…would he therefore be under its control? Did Cooper retain his own identity? They would have to listen carefully to what he said and make their own assumptions. He breathed in deeply one more time then joined the other leaders.

~

Cooper felt impaled by their glares the moment his heavily armed guard escorted him into the chamber. There were no false pretenses, only unbridled looks of contempt and suspicion. Cooper offered them a courtly bow but was not surprised when they did not return the courtesy. It took all of his willpower not to smirk at the cold deference paid to him by the Herkahs. *It's good to be king!*

"What is happening in your city, Cooper?" demanded Alyxandyr.

"That's a long and complicated story…"

"Condense it for us," Mason's deep voice cut through Cooper's arrogance.

"About a year ago a stranger came to Kepracarn. He told me that there was treasure buried on the desert ins…"

Allad's eyes glinted dangerously across the table from him.

"…on the Herkahs' lands. He had a map but no diggers and offered a percentage of the gold in exchange for workers. I agreed and sent out an expedition with him."

"Why not kill the man, take the map, and unearth the riches yourself?" asked Mason.

"That thought might have crossed my mind but this was no ordinary man, *Brother*."

Mason cringed at the mere mention of such a connection;

Cooper forced himself not to further exploit it.

"The stranger did not have the map with him, claiming it was at the dig site. I agreed to accompany him, finalizing my scheme on the way to the location. Fifty men came with me and never returned to the city." Genuine fear and hatred began to filter into his voice as he continued speak.

"We dug for days, carting away loads of sand yet never found a single thing. I was beginning to tire of this fool's errand until we uncovered a flat rock placed over a hole in the ground. The excitement rippling through the camp was short-lived, for when my men pried it open…"

Cooper closed his eyes and watched as the scene replayed itself behind his lids. Sweat glistened off the workers straining to hoist the cap off the opening. The stranger seemed to stand a little taller and the hands resting on his hips looked larger than Cooper remembered. The men groaned in unison, their exertions inched the cover to the side exposing the opening. The stranger stepped to the edge and stared down into the blackness, then spoke in a tongue foreign to Cooper. At first nothing happened, then the screams and shrieks rose up from the depths. Soon a noxious mist curled up from within the darkness, spreading over the lip and staining the white sand all around it. Cooper backed away from the menacing fog, seeking an explanation from the stranger who welcomed its embrace. The rangy man with the weathered features began to alter right before his eyes, growing in height and girth until he towered over him. His once tattered and dusty cape billowed behind him like an ominous cloud promising severe weather.

The haze infused itself into his men, their cries and howls cherished by the monster standing in the middle of the upheaval. The king watched helplessly as gangly things with matted black hair scampered out of the cavity. They immediately set themselves upon his men. They ripped them apart, gorging on their flesh and each other if one got too close. Cooper dropped to his knees, cowering as the madness persisted all around him. It intensified as the fiend strode toward him, his massive legs pushing aside everything in their path.

196

"Rise!"

Cooper could not speak let alone force his rubbery legs to support him. He remained on his knees swaying with disbelief. A black gloved hand shot out from within the immense cape and yanked him unceremoniously to his feet. Tears of pain and panic blurred his sight. He wiped them away and saw the ultimate betrayer. Antama, his companion for decades, stood unmolested in the center of the horror, her flawless features radiating sheer contempt for him. Confusion filled his mind. She had access to everything, including his decision-making. It had not been enough for her. She wanted to be queen and allied herself with this demon to fulfill her wish. He watched Antama lift her arms to permit the red mist swirling at her feet to flow up her body. It crawled upward with tiny talons that sliced into her flesh; her blood was indistinguishable from the haze. The fog finally enveloped her then immediately retreated into her body. …

The group sat shocked and silent throughout his account for many long minutes after he had finished.

"Your greed set the evil free!" Mason was aghast.

"I wouldn't have complied had I known what he was! Give me a little credit!"

Cooper rose from his chair, his hands balled up in fists. Mason pushed his seat back more than willing to fight his brother.

"Stop it! Both of you!" demanded Alyxandyr.

"King Cooper," Zada's clear voice cut through the tension. "Please proceed with your report."

Mason resumed his seat; the brothers continued to glare at each other for a few seconds more. Cooper straightened his shoulders then sat down in the chair.

"I was brought back to the city. Mahn had taken it over while I was at the site. I was kept prisoner in one of my rooms. The only contact I had was with the Vox and, on occasion, with Mahn. He did not kill any more of my people, but he should have. They became like rats, scrounging around or fighting for pieces of food; living in filth and despair. This went on until he decided the time was right for me to come here."

Some of his equals exchanged wary glances while others stared off into the distance, picturing the horror he had described. He endured the scrutiny of all who looked upon him except for Zada. Her gaze was steady and direct, lacking any animosity but radiating danger nonetheless.

Cooper purposefully hunted the Herkahs. His one and only desire was to kill them…well, for pleasure. His victories were rare and cost him many men. That didn't matter for the surge of power and excitement those scarce conquests gave him made it all worthwhile. The nomads had every right to slay him where he sat - he certainly would have if their roles were reversed- but they remained calm and non-threatening.

"Why do you think this Mahn forced you to our gates?" asked the elven king after a long pause.

"My guess would be to help precipitate your downfall."

"And how would you fulfill such an obligation?" Mason's deep voice reached across to his brother, its touch squeezing his innards as effectively as Mahn had. Cooper would never admit it but he was even more afraid of Mason than Allad.

"I don't know."

Mason, however, did know. His brother's craftiness, intelligence, and patience were weapons he used with great pleasure. His methods had allowed him to remain king for all of these years. Mahn sensed these things and knew such duplicity would work in his favor. Cooper's danger lay in the fact he could create havoc, doubt, and distrust amongst the fragile alliance guarding the city. It was imperative the king be isolated, his communication restricted to a chosen few who would not heed his snake-like words. He whispered as much into Alyxandyr's ear. The king agreed and ordered Cooper to wait outside the chamber, while they listened to Mason. They decided to secure Cooper in the room Ramira had recovered in; the Herkahs would stand guard. The nomads escorted him to the chamber and locked the door behind him.

~

Ramira dunked the washcloth in the water, wrung it out then

placed it across her face. The house was hers until later on. Ramira heard someone enter the house and saw Danyl through the partially open door. She pressed her body against the side of the tub; her arms and hands rested on the edge. He sat down on the chair beside the bathtub. That peculiar sensation flared to life once again. The fire burned away their inhibitions and the world beyond the room. The elf closed the remaining distance between them until mere inches separated their faces.

Danyl traced her features with his index finger. He leaned forward and kissed her, his hands caressing her wet arms and back. Her limbs snaked up his forearms; the pair rose to their feet as one, never breaking their embrace. Danyl lifted her out of the tub and wrapped a towel around her. He removed his sodden tunic and dropped it on the back of the chair. The elf scooped her up in his arms and carried her up to her room, pulling back the covers before placing her on the bed. Danyl lay down alongside her and kicked off his short boots. He gazed into her eyes, the passion reflected within them matching his own. Danyl took off the rest of his clothing and joined her beneath the covers.

~

Sophie walked into the kitchen. She glanced into the bathing chamber, and then approached the tub. She reached into the cold water, yanked out the plug and blew out the lamp next to the half-full glass of wine. She picked up the tunic carelessly tossed on the back of the chair and stared at it for a moment. Her gaze traveled to the ceiling then back to the garment. She headed upstairs and softly knocked on Ramira's door. Sophie pushed down on the handle and cautiously entered the room. Her eyes adjusted to the moonlight flowing in through the balcony window. Sophie gazed down at the bed and pressed her lips together.

Danyl slept behind Ramira. His arm was draped across her slumbering form; their clasped hands were at her side. The couple dozed peacefully beneath rumpled blankets, their content faces framed by damp hair. Sophie looked away and retrieved his trousers, hanging them and his shirt over the armchair. She left the room and stepped out into the hallway, glancing back once before closing the door.

~

He emitted a low hiss of satisfaction as the Source of Darkness' approximate location appeared before him. He had been searching for it for a long time and it now lay within his grasp. He could not go and take it, but he could make it leave…force it to expose itself then reach out and take it. Mahn focused his gaze on the squalid conditions within Kepracarn. It was a most welcome sight, one he planned to heap upon the rest of the land once he had the power.

He drew great satisfaction from the starving forms using their precious strength to wrest a morsel of food from someone even weaker than they were. Perhaps he would let a few mortals remain alive so their last instincts for survival could amuse him. He could throw a few crumbs between two of them and watch. Maybe not, he sneered at the wretched things below him. He would be Lord and Master of everything soon enough, then he could decide what their insignificant fates would be. He turned as the doors behind him opened, admitting one of the Vox. The Herkah shell was inhabited by a fearsome demon that made him pause in admiration. It bore a message.

"Cooper has entered the city and the beast, as expected, has been slain." The choked wheezing sound due, he was sure, to the still living Herkah struggling within its violent internal embrace.

"How long before these creatures are ready?" He indicated the contemptible figures below the window.

"They can be ready within days."

"Good. Have the three been dispatched?"

"Gone since this morning," it breathed heavily. The sound was very deceiving, for the Vox could run and fight for days without tiring.

Mahn nodded; the Vox slipped away leaving the evil to contemplate his plans once more. If the Source of Darkness abandoned the city soon, then his armies could be at Bystyn's gates within two weeks. If it did not, then the snows would hamper but not stop his advance. His legions would hammer the allies if the Source of Darkness managed to slip through his fingers for a few days or weeks. His army would weaken the allies' defenses, making it easier to annihilate them. He had sensed the elven magic beginning to awaken, but there was no one within the city who proclaimed to be its bearer. The White Witch had bestowed the sight upon the nomad, a burden he planned to exploit to the fullest. He anticipated tormenting her and the White Witch. He could not wait to exterminate her followers: without them, she would fade into obscurity, a forgotten symbol wasting away into oblivion. No, not killed but absorbed into his dark realm - an even better fate.

He began to roar with anticipation, imagining the souls he would eat. The most gratifying ones would be the shrieking mortals running over each other to get away from him. His hatred and bitterness radiated outward, and spread down the side of the building and out into the street. It not only drove the pitiful humans to escape its horror but scattered his minions as well.

~

Zada gasped for air as Mahn's twisted jubilation traveled to her sensitive sight. Her hands clutched at her throat; the rancid odors stole her breath even from this distance. Clare rushed over to her, grabbing her just as she began to topple forward. The dwarf queen met Alyxandyr's eyes as she held the woman in her arms. There was no need to speak for they could well decipher the nomad's reaction. Alyxandyr turned around, clasping his hands in the small of his back as he stared out the window into the rainy afternoon. They were all so different, yet the one thing binding them together was the need to persevere against things they could not understand. They were offering their faith and lives and the king had nothing to give back except for a place to die. That concept made his blood run cold. His sons came and stood beside him, their hands on his shoulders. The evil grew in power every day, his plans for the mortals well underway. Mahn and his slaves were coming to Bystyn. The elven king looked down at the dwarf queen who still held the Herkah in her arms,

201

then glanced over at the Khadry. They were all bound to one another regardless of their beliefs. Alyxandyr realized that thread was hope.

~

Laden with packages, Ramira entered the kitchen and stopped in her tracks. She could not believe her eyes as the most powerful leaders in the land crowded around Sophie's table, enjoying platters of food and a variety of beverages. Seven, Clare, Alyxandyr, Zada, Allad, Danyl, and Styph greeted her and then resumed their feast. Sophie took the supplies and Anci shoved a bowl and spoon into her hands before Ramira could utter a single word.

"You'll trip over that if you don't close it," chuckled Seven, pointing his chin at her jaw.

"They've already opened every drawer and cupboard looking for food, girl, and they'll look in there for more, too," muttered Sophie.

"What…?"

Sophie gave her a healthy serving of stew then sat her down between the elven king and Danyl. The space was barely wide enough for her slim frame but none other was available. She began to eat, lightly pressing herself into Danyl who softly nudged her shoulder with his.

Seven finished first and produced a bottle of his clear poison. Not to be outdone, Allad deposited his version of the drink on top of the table, much to the delight of the dwarf but not of Clare or Zada. They initially gave their respective mates a look of warning then thought better of it: nights like these would be few in the coming weeks. Ramira subtly glanced from one to the other. Seven was his usual animated self; Allad was remarkably handsome as he smiled and laughed next to the dwarf king. An impish air surrounded Styph who smirked at his brother across the table. Alyxandyr participated in the fun but his tense body felt like a brick wall against her side. She hesitantly placed her hand on his brawny arm to get his attention, and then held her breath as his commanding gaze landed on her. He seemed to grow in stature without ever moving a muscle.

"Yes?" The king's voice was both gentle and direct.

"Could you please pass the..." What had she wanted? She glanced down at her bowl then over to her glass. Yes, that was it. "The wine?" Ramira watched the elven king fill her glass then thanked him.

Ramira noticed the shadows crossing the terrace, the ever-vigilant guards keeping their distance while protecting their charges. The peril emanating from the west hovered outside the kitchen and only the good-fellowship shared here kept it at bay. For the time being, anyway. Danyl reached for her hand under the table and gently squeezed it. She shifted her focus to the prince, the love they had shared shining from his eyes. Ramira desperately tried to restrain the blush creeping up onto her cheeks. Relief came in the form of a glass Alyxandyr handed to her. Ramira hastily downed Seven's concoction. She shivered as it burned everything on its way to her stomach and helped, she hoped, to explain the flush on her face.

"Easy, child!" warned Clare.

"You know what happens if you drink those too quickly?" Seven asked with a wink.

"You wake up with a head that won't fit through the door and drink everyone else's tea?"

"No..." Seven pointed a finger at a grinning Danyl.

"You get lectured by Clare while holding a cold cloth to your forehead?" Styph offered an amused Clare a stately nod of his head.

"No!"

"Your tongue becomes so loose it falls out of your mouth and trips you?" The dwarf queen jabbed his side for extra emphasis.

Seven pretended to glower, brightening immediately as Allad poured him a glass of Herkah liquor. He slapped Seven on the back; the dwarf panicked as the liquid threatened to spill over the rim.

~

Zada studied Danyl and Ramira, noting the understated

changes in their behavior toward one another. His gaze lingered on her face; his body responded as she leaned closer against him. The nomad smiled then frowned slightly as she remembered what the elf bore, and how he had unknowingly used it to snatch Ramira out of the evil's grasp. The power elevated him beyond the mortals gathered here, including the woman he had chosen as his companion. She tuned out the stories and laughter as an interesting thought presented itself to her. The Elven Might had been buried deep within Ramira and should have somehow affected her. She showed no outward signs that it had or of any delayed aftereffects from the Kreetch's poison.

She carefully focused her inner eye on the couple and took a sharp breath at what she saw. A faint, greenish haze rolled around Danyl's body much like the lazy mists after a cool summer rain. It diminished when the contact between the two of them was broken then reemerged when they touched once more. The longest of the tendrils swirling around him wavered, becoming more brilliant every second. It swayed in warning over his head like some cobra readying to strike, hypnotizing Zada with its deadly dance. The Herkah attempted to move beyond the boundaries of her sight toward it until her inner eye abruptly ended the trance.

The conversations sounded loud and the smell of food and tobacco smoke overwhelmed her senses. Perspiration trickled down the side of her face as she dared to look at the prince, who sipped unaware from his goblet. Zada kept her cold hands in her lap, her awe much more difficult to conceal.

Allad tapped her arm and interrupted her thoughts: it was time to go. It had been a long and delightful evening but their stifled yawns urged them to bed. They shuffled, still laughing toward the front door, leaving Danyl and Ramira alone for a few moments. He wrapped his arms around her, kissed her lightly on the lips then gently caressed her flushed cheeks.

"I don't suppose I could convince you to return to the castle with me," he whispered to her.

"The temptation is there," she shyly replied, "but I have to stay and help Sophie clean up."

"Eventually that will change, Ramira. You know that, don't you?"

"Yes," she sighed touching his face.

He nodded, and then joined the group walking back to the castle surrounded the guards.

"You were rather surprised to see them all in here," Sophie said as she cleared the table of the glasses and empty plates of food.

Anci shuffled sleepily up to her room, the two women smiling and shaking their heads at the exhausted girl.

"So much power in such a little room…"

"They always end up here when they visit; it's just that this time there were more to share in the friendship."

"Sophie?"

"Yes?"

"You aren't angry with me about the other night, are you?"

Ramira and Danyl had awoken and found his clothes neatly folded on the chair beside the bed. Sophie had not mentioned a word about what had transpired, but it was her house and she had a right to speak her mind.

Sophie thought back to the few precious years she had spent with Anci's father. She had first seen Tabryn, the king's quiet cousin, in the garden where he spent a great deal of time reading beneath a bower heavy with white clematis. He had invited her to sit with him, telling her about the city she had recently begun to call home. Sophie remembered his kindness and attentiveness, and the pure joy he elicited from her soul. He died after falling from a horse shortly before their daughter was born. She missed him dearly to this very day.

"No, child," Sophie said softly, cupping Ramira's chin in her hand. She untied her apron and went to bed, pausing at her door as the memories persisted.

~

Ramira sat down in front of the hearth, the unmistakable stirrings in her mind telling her she would not sleep well that night. The foreboding dreams hovered at the edge of her consciousness, promising to assail her the moment she closed her eyes. She began to rock back and forth in the chair, the motion offering her a measure of comfort as she focused on the woman from her childhood. She imagined the arms enfolding her and the unmistakable kiss on the top of her head; the far-off humming echoed within her mind. The memory numbed her fears, replacing them with a sense of security that only true devotion could instill. Love from this woman flooded into her being allowing Ramira to fall asleep without dread.

~

Autumn slipped into the land; the nights became a little cooler and faint hints of color painted the leaves. This time of year was usually the elves' favorite. They labored in the fields filling their larders with vegetables, fruits, nuts and roots from the forests. The elves stocked up on meat and fish; the smokehouses were busy day and night. The Herkahs offered up their spices; the Khadry hunted deer and the dwarves brought in wagonloads of wood. The city had doubled in size and everyone had an obligation to contribute.

The highlight of the season was the harvest festival. Carts of food and drink would sprout up on the plains where competitions of strength and speed; games and entertainment abounded. The celebration lasted for several days, after which many would leave the city and return to their outlying homes for the long winter. The king could not chance holding the celebration on the plains, opting to have it in the city instead. It was better than nothing and would at least alleviate some of the growing tension.

Alyxandyr watched the festival unfold where the two main avenues intersected. He could see groups of singers and musicians milling about the partially filled square; bright awnings covered stands of food and drink. He was pleased to see black and brown garb mixed in with the green. The festive distractions appealed even to the Herkahs. Alyxandyr re-entered his chambers and the matters at hand.

More than one patrol had reported seeing Mahn's army already on the plains far to the west; its size grew with every account. Mahn had grown enough in power to mobilize his legions and begin the trek east. It would not be long before it halted in front of the gates. Zada had sensed Mahn concentrating his search in the surrounding area, the Source of Darkness' nearness both alarming and relieving. He returned his attention to the map strewn across his desk and the reports streaming in from all parts of his lands. Alyxandyr read one then made a short notation on the map using the patrols' information from that area. He repeated this several times and noted that a pattern was developing. There was little movement from the northeast and south; the bulk of Mahn and his army flowed toward Bystyn from the west. They did not seem to be in any hurry, which pointed to one important reason: Mahn did not possess the Source of Darkness. What were the chances of finding it and using it against Mahn? If nothing else, they could conceal it from him.

That was a foolish notion because power, especially the evil kind like the Source of Darkness, would never allow itself to remain hidden. The Source of Darkness was an indestructible form of magic, so what were they to do with it if they chanced upon it? The king leaned back in his chair, his interlaced fingers behind his head while he scanned the map. They were missing something.

"Where are you?" he asked the Source of Darkness in quiet tones.

~

Ramira sat next to Sophie on the front stoop, the more restrained version of the autumn celebration drawing more people in the early afternoon hours. Groups of Herkahs mingled with dwarves, elves, and even a few Khadry. A Herkah stand to their right drew mobs of people wanting to purchase their meats and sweets. The elves had developed a taste for nomad food and one of the Herkahs made several trips back to the camp to restock her supplies. The singers, musicians, and dancers lifted the folk out of their anxious moods. The dancers wore brightly colored costumes and twirled to the beat of drums and flutes. Many sang along or simply clapped; a few even danced to the catchy tunes.

The food carts became focal points where many gathered to chat.

Sophie glanced over at Ramira and frowned. The dark circles under her eyes had become more prominent. She appeared drawn of late and Sophie knew her bad dreams were robbing her of more than just sleep. Could the aftereffects of the poison be to blame for that? It would break her heart if one of the Herkahs had to…she couldn't finish her thought. The overall pain her death would cause would be too much to bear. Sophie reached over and gently squeezed Ramira's hand, who rewarded her with a tired smile. With any luck, all of this would soon be over and they could return to their normal lives.

Ramira appreciated the touch more than Sophie could know; the nightmares invaded her daylight hours. Although she still sensed a presence in the house, she had ceased searching for it. The knives never left her side and provided some measure of comfort. Danyl's visits were brief and rare; he was heavily involved in the planning process. His closeness offered her a measure of quiet but she could not shadow him during these dismal times and so suffered them alone. The claw marks had healed, but bothered her, especially when she sensed the phantoms about. Cool cloths were unable to alleviate the burning, forcing her to endure their discomfort until her hallucinatory feelings subsided. Ramira assumed Allad and Nyk experienced the same annoyance, and made a mental note to ask them. Perhaps the nomads had some sort of balm to ease the ache. She clung to Sophie, the woman's touch easing some of her apprehensions while watching the passers-by enjoying the festivities in the street. Ramira longed to join them but felt too drained to leave the stoop. Perhaps a nap would help. She excused herself and went upstairs to lie down for a while.

~

Danyl's corridor dream had invaded his sleep several times over the past few weeks; he decided to reveal them to Zada. She listened intently as he recalled the endless gallery, the locked doors, and the water dripping from somewhere off in the distance. His confusion regarding the direction he was moving in piqued her interest.

"Many believe their lives are mazes they cannot escape from," she said. "In truth, a person's life is very simple and straightforward. We are all free to make our own choices in life. The problem, Danyl, is that the option to escape one's 'maze' is more daunting than the 'maze' itself. The doubt generated by leaving a known or accepted situation inevitably keeps us locked within the labyrinth."

"So my choices lie behind one of the locked doors?"

"Or at either end of the corridor." She gazed at him, wondering if he knew what thrived within him and how he would react once that truth revealed itself.

"Zada," he peered intently into her eyes, "what did you see the night I denied the demons Ramira's soul?"

She should have anticipated his question. All she could do was stare at him in silence for a long time.

"What did you see?" he persisted.

"I was astonished by what had transpired, that's all," she replied honestly.

"Zada," he took her trembling hands into his, "did something help me pull her away from him? Am I the bearer?" he asked quietly.

"What do you think?"

He *had* been thinking about it since that night; there was no way for him to have confronted Mahn's power without any of his own. There had been a steady yet faint pulsing sensation deep within him, one he had never encountered before that night. The feeling was unfamiliar yet intimate at the same time. This presence had entwined itself with his soul.

"What am I supposed to do with it?"

"I don't know, Danyl, but I think you should keep this information to yourself for a while."

"Why?"

"You must be allowed to come to terms with what you house, for the Green Might is an extension of who you are. The only person who can fully judge you is yourself, and if you cannot do so, then the power will be useless."

"The Green Might arose because I wanted to save her life," he said after a long pause.

Zada remembered Ramira's single-minded determination to eradicate the demons when she approached the house. She had executed the Kreetch as if that had been her only purpose in life. The amount of venom inflicted into her should have immediately turned her into one of the demons, yet she not only survived but showed no ill effects. None that were visible anyway. What was it that allowed her to endure the demons and, in a roundabout way, the elven magic?

She glanced at a pensive Danyl, the burden he carried not one she wanted to bear. She lifted his chin, the bewilderment on his face giving an innocent cast to his features. He was like a small child given his first important task and not knowing how to accomplish it. The Herkah wished she could tell him something to ease his confusion, but he was the bearer and would have to figure it out on his own. The heaviest burden would fall upon his shoulders. She and the others would lead their people to death; it would be his lot to brandish the final weapon. If he failed to find the courage necessary to allow the power to infuse itself into his being, then they were all doomed.

"Danyl," she whispered, "never forget that the Green Might chose you for a reason."

"And what would that be?" he asked.

"It will share that with you when the time comes."

~

Ramira awoke with a start, her instincts fully roused as they sensed a presence lurking just beyond the edges of her perception. This sensation was different from the others; she could not ignore it. The sinister echoes buzzed around her head like so many hateful flies. She was growing tired of these perceptions and wondered if she were going mad. Worst of all, she was beginning to believe these terrible things. They erupted at will showing her horrible images of what had happened in the past and implying the same fate would befall those in Bystyn if she stayed. Ramira began to give credence to the promise of sparing the city if she abandoned it. She was too exhausted to fight their tenacious hold on her psyche.

Ramira could not dislodge the obscure pledge from her mind. Her nightmares chipped away at her resolve; the darkness pushed aside all reason. Was she willing to forsake this place and the people she loved and respected? Was she ready to run away and draw its loathsome ire away from these gray walls? What then? Where could she go? She knew she could not head west or east and certainly not north into the impenetrable mountains. South remained her only option. What if the voices were lying? What if they were rooted in her subconscious doubts?

Ramira dressed then stood on the little balcony overlooking the wilting garden. The cold early morning air made her shiver; the first tinges of color stained the eastern horizon. She was a mystery even to herself, but she would not allow that unknown secret to jeopardize innocent lives. Her thoughts stayed with her all day and well into the next night, tormenting her with things she could neither prove nor disprove. The treacherous whispers seemed to sense her bewilderment, and increased the frequency of the images at a frightening pace.

All those she loved suffered horribly from every vile infliction known; their eyes focused on her as they appeared and disappeared at will. Zada and Styph mingled with faces she did not recognize; Anci's emaciated body brushed past her to join them. Ramira felt something grab her ankles and, upon looking down, cringed. The elf and dwarf kings lay twisting on the ground. Then the worst likeness emerged: Danyl. Torn apart by wolves and covered with flies, he managed to hold out his hand to her as he sought to pull her into this ghastly scene. She could take no more.

~

Sophie hummed softly as she set the table then stirred the contents of the pot. She sampled the stew, added a few more herbs then mixed it a few more times. She wiped her hands on her apron and noticed how quiet the house was. Anci would be home from visiting her uncle soon and she had no idea where

Ramira had gone. Perhaps she had run out to do an errand or two. Sophie furrowed her brows, an unknown nagging tugging at the back of her mind. She shook her head and placed a plate of freshly baked bread on the table. Anci walked into the kitchen, and gave her mother a hug.

"A gift from Zada," Anci said excitedly as she unfolded a parcel. Sophie's mouth began to water at the sweet bread drizzled with honey and nuts; it was still warm to the touch.

"I'll have to repay her kindness. Did you see Ramira at the castle?" Sophie hoped Danyl and Ramira had been able to find some uninterrupted time together, a luxury of late.

"Danyl spent the whole day with Nyk and Styph," Anci replied pouring mugs of tea.

"Did she happen to mention her plans for today?"

"No."

Sophie looked down at her daughter without really seeing her, a wave of uneasiness enveloping her thoughts. Ramira had appeared more tired than usual of late; the dark circles and withdrawn gaze a testament to the nightmares she refused to discuss. Sophie marched upstairs and entered Ramira's room. Everything was tidy except for a partially closed drawer. Sophie pulled it open. Ramira had kept the clothes she had arrived in within it and it now lay empty. All the other drawers were still full. She ran downstairs, the look on her face beginning to scare Anci. She flung open the pantry door, her gaze resting on the vacant hook that had held the travel pouches. Ramira had gone away.

"Mother?" Anci's timidity brought Sophie back to reality.

"Stay here," she told the girl as she grabbed her shawl and headed up the avenue.

~

Danyl stared at her, as perplexed as the others seated around the dinner table. Why in the Four Corners of the land would Ramira suddenly decide to leave? She slipped out into the night to go…where? Where was she heading and why?

"I think her nightmares had something to do with her leaving,

212

Danyl," she said, both hands flat against his chest. "She tried to hide it but it showed in her eyes."

"I should have been more insistent she tell me what they were," he said.

Danyl walked over to the window, straining to see a figure swallowed up by the darkness. He felt the first tinges of alarm worm their way into his heart; the guilt of not being there for her began to settle in his mind.

"She wouldn't have told you and you know it," she corrected him.

Zada recalled the conversation she had had with Danyl another night and the thoughts those words had elicited. There was more here than they knew or understood. It wasn't so much that the pieces of the puzzle were missing, but they had yet to identify the ones that were all around them. Ramira, she was sure, was a part of the mystery and had left Bystyn in the middle of the night to escape her bad dreams. People had nightmares all the time, but trying to run away from them was pointless. The bad dreams seemed to stow themselves away in your satchel along with a fresh change of clothes. Had the Kreetch's venom intensified her nightmares? Was she heeding their silent call? Is that why she left?

"Danyl," Zada asked, "when did you first meet Ramira?"

He dropped his gaze; the room went silent.

"Tell them, Danyl," Sophie urged him.

Alyxandyr narrowed his eyes then stared from Sophie to his son as he waited.

"She is the one that saved my life months ago along the Broken Plain," he confessed, silently apologizing to her.

The king raised his hand to still the chorus of questions erupting in the room.

"She was in that cave *before* you got there?"

"Yes, Zada, she woke up when she heard my cries for help. Why?"

"All of the caves we've found run from the desert straight through to the Broken Plain," explained Allad. "Some disappear into an abyss or underground streams but go through nonetheless."

"This one was blocked with debris and had been for a very long time," explained the prince.

"Did you see anyone else in that area?" Allad asked, his eyes bright points of light.

"Not that I can remember."

Zada sighed deeply. She saw how nervous and restless the prince was, the only thought in his mind was mounting a search party. That was not a good idea, not yet anyway. Mahn had been probing for the Source of Darkness in this area, and she was sure more Kreetch would follow on the heels of their dead brethren. An indiscriminate hunt, therefore, would be foolish. The Kreetch had been at Bystyn's gates and that meant Mahn had already deduced where the Source of Darkness was located. The elven magic provided a sort of barrier against him, especially if his own power had not yet fully developed. He could not come and get what he desired, but he could have it come to him. The woman with no past, tormented by nightmares, and defiled by demons was suddenly gone, flushed out of Bystyn like a pheasant from the grass. Zada turned white and started to shake as the implications slowly manifested themselves in her mind.

"Zada?" Seven called to her then glanced over at Allad.

"I think," she finally managed to say, "we had better have a very private meeting and you had best invite Gard."

~

There were twelve gathered in the king's private chambers, who listened with varying degrees of disbelief as she revealed what she believed was the truth. Their faces registered everything from dismay to impassivity, yet none dared utter a single word while the Herkah spoke.

"Mahn became aware of the Source of Darkness right about the time you were saved by Ramira, Danyl. He was unable to recognize it for what it was or he would have taken it at that moment. The same reason for him not detecting it allowed it to travel east to Bystyn. He must have taken control of Kepracarn then as well, since he would need a base of operation. Once he established himself, he unleashed his ilk upon the land seeking souls for his army while scouring the area for the Source of Darkness. Not finding it near the desert forced him to broaden his search here."

"What are you insinuating, Zada?" asked Mason.

"I think that Ramira houses the Source of Darkness."

The ensuing silence was deafening. Even Danyl was too shocked to voice his opposition to such a preposterous idea. The same thoughts and series of events played through all of their minds until they realized Zada's words made sense. The degradation of the land by the evil began when Danyl was nearly lost all those months ago. Ramira, apparently unaware she carried the Source of Darkness, followed him to the city with Mahn trailing behind.

Danyl could not believe the woman he loved harbored such evil. She had toiled long and hard to help everyone around her without ever complaining. The prince could not look beyond her caring and loyalty to accept the logic in Zada's words.

"Now, I cannot even begin to figure out Ramira's past, but she does bear some Herkah traits. Her abilities with the knives, her clothing choice, and, according to Danyl, the briquettes she used in the cave hint at such a connection. The Herkahs, however, have never seen her before. Mahn does not know what she looks like, depending instead on the dark magic to guide him to her. Once he knows her approximate location, he will send the Vox after her. They, too, will be directed by something other than her appearance."

"Why do you believe he does not know who she is?" asked Styph.

"Ramira has been wandering the land since her emergence from the cave, but has yet to be confronted by any of his minions. The Kreetch incident must have been purely accidental. Her brief connection to Mahn via the poison confirmed that the Source of Darkness was in this area."

"That also might explain why the poison did not transform her into one of thc demons," suggested Clare.

"It's entirely possible that the Source of Darkness negated

their effect," added Seven.

"Or maybe it absorbed their venom," muttered Gard, his animosity towards Ramira for bringing the evil into his home clear in his tone.

"That's not fair, Gard," Seven reminded him. "Regardless of how things appear, I doubt very much Ramira chose to be the bearer."

"Whether she embraced it or not is no longer an issue," Mason's deep voice stilled any further discussion. "She has it."

"The nightmares, then, were focused in this direction with Mahn hoping it would affect whoever had the Source of Darkness and force them out into the open," stated Alyxandyr.

"Exactly," replied the nomad.

"So, he is hunting for her but still doesn't know what she looks like or which way she is going?" asked Clare.

"As long as she refrains from using the power, if indeed she is even able to, yes."

"So that brings us back to why she left," said Nyk.

"What would be the one thing that would make her leave, Danyl?" asked his father.

"She would only go if she thought any or all of us were in danger," he replied after a long while.

"Mahn must have been sending her twisted half-truths and outright lies. She took the only measure she thought would help us all," Zada said. The Herkah could not even begin to imagine what sort of horrors he had inundated her with and that, along with her unknown past, pushed her out the gate.

Danyl closed his eyes; Gard remained quiet in his chair. Zada thought back to when Danyl yanked her from Mahn's grasp and realized that the Green Might had reacted to the Source of Darkness. The elven magic had helped him avert a disaster but did not exterminate the dark power.

"So, what do we do now?" asked the crown prince.

"We have to find her," stated Allad.

"Find then kill her?" Gard barely kept the bitterness out of his voice; he ignored Danyl's glacial stare.

"No, Gard," Zada explained. "We don't know how that will

change the outcome, if at all. Besides, slaying her then finding out she would be more helpful to us alive is a mistake that cannot be undone."

"So what is to be done, Zada?" asked Mason.

"We have to catch her before he does, Lord Mason. The only advantage to her being out in the land is we will have more time to work on our own defenses."

"She bought us a little extra time," Seven mused aloud.

"Yes, Seven, but unfortunately she shortened her own, which is why we have to move quickly. A small group with an experienced tracker should go after her. I must insist at least two Herkahs go along to battle any demons that will surely be hunting for her."

"Wait," she said stopping them all from volunteering at once. She looked at Alyxandyr: he would decide who went to their likely deaths.

"I think it is only fair that one from each race gathered here should go, but each will choose who shall represent them."

"I would have no other dwarf take my place and any arguments," Seven lifted his hand, "will fall on deaf ears."

Gard rose from his chair, as did Allad and, of course, Danyl. Lance took his place beside the prince.

"There stands before us more royalty than we can possibly spare," objected the king looking from one to the other.

"If we fail we won't have to worry about that, now will we?" Seven locked eyes with his longtime friend forcing the king to nod in agreement.

They planned to leave at sunrise the following day, the impending bad weather a fortunate occurrence that would allow them to ride out cloaked and hooded. Lance and Allad left to see to the provisions and the horses while the rest worked out a basic plan. Since only those gathered knew of the search, the group would be on their own.

"I cannot watch you with my inner sight for Mahn will eventually sense it and take an interest. I will, however, be able to see or feel any use of magic or whether or not you encounter any demons."

"Zada?" Danyl asked, as the two of them stood alone in the room. "If this Source of Darkness is so sinister, why did Ramira slay the Kreetch? Why did the elven power aid and not destroy her?"

"I don't know, Danyl," she replied. The dark magic should have embraced the Kreetch, yet she slaughtered the demons instead. Ramira had failed to save the couple, the tears streaming down her face marking her grief while the vile blood of the Kreetch still dripped from her knives. The Source of Darkness allowed her to destroy one moment then mourn the next…or did it? What exactly was this foul power embedded within the fair Ramira?

"What are the chances of encountering Vox, Zada?" he asked.

"You must not engage them, Danyl. Leave the fighting to Allad and Haban and heed their commands when they do so," she emphasized then touched his cheek before leaving the room.

Danyl poured a glass of wine and walked out onto the balcony, the crisp night air proclaiming a change in the weather. Winter was about to smother the land under a thick blanket of snow. He had been looking forward to spending more time with Ramira during the long, dark nights but her flight had changed all of those plans. Why hadn't he insisted she reveal her nightmares to him? Why had he relented in allowing her to return to Sophie's home? Why hadn't he visited more often to see what was happening to her?

~

They gathered early the next morning, out of sight beneath the arches leading to the rear of the castle and the stables. Zada nodded at Haban, then handed each member of the company a small scabbard they tucked away within the folds of their cloaks. They embraced each other, and then the members of the group mounted their horses. The time to leave was upon them.

"All Herkahs wear one of these," she explained in the crisp darkness. "If you are about to be killed by a demon use it and spare yourselves the agony of becoming one of them. May your journey be swift and your hearts remain pure."

They urged their horses forward, exchanged silent farewells, then rode down the avenue and out the gates beneath a cold rain. More than a full day had passed since Ramira left, but she could not have gotten very far on foot. With any luck, they would be back by the following sunrise.

Gard found the trail amid the rain and misty shadows and it ran, as they had surmised, south toward the Ahltyn River. They followed the trail until sundown without any luck. They made camp after dark, sharing a meal and discussing her possible whereabouts. Each also silently wondered if Ramira had any idea what she carried and prayed she would not use it.

PART II

SEVEN

Ramira eyed the house as she went by, the memory of what had transpired there still fresh in her mind. She loathed the things that murdered the gentle old couple. The house remained unoccupied, boarded up as if to contain the horrors that had occurred within. Ramira could feel the bile rise up in her throat, the keen desire to inflict more damage onto the demons tempered only by their absence. There would be no mercy if she crossed paths with them in the future.

Ramira turned south crossing the Ahltyn by the light of the moon, which was now at its highest point in the sky. The first fingers of clouds began to obscure the moon; the change in the wind promised bad weather. She knew they would search for her and covered a lot of ground by mid-morning. The driving rain did not deter her. She finally crawled into a clump of trees and brush to sleep for a few hours, exhausted from walking since late evening. She awoke to the sounds of thunder in the late afternoon. Ramira scrambled far enough out of her hiding place to check her surroundings. Satisfied she was alone, she grabbed her things and set out once more, her mind on the friends she had left behind.

Was she doing the right thing by leaving them? Would what she was doing really matter in the end or should she have stayed and enjoyed her last days with them? It didn't really matter for she was apparently the cause of not only this misery but the one from her past, too. People died, and worse, because of her and now the same fate hovered over the elves, dwarves, Herkahs, and Khadry. Ramira was suddenly ashamed of her intimacy with Danyl, for she had done nothing less than taint him with her own brand of evil.

Oddly enough, the images and whisperings that had driven her from Bystyn were virtually silent out here. She could sense them on the edge of her consciousness but they did not torment her as they had in the city. The rain and impending darkness would make travel difficult, compelling her to find a suitable place to spend the night. She spotted a cluster of boulders under an overhang where she could remain dry and watch for any unwanted company. After a short climb, she settled in under the shelf and pulled her knees up to her chest. It had been two days since she left. Her exertions and the cold made her hungrier than usual, but she forced herself to eat sparingly. Ramira had provisions for at least another week, but the unfamiliarity of the land demanded she ration her food. She had no idea what to expect in the south and did not know if the people living there would be hospitable to strangers. She ate without tasting the dried meat, fruit, and cheese. Ramira washed her meal down with water as she contemplated her direction. How long would she be able to run and how would that really affect the outcome to the north? Did she actually believe the evil would spare the city because she was gone? What exactly was she running from?

"You're running from yourself, you dolt," she quietly chided herself.

Ramira leaned back against the rock and drew her cloak more tightly around her body; the brittle night air was balmy compared to the chill residing in her soul. She was still on elven lands and could easily march right back the way she had come. She would face Danyl's and Sophie's searing reprimands, their welcoming the admonishments would sound like music to her ears. She began to doze, the sound of the icy rain lulling her mind into a restless darkness.

~

Ramira awoke to a chilly and misty dawn, the rain leaving the earth soggy. She stretched her cramped muscles and ate a few bites of food before starting on her trek. She was careful not to leave too many tracks in her wake, but knew the elves could trail her even if she left nothing behind. She walked steadily on, trying to put as much distance between herself and her friends as she could manage. Ramira kept near the tree line, her senses straining to capture any sound of pursuit. She heard hooves later that day and scampered into the brush as an elven patrol rode by. When they were well out of sight, she emerged from her concealment and resumed her journey. She spotted no one else that day or over the next few days, their absence both a relief and a worry.

Ramira swung around a vast outcropping of rock, one driving her due east for nearly a half-mile before it disappeared back into the earth. She came upon a thick stand of hardwood trees interspersed with pines and, after taking a deep breath, walked beneath their boughs. The ground here was level although there was an occasional exposed root or fallen log. She remembered looking at the maps in Karolauren's study; the huge rock she had maneuvered around marked the edge of Bystyn's lands. If her memory served her correctly, there would be a neutral zone between the elves' boundary and the southerners where a traveler might cross without trespassing on either land.

A crow landed on a branch several feet to her right. It cawed loudly; its black brethren answered from somewhere in the distance. The sound was loud, echoing hollowly in her ears and through the endless rows of trees. It called out a few more times before flying away. Ramira was able to hike for another hour before the light began to fade; her breath obscured her view each time she exhaled. She pulled her thick cloak more tightly against her frame to ward off the chill; her cheeks and nose took on a rosy hue. She wished she were trekking home to Sophie's house after a long day's work where the fire crackled and a pot of stew simmered over the fire. For a brief moment, the trees and boulders disappeared leaving her within the confines of the kitchen until a root tripped her and jarred her out of her reverie. Ramira picked herself up off the ground and rubbed her stinging knee. Caw. She glared at the crow mocking her predicament. She picked up a rock and threatened the bird with it. Caw. She let it fly and watched as it skimmed along the bottom of the branch and ricocheted off in the distance. Caw.

"I would have hit you had it not been for the fading light," she muttered at the departing crow, raising a brow as it emptied its bowels in response to her boast. The daylight quickly began to wane, the pale gray giving way to the night. Alone once more, she crawled beneath the drooping boughs of a pine for a few hours of rest.

~

The frigid air seeping through her blanket and clothes woke her near moonset. She sat up, pulling her knees to her chest and the blanket closer to her body; her breath masked her view. She began to shiver with cold, a predicament that would get worse if she did not find some shelter soon. A few hours of rest in a cave or barn would be ideal. She gathered her few possessions and left her soggy refuge behind, carefully walking on the slick ground to a more suitable place. The land started to slope downward, making her footing more precarious. Her backside landed on the hard earth on more than one occasion as she continued. She rested against a tree and stared at the sun rising behind a bank of ominous gray clouds. The wind bit into her dirty face and stirred her limp hair. Her gloved hand reached up and flipped her cowl over her head then tugged it closer under her chin.

"Come on," she scolded herself, "you don't have much time."

Ramira wound her way through a stand of oaks and maples, the thorny brush, roots, and rocks hampering her progress. The frozen rain came down slowly at first then with greater force; it coated her in ice within minutes. The extra weight on her exhausted and famished body slowed her down. She passed beyond the last of the trees and stepped into a clearing. A large barn stood to her right and beyond it a farmhouse. She dropped behind a pile of wood as a door slammed, the rusty axe stuck in the chopping block impeded her view. She watched a man bundled up in a heavy coat head toward the barn.

"Uwing!" he shouted. "Uwing! Where'd that lazy little bastard get off to now?"

"Coming Papa!"

Ramira spotted a small boy, his shirttails sticking out from under his short jacket. He ran over to his father, halting just beyond his reach.

"Those damn rats ate through the sacks again! You were supposed to keep an eye out for 'em boy!"

His hand came up and across the boy's face before the child could react. Ramira could see the red mark even from her vantage point.

"I'm sorry Papa…"

"Get in there or I'll whip your hide!" The man grabbed the boy by his collar and yanked him into the barn.

The sleet began to hurt but she could do nothing but wait until the man was back in the house. She shifted her body, ignoring the subtle crackling of her cloak. Her fingers and toes grew stiff and unwieldy; her stomach growled. Her eyelids drooped and only her rubbing kept them from staying closed.

"Now kill those vermin or else!"

Ramira waited for a while longer then cautiously crept toward the barn. She sidled up against the rough-hewn boards and inched her way to the window at the end of the building. She carefully lifted the wooden slat just high enough to peek inside, breathing a sigh of relief as she stared at the back of a beam. Ramira looked around then sneaked into the barn, holding the shutter to keep it from banging against the window frame. She crouched down, listening for any sounds. Ramira heard flames feeding on wood then a tap-tap-tap noise. She eased her way over to a punched out knothole and looked through it.

The boy, Uwing, sat in front of a potbellied stove holding a long, thin stick and letting its tip hit the worn floorboards. His nose was runny and the welt on his face covered his entire cheek. He wiped his nose with his sleeve and scooted closer to the stove, humming softly to himself. Ramira glanced over to bales of hay stacked in the corner then at the sacks of provisions hanging from the rafters. Small round protrusions…nuts? Larger chunks…potatoes? The rounded pouches might contain flour or meal, a virtual banquet dangled from the beams. Ramira exhaled slowly as weariness sapped the remainder of her strength. She crawled over to the hay, being extra vigilant as she passed by the opening to the main part of the barn. She wormed her way behind the bales, pushing the front section forward to create a space for her to lie in. Cold and hunger were her companions as she fell into a dreamless sleep. Ramira slept through the morning, never

225

hearing the man chop wood or the squeal of the pig he slaughtered. She never knew the cows were being milked or the man coming in to spread fresh straw for the animals.

He cut the twine on the bales then jammed his pitchfork into the straw to work it loose. His downward thrusts moved toward the back then, when he had loosened enough straw, he tossed forkfuls over into the stall.

Ramira shuddered as the cold invaded her sleep. She forced her eyes open, the gunk nearly sealing her lids shut. Funny…she could see the back of the stable. A shape loomed over her holding something long and slender in his hands. Was that light reflecting off metal? She instinctively pushed herself against the uneven planks as the prongs bit into the hay where she had been a second before. Had she been found out? Was this person trying to kill her? She slipped into the space between the bales and the wall as the pitchfork stabbed down once again. Man…boy…barn…Sweet Mercy! Ramira was fully awake, her hands gripping the hilts of her knives. One of the tines buried itself in her forearm. She sucked in her breath; the piercing brought tears to her eyes but she did not yelp in pain. He brought the pitchfork down repeatedly, catching bits of her clothing but no more flesh. The man moved away and didn't come back - he was finished.

"Let's go, boy. Suppertime."

Warmth oozed from the puncture wound, which she hastily bound with a strip of cloth. She left her place of concealment, ignoring the nervous horse and cow in the stalls next to her. She peeked around the corner; her arm throbbed. Ramira glanced at the milky light visible between the breaks in the barn walls, then at the bags suspended from the crossbeams. She approached the ropes wrapped around the cleats and lowered each one, filling her pouch with as much as she could carry. She went over to the stove and held her hands out to the heat, squashing the urge to hug the glowing stove. The warmth made her fingers tingle. It felt so good to be near heat…it made her want to lie down and sleep alongside it. Her knees began to buckle and only the man's voice broke the stoves hold over her. She slunk out the way she had come, shivering as she disappeared into the gathering darkness.

~

The company set up camp beneath a clump of pines, their full branches arching and interlacing overhead like a natural, aromatic ceiling that kept out most of the sleet. They were already wet, but the briquettes Allad lit provided some heat and warmed their meal. Their horses tended to and their bellies full, the companions, each lost in their own thoughts, sat around the embers.

"We should have found her by now," stated Danyl, troubled why their combined tracking skills had failed.

"Evidently she does not wish to be found, Danyl," Seven reminded him as he stretched then inched closer to the fire.

"The few telltale signs she couldn't erase are all we have," interjected Allad.

"I'm sure we chose the right direction; it's just a matter of finding the hare before she hops down into a burrow," Seven said as he passed an ale skin to Haban. The Herkah uncorked it, took a swig then shrugged in response. Seven shook his head in mock disgust.

"What does the land look like from here to…say another twenty miles farther south?" asked Allad.

"The forest stretches in a wedge shape to the west growing wider as it heads in that direction," explained Danyl. "The land itself eventually turns into rolling hills with an abundance of boulders. The rivers and streams there are easy to spot because they are surrounded by vegetation."

"Sort of like the oasis in the desert," said Allad.

"You'll find fresh water and some food there," finished the prince.

"What of those who live on the other side of the forest?" asked the nomad.

"They do not mingle with those on the elven side of the woods," began the prince. "They are, for the most part, a sturdy lot eking out a meager living while trying to avoid scattered roving bands of marauders."

"Something to look forward to," muttered Seven from within his blankets, visions of Rock Lords appearing in his head.

"In any case, they would be more apt to avoid rather than confront us," finished the elf.

"The bandits or the folk?" asked Seven.

"Both, Seven."

Gard and Lance took the first watch yet sleep did not come easily for any of them. Her faint tracks told them she was heading steadily southward, but she should not be that far ahead. Had they missed something? Danyl and Seven took over the sentry duty during the night. Haban and Allad stood guard in the wee hours of the morning and watched the pale sunrise behind a milky sky. They stretched their stiff muscles and shared a quick meal before gathering up their gear.

"So much for finding her before sunrise," muttered Seven as they mounted their horses on the sixth day out of Bystyn.

The dwarf king could not fathom how someone traveling on foot in an unfamiliar area could so elude them. He as well as the others could not seem to shake the feeling she was nearby, but even with their keen eyes and sharp hearing could not detect any movement.

"We might have passed her by along the way," suggested Gard.

"Maybe," replied Allad. "I don't think so. We aren't traveling very fast and it would not be difficult for her to keep pace with us."

"Do you think she is shadowing us?" asked Danyl.

"It certainly would be more difficult for us to follow the tracks that are behind us, now wouldn't it?"

They rode on for most of the morning, aware of the changes in their surroundings as they crossed into the south. The watery sun trying to break through the thick clouds made everything appear washed out, a depressing sight to the frustrated trackers. They were mindful of the weather; more than one careless traveler disappeared in a sudden storm. The company studied the line of short, rolling hills farther to the south, which were interspersed with stunted trees and large boulders. The rocks, bleached by the sun, reminded them of pieces of bone sticking out from the ground. They wondered if Bystyn's verdant plain might end up like this if they did not succeed in finding Ramira. Even if they did find her, that shared image might still happen. They stopped once to rest then resumed their search, coming upon a drab town near sunset. Gard, Allad, and Seven wormed their way between some bushes on a hill overlooking the town to study it.

The buildings were mainly one story and constructed of slats of wood with weathered tin roofs. The lights shining through grimy windows fell in colorless pools upon the roughhewn boards; debris and rickety chairs littered the sagging porches. A raucous group of men left a tavern, their voices reaching them from their place of concealment as they staggered into the street. A slightly built figure suddenly darted from an alleyway, immediately catching the attention of the group as it ran down the street. The inebriated men were unable to catch up; their curses and shouts fell short of the escaping figure. Others ventured out into the street and accosted the men and, within moments, fights broke out. The figure took advantage of the distraction and disappeared into the falling darkness.

"I think I prefer spending the night in the cold and damp over that," stated Seven jerking his thumb at the town.

"I agree with you," replied Gard.

The three of them returned and reported the news to their companions. They rode on for a while longer, intent on placing a bit of distance between themselves and the collection of shabby buildings and short tempers. They found a place to spend the night and filled their stomachs with warm food. The night air grew crisp and their surroundings very quiet.

They rose shortly before dawn and were about to mount their horses when a slight sound caught their attention. They pretended to adjust their equipment while Lance slipped away unnoticed, returning almost immediately with a struggling figure in his arms. His hand covered its mouth. Danyl thought it might be Ramira, but the girl in Lance's grasp was too slight and Ramira would certainly not grapple with the captain. Danyl stared hard at the young girl's wide blue eyes and short-cropped brown hair; her defiance was composed of fright more than bravery. The prince nodded to Lance who removed his hand from her mouth.

"Who are you?" demanded Danyl, trying hard not to laugh at her faltering bluster.

She lifted her head but remained silent until Allad faced her. His hawkish features warned her to respond or certain consequences would be unleashed. The nomad, too, worked hard to keep the amusement off his face.

"He asked you a question."

"My name is Cricket," she finally managed to say, her nerve slowly waning.

"What do you want?" asked the prince.

"Nothing…I…" she sputtered, her hand nervously clutching at a little leather bag attached to her belt.

"You wouldn't happen to be a thief now, would you?" inquired Seven, eyeing the bag and remembering the group of men looking for a slight figure the previous evening.

"No! I'm no thief!" she replied defiantly.

"So why have you sought our company?" asked Allad.

"I just happened upon you, that's all," she said. She swallowed tensely

"That scuffle last night would not have been due to you now would it?" asked Danyl.

"Yes," she finally admitted. "My brothers have little love for me."

"'Brothers', eh? Well, Cricket, what do you want us to do? Maybe bring you back to them?" asked Allad.

"No. I can't go back… they'll kill me."

Danyl held her chin with his thumb and index finger and forced her to look into his eyes. He realized family or not, those men would surely harm her. To take her along meant possible problems down the road if they were to meet up with the men. He couldn't leave Cricket behind. He shook his head.

"What do you want us to do?" he gently asked the girl.

"May I stay with you?" she begged in a small voice. "I promise I won't be a problem."

"What makes you think you can trust us not to harm you or bring you back to your 'brothers'?" asked Seven.

"Because you are not like them."

"Well then," said Danyl after a long pause. "You can come along but the first mistake you make will be your last one, understood?"

Cricket nodded, the relief in her eyes stilling even Gard's protests. Danyl helped her up behind him as they resumed their search for Ramira, the day bright and clear but their cloaks pulled close.

Cricket burrowed up against the elf's back, silently thanking him for trusting her. She knew the men would be looking for her and hoped her newfound companions would be able to protect her if they found her.

"What's to be found in these parts?" Seven asked her.

"You aren't from around here, are you?"

"We wouldn't be asking you if we were, now would we?" was Gard's terse reply. He did not think it was a good idea to bring this stranger with them. Their dire quest and the possibility of demons were enough problems.

"There are a few towns and villages like the one I left and some farms scattered about," she eyed the Khadry but said nothing else.

"How do they react to strangers?" asked Allad.

"Not very well," she replied.

"What do you mean, Cricket?" asked the prince.

"There have been some odd things happening around here of late," she stated, the hint of fear in her voice muffled against the elf's cloak. "Even those who usually are to blame for such things don't leave town much anymore."

"Like your 'brothers'?"

"Yes. They can't bully what they can't see."

"What do you mean by that?" Seven stared at the girl then at his companions.

"Bodies have been found…horribly torn apart. No animal can do such a thing."

"Have you seen such things?" asked Seven.

Cricket closed her eyes, trying to erase the images that would never go away. She vividly remembered one night a week or so earlier. She had crept along the dingy alleyways behind the shops in search of anything of value, when she stumbled upon two terribly mutilated bodies. She could neither scream nor move for several long moments. Her scream woke the entire town up. The residents had raced to the alleyway and stared with horror at the corpses ripped to shreds. Everyone, even the worst of the bandits, had paled at the ghastly scene in the alleyway. Danyl could feel her hold tighten on him as she spoke the words.

The king and the prince locked gazes. Allad exhaled heavily for it was the Kreetch had invaded this part of the land, too. They would need to be extra vigilant in their travels. They hoped Ramira would be alert to the dangers here then remembered what she had done to the Kreetch at the house. If there were Kreetch, the Radir and Vox would not be far behind. They rode on in silence, the morning turning into afternoon before they stopped to rest for a while. Cricket never ventured far from Danyl.

"Cricket, have you seen any other travelers…a woman, perhaps?"

"I've seen many women. What does she look like?"

"She has long red-gold hair."

"No one like that. She must be pretty special for you to be looking for her."

"Yes, she is," he said, his gaze dropping to the ground.

"Is there any place safe for a lone traveler in these parts?" inquired Seven. The dwarf frowned when she shook her head.

"Cricket, if you were a stranger in these parts and realized you couldn't go into the towns and villages, where would you go?" Allad asked quietly.

"I don't know, but there are a lot of places she could hide in like abandoned farms or the thicker woods in the south," she said pointing to their left. "She could find shelter among the hillocks that are common to the east of the town I came from, too."

"Where would you have gone if you hadn't found us?"

"The knolls."

"Why?" asked Seven.

"Because you can hide yet still see all around you."

Cricket looked from one face to the next, noting they all shared a variation of the same emotion: uneasiness. Allad and Seven's concern was steeped in the urgency of finding a friend; Gard's held a tinge of bitterness, and Danyl's filled with sadness. In any case, they all wanted to find a certain woman as soon as possible. Why? Did she steal from them?

"Wasn't that the area where we last saw some of her tracks?" asked Gard.

Ramira had undoubtedly scrutinized the collection of grungy buildings to determine if it was safe - and wise - to seek shelter there before coming to the same conclusion they had. He and his companions had continued to travel west while she had more than likely chosen a different path. The Kreetch's handiwork told them the demons had penetrated the Southland, but how far east had they traveled? How many of the evil's ilk hunted for her here in the south?

"It was," confirmed Seven, "and it's only about a half-day's ride from here."

They stopped riding and discussed what Cricket had told them. It was possible they were heading in the wrong direction. There were many risks in going back, not the least of which was running into the men Cricket had fled from and the Kreetch roaming freely there. If Ramira had gone the way they were now riding, they would lose a great deal of time by turning back; any signs she may have left would surely disappear. This direction, however, headed west and none of them, including Ramira, wanted to end up on Mahn's doorstep.

"Gard?" Danyl addressed the Khadry. "What do you think about riding to the knolls?"

"I think we should turn back," Gard replied after a moment's hesitation.

"Allad?"

"That might be the best place for her to hide."

Seven, Haban, and Lance agreed. Danyl nodded; they turned back and head for the hillocks, a nervous Cricket clinging to the prince's cloak. No one needed any reminders to increase their alertness.

~

Ramira rested in the shadows of a mound; a gnarly pine grasped its side and bent outward at an awkward angle. She opened her pouch and frowned: there was only enough food to last a couple days. She sighed and ate while surveying the area around her, the prospect of being hungry in this odd land not a pleasant thought. How far could she go before she ran out of land? Then what? Head back north to Bystyn to see if everything had settled down? Was she shirking her duty to those whom she had come to love by abandoning them? Why had the voices become silent? They had not tormented her for many days now. That left her mind free to contemplate how insane it had been to leave in the first place. She rubbed her face, her dirty hands smearing the road dirt across her cheeks and forehead while strands of hair stuck out at odd angles. She undid her braid and removed the hair clip, lovingly holding it between her fingers as she stared at the little bird in the apple tree. Jack. The kind elf's face appeared before her until tears welled up and blurred the image. She could not save them - she had been too late. The rage toward the demons began to roil deep within her once more. Her chest began to heave in unison with her increasing heartbeat as she fought to contain the loathing for the foul beasts.

Ramira forced the image away while combing out her hair. Her sense of failure manifested itself in her strokes as she pulled out strands of hair and tossed them on the ground beside her. Finally free of the tangles, she re-braided it, replaced the gift, and prayed for their forgiveness. How many others should she be asking for mercy? She shook her head and got to her feet, resuming a trek to nowhere with a heavy heart and a lonely soul. She had just crossed over the next hill when the sound of hooves echoed toward her. She peeked from her hiding place and spotted a group of riders. They were not elves. They were men, their menacing faces and array of weapons on full display. She cursed under her breath as they neared her cover and stopped. They argued violently amongst themselves, shouting and pushing each other until a fight broke out. The apparent leader ended the scuffle by grabbing both brawlers by their shirts and smacking their heads together. Bloodied and dazed, the aggressors glared at each other but refrained from throwing any more punches.

They were close enough for her to smell their sweat. Had they detected her? Had she been careless? She heard them curse then spit on the ground as they discussed a young girl, Cricket was her name, and what they were going to do to her once they found her. They were determined to find her at all costs.

The tallest of the men was the most irate. He loudly proclaimed he was going to enjoy whipping her once he had his hands on her. She had a feeling he was not going to stop with just a simple beating. Ramira withdrew into the brush, waiting until they were far away before continuing her own uncertain journey. Much to her dismay, the men scattered and began to search the hills in her immediate area. It didn't take long for one to approach her hiding place. He didn't dismount, taking advantage of his elevation to hunt for the girl. Ramira looked around for better concealment and spotted a fallen trunk over a small ditch to her right. When she tried to squirm in that direction, the strap from her pouch caught on a branch and kept her rooted in place. She could not move forward or backward without breaking the branch. Ramira held her breath, the gap in the branches in front of her offering him a clear view of her predicament. She slipped the knives from their scabbards, preparing to cut the strap and, if need be, the man. The horse came nearer until it passed by right in front of her. The rider never noticed she hid a few paces away.

"Not here!" shouted one of the men who rode over to the next hill.

One rider positioned himself on a knoll to watch for anyone trying to scamper away from them. Ramira lay still. It was getting too dark to resume her trek, especially with the men in the immediate vicinity. She sighed and was about to sit up when her instincts warned her of another presence nearby. She strained her ears but heard nothing. Her hands automatically tightened around her knives as that peculiar sensation she had experienced at the couple's home grew. This time the feeling was deeper, more sinister and made the hair stand up on her neck and arms. Ramira waited then saw a pair of Herkahs walk in the opposite direction from the men. The urge to greet the nomads stuck in her throat as the wave of evil washed over her. It took all of her will not to rush forward and force an encounter with them. One of the Herkahs paused, as if it sensed something. It moved away when Ramira suppressed her reaction. She knew what they were but what were they doing in the southland? What were they looking for? It was becoming very crowded in this barren land. It was time to head in a more westerly direction. She freed the strap then retreated as far back into the brush as she could wiggle, her eyes and ears straining to detect any more unwelcome visitors. The shadows around her grew longer as night claimed the land. She was safe within her thorny confines, but that did not calm her apprehension. Mahn's vilest minions stalked the land, forcing her to reconsider her plans. She had to circumvent them but how could she do that without knowing where they were heading? Was she foolish enough to track them, then head the other way?

Sleep did not come easily that night. She awakened every few minutes expecting to find the Vox's face inches from her own. Ramira was not concerned about the men but the two high demons were another story. As menacing as they were, she had wanted to challenge them with the same irrational impulse that had surfaced when she confronted the Kreetch. What stayed her hand this time was a mystery. She finally slept the last few hours before dawn.

~

Cricket pointed them south to the haphazard hills dotting the land, they ran, she explained, farther south for about twenty or thirty miles. The members of the company thought it would be impossible to find Ramira in such a broad expanse, but their choices were limited. The trees wore very little of their autumn regalia and that meant time was running out. If they wanted to return to Bystyn before the first snows fell, they had to do so soon. Once snow covered the land, it would be tough to survive. They stopped amid a cluster of pines, eating a quick meal while their horses rested. They walked around the closest hills for any signs of Ramira's trail, keeping a sharp eye out for intruders.

Haban examined a small hill. A snapped branch and scuffmarks in the dirt made him pause; he carefully pulled the limb back. Someone had recently been here and, as he turned his head to alert the others, discovered fine filaments caught in a bush. He plucked the gossamer threads from the bough, held them up to the light, and recognized what they were.

"Allad!" he called quietly, re-emerging from the underbrush. Haban's companions came running, skidding to a halt in front of him. He lifted his hand.

"Ramira's hair!" Seven said excitedly.

"Where did you find them?" demanded Danyl.

The companions followed Haban back to the hill. They searched it again but, other than a few more strands of hair and some boot marks, little else marked her presence.

"The trail is fresh, Danyl. She was here within the past day," stated Lance.

Danyl stared into the thicket. He imagined her sleeping through the night with her nightmares as her only companions. Their decision to return to this place had been the correct one, thanks to Cricket. With any luck, they would find her sometime in the morning. He didn't know whether he should first hug or reproach her.

"We have company," Gard nodded toward the riders approaching them.

Cricket disappeared into the thickets.

They watched the men advance, unsure if they were the same group from town.

The riders reined in when they got close and stared down at the odd collection of individuals. The biggest man in the group edged his horse forward, nodding once in greeting even though his eyes remained unfriendly.

"Seen a young girl, skinny with short brown hair in your travels?"

"No," replied Lance, drawing the big man's eyes in his direction.

The man studied the captain and noted his ready stance and impassive features. A dwarf, some elves, and a dark fellow made for very strange company, especially traveling this far south. Their lot stayed on the other side of the forest and rarely ventured beyond it. They didn't look like outlaws, but he surmised they wouldn't be easily intimidated, either. He scratched at the scraggly growth on his dirty face and wondered what brought them here.

"Don't you want to know why we're looking for her?" he asked.

"No," Lance replied in a disinterested fashion.

"Well, if you do run across her, she's a thief and has something of mine," the man persisted. "I want it back."

He locked eyes with the captain then turned away under Lance's steady gaze. He jerked his head to the side and rode away with the others. The company remained where they were, watching as the men rode off in the town's general direction.

"They'll be back," muttered Seven.

Danyl only half heard him; his attention was focused on the silken hair in dangling from his fingers. He had so many questions to ask her, but the only thing he wanted to do was to hold her and never let her go. He didn't care whether she housed the Source of Darkness or about the nightmares. Wasn't it so much better to face their fate together?

They searched for Ramira all afternoon, their frustration at being so close palpable. The long shadows spilled across the land. The hills facing west glowed in a soft orange light; the eastern sides were nearly lost in an inky blackness. Tired and disappointed, they decided to make camp for the night.

The men from town would undoubtedly keep an eye on them. Ramira was somewhere in the vicinity and those men were not going to stop the companions from finding her. A cold breeze blew across the open land; it moaned as it brushed through the stunted pines dotting the landscape. The sound was disconcerting, reminding them of souls crying out across a void. Even the normally unaffected Lance nervously surveyed the night, his hand never far from his sword. They took turns standing guard yet no one slept well that night.

Cricket reappeared well after dark and wriggled into Danyl's arms; her shaking was due to the men and not the chilly night. The elf knew the men were no competition for him and his comrades, a fact Cricket had yet to discover. With any luck, they would be able to avoid any conflicts with them. He felt sorry for the girl. She had evidently lived a rough life, a group of strangers her only refuge.

"What did you take from him, Cricket?" he asked.

"A stupid stone."

"A 'stone'? You mean a jewel, don't you?"

"No, not a gem, Danyl, just a blue stone."

"Show it to me in the morning?"

"Yes," she said then fell into a fitful sleep.

~

Ramira sat with the blanket pulled close to her body, one she hadn't washed for quite some time. She wrinkled her nose. She guessed it would be even longer before she'd feel any steaming waters again. The thought of being clean only made her long for a bath even more. Her once bulging pouch lay flat against the ground, the few crumbs within barely enough to satisfy an insect. She had eaten the last handful of nuts early this morning, the mouthful of food leaving her even hungrier. She needed to find provisions. Ramira drank some water then placed the half-empty canteen down beside her. Sleep eluded her even though she was exhausted. She tossed and turned on the hard ground, the rocks and lumpy earth digging into her body. She gave up and sat with the blanket wrapped around her. The moonless night fused everything together, even the hand she held up in front of her face. Ramira glanced up at the tiny pinpoints of light feebly twinkling within a sea of black, then out over the murky landscape. She jumped as an animal screeched with pain, then pushed back against the rocks as the mountain cat padded by with something suspended from its jaws. An owl hooted off in the distance. The wind whistled eerily through the scrawny trees, the sound the loneliest she had ever heard. The Vox roamed somewhere in all that forlorn darkness, a fitting backdrop for such immoral creatures. She thought about the Vox and wondered what they were doing so far south from Bystyn. If there were Vox then the Radir and Kreetch would also be in the area. She felt an inherent corruptness rising to the surface of her consciousness whenever she was near the demons. It was a vile sensation, one she abhorred, but one which she was powerless to fight. Was she nothing more than a demon hunter? Did the exposure to the vile poisons provoke her dreams? She squeezed her eyes shut.

The sun would rise in a few hours. Ramira began to doze, her exertions demanding rest. She tried to remain aware of her surroundings, but her mind and body shut down. She curled up, tugged on the blanket once then gave in to her weariness.

~

The company awoke at dawn, the thick gray clouds hovered low over the horizon. The drop in temperature was an unexpected, and unwanted, dilemma. The impending storm would reach them in a few hours; the companions hastened their search for Ramira. Before they set out, Cricket reached into her pouch and produced the stone, one that Danyl carefully studied. It was the size of an egg and fit into his closed hand; its deep blue hue unmarred by any facets. He handed it to the others. None of them thought the stone was of much value. Danyl thought that it resembled the beads on the bracelet. He handed it back to the young girl then set out to find Ramira.

They had been looking for several hours when Haban spotted a pair of Herkahs approaching them from the northeast. He motioned to Allad. The nomad knew no other Herkahs should be in the area. He barked at Haban; the nomads removed their shirts as they prepared to face their ultimate nightmares: Vox.

Allad and Haban inhaled deeply, their eyes never wavering from the approaching demons. Haban's fingers twitched at his side. He had managed to battle one Vox and barely escaped with his soul intact. Haban had removed Zada's knife and was about to plunge it into his own chest when the Vox slipped. Haban twisted around and drove the blade into the demon. The memory lingered to this day and reminded him any mistake, no matter how insignificant, would prove costly.

Allad had fought several of the Vox and understood the necessity of slaying his own kin to kill the evil dwelling within them. It was a somber task devoid of satisfaction.

"Stay here and do not interfere," commanded Allad, his black eyes pinpoints of determination. "If one of us falls, ride away as fast as your mounts will take you."

He nodded to an anxious Haban then the two of them walked over to intercept the Vox.

"Sweet Mercy," Danyl exhaled. "Those things look just like our companions."

Lance, Gard, and Seven formed a little group pulling a terrified Cricket into their midst. They watched the Herkahs and the demons approach each other. All four studied their foes for a moment before the larger of the demon-Herkahs chose Allad, leaving the other one to face Haban. The ensuing clash was swift and frightening as the two pairs wielded their weapons against each other. Those watching swore there was fire flying from their knives. Allad kept pace with his demon but Haban was not as adept as his opponent was and began to retreat. Haban did his best to deflect and attack but the demon was much stronger than he was. He soon went on the defensive, parrying thrusts to save his life. Haban was one of the best but Mahn had sent Vox that were even better. Allad was able to stand his ground.

Seven now understood why the Herkahs so feared the Vox; the high demons exuded a sense of power and doom. He could not even begin to imagine what the spirits of the Herkahs, imprisoned within their own bodies, were experiencing as they fought their kin. They undoubtedly prayed for freedom from the abhorrent parasites compelling them to corrupt their clan. That liberation came with a price, one they were more than willing to pay: death. The dwarf king glanced at Lance, the stunned look upon his face giving way to resoluteness. If one of the Herkahs fell, Lance would be the first one to defend him.

Gard's gray eyes absorbed the skillful and deadly techniques

241

used during this macabre fight. His friends sought to kill; the Vox were determined to add two more demons to their ranks. He had seen the Herkahs do battle before but not at such a high level of mastery.

The fierce combat mesmerized Danyl; the graceful and fluid motion disguised the intensity of the confrontation. The Vox wanted the blood of the Herkahs; the nomads were resolved not to give in to them. He heard Cricket whimper, her trembling body pressed against him. The young girl had seen plenty of terrible things in her life but none more terrifying than this. He slipped his free hand over her cold one her fingers nervously tried to intertwine with his.

~

Ramira left the confines of her shelter and headed in an easterly direction. With any luck, she might catch a small animal or stumble across someone who would share some food. She would steal if she had to. She walked on sipping from her canteen now and then, mindful of the gray day growing darker. The weather discouraged the woodland creatures from venturing too far from their burrows. Hunger might be her companion again this night. A thick stand of trees surrounded by barbed undergrowth forced her to retrace her steps toward the north. She walked for several miles until she located a break in the thorny shrubs. Ramira decided to take a chance in maneuvering through them. The inch long spikes exacted their payment for her passage as bits of cloth and blood adorned their points. Ramira finally made it to the other side, wiping away the blood trickling down her cheek with the back of her scratched hand.

"Wonderful," she muttered aloud. "More boulders and bony trees. Am I the only human here?"

Ramira refilled her canteen at a nearby stream then crossed it stepping on the rocks poking up above the water. She almost slipped into the chilly water but managed to regain her balance and reach the other bank. She glanced back at the thorn-encrusted trees running for several miles east; the stream flowed directly into the heart of it. It would have been a long trek had she chosen to parallel it. This entire area was composed of one barrier after another, hindrances that became more imposing the farther she traveled. The hills were scalable, but the bristly thickets were another matter. They grew in clumps of varying sizes and widths: some no higher than her ankles, others larger than houses. Ramira spent more time skirting them than she wanted to and made little headway as the day wore on. She finally broke free of them hours later, sighing with relief at the line of bent pines and slabs of stone directly ahead of her. Ramira glanced up at the bulky gray clouds pressing down upon the earth then over to the protective canopy of the trees.

"Well…it's better than nothing."

Ramira heard hoof beats and immediately hid within a cluster of boulders. Her first thought was of the men searching for Cricket and decided it was prudent to hide. She wriggled her way forward and peered through the underbrush at the riders. She recognized them even from this distance. Ramira had expected a search party but not one comprised of the individuals who slowly rode closer. Perhaps she was being too bold in thinking they were looking for her; maybe someone of importance warranted such a company. A spark erupted in her breast, one fanned into a flame by the longing to be with her friends once more. She yearned for their contact then squelched that desire as the embarrassment of her actions surfaced. She should never have left and seeing them here amid the dangers lurking everywhere only made her feel even guiltier. She had done what she thought was right but was it reasonable or did she just use that as an excuse? She glanced at Seven, the dwarf king's usually capricious demeanor replaced by a dark determination. Allad and Gard shared a similar expression while even the normally stoic Lance showed signs of trepidation. Ramira did not know who the young girl was but the frightened creature kept close to Danyl. She missed him the most. His presence had not only calmed her but had chased away the foreboding shadows that stole her sleep.

It would be a simple thing to emerge from her place of concealment and beg for their forgiveness. She dropped her head in remorse and tried to block out their tense faces. Ramira began to back away from those she loved then abruptly froze; a sense of foreboding washed over her in repulsive waves. She scanned the area for the demons, detecting them as they rounded one of the knolls directly in front of the group. She watched with apprehension as Allad and the other Herkah removed their tunics, and approached the demons with great courage.

The Herkahs fought the demons with every ounce of their being but the dark spirits hacked and slashed at them with an otherworldly ease. The young nomad's desperate attempts to ward off the Vox's endless strokes sapped him of his strength and forced him backward. He was tiring and would soon be unable to defend himself. The Vox feigned a blow to the right then sliced upward from the left as Haban sought to block the blade. Blood poured from the deep gash to his side. He glanced over at Allad wanting to help; darkness began to blur his vision as the Vox surged forward to finish the nomad. The demon was about to recruit another Herkah. Haban had other ideas however, mustering enough strength to pull out Zada's knife and plunge it into his heart. The Vox's choked hiss of denial accompanied Haban's body as it fell at the demons feet. To the dismay of the mortals, the demon began to advance upon the group clustered together near their horses. Allad had warned them but, danger or no, they refused to abandon him. They drew their swords in unison to fight what would surely consume them.

Ramira turned toward the members of the company. Her hands had already removed her empty pack and cloak yet she never noticed the chill in the air. She burst through the brush and planted herself between the demon and her friends. Hatred rose in her stomach, fueled on by the determination that these vile creatures were about to befoul her friends. She did not, could not, look upon their faces. She heard their shocked reactions as she challenged the Vox.

"You will not take them!"

~

Zada and Clare descended the staircase to meet with the king when the nomad froze in mid-step; her eyes were wide with alarm. She would have toppled down the stone stairs had Clare not grabbed her. The dwarf queen immediately relinquished the contact as the abhorrent feeling flowed from Zada into her. Clare shouted for the king but remained by Zada's side. Alyxandyr and Styph ran to the women. They gasped at the toll the vision was taking on the nomad. Her face took on an ashen cast; sweat beaded down her face as she struggled to keep the image in her mind.

"Vox...Haban has fallen...Allad is barely keeping the other one at bay," she told them in a raspy voice.

"How many Vox? Are the rest hurt?"

Alyxandyr's worst fears manifested themselves. He should never have allowed those individuals to go; losing them would be a huge blow in their fight against Mahn.

"Two Vox...the rest are alive."

"Have they found Ramira yet?" Styph's intense voice echoed in the stairwell. He wanted nothing more than to stand beside his brother and friends to confront the evil advancing upon them. He hated this feeling of powerlessness.

Zada's inner sight opened up once more, ruthlessly swallowing her up while forcing her to witness the continuing horror. Thrust into that black tide of energy where mortals were not meant to be, she prayed she had the strength to escape its grasp once the vision ended. The journey back to the fight terrified her. She sped across the plains with such velocity that not one thing could be identified. Boulders, houses, trees, and everything else along her path appeared smudged and indistinct. She existed in that in-between place where the cries of the damned accompanied her crossing; the indecent chorus was a fitting backdrop to the passage she was rushing through. Then everything abruptly stopped.

Zada watched Ramira emerge from the edges of her vision, her features reflecting a single-minded determination. Zada flinched, the reaction much stronger than the day Ramira battled the Kreetch. The Herkah observed the efficient slaying of one Vox then Ramira's deliberate focus on the one closing in to kill Allad. To her surprise, the Vox ignored her mate and concentrated instead on Ramira. The ensuing fight between the two made her blood run cold. For a brief second the brown woman appeared to her, her face lined with worry for, strangely enough, both Ramira and the Vox.

~

Few individuals other than the Herkahs had seen the Kreetch's mindless ferocity. They fought with little regard for anything except their desire to inflict pain. The Vox battled to impose terror upon their victims. The bodies they inhabited had at one time been perfect fighting units and the dark spirits now occupying them added their own strength. Who better to send into combat than a Vox-possessed Herkah? A Herkah's technique, resilience, and mastery with the blades was extremely difficult to duplicate, let alone defeat. Commanding one was the next best thing. The Vox sensed victory and planned to add the members of the group to their terrible fraternity.

Allad was immensely impressed with this Herkahs strength and skill. He was lightning fast, each swing of the blade meticulously timed and executed. He had to concentrate on the task at hand because losing was not an option. He glanced at Haban and cursed under his breath; if they were both to die, the remainder of the company was doomed. The nomad knew even with his warning they would never abandon them. He grimaced as the demon sliced across his chest, the blood seeping from the wound mixing with the sweat covering his abdomen. He feinted to the right then brought his blade up near the demons side; it sidestepped the knife and immediately recovered to stab back at him. Allad chanced a quick glance at the other Vox heading for his friends.

The demon rose and advanced toward the group when a figure emerged from between the hills and scrubby pines. The companions could only stare in shock as Ramira placed herself between it and them. She remained perfectly still except for a strand of hair lazily circling her face as the cold wind blew across the land. The demon took a tentative step to the side, cocking its head at this unexpected threat. The Vox wiped his blades on his trousers.

Ramira set upon the Vox with a savagery stunning even the demon, her knives blurs of motion as she forced him to retreat. She hacked at the demon, compelling it ever backward as it fought for its life against this unforeseen threat. It lost all the ground it had gained against Haban within moments. It was no match for the rigid woman pursuing it back to its companion with a ruthlessness that made them all pause. The Vox was now on the defensive. The soul of the imprisoned Herkah knew its time was at hand to accost the demon from within. The soul could do little damage, but it did distract the demon, allowing Ramira to dispatch the creature. She glared with hatred down at the twitching form, and then turned to the Vox holding Allad in its death grip.

~

Danyl and the others watched as the Vox lost all interest in an exhausted and wounded Allad, swatting the nomad away as it turned to face Ramira. Had the demon sensed the Source of Darkness and sought it for his own? Were the Vox capable of wielding it? Allad tried to intervene.

"Go! Take the others and leave!" she ordered.

Allad, like the others, was not about to abandon her: they would all stay and live or die. Allad staggered back to his friends, constantly looking over his shoulder at the life and death battle behind him. The confrontation reminded him of a brutal dance between an apprentice and master. Ramira was much smaller and weaker than the demon, depending upon her resourcefulness to keep pace with the Vox. They battled back and forth, both sets of knives inflicting wounds while neither gave any ground. The Vox finally outwitted her. He grabbed her from behind with one hand and lifted his blade to her throat with the other. Allad could feel their mortality begin to slip away from them: if she succumbed to his blade, they were all worse than dead. He heard Danyl give a strangled cry of despair, Cricket began to sob while Lance and Seven stood still.

~

Ramira somehow knew this thing's style and kept pace with the thrusts and parries. Although it had plenty of opportunity to kill, it bided its time. It was playing with her, fighting as if this was nothing more than an exercise. She surged forward, initiating the attack then rolled to either side to thwart its advance. The combatants ended up exactly where they had started from every time. The final fake lunge caught her quickly from behind. The Vox's blade rested against her neck; one of her arms was wrenched upward behind her back. Her mind raced as to how to defend this position when she noticed the Vox's hand.

The scars on her shoulder and thigh flared briefly in response to the likeness between his thumb and forefinger. Ramira stared at it without breathing; she stared without blinking at the coiled and hooded snake undulating imperceptibly in the gray light. Its movement mesmerized her, making her forget where she was and what she had been doing. Dumbfounded by what wavered inches from her face, she was powerless to stop her guard from dropping. She sensed the faint essence of what still existed inside the Herkah's body, a spirit ravaged by the presence of the Vox. His soul surged forward one last time to give her a chance to defeat the Vox and to set him free.

The host's sudden resurrection surprised the Vox who turned inward to restrain it. The distraction lasted just long enough for Ramira to bring her free hand up and block the Vox's blade. The edge of her knife rested between his haft and blade for a split second before the black dagger sliced cleanly through it. She twisted in its grasp and looked into the Herkah-demon's face; the sinister light return into the eyes. She felt no pity when she brought both knives down into its chest and remained motionless while the demon violently grabbed at the air in front of her. The dead demon-Herkah collapsed on top of her without warning, pushing her roughly to the hard ground. The impact knocked the wind out of her; the added heaviness made it difficult to breathe. Ramira hovered on the verge of unconsciousness.

Then the world she existed in disappeared. She felt the spirit within hover at the edge of her senses, the snake uncoiling and gliding toward where she lay. The serpent stopped then gradually rose from the ground, growing in height and breadth until it took on a human form. Its black color melted into a warm brown hue covering the man from the top of his cleanly shaven head all the way down to his feet. The towering man knelt at her side, his large hand gently caressed her hot face. His black eyes radiated an inner peace.

"Horemb?"

"I am free now, child. You do not have much time. Flee with your friends."

"Horemb…please…"

"Go. Do not let us die in vain."

Ramira watched him rise and walk away, then dissolve into a fine white mist. His body began to crush the life out of her, but instead of pushing him off, she weakly embraced him. She was finally able to hold someone from her past, even if his spirit no longer dwelled within his body. A tear rolled down the corner of her eye as she fumbled for his lifeless hand. She clung to it like a small child holding fast to its father's hand, afraid that she would be lost forever if she let go. Horemb's dead embrace kept her anxieties at bay, the feel of his body a link to her past. The world around her became indistinct as his corpse pressed down upon her. She refused to relinquish the contact with her beloved mentor and friend.

~

Zada collapsed into a heap, the strain of enduring the vision too much to bear. The king carried her to her room and placed her on her bed. Clare dabbed at her burning face and neck with a cool cloth. The nomad slowly began to recover and looked up into the anxious faces staring down at her.

"The Vox are dead and Ramira is now with the others."

"They will be heading back to us," murmured the king.

"They are still far away, Father," Styph reminded him.

"We need to send out patrols to intercept them when they return to the lands."

"We don't know where they will be coming from, Alyx," stated Clare.

"Then we will have to guess."

Zada closed her eyes, relief and sadness flooding through her being. Mahn had been denied the dark magic yet again, and she could well imagine how angry he must now be. He had sent his best and she had beaten them. No, that wasn't quite right. The large Vox had revolted against its demon to aid her. Her inner eye unveiled a thread of devotion between them and it explained the sorrow on the brown woman's face. She developed a headache; the aftereffects of the extreme effort she had required to keep the connection open. Zada drifted off into an unsettled slumber.

~

Ramira lay on the ground, the effort of fighting Horemb/Vox leaving her completely spent. Horemb had taught her how to wield the knives she had taken from the red woman. Ramira had killed him. Who were the others that had died for her? What part had they played in her life? Her mind began to reel prompting her to clutch Horemb's hand more tightly. She shivered as the warm blood cooled in the frigid air. It took several moments for her to realize that his body no longer pressed against hers. She tried to focus on the anxious faces peering down at her but the disconnected feeling between her body and mind left her disorientated. Ramira closed her eyes and willed her friends to leave her alone. She didn't deserve their loyalty or understanding. They poured water over her face and neck forcing her to return to the rolling plain.

"Ramira? Are you badly hurt?"

She looked up as the prince gently shook her back into the present. She tried to turn her head but he forced her to look into his eyes.

"Ramira!" he called to her again.

The opaque sun slipped behind a bank of dirty gray clouds; a foreboding stillness settled upon the land.

"Get her up," Seven ordered.

250

Ramira felt herself float in the air; a pair of arms supported her. Gooseflesh erupted all over her body; her head slumped against her chest. She grieved for the man who had given her hope.

The land slowly became more distinct to her, as did the cold seeping into her flesh and bones. She shivered even after Danyl wrapped his cloak around the blanket that covered her. Ramira felt Danyl's arms around her and the thumping of his heart. She heard her companions speaking of finding shelter from the threatening storm. The nervousness in their voices penetrated her semi-conscious mind and yanked her to consciousness.

They halted within a cluster of pines and stared at a dingy inn a short distance ahead. An enclosed porch fronted the weathered L-shaped building; a covered walkway in need of repair led to the barn. The ground in front was devoid of grass. Lights shone through the thickly paned front windows and from one of the upstairs rooms; they could hear neighing from the barn.

"We are out of options…and time," said Seven flipping his hood up to ward off the sleet beginning to fall.

The dwarf king glanced at Allad and frowned. The Herkah needed his wounds attended to as soon as possible, as did a slouching Ramira.

"There doesn't seem to be too much activity," Lance said, his breath screening his face.

"Go down and find out," ordered Danyl.

Danyl held the reins in one hand while keeping Ramira upright with the other. The prince glanced over at Cricket, whose frightened gaze briefly met his. He offered her a little smile of encouragement but the young girl's fear and confusion would not abate. Cricket stared at Ramira then at the elf.

Seven understood Cricket's response to Danyl's genuine affection. He felt sorry for the young girl who grew up without any loving guidance.

"I think we are going to be kept inside for several days."

"Maybe," she muttered.

"It'll be nice to sit in front of a fire with a full belly, a drop or two of ale, and a stack of winnings from a card game."

"There is no card game I can't win," she stated, her focus drawn away from Danyl and Ramira.

"Are you challenging me?" asked the king.

"Maybe."

"Such a young thing like you can't play anything but easy games."

"I've taken my share of coins," she rebutted, the dwarf's dare too much for her to ignore.

"Name your stakes," he chuckled.

"What have you got?"

Seven laughed for the girl had no idea she rode with a king, two princes, a Lord, a high-ranking captain, and a magic sought by the most evil of all creatures in the land. Seven liked the girl's pluck and the way she tried to hide her fragility behind a veil of bravado. He shrugged, for most young people her age did the same but she did it in a very endearing way. Her infatuation with Danyl would, hopefully, be short lived.

"I'll be able to tell you when I search through my pockets."

She was about to answer when Lance returned.

"There are many rooms available," he began, "and few people about. There is a group of four already in the tavern and another pair securing their horses in the barn."

"What did you tell them?" asked Danyl.

"Seven seek shelter. They demanded payment up front for one night and everything else would be extra."

"Not very trustworthy, are they?" grumbled Gard.

"Many don't pay in these parts," Cricket stated quietly from behind the dwarf king.

Snow and sleet began to fall more heavily.

"I think we should be safe for a day or two…at least while the storm lasts," said Gard.

"Then we should get going before we die in this snowstorm," warned Danyl while urging his mount down into the hollow.

Lance and Gard took their horses to the barn while the others entered the inn. The four other travelers were eating, the scrutiny of both groups brief yet thorough. The rotund innkeeper with the filthy apron welcomed them, the coins he was about to make already jingling in his mind. His mate, a tired looking woman with a long face, came out from the kitchen wiping her hands on towel. She eyed the extra mouths she would have to feed. She gave them a wan smile and invited them to a table in the far corner. The woman returned with plates and silverware just as Lance and Gard walked in and brushed the snow off their cloaks. They hung them to dry by the fireplace. The innkeeper's wife placed a tureen of soup in the middle of the table and a stack of bowls beside it.

"How skilled are you at sewing?" asked Allad gripping his side.

"I once managed to thread a needle after only four tries." Seven squinted while mimicking threading a needle with shaky hands.

"Can you mend my wounds without sewing my tunic into them?"

Allad watched Seven drink down an entire mug of ale then wipe the foam from his upper lip.

"I can now."

Seven and Allad disappeared upstairs, their companions grateful for the hot food and warm shelter. Ramira's stomach growled so loudly that even Gard heard it from across the table. She never looked up while eating or drinking her tea. They ate in silence until the dwarf and nomad rejoined them.

"And?" Danyl asked Allad.

"I will not have to wear this garment for the rest of my life."

They shared a rare moment of laughter, ignoring the sleet hitting the windows and the darkness that had nearly taken them.

"We made it just in time," Gard stated filling his mug with ale.

The howling wind smashed something against the outside wall causing everyone to jump. The wind howled and continued to batter the glass with sleet.

Ramira ate out of necessity though her friends could see food was the farthest thing from her mind. She knew she would have to explain her reasons for leaving the city an act leading to Haban's death and placing all of their lives in great peril.

They ate their fill then sat around the table, the smell of tobacco from Seven's pipe lifting into the air. Allad leaned back in the chair to alleviate some of the pressure on his wounds; Gard rested his chin on fists so tightly clenched his knuckles appeared white. Seven and Danyl were engaged in a discussion concerning their depleted provisions; Lance reminded them of things they had overlooked.

"Good woman," Ramira called to the innkeeper's wife. "A bath, please?"

She crooked her finger and led Ramira to the rear of the inn by the kitchen. The woman handed Ramira a towel and a sliver of soap.

Ramira checked her wounds, grateful none needed stitching. She filled the tub twice before feeling clean enough to sit and soak in the warm water. The only sounds infiltrating the room were muted voices and the clanging of pots from the kitchen across the hall. Ramira quietly mourned Horemb's passing, killing the only link to her past before she could speak with him. Her mind replayed the moment she drove the blades into his chest, the pain exploding within her own heart as nothing but the hilts protruded out.

Horemb had saved her life by drawing away the demon and she had given him his soul back when she executed the Vox. That did little to assuage her guilt. She closed her eyes and allowed the striking snake to fill her mind: it morphed from a hand into a body. It relinquished its hold on her from behind and stood before her.

Horemb's deeply tanned body glistened with sweat; gold armbands covered his bulging upper arms. He wore a loincloth held in place by a leather belt; numerous scars marked his body. He smiled down at her; his powerful hand reached out and cupped her chin. The image began to fade away leaving her alone with a single tear running down her cheek.

Humbled by Horemb's sacrifice, she rose from the cooling water. She washed her clothes and hung them on a clothesline strung behind the massive fireplace. Ramira changed into her spare clothes then walked back to her companions. She sat beside

Seven while Danyl headed for the bathing chamber. She and the elf would go to their room where she would have to explain her actions. The dwarf took her hand in his and squeezed it.

"It's good to see that you are well," he said. "You are as hard to find as my concoction when Clare gets hold of it."

"I'm sorry for all of the trouble I've caused. Why you think I'm worth it is beyond me."

Her companions exchanged knowing glances. She stared from one to the other as a sense of uneasiness began to grip her. Danyl would probably have come after her but not Gard; Allad and Seven might have sent men with the search party while remaining in Bystyn. She glanced at Gard, the unmistakable coldness shining from his eyes confusing her. She turned her attention to Allad. The Herkah held her gaze but kept his sentiments to himself. Her fingers curled more tightly around the king's hand as Danyl strode over to them, the look of betrayal prominent on his face.

The storm raged on; the afternoon as dark and dreary as the night. The other travelers retired to their rooms; the innkeeper and his wife were busy in the back of the building. It was time to plan their return to Bystyn.

"Cricket," whispered the king, "how far west have we come?"

"From what point?" she asked keeping her voice low.

"From the eastern edge of the forest."

"About here," she replied using the boards and cups on the table as reference points. Seven and the others immediately knew they were too far west to cut straight up and onto the plains. If Cricket was even remotely correct, they had to travel several days east then north in case the enemy had infiltrated beyond the first third of the plains. The Vox's presence in this area alluded to that distinct possibility. Mahn knew the Source of Darkness was somewhere here in the south. He would undoubtedly be better prepared the next time the dark magic revealed itself. Would a day or two be sufficient to avoid Mahn and his army marching from the west?

"We should discuss this later," said Lance as two of the other lodgers came downstairs to sit by the fire. Danyl agreed then lightly nudged Ramira. It was time.

Danyl closed the door and immediately embraced her, the contact releasing the pent up frustrations that had plagued them both for so long. She began to cry; he encouraged her to purge the darkness gripping her heart and soul. Ramira finally ran out of tears and readied herself for the questions he was sure to ask. He did not speak right away, tending instead to the cuts inflicted by the Vox.

"I cannot begin to apologize enough for the trouble I've caused."

"What made you leave?"

He listened to her recount the whispers and the empty promises made by the unknown voices; her nightmares filled him with revulsion. They clung to each other as she told him about her flight from Bystyn. Then quietly, almost reverently, she told him about Horemb. He heard the respect and love in her voice and held her more closely while she mourned his passing. The bearer of the most appalling of all powers in the land trembled in his arms and begged for his forgiveness. He had two truths to tell her and wondered what they would do to her and to them.

"Ramira," he lifted her chin so he could look into her eyes, "I know why those things have been happening. You house the Source of Darkness. Mahn is hunting for you. He drove you from the city to make it easier for him to get it."

Her mouth opened in disbelief. The idea that she was the cause of all of the death and destruction was too much for her to bear. In essence, her dreams had revealed the truth and her friends, knowing the danger, came for her anyway. She felt his arms around her, holding her close as she grappled with the awful truth. Ramira lay her head on his shoulder and stared unblinking at the worn wall behind them. She did not deserve such loyalty and dropped her head in shame.

"You shouldn't have come looking for me, Danyl. Now you are in even greater peril than before."

"Things will get worse whether we are here or back in

256

Bystyn, Ramira, the only difference is the Green Might will be able to keep Mahn at bay."

"You've found it?" she asked.

The second truth was about to be revealed. She believed Mahn would obtain Danyl's power through her and would do anything to keep that from happening. She avoided him back in Bystyn because he was a prince: what would she do once she found out he had the magic? He took a deep breath and made her look into his eyes.

"Yes. I'm the bearer," he said quietly.

"You?!"

Ramira stared at the elf then tried to break the contact between them. His grip remained tight, loosening only when she began to relent.

"Yes. Ramira, the others know about you but not about me and it is best that we keep this between us."

"Is the city vulnerable now that you aren't there?"

"I think Mahn is so intent on finding you that Bystyn is the least of his concerns right now. It is, however, important that we get back as soon as possible."

"That's why you were able to save me from the demons after the Kreetch poisoned me, isn't it?"

"Yes. Your power ignited mine and it protected and guided me when I searched for you. If you hadn't been poisoned then who knows when the Green Might would have awakened."

Ramira intertwined her fingers with his while absorbing the truth of his words. She now understood what that strange sensation was that surged upward whenever they embraced.

"Things would be very different had you not heeded my cries for help or chosen not to follow me to Bystyn. Fate, it seems, is intent on keeping us together and I, for one, am grateful for it."

"You should be angry with me, Danyl," she said in a small voice.

"I'm not angry, Ramira, just terrified of losing you. Promise me you won't run away again or use the Source of Darkness?"

"I won't disappear and I don't even know how to wield the power."

"If you brandish it like you do your knives then...."

She gazed up at him, the innocent appeal to shield her from the evil an arduous task, but one he was willing to accept. He kissed her forehead then tenderly traced the contours of her face with his finger. He offered her his quiet reassurance while she wrestled with the truths he had confessed. He somehow knew she would draw on her inner strength and courage to accept what had befallen them, then place her trust in the bond they shared.

"Danyl?"

"Yes?"

"No matter what the future holds for us, I want you to know that I love you and I would never do anything to hurt you or anyone else. I don't know why I am the one that holds the dark magic, but I do know that I won't let him take it. This I swear to you here and now."

"We all trust you, Ramira, and if we can't have faith in each other than Mahn has already won. As to your love..." he leaned forward and gently kissed her, the need for her closeness greater now than before.

They both understood she was a danger to them all but, with her return to Bystyn she would at least be out of Mahn's grasp. He would come for her. The only thing hampering the immediate dispatch of more Vox was the weather. It would hinder both the pursued and the pursuers. What would happen once they reached the plains on the other side of the forest?

Zada, he was sure, had 'seen' the confrontation and would have informed his father and the others about it. The most logical thing to do would be to send patrols to specific areas from where they might emerge. What if they came out miles away and needed immediate help? All they could do was head back to the city as quickly as possible and hope for the best along the way. If they encountered any more Vox between now and then, they would have to rely on Allad's and Ramira's talents. They lay down on the bed together, the elf holding her tightly against him. She shivered beneath the blanket; her eyelids slowly closed. Danyl fared little better. An undercurrent of need flowed from one to the other. Their union was brief, an antidote for the emptiness

258

that had haunted them for the past several weeks. The Green Might and the Source of Darkness merged then separated, leaving a twinkling silver grain in their wake.

~

Seven quietly entered the room with Cricket and walked over to the sleeping pair. The peaceful looks on their faces tugged at his heart. He missed Clare and envisioned himself curled up beside her. The dwarf king rubbed his tired face then pulled the blankets up over their shoulders. The dwarf steered Cricket to the corner bed and patted her affectionately on the head before sitting down in front of the fireplace. Allad opened the connecting door between the rooms and glanced at Danyl and Ramira. The king noticed the imperceptible nod of his head and invited him to sit in front of the fire with him.

"I wish we had some news about what is happening in Bystyn," said Seven pouring them each a cup of ale.

"Unfortunately we are blind, Seven, and must therefore make more assumptions than is advisable."

"How much could have happened in the time we were gone?" asked the dwarf king.

"How much indeed?"

Allad glanced past Cricket, who stood in front of the window looking out into the dismal storm. Bits of sleet whipped against the panes, hurled about by the wind as the blizzard brought this part of the land to a standstill. At least they would be able to rest properly for a couple of days. They might need the extra energy for the return trip. How far had Mahn advanced upon the city during the time they were away? The Vox were already far to the east in the southern portion of the land. They scoured the area for the Source of Darkness and strategic advantages. Mahn would attack from the west and the south. He said as much to Seven, who agreed with his assessment.

"That would make the most sense. Will he be able to get enough bodies to do that?"

"The only thing he lacks the most are Vox," replied the nomad.

"Well, he lost two and was denied two…I'd say we were most fortunate, wouldn't you?"

"Absolutely, my friend. I know I am pleased to be sitting across from you right now."

Both knew fortune would not always smile on them. Allad checked his injuries while the dwarf king stared off into the distance. His face suddenly lit up; a wry grin spread across his weathered features.

"Here."

The king poured them both a small amount of his potion from a flask he pulled out of his tunic pocket. The Herkah shook his head and chuckled softly; they raised their glasses to one another and then swallowed the drink in one gulp.

"Did you sneak this out while Clare wasn't looking?"

"No, my friend," he grinned then refilled their glasses. "My sweet love packed it for me."

"She did, did she?"

"Yes, but I packed these!" he confessed while lifting the flap on his pack. A half dozen more flasks were carefully wrapped and securely tucked away within it

"I've seen babies with less swaddling," stated the nomad with a stifled laugh.

"Drink up, Allad, and get a good night's sleep. We all could use one."

The king finished his drink, grabbed his blanket, and followed Allad into the adjoining room. Cricket stared at Danyl and Ramira for a while, the tinge of disappointment eventually vanishing from her face.

~

Alyxandyr finished reading the stack of reports then toss the last one onto his desk. Mahn was already marching toward Bystyn even though he did not possess the Source of Darkness. The demons had ravaged everything in their path; those they had not slain hid in the forests surrounding their homes. They had lost four entire patrols and the city teemed with people. The elven king knew chaos was their worst enemy. He and the other rulers made it clear that anyone found guilty of inciting disorder would meet with the harshest of punishments. Alyxandyr looked up as Nyk, Styph, Mason, Zada, and Clare entered his private chambers.

"Any more visions, Zada?" he asked

She shook her head. He watched Mason unroll a map, placing objects on its corners to keep it from curling back up.

"What did you see regarding their surroundings, Zada?" inquired the First Advisor.

"Rolling hills…lots of boulders…it was cold because I saw their breath. That's all."

"That would put them in this general area," said Styph pointing to the map. "There's nothing in that region except towns filled with thieves, murderers and the like."

"We know that Mahn's army was spotted here," the king indicated an area with his index finger, "and that it has reached the hollows."

"We lost a patrol here," Styph pointed slightly west of the hollows. "So for now that would be his farthest push east."

"It's a two or three day ride from the northern fringes of the forest to the gates. They still have to get through the woods," explained Mason. "We can't help them until they get to the plains, and even then they might be too far west for us to be of any significant aid."

"Mahn knows he has lost two of his Vox and that the Source of Darkness is in the area. He will send more demons to find them, probably Radir for he cannot chance losing any more Vox. The Radir are not as powerful as the Vox, but they blend in better with their surroundings and can be more easily replaced," stated Zada.

"Exactly who or what are these Radir?"

"They are flesh and blood men who are under Mahn's influence, Seven."

"Not full of poison like the Kreetch?"

"No, Styph, and they cannot possess like the Vox."

"Then Allad and Ramira will be even busier fighting them," muttered Alyxandyr.

"Not really, Alyx. They are formidable but can be killed by the others."

The noose was tightening around their necks, and their only way of defeating Mahn was roaming around in the southlands. It was imperative Danyl and Ramira return to Bystyn before the enemy cut them off. The allies had lost control of half the plains to the west, making it difficult to gather information and plan reprisals against Mahn.

The elven king studied the map. He followed Mahn's progress westward to Kepracarn. Mahn originated from somewhere in the desert; he used Cooper's city as his base of operations. Alyxandyr cocked his head to the side, envisioning how he would attack Bystyn. The elven king would spread his armies to the northeast and southeast, effectively surrounding then isolating the city. There had to be a weakness, though. There always was. Perhaps Cooper had some information that could help them. Alyxandyr sent four Herkahs to bring the king to his chambers, much to the dismay of those gathered.

"I hope you have everything you require," Alyxandyr greeted the king. He offered Cooper a glass of wine and then waved him to a seat.

"Actually, my treatment is better than I had anticipated," he replied.

He lifted his glass to those gathered in the chamber. Cooper ignored their cold responses but took note of who was not in attendance.

"Is there anything else you can tell us about Mahn?" Alyxandyr asked.

"A few of your kind came out of that hole, too." He glanced at Zada, who impaled him with her hard gaze.

"'Your kind'…what do you mean by that?" demanded the Herkah.

"Vox."

Cooper shuddered inwardly at the thought of either Allad or Zada as demons, especially Allad. The Herkah was a formidable enough foe without the added impetus of a demon controlling his highly skilled body.

"How many, Cooper?" demanded the elven king.

"I'm not sure…a dozen, perhaps a few more."

"How many guarded you in Kepracarn?" inquired Styph.

"Two…two others escorted me out the gates."

"We've lost six of our people in the past few years," said Zada. "I can't imagine where he'd get the others from."

"Are there small groups of Herkahs living away from the tribe?" Mason asked.

"Not to my knowledge."

"There are two fewer Vox to contend with," stated Alyxandyr.

~

Cooper stared into his glass, the interrogation demeaning but necessary. He hoped he could discern things from them to advance his own cause. They did not have a chance against Mahn even if he didn't control the power he sought. It dawned on him that they were waiting for him to acknowledge something. The king shifted in his seat then re-crossed his ankles. Where were the other leaders? Clare was here but not Seven. Allad was absent as were Danyl and Gard. One or maybe two might be ill or off on some errand, but all four? In addition, what did the elven king mean when he said there were two fewer Vox in the land? Who could possibly have killed those monsters?

"What's going on?" His voice was laced with suspicion.

"What do you mean?"

"Don't trifle with me, Alyxandyr." Cooper's anger rose up from deep within him.

"What is it that you wish to know?"

"Where are Danyl, Seven, Allad, and the Khadry prince?"

"They are currently busy with various duties," stated the king pouring himself a goblet of wine. "Why do you ask?"

Cooper knew his chances of acquiring Bystyn as payment for his allegiance with Mahn were non-existent; allying himself with the elves galled him. He would share in the elves' and their allies' fates. There was nothing to gain no matter where he placed his fealty, an entirely unknown situation for him. Cooper knew death waited for him in the end. The king decided to play his hand and hoped he could bluff his way out of his situation.

"Are they out looking for the Source of Darkness?"

"Why would they be looking for the Source of Darkness?" inquired Alyxandyr.

"Is it nearby? You have it, don't you?" His mind began to establish a variety of scenarios.

"We do not."

"But you know where it is."

"We do not," repeated the elven king.

"Where are they, Alyxandyr?"

Cooper saw the concern flicker in the elven king's eyes, a reaction shared by the others. Cooper felt a stab of panic in his chest. The only way to beat Mahn and save his own skin was to wield the Source of Darkness.

"Alyxandyr, Mahn is also searching for the Source of Darkness and will destroy everything if he obtains it. Now, where are they?"

"At what point did you become the inquisitor?" Styph's voice was steeped in rage.

"When my life became an issue."

"Why should I tell you anything? What could you possibly reveal to us that would help our situation?" inquired the king.

"Because the last thing I want is to become like them!" he hissed between his teeth and pointed to the west.

Those gathered stared hard at the undisguised candor in his voice and on his face. None of them wanted to become a tortured tool of the evil, either.

"What do you know?" the king persisted, his patience wearing thin.

"Mahn sent a contingent of demons south then east through the southern forest when he released me. Now you."

"We are aware of that, Cooper."

"Mahn has plenty of power."

"We know that."

"He can't use his full might without the dark magic."

"We know that, too," replied the elven king.

"What don't you know?"

"Why all of this is happening."

Cooper had no idea why and suddenly didn't care. His ruse had failed to acquire any information that would help him out of this dilemma. He was tired of everything and wanted nothing more than to return to his prison and sleep. Would he have been better off had he made a pact with Mahn like Antama had? The red mist engulfing her filled his mind and re-ignited his hatred for her.

"Cooper?" Mason's voice cut into his thoughts like a knife.

The king glared at his brother.

"Antama made a bargain with Mahn. I think the crimson haze might have been yet another fiend."

"Something else to contend with," muttered Styph.

"So it seems," replied Cooper. He drained his glass and set it on the table. "I'd like to leave now."

Alyxandyr eyed Cooper and saw a king bereft of his kingdom. Mahn would have wrested away all Cooper had, regardless of how intelligent the king. The evil could not have inflicted a greater emotional and mental pain upon him. Cooper deserved to be humbled, but not in this fashion. Alyxandyr nodded at the Herkahs, escorted him back to his room.

"Antama finally found her road to power," stated Mason. "Her knowledge, fighting skills, and lack of remorse makes her a menacing foe. I am not surprised that she allied herself with Mahn."

"I don't think anyone 'allies' themselves with Mahn, Mason. I believe he has some use for her at some point," replied Zada.

She was at a loss to explain this red demon, for she had never sensed it before. What else arose from that foul hole?

"We all have much work to do if we are to survive," said the elven king rising from his seat. The others followed suit and silently resumed their duties.

~

Mahn reviewed his army standing silently before him from atop a mammoth black horse. The Vox lingered along the edges of the huge group like dogs keeping a flock of sheep in line. They all waited for the signal to march east. Mahn wondered what had killed the two Vox he had sent in search of the Source of Darkness. He had sensed no magic, only an increase in exertion then a sudden separation from them. That meant there was someone out there with the capacity to beat them in combat. This unexpected revelation troubled him, but not enough to alter his plans. The third Vox was already in place and would remain there until the fighting began. It had only one purpose, one that would devastate the hated Herkahs. A low hiss of satisfaction issued forth from the cowl as he imagined the Vox completing his task.

Mahn opened his mind and scanned the land for any magic. There was nothing, not even a flicker of green from the city. The elven magic had flared briefly; its current dormancy since the dark magic departed the city mystified him. He tapped the pommel of his saddle with a gloved finger, the blackness issuing from his cowl pointing in Bystyn's direction. Mahn converged all of his appalling energy into a point and let it fly straight into the heart of Bystyn. The arrow of darkness darted past trees, over the cold ground and then up the main avenue to the castle. It sliced through the thick oaken doors and up the staircase, impaling Zada with its despicable barb. Mahn sneered with pleasure as he watched the Herkah witch clutch at her chest and gasp for air. Her face turned nearly purple and, as his power dissolved, she collapsed in a heap. Mahn refrained from using his unseasoned might too soon.

The Green Might, however, did not respond to his probing. It remained silent, almost uninterested in his attack on the city. It did not matter because the elven magic alone could not harm him, especially if he had the Source of Darkness. Besides, he planned on extracting the Green Might from the bearer and adding it to his own. The thought of so much power fine-tuned his senses. He could hear his army breathing and smell their sweat. He focused on their vacant faces; every pore was as deep as a crater and every hair as tall as a tree. Their leather jerkins creaked loudly in his ears. He sensed the souls imprisoned by the demons, their silent cries echoing hollowly within their bodies. They all yearned for death, an end he was not yet about to grant. Soon he would have scores more to torment, an eternity of spirits to break.

He nodded toward the Vox; they herded the vast army east while he followed behind them. The weather was cooperating but he sensed it would soon change. Mahn was unconcerned for the black horde spreading out before him like some hideous disease. They would drive on, heedless of hunger or exhaustion. He turned toward an approaching Vox.

"The Radir are in the forefront," it wheezed, then rode back to the army.

Mahn was pleased. The first wave of his army would inflict a great deal of damage on the defenders. He relished the thought of demonizing them and the ensuing pandemonium that would erupt in the city. Such a plan would have a devastating effect on the others and would stir up old animosities amongst the races. It would be difficult enough for the allies to fight his army without the added burden of cutting down their own men. Mahn pictured the turmoil that would cause and wished that moment was already here.

"Soon enough," he hissed with satisfaction.

~

They met for the morning meal at the same table as the previous evening the storm still raged outside. Two men seated on the other side of the room spoke in low tones with each other; the other two were absent. Allad and Seven returned from checking on their horses. The woman placed fresh bread, cheese, and a variety of sliced meats on the table then refilled the teapot. The innkeeper brought in armfuls of wood for the fire.

"It felt great to sleep in a bed," said Seven helping himself to the food.

"I think you'll get the chance to do that for at least one more night," Allad informed him. "This storm won't stop before late afternoon."

"That didn't hinder two of our friends from leaving early this morning. Must have been a damn good reason to go out in this weather," said Seven.

"We'll have to be extra vigilant, won't we?" said Danyl.

"I asked the innkeeper about acquiring some supplies," Allad stated while reaching for another slice of bread. "He told me he could spare maybe a few days' worth if we were willing to pay for them."

"I expected nothing less," muttered Danyl as he placed his fingers around his mug for warmth.

"Do you think the weather has affected Bystyn?" the nomad asked the prince.

"No. The storms usually swing northward. The last place I'd like to be is outside the city when the weather does change."

"Perhaps we can leave if this clears up in the early afternoon," suggested Seven. "I know we'd all like to get back as soon as possible."

"I agree," said Gard. "It'll be difficult traveling regardless of when we leave."

They kept themselves occupied most of the morning while they waited for the weather to break. Danyl and Ramira managed some private time together while the others remained downstairs. The ever-present Lance guarded them in the hallway. It began to get lighter late in the morning; the snow finally stopped around midday. The rested and provisioned company headed out. Thoughts of seeing the gray walls of Bystyn filled all their minds. The group saw no other travelers during the afternoon and decided to head in a northeasterly direction back toward the city. They spoke very little, keeping a sharp watch on their surroundings. The companions continued until the sun began to set the dirty gray clouds stretched across the horizon. They made camp along a small hill.

Ramira hesitated when Danyl held up the corner of his blanket. She still felt guilty for putting them all in jeopardy but the elf insisted and she complied. Their nearness reassured each other.

"I'm going to lock you in my chambers when we get back to Bystyn," he whispered in her ear.

"Wouldn't a mad woman with a pair of knives make you think twice about that?"

"I'd take them away from you."

"You'd still have to contend with my madness."

"True."

They were both quiet for a few minutes.

"Danyl?" she whispered.

"Yes?"

"Can the two of us go away together when this is all over?"

"I think that can be arranged," he replied pulling her closer.

Seven rested his head on his hands; he studied his companions. Danyl and Ramira were where they belonged-together; Gard and Allad were guarding them from somewhere in the shadows. Cricket, he noted, had been watching the pair but soon grew either too tired or resentful and turned her back on them. The prince undoubtedly elicited a variety of feelings from the young girl, emotions she had never known. He guessed she was about Anci's age. The king wondered if they were bringing her to an immediate death. There were going to be some very frightening and trying days ahead of them. If they managed to get back to Bystyn with Ramira, at least they would have some chance against the evil. If they failed or if Mahn took her, then all they could do was to fight and hope for a miracle.

Was there anything about her magic that predicted how it was to be used? Mahn, after all, was destructive, but Ramira, who held the power within her, was not. Granted, the young woman could destroy demons in a way that was alarming even to a seasoned veteran like himself. Her loyalties, however, were not in doubt. She had not abandoned them; she had left because the voices threatened to demolish the city and all those who lived within it. She believed she was distracting Mahn away from those she loved. Did that mean the magic she held reflected what was in her heart? If the Source of Darkness were a malevolent power, would not that evil somehow taint her heart and soul? Seven knew individuals steeped in corruption that showed no signs of guilt or remorse. They could also never love. He saw the love Ramira held for them all. Seven rolled onto his back and stared at the intertwining branches. Each tree was capable of supporting itself, but an entire forest of trees could provide comfort for a myriad of creatures. The strength of the oaks and the graceful birches would stand beside the fragrant pines and the sturdy maples. Seven liked being a part of the forest.

~

They resumed their trek at dawn. The companions picked their way over fields of boulders and through broad stands of hardwoods. They stayed hidden amongst the plant growth as they passed by a house to their left. They heard pigs squealing and cows lowing near where smoke curled out of a chimney visible above the treetops. Chickens squawked with indignation as something chased them around the yard, the excited barking of a dog pointing to a likely culprit. A woman called out and moments later children answered from a distance. The noises became indistinct then faded away as they maneuvered past hedges festooned with fat red berries.

Seven plucked one from a branch and immediately regretted doing so. The berry was sticky and it took several quick flicks of his wrist to get rid of it. He watched the berry arc gracefully then land on an unsuspecting Allad. Cricket shook her head and smirked at the dwarf king, who held his stained finger to his lips. He winked at her then shrugged his shoulders when Danyl glanced over at him.

"Behave or I'll tell Clare," Danyl playfully whispered to him.

They stopped at the edge of the haphazard row of shrubs and stared at the dark canopy on the horizon to the north. The forest separating the elven lands from the south appeared like a smudged line of green and brown; it stretched in a straight line from the east to the west. Barring any unforeseen problems and with a little luck, they would be on the other side within a day or two.

"Danyl," Lance warned.

"I see them, Lance. Remember we are just a lowly group of travelers."

They rode on, casually glancing at the approaching men and silently cursing their imminent arrival. They would be outnumbered two to one if forced to fight. He recognized some of the men; Cricket's whimper confirmed his suspicions as she pressed her face into his back. The strangers continued to angle toward them. The large man reined in his horse several yards away and nodded tersely at Lance; his eyes glittered dangerously.

"We meet again," said Lance.

"So it seems," he replied then spat on the ground, the brownish stain stark against the snow. A lecherous look crossed his features when he saw Ramira, who glared defiantly back at him.

Ramira studied his men, staring hard from one to the other. Her hands snaked down to her blades, the sudden sensation to hunt overwhelming her. Her companions and the men wondered what she was looking for, but only the former knew: demons. Ramira fixed her attention on two men at the rear of the group. Their coarse smugness was indistinguishable from the other men. It took every ounce of willpower to keep her hands from instinctively sliding out her knives.

"What do you want this time?"

"Who's behind the elf?" demanded the man.

"A fellow companion."

"I'd like to meet this 'companion'."

"I don't think so."

"You gonna stop me?" he barked at Lance then urged his horse forward.

Ramira intercepted him. "I will," she warned pulling back the edges of her cloak.

The man laughed at her.

"Not likely," he replied reaching over to grab her.

He winced in pain as she swung her blades up and across his hands, the motion so swift all anyone saw was a streak of black. The sound of metal scraping against scabbards filled the air.

"If that's the little thief then you will all die," he growled as he and the men converged on them.

The company formed a loose circle and faced outward; the clanging of steel on steel echoed beneath the milky sky. The men realized that they faced well-trained warriors; their numbers meant nothing to their adversaries. They decided this battle would not fall in their favor, and hastily retreated. Ramira waited for the demon to dismount and approach her.

"Vox, Allad?" asked Seven in hushed tones.

"No, Seven, Radir. Don't Danyl," he cautioned the prince who moved toward Ramira.

She threw her cloak over the saddle then unsheathed her knives. The nomad took his outer garments off as he readied himself to help her if she needed him.

The Radir was a demon with characteristics of both the Vox and the Kreetch. Although able to occupy and properly use its host, it stayed unrestrained like the Kreetch. This demon abandoned the normal movements of the body it occupied and began to flail and slash at Ramira with glee before she killed it. She turned toward her horse when a form flew at her from behind a cluster of boulders. A third appeared from within the hedges to their right. Allad immediately intervened and dispatched it. She slew the third Radir in rapid fashion, but not quickly enough to dodge the sword it swung at her. The weapon glanced along her side, slicing through her tunic into her flesh. Ramira shook off their concern and hurried to her mount. They raced as one for the dark line of trees that were still too far away.

So many demons in this part of the land meant that the forest could be teeming with them as well. Time, they knew, was running out for them. They had many miles to go before they passed through the woods and onto elven lands. What, they wondered, would they find on the other side? The companions urged their mounts on, not stopping until early afternoon and only then because the animals were exhausted. They rubbed them down then rested for a spell; three pairs of eyes continuously scrutinized everything around them.

"Radir can be slain by anyone skilled with a weapon," explained Allad. "The best way to slay them is by slitting their throats."

"I've seen men like that in the town," Cricket said in a small voice. "I just thought they were the crazy sort and avoided them."

Cricket remembered seeing them scattered in the city, shunning everyone, even each other. Their faces were vacant but something lurked just beneath the surface of their skin, something that warned her to stay away from them.

"They were in your town before we met?" asked Danyl.

"Yes, for about a month or so."

Seven exhaled sharply. If they were already prevalent in these parts then the companions would stumble across more of them before they got back to Bystyn. Their trip through the forest would be an interesting one to say the least. Their choices, however, were limited. They had to take a chance and follow the most direct route back. At least they could fight the Radir and not depend upon Allad and Ramira to do the work for them.

Gard kept his anger for Ramira locked away. They were in this predicament because she had fled the city. Granted, they would be taking back a great deal of information, but it did not appear as though they were going to make it to Bystyn. She had what the evil wanted. Why not let her unleash her might and destroy him? She was unwillingly enticing him to the very gates of the city; Mahn would rip apart every wall to get to her, killing many along the way. The odds of their demise had increased dramatically over the past few days. And for what? To protect one form of evil from an even greater one? What if she needed to be slain? He was the only one in the group who would drive his sword into her. Gard's dark expression focused on Ramira. He noticed Allad staring at him; Gard turned away and finished adjusting his saddle.

They rode for several hours then rested for one, the pattern never varying until the forest loomed ahead of them. An undulating mist concealed the roots and prevented the group from seeing very far into the woods. The prospect of riding within that eerie labyrinth was not a pleasant one.

"This feels wrong," stated Gard.

"I agree," replied Lance. "We could follow the same route north."

"A good suggestion but a bad idea," said Allad.

The Herkah pointed toward a band of riders heading in the direction Lance had indicated. It was becoming very crowded in this area. The drab, homespun clothing and large horses identified them as men similar to Cricket's pursuers. They could also be part of Mahn's conscripted army. The companions wanted no part of either one.

"I get the distinct feeling we are being hunted," Danyl stated while watching the riders head south toward Cricket's town.

"They might have been alerted by the two men that disappeared from the inn," suggested Lance.

"Those 'men' could have been Radir," stated Allad.

"They could have been a lot of things, none of which I care to think about so far from home," Danyl muttered aloud.

"Cricket? Are there normally so many people traveling in these parts this time of year?" asked the king.

"No."

"Well, trap or not, we have to get to the plains," said Danyl looking across the now empty area. "Let's go."

They surged forward, watchful of every tree and cluster of rocks as they raced toward the dark line of trees. The fog seemed to writhe the closer they came until the rising sun burned it away. Its departure was not reassuring, but at least they would be able to see what littered the ground while riding through the woods. They entered the outer ring of trees and were immediately aware of the silence. Nothing flew or scampered out of their way as they continued through the unusual stillness. The only sound was the muffled hoof beats as they galloped over the terrain. Cricket was terrified and clung to Danyl; everyone peered nervously into the murky shadows for any signs of danger. It did not take long to reach the center of the woods; this end of the forest was no more than a few miles wide. Gard, the most experienced tracker, chose the fastest way to the plains. They had been riding for little more than an hour when the trees began to thin out ahead. A brief surge of relief washed over them for the elven lands were only a short ride away. A rustling sound on their left caught their attention; it arose from their right moments later. A renewed sense of urgency spurred them on.

Shadows darted amongst the trees, appearing then disappearing at will from every direction except from in front of them. All they could do was hope to outrun the specters. The phantoms could have confronted and annihilated them within the woods, yet chose not to.

"Don't stop and do not get separated from each other!" shouted Gard as the forest gave way to the plains.

Ghostly riders moved out from within the darkness of the trees and converged on the company. The companions' tired horses could not outrun the fresh mounts waiting for them on the plains. Fighting such a large host was out of the question. There were wider swatches of open ground around the trees now and the nervous horses, sensing this change, began to accelerate. They hurdled over the occasional fallen trunk or clump of bushes to escape the threat, needing little prodding from their riders. The plains gave the companions a renewed sense of hope, an optimism that was, unfortunately, short-lived.

They burst through the last line of trees and finally rode onto the snowy plains. To their dismay, a line of black garbed riders surged toward them from the west, forcing them to angle farther to the east.

Cricket clung to Danyl; she stared wide-eyed at the black horde closing in on them. She saw the grim determination chiseled on her friends' faces; their free hands rested on their swords. Panic began to grow in her stomach as the cold reality of their predicament took root in her heart. She had seen much death and despair in her short life but nothing like this. These things were unlike anything she had ever seen before. All she could do was to place her trust in the people around her, and pray that a miracle would save them.

Gard cursed under his breath. Outnumbered and atop tired horses, the group from Bystyn was riding to their death. No, there was one option, although that was the very thing that gave them a chance of defeating the evil…or was it? He glanced over at Ramira: a fierce resolve glittered from her eyes. She looked past him at the advancing enemy, her features blazing with the same coldness she bestowed upon the demons. Awe and dread paralyzed Gard as invisible ripples of energy radiated off her. It reminded him of the electrical current in the air before an impending storm. He second-guessed his desire for her to wield the Source of Darkness, but what choice did they have?

Ramira realized time was running out for them. There were too many to fight and the horses were already lathering down their necks and across their legs. She had to do it…she had no choice. She closed her eyes, daring to face that which existed deep inside of her. It responded by pulsing to life and filling her mind with an image that lasted no more than a few seconds…

She stood on a balcony overlooking the sparkling white sands. The full moon ignited them until she gazed upon a sea of shimmering diamonds, amethysts, and sapphires. She was naked; the cool night air blew across her skin. Three different hands rested lightly upon her shoulders.

The moment has arrived, Ramira, for what you wield will reflect what is in your heart. Will your fire be black or will it be amethyst…

Ramira knew Mahn would swoop down and snatch her away if she used the Source of Darkness. Not using it would insure a fate worse than death for her friends. Protecting the Green Might was crucial. Even if Mahn were to take her, he would still need time to move his army across the plains and to wrest the Source of Darkness from her. That, she swore, would be no easy task. Ramira inhaled deeply and prayed that she was doing the right thing.

Ramira caught Lance's attention and motioned for him to keep riding. The captain stared hard at her then realized she was going to confront their pursuers. He was about to protest but the look on her face forbade any argument. She conveyed the same thought to Allad. The nomad opened his mouth to object but she had already reined in her exhausted horse. The group had ridden about a quarter mile before Danyl noticed her facing the oncoming horde. The thundering hooves approaching her muffled his horrified shouts. She removed her gloves and cloak then summoned the power.

The darkness and stillness within alarmed her. If she could not coax the Source of Darkness to life, then they were all lost.

She searched frantically for it and finally sensed a faint pulsing deep inside her soul. She fervently hoped that it would not betray her as she roused the slumbering power to life. Ramira gathered her courage to confront the Source of Darkness and was shocked at how benign it appeared. She had expected a raging vortex, not the subtle emanations from an innocuous ember. She reached out and touched it, the immediate reaction unsettling her to her core…

The dark magic sprang to life in her midsection; it felt as if she had swallowed an entire skin of Seven's concoction. It spread outward to her arms and legs then up into her head. Its heat threatened to burn the flesh from her bones. The Source of Darkness blinded her and, when she was able to see again, watched the black garbed riders approach her in slow motion. Their mantles billowed up behind them like great black sails while clumps of frozen snow and sod, kicked up by their horses, arched sluggishly behind them. The sound of hooves striking the hard earth echoed hollowly in her ears, and matched the rhythm of her pounding heart. Ramira dared not turn around and look at her companions, especially Danyl. She planted her feet firmly on the ground and brought the palms of her hands together. What color will the Source of Darkness be? Black or amethyst? Ramira took a deep breath and let the fire explode into the onrushing riders; the power blinded her.

I am not like you! She silently declared.

~

Danyl howled with fury. The very thing they had tried to avoid was happening. She had promised not to use the power and had broken that vow. He had to intervene before her fire became a beacon for Mahn. The roar of thunder accompanying the dazzling light drowned out his cries. It never occurred to him to use the Green Might, which remained idle deep within his soul. It took the combined efforts of Lance, Gard, and Allad to hold him fast while they watched her face the enemy alone. They shielded their eyes from the brilliant lavender fire that ripped into and disintegrated their foes.

277

Zada collapsed as the Source of Darkness tore into her inner sight, its potency stealing her breath. The Herkah felt the eruption scorch every fiber of her being even at this distance. Zada sensed the ancient powers responding to it, rising like mammoth waves from the recesses of time. She slid to the tiled floor in shock. An attendant shouted for help, then tried to prop the nomad up against the wall. He instantly backed away when her vision burned into his mind. Fear and awe flashed across his features but he did not abandon the Herkah. Seconds later Styph, Clare, and Mason crouched down beside her. Zada's shocked features portended grave news.

"She used it…"

"What?" asked Mason.

Zada shuddered as the dismal mist raced over the miles to the coveted prize. She sensed the triumph within that horrible fog and winced as it closed the distance. Mahn's search for the ultimate treasure, and their destiny, was over.

"Ramira wielded the Source of Darkness and Mahn is speeding across the land to get her."

"Sweet mercy," muttered Clare, wiping away the sheen of sweat from Zada's pale face.

Mason's face was ashen. Their survival depended on the company bringing her back to the city.

"Why is she wielding it?" asked Styph.

"She destroyed the riders sent by Mahn…horsemen planning to capture the group on the plains."

Mason nodded. The loss of the dwarven king, the Khadry, the Herkah Lord, and the elven prince would be disastrous. Ramira sacrificed herself so her companions could escape.

~

Ramira dropped to her knees, the unfamiliar power too much for her to bear. It abruptly resumed its place within her soul. She gasped for air while trying to remember the color of her fire. Ramira managed to stand up then turned toward her companions. She needed Danyl to hold her and shield her from the horrible images streaming into her mind. A black cloud sped across the land. Ramira tried to run away from the whirring mass. She managed a few steps before falling hard on her hands and knees. Panic grabbed her as the edges of the buzzing haze reached out and engulfed her. Its repulsive touch was overwhelming. She lapsed into unconsciousness as the black mist carried her away.

~

An odd silence descended upon the land as if the earth itself held its breath. The company gathered around her cloak and gloves. Gard exhaled sharply; Lance continued to scan for danger. The Herkah and dwarf sat speechless in their saddles. Danyl jumped off his exhausted horse and paced back and forth.

Cricket clung to Seven while the others tried to calm the livid prince. Danyl finally quieted down and listened to reason.

"There is nothing we can do for her now, Danyl. We have to get back to Bystyn and prepare for the worst."

"We have to do something, Allad!"

"What shall we do? Ride up to Mahn's gate and demand her back?" retorted the Herkah.

"The only thing worse than having lost the dark magic to Mahn is having our Vox-possessed bodies free to roam within the city," stated the nomad.

"A disagreeable predicament," added Lance.

"We are in grave danger here, Danyl. We must leave," urged the Khadry.

The prince stared down at her things, his mind reeling with possibilities, none of which were pleasant. They were right. He regained control of his emotions, mounted his horse and headed north. They rode well into the night, wanting to put as much distance between themselves and Mahn as possible. They rested for a few hours shortly before midnight and ate the last of their food. Sleep eluded them all. They were up well before dawn, keeping a sharp eye on their surroundings as they rode toward Bystyn. Their goal had been to find and bring Ramira and the Source of Darkness back. It was now in his possession.

Allad and Seven locked gazes then looked at Danyl. The elf

stared ahead; his face was unreadable. The group stopped around mid-morning and rested. Gard passed around the last of their water.

"I could use a few sips of your poison, Seven."

"Soon, my friend, soon," replied the dwarf king tiredly.

"We should be back before sunset," stated Lance. "Danyl?"

"Hmm? Thank you," said the prince taking the canteen from the captain.

They mounted and were on their way again, all of them eager to get back to the city. They journeyed on until they ran across a patrol an hour south of the city. It wasn't long before they saw Bystyn's gray walls looming in front of them. They could now formulate a plan to help Ramira. Danyl's mood, though, remained dark.

PART III

EIGHT

They rode under the gates, ignoring the people welcoming them. They had failed in their quest to bring Ramira back. The horrors encountered along the way added to their sense of foreboding. Even the relieved faces of their friends and families failed to still their trepidation. They exchanged warm embraces then were ushered into the castle.

They ate out of need; they bathed to refresh their filthy and sore bodies. Mason reminded them that Ramira had allowed the heart and soul of those gathered to return unharmed. The members of the company sat glumly at the conference table listening to what had transpired during their absence.

"We must rally around each other," began Alyxandyr. "He has the Source of Darkness, but I sincerely doubt Ramira will simply hand it over."

"How can you be so sure?" demanded Gard.

"Her loathing for his minions is no secret, Gard," Zada said.

"How can you be so sure?" he persisted.

"Because she promised, that's why!" shouted Danyl.

He stood up and challenged the Khadry. She had also agreed not to wield the dark magic or abandon him. Her betrayal still ripped into his heart.

"That's enough!" roared the king, "I will have no bickering!"

Styph and Nyk pushed their brother back down into his seat. Exhaustion stole what little strength the companions had. Alyxandyr sent them to their rooms to rest. Danyl entered his chambers, the very rooms he had threatened to lock Ramira into when they returned. He flopped down on the bed and closed his eyes. The annoying stone maze appeared in his mind...

He tugged violently on the locked doors then banged on them with his fists until his hands bled. He shouted and screamed; the echoes mocked his dilemma. He began to run down the hall, stopping now and then to try the doors but they remained closed. He was lost in a maze that was nothing more than a straight line…

Danyl awoke with a start; his body was covered in sweat. He peered at the bland light seeping in from between the drawn curtains. He exhaled slowly then remembered that Mahn had her. She was gone. He pushed a section of his light brown hair from his forehead then buried his face in his hands. He sat that way for a long time, trying to purge the emotions threatening to overwhelm him. The empty feeling became numb; a tendril of the Green Might reached out to soothe him. Danyl lashed out at it then at himself. Why hadn't he brandished his power to save her? He rose and dressed, then poured himself a cup of water and drank it down in one gulp. The prince needed answers. He headed for the great hall and the tapestry.

He stared up at it, willing it to tell him its secret. The first elven king continued to gaze at him while his people moved on toward their final destination. Alyxandyr was watching someone, of that Danyl was sure. He could see the concentration on the king's face as he strained to peer into the far left corner of the tapestry. Who hid within the vegetation? Who lay concealed within the shadows? He and Karolauren had combed through every possible tome, diary, and list that existed within the library yet never found a single clue.

You are looking too hard.

"What…who's there?" he shouted.

The elf was in no mood for pranks. He saw no one; the voice remained silent. He was tense and tired; his mind played tricks on him. He rubbed his eyes.

You are looking too hard.

Danyl did not speak nor look around the room. He knew the voice existed only inside his mind. Where were the answers he was looking for? Were they with the Historian? Did he overlook something? Did he not listen well enough to his lessons? He realized how similar his and the dead king's features were; both possessed the Green Might. He held his hands up and stared at the palms then turned them over. Ramira had brandished the Source of Darkness with her hands. He closed his eyes and concentrated on the mysterious ember intertwined with his spirit, first willing then begging it to rouse itself. The magic would not budge. He tried repeatedly until he ran out of ways to coax it to ignite. Nothing. He was about to give up when the voice returned.

You think too much.

"I am a descendant of the first king and I house the Green Might: I demand that it fly forth from my hands!"

Do not be arrogant.

"I am not arrogant!"

Danyl dropped to his knees. Who was he to assume he could use the Elven Might at will? He was nothing more than an ordinary person composed of flesh and blood. His only distinction in life was the title before his name; a title passed down through his family and not one he had earned. What he housed was a precious responsibility, one he should honor and respect. He should hold that privilege in the highest regard and not treat his legacy lightly.

Danyl stood in the midst of his ancestors, individuals greater than he ever could aspire to be. He suddenly felt ashamed and wanted to take his contemptuous presence away.

The elf headed for the huge double doors and tried to open them. They would not budge. The lesson was not over. The price turned to face the judgment of the kings and queens of the past. They remained silent yet he could feel their presence everywhere. Their thoughts, emotions, and unfinished deeds hovered in the hall. They no longer walked the land but their spirits, still resonating with their beliefs, prevailed. Their passions were by far the most prevalent traits, guiding them to succeed. He felt them surge around and through him like some unseen wind blowing from a distant place. What was his passion? What made his spirit soar? Up until a few months ago, his obligation to the city was his driving force. Then Ramira entered his life and mirrored his commitment. Their bond strengthened even though she struggled to protect him from her unknown past. The thread binding them together, however, refused to break: love.

Sophie grew to love Ramira and treated her like her own daughter. Seven adored Ramira, as did the slain couple. His own passion for her resided in his soul. Danyl looked at his mother's bust and remembered how animated his father had been while she lived. His love for his people and friends had not abated, but the light that had flared in his heart burned to ash the day she died. Her quiet strength and gentle presence had offered him more courage than he could ever know. Now bereft of her presence, his father faced their terrible fate without her kind-hearted guidance. What would he have to confront without Ramira's presence? Indeed, what would he have to do in Ramira's presence when Mahn brought her to the gates of the city?

You must believe.

He did believe…in her, his friends and family, and in the conviction of those who were about to face their most trying hours. Did he think he would falter when the moment came? He could not afford to fail. Too much was at stake, but what would happen if he did? What would the consequences be if he were unable or incapable of wielding the magic? The great hall began to flicker and dim, replaced by a vision that made his blood run cold…

The great hall was vacant and crumbling. The windows were broken and the items that had sat upon pedestals and hung from walls lay strewn on the floor. He looked down at his mother's broken bust and took a step backward as he sought to escape the glare of her one remaining eye. The tapestry was nothing more than a few tattered pieces held in place with rusting nails. Vegetation grew along the broken stones and dirt; dust hid the fine granite floor. A cheerless light spread into the corners of the destroyed room, illuminating the ruins in a macabre sort of way. Danyl did not know if this was what could or would happen to Bystyn and its people. It took all of his will to wait and see what the vision wanted him to know. It didn't take long. Soon the grayish light began to penetrate the dark recesses of the chamber, scattering the apparitions Danyl did not recognize. Was this their future if he was unable to wield the Green Might? Would he be unable to use it because of his arrogance? Was this a portent if Ramira was incapable of keeping the Source of Darkness from Mahn? This was as frustrating as that damn maze and…the maze. It was as enigmatic as the hall. Physical force could not open the doors; he was unable to find the right direction to set the magic free. The only time he was able to wield the power was when Ramira began her headlong spiral into the waiting hands of Mahn. What had activated the magic and allowed him to retrieve her from those apocalyptic hands? What was the catalyst? Danyl heard the lock open and knew the lesson was over. He bowed respectfully to his ancestors and left the hall. The Green Might throbbed in his soul.

~

Ramira roused herself from the horrible experience on the plains and opened her eyes. *Please let them have escaped*, she silently implored. She rose unsteadily to her feet and stared at her strange prison. The demons moved in the darkness just beyond the strange light glowing all around her. She stood on a round platform; random twisting staircases disappeared into the inky heights above her. Blood red curtains woven of the lightest of fabrics surrounded the stairways, their origins somewhere high overhead. They stirred and floated independent of any breeze, partially obscuring the steps. One of the staircases led back to the world of light. They mocked her predicament as they stretched upward into the blackness.

Ramira glanced down and saw a black, long sleeved dress composed of the same material as the curtains; its touch made her skin crawl. She tried pulling then ripping the fabric but it refused to come off. Ramira ignored the attire and decided to try one of the stairs. She approached it and heard claws skittering across the stones somewhere just beyond the light. Demons guarded the staircases. She reached for her knives and was surprised that she still possessed them. The cold feel of their blades was reassuring.

She thought back to her last moment's on the plains. The Source of Darkness' intensity prevented her from knowing the outcome. She was here but what had happened afterward?

"Much occurred after your departure," a smooth voice hissed from beyond the light.

Ramira turned and tried to distinguish from which direction it came.

"What do you want?" she demanded.

"You have eluded me for a very long time, but that only makes this moment so much sweeter," he replied.

"I will not give you what you want."

"I intend to take it from you."

A tall and burly figure cloaked in black walked onto the platform. Every step closer made it more difficult for Ramira to breathe. She gathered her courage and tried to peer into the black cowl, but could see nothing within its ominous depths. The demons haunting the edges of the darkness stirred at his presence. Mahn ignored them. His entire being concentrated on the woman composed of the hues of the setting sun. His gloved hand reached out to her, compelling her backward. A deep grumble resonated from within the hood. He sensed her fear and repulsion; those responses would be quite useful when the time came to rip what he desired from her. He hissed with delight.

"Your mind and soul were tainted by those who thought to spare themselves from what you contain. The High Priestess learned her lesson too late and paid for it with her life. She lost the very implements necessary to remove the Source of Darkness."

"What are you talking about?" she said, the image of her stabbing the red woman flashed in her mind.

"The fools believed they could avoid the inevitable by teaching you about 'good', but they disregarded one basic truth."

"What is that 'truth'?" she said in a voice smaller than she had intended.

"The 'truth' is that no amount of 'good' can wash away the black fire residing within you."

Ramira stared hard at Mahn, her uncertainty gnawing at her once more. The Source of Darkness' color and her friends' fate remained a mystery to her. They had to have survived. She could not, would not, harm any of them. She watched as Mahn backed away and, as repulsed as she was by his presence, she needed him. She could sift through his lies and piece together enough information to make up her own mind. The dais was hers once more. She searched for the good in her life to refute Mahn's words. She sensed Mahn somewhere in the shadows, leaving her to drown in her own doubts. She remembered the 'fools' Mahn spoke of and concentrated on the few memories she retained. She recalled the warm feeling of the brown woman and the gentle satisfaction Horemb bequeathed onto her. She envisioned the warmth of Sophie's kitchen, the well-worn wooden table a beacon for those seeking comfort and companionship. Then there was Danyl.

She had tried not to get involved with him but that which bound them from the very beginning would not break. They overcame numerous obstacles along the way and ultimately accepted their fate. She could not say whether that was a good or bad thing.

"You were instrumental in the downfall of your own people, and I will have the pleasure of watching you perform that same accomplishment on these mortals."

"I am not like you!" she protested in the eerie light.

"You are quite correct, Ceraphine, for I am like you."

"What did you call me?" she asked in a whisper.

"Ceraphine."

"What does that mean?"

"It means 'queen' and you, Ceraphine, are the last queen of Thebes."

"I am no more a queen than you are merciful," she snarled. Her patience, her very tolerance for this evil was beginning to slip beneath the waters of her own self-doubt.

"Do you not remember the pact you and I made?"

"I would never bargain with you."

"You told me that you'd give me the Source of Darkness if I spared your people. You reneged and I obliterated Thebes. If you repeat your mistake this time, all you know will be gone."

"No."

"You are in no position to argue with me, Ceraphine."

"I am not disputing you, I am telling you!" she stood erect, daring Mahn to gainsay her.

"That same pride cost the lives of your people, those on the plains, and will doom those in the city."

Ramira forced him from her thoughts, wondering if he might be telling her some measure of truth. Her nightmares revolved around death and destruction yet her mind would not reveal what had really happened. Had the guilt of having inflicted that devastation locked her memories away? She sighed and sat down upon the smooth floor. She drew her knees to her chest then buried her face in her arms. They had to have survived! She couldn't have killed them, too. She lifted her head and stared at the staircases, the crimson material still rippled without a breeze. She knew her past would eventually reveal itself. Would she be strong enough to face the truth when it finally surfaced?

~

Zada stared out into the gloomy darkness pondering Ramira's fate while fretting about everyone's destiny. Her actions had allowed the Green Might to return to Bystyn. She shuddered to think of what would have happened had Ramira obeyed the order not to use the Source of Darkness. Had she given them enough time to succeed? Mahn's vast army would arrive on the outskirts of Bystyn within the next few days and lay siege shortly thereafter. Mahn would make quite an entrance, but she doubted he would tear the dark magic from Ramira prior to his arrival. She guessed he would do so in front of them all, further shredding the already fragile confidence keeping the allies together. That, too, granted them an edge; they had to make sure they did not squander that extra precious time. She saw Danyl's reflection in the window as he came up behind her; he placed his hands on her shoulders to comfort her.

"I should be the one consoling you, Danyl."

"Your presence is soothing enough, Zada."

"I know this is hard to believe, Danyl, but she gave us a chance," said the nomad after a while, hoping to ease his loss.

"I know, Zada." The reality of Ramira's actions, as painful as they were, had finally set in. His inability to help her, though, gnawed at his heart.

"I don't think he will take the Source of Darkness from her until he arrives. That sight will be detrimental to the spirits of those who will face him and his army."

"He plans on inflicting every possible horror upon us, doesn't he?"

"Yes."

The Herkah turned and faced him. The bulk of the responsibility lay upon his shoulders. Was he capable of destroying Mahn by killing Ramira? Could he be convinced that doing otherwise would effectively assure their defeat?

"I have tried unsuccessfully to revive the Green Might."

"All things will fall into place when the time is upon us," she said, then gently touched his cheek.

"I dreamt of the maze again, Zada. The doors will not open and my reaction to them is becoming violent."

"Perhaps you should not fight it," she suggested, then patted his arm before leaving him to his thoughts.

~

The Herkah returned to her room. She stuck her hands in her pockets; her fingertips brushed against the bracelet. She pulled it out and held it up to the light. Enough beads had been broken to reveal gaps in the bracelet yet a silent voice urged her to break another one. She remembered the brown woman's warning; time was running out and they needed answers. She took a deep breath then sat down and smashed one of the beads. For a moment nothing happened, then her chamber disappeared...

She was back at the platform in the desert just before sunset. The Place of the Horii remained intact. A slight breeze lifted up from the desert carrying with it a most wondrous fragrance. The scents intoxicated her even within this memory. She lifted up her arms and tilted her head back, inviting the perfume to invigorate her soul as she stood upon the sacred dais. Zada glanced down and was astonished to see the plain homespun clothing she wore. She believed she should have been clad in the finest attire, but the bracelet's owner thought otherwise. The bracelet. She lifted up her arms and there, on her left wrist, was the trinket. Her skin reflected the soft red and golden hues of the setting sun. What was the bearer of the bracelet doing at the Place of the Horii? It was hallowed ground; one that did not respond kindly to those who were unfit to stand upon its ancient stones...

The image withdrew leaving Zada with more questions than answers. The Horii had accepted this woman. She knew the beads showed only snippets of this woman's life, but it was becoming clear she had occupied some powerful position. Her clothing and the fact that she preferred the love of the humble brown woman told another story. She thought of Mason and Sophie, whose fates would have been much different had they chosen to remain in Kepracarn. Could this woman also have faced the same sort of situation? The unknown woman stayed at arm's length from those who ruled. Zada gritted her teeth and crushed one more bead...

She stood in a stone chamber; beautifully painted river scenes adorned the far wall. There were tall reeds filled with waterfowl; fish swam in water so blue she was tempted to dip her fingers into it. Blossoms floated upon the water, their pink petals contrasted perfectly with the brilliant green leaves. The colors were vibrant, their rich hues soothing to the eye. A series of pure white, nearly transparent drapes separated her from a wall hung with mirrors. She could see her shadowy form as she moved along the fabric. Zada silently pleaded with the indistinct woman to part the curtains and stand before the mirror. The woman, however, was not interested in seeing her reflection and continued to walk parallel with them. Zada approached the end of the row of curtains, her heart racing in anticipation as a gap appeared between the curtains and mirror. She was about to unmask the woman's identity, but the woman turned the corner ending the vision...

Zada's frustration at coming so close to knowing this woman's identity encouraged her to crack another bead. The visions, however, were taxing and pursuing them in her tired condition would lead to problems. She rubbed at her face, stared at the bracelet again and then placed it back into her pocket. Other images might reveal this enigmatic woman, but she did not have the strength to find out. She sighed and wondered what was keeping Allad. He should have been back from the meeting with the king. Zada left her room and headed downstairs to the council chamber; it was empty. She was about to go back upstairs when she espied the Historian, arms laden with books, disappear into the library. She rapped on the door and entered the chamber. He sat up straight to see over the piles of books on his massive desk. She smiled in greeting, marveling at how much energy and enthusiasm he had for his tasks.

"Good evening, Zada."

"Good evening to you, Historian," she replied then took the seat beside him. "What keeps you up so late?"

"I wanted to finish the inventory of the scrolls," he responded, pushing his list aside and openly staring at the Herkah.

"What?"

"I would like to write down your histories, if I may, after all of this nonsense is over with. I think it will be important for everyone."

"You are saying that it might help others from developing an imaginative description of my people?"

"Yes, in a manner of speaking."

"Won't they be disappointed that we do not eat our young or use the skulls of our enemies to drink from?" she laughed softly as his face reddened.

"Well," he sputtered, "those without the benefit of having met you might think of things like that."

Zada laughed; Karolauren's face soon mirrored her mirth. She noticed the fragile glass holding the deeply hued liquid. The Historian followed her gaze and picked it up from the shelf behind him. He handed it over to her. She deftly pulled out the stopper and sniffed the contents. Zada gaped at the bottle then over to the Historian.

"You removed the plug as easily as that damn girl...Zada? What is it?"

With trembling hands, the Herkah reached into her tunic and withdrew a small phial hanging from a silver chain around her neck. She uncorked the delicate glass vessel then held it up for him to smell. She swapped her phial with the perfume bottle and watched his reaction.

"That is Queen's Blood, Karolauren. The dried residue along the sides is all that remains. Only the chosen Herkah leader receives this ampoule, an object handed down through the generations. Where did you get that bottle?"

"It has been so long I have forgotten...would you like some of it?" he asked.

Zada reverently fill her container. She beamed with gratitude, embarrassing the Historian who pretended to shuffle some papers.

"Queen's Blood, Historian," she explained repositioning the treasure against her skin, "is the rarest thing in the land. Those who first combined the extraordinary ingredients are all gone as are the elements needed to make it. It was a scarce and highly prized thing worth more than all the gold and jewels in the land. It is a link to our past."

"Interesting," he muttered to himself while staring at the bottle.

"Karolauren, who was the girl that removed the stopper?"

"Hmm? Oh, Danyl's companion," he replied distracted by something other than paper.

"Ramira?"

"Yes, this is why it stays in my sight all the time."

"What was her reaction when she sniffed it?"

"She seemed to enjoy the fragrance...that was all," he replied. "She dabbed some on her neck, too, if I remember."

Zada traced the bottle and stopper with her fingertips. The fragile piece survived for centuries but how did the elves acquire it?

"What do you know about this bracelet?" she asked handing it to him.

He murmured several words in the old elvish tongue while surveying the damage. Zada revealed the visions she had seen, the Historian never blinking once the entire time.

"The beads have somehow been able to retain the memories of its wearer. These recollections are released, so to speak, when they are broken."

"Who else knows about them?"

"Danyl."

"I should have known that boy would somehow be involved."

"Don't blame him, Karolauren, for he only did what it asked him to do."

"I suppose we should break the rest of them then," he mumbled sourly taking out a small knife.

"No, Historian," Zada stopped him. "It's a little more complicated than that."

"How do you mean?"

"There is a chance that whoever smashes the glass might well be stranded in the memory, and possibly at the mercy of whatever destroyed the owner."

"We have to tell Alyx, Zada."

"I know. Why don't we go to see him together?"

~

The king and Mason listened to what was said, then called for Danyl to join them. Alyxandyr was unsure of the bracelet's importance; he didn't like being ignorant of its existence, especially during these trying times.

"Are willing to part with this bauble, Karol?" he asked the Historian, who shrugged in assent.

"You realize we may well have to break the rest of the beads," Zada said to the stick-like figure nearly lost in the chair across from her.

"Yes…yes…" he grumbled.

"Are you strong enough to shatter one in front of us?" the king asked the Herkah.

"Yes," she replied.

She took the bracelet, placed it on the table, and broke the tiny stone closest to the clasp...

The wearer stood upon the side of a mountain overlooking an impressive city. High, cantilevered walls glowed like pearls beneath the sun; its main gate was flanked by a dozen tall pylons. The multi-colored pennants flapped in the breeze over people streaming into and out of the rectangular entrance. Watchtowers dominated each of the four corners of the broad complex. Guards patrolled the parapets beneath more bright standards. Two main avenues, not unlike those in Bystyn, intersected in the center of the city. That is where the comparison ended. Bystyn's streets were open to all; this city kept the majority of the population cordoned off behind a massive brick wall. The upper portion of the city was dazzling to behold, especially the palace. It was a monumental structure atop steps too numerous to count; it was accessible by a road lined with carved figures interspersed with fountains. Tile covered conduits paralleled the streets and fed the fountains and vast tracts of greenery. Sunlight reflected off capstones adorned with beaten gold; the granite pulsed with a soft pinkish hue. The lower half of the city was completely different. The narrow and winding streets were crowded with people, carts, and animals; the rooftops were covered with ragged awnings. It was almost impossible to keep the alleyways clean. People purchased items from pushcarts or backed up against the walls to let wagons pass by. No precious metals shone from the drab walls...

Zada remembered the plain garments the brown woman wore, her callused hands, and the sparseness of her home. Those were signs of a people who labored for a few privileged individuals. They evidently did not partake of the bounty they worked so hard to provide.

"There is no more?" asked the king, his eyes riveted to the spot where the vision had been moments before.

"No, these are only brief flashes of time."

"I'd like to see more," said the Historian.

"The city was as beautiful as it was ugly," said Zada.

"It seems as though those who ruled had not learned, or had forgotten, the lessons taught to all who must care for their people," began Alyxandyr. "That usually means a collapse is imminent."

"Mahn sensed the apathy and used it to his advantage," stated Mason, silently questioning what he had just seen.

"Or perhaps he had been awakened by someone who planned on using it to their advantage," suggested the king.

"What do you mean?" asked Danyl.

"The city was in a state of decline. Cooper experienced the same thing when he had his father killed and took control of Kepracarn."

"He's right, Danyl," confirmed Mason. "Our father became disinterested in everything other than himself and Cooper, along with a few other determined individuals, used that to oust him and ascend the throne. The people of Kepracarn had to believe things would improve with Cooper. Although their lives did improve, they found out that Cooper liked to indulge himself, too. The only difference was my brother understood he had to make some concessions to his people to retain control."

"The owner of this bracelet evidently saw things quite differently, and I have to wonder what she could have done about it?" asked Alyxandyr.

"Probably nothing," conceded Zada, "except for the fact that Mahn arrived and hastened the decline."

"Then why was her bracelet found amongst the first king's things?" asked Danyl. "That's the mystery for me. He either took it from her, found it or she gave it to him."

"The elves passed near that city about the same time it was destroyed," stated the Historian.

"Do you think she warned him of what was happening?" asked Mason.

"I think there was some sort of contact between them," stated Karolauren, "or we would not have this in our possession today."

"If we speculate she did warn him, knowing her city was doomed, she could have saved the elves' lives."

"True, Alyx," Mason commented. "And that would explain the Herkahs, too, for did you not say your origin lies within the city, Zada?"

"It does, Mason. It also means that perhaps she also helped those unaffected by the ruler or Mahn to flee the city before it was laid to waste."

"We are making a lot of assumptions out of one vague image," muttered the Historian.

"Indeed we are, Karol, but these guesses are making the most sense," the king argued.

Zada stared at the trinket, its fragile blue beads as much a link to her past as the Queen's Blood. Karolauren was right, maybe they were reading too much out of one vision. Karolauren slid the bracelet over to her; she cracked another bead before anyone could stop her...

The owner of the bracelet walked up the avenue ignoring the extravagant objects flanking her. The guards gave her a wide berth when she climbed the wide stone steps leading up to the colonnaded palace. She entered the cool darkness and escaped the burning sun. No one dared to meet her gaze. She headed straight down the airy hall, forced open a tall set of richly carved black wooden doors, and let them slam behind her. She stood in front of a throne embellished with gold and jewels; finely painted jars holding tall, blue-green feathers flanked it. Behind the throne was a wide balcony and beyond it a lush garden. The image of the queen standing victoriously over her enemy, her foot placed on his neck and holding a scepter loomed on the wall beside the throne. A figure emerged from one of the rooms to the right of the dais; loathing radiated from her cold features. The closer the wearer of the bracelet came, the more the red woman cringed...

"That was interesting," the king exhaled with some apprehension.

"The ruler of the city?" asked Mason.

"I don't know...perhaps," said Zada picking up the bracelet.

"Zada? Is there any way, any way at all, you could see how Ramira is faring?" asked Danyl.

"It would be too difficult, Danyl, especially if he is preparing her for his final assault."

"You mean poisoning her mind against us?" inquired Mason.

"Something like that," she replied quietly.

"So," the king recounted. "We've seen the city, this confrontation, the brown woman, the Place of the Horii twice, and also the bald man. Danyl explained to us how Ramira met the man who had taught her how to fight. Is it possible that the bracelet belongs to Ramira? After all, if her memories are inaccessible to her..."

"...then they would be to Mahn, as well," Zada finished for him.

"That would make her a thousand years old!" Danyl exclaimed.

"Yes and no, Danyl, for the dark magic would have contained her in a way that, well, stopped time for her." Zada's excited voice filled the room.

If their theory was correct, Mahn was finishing what he had started centuries ago. The Source of Darkness concealed Ramira from Mahn until a power equal to his could arise and challenge him. Fate had decreed that time was now. Destiny had set the stage for the ultimate battle but could not dictate the players' reactions.

Ramira might not have heeded Danyl's cries that night. She could have chosen not to follow him to Bystyn. Allad had taken great risks in allowing Nyk and Ramira to live. Sophie could have turned Ramira away instead of letting her live in her home. There were so many variables; each decision was based on emotion - the hardest thing of all to predict. They now stood at the edge of their existences, but their circumstances seemed less dire than they had first believed. Mahn had what he wanted but was it what he expected? What exactly was the Source of Darkness? Was it evil? How could the dark magic steeped in all things amoral, burn with an amethyst fire instead of black?

What had transpired to change it? Did fate somehow intervene? Zada thought the brown woman, the bald man, and the spirit tainted by the Vox were in some way involved, but she could not quite fit those pieces together. They appeared to be very prominent in her life, if indeed this was Ramira's life. It had to be, for nothing else made sense, even though this too, seemed highly unlikely. She looked over at the prince who stared at the floor between his feet, the information frightening him in a way she could not even begin to understand. He and Ramira had formed their bond long before each knew what the other housed. They would have to hold fast to what they learned about each other if they were to survive. She did not envy their positions and hoped that very connection would give them the strength to do whatever fate had in store for them.

"You give new meaning to loving an older woman, son," the king gently teased him.

Danyl dropped his head to his chest and closed his eyes, envisioning her in his arms, in the darkness of Sophie's terrace. The warm summer night filled with the sounds of insects and birds. Did the magic protect her for all of those centuries? He knew the bearers of the elven magic lived longer - providing they survived wielding it. If she warned the first king then…was that what he was staring at in the tapestry? He rose without a word and returned to the Great Hall, planting himself in front of the mural while staring hard at the king. He inhaled and exhaled several times then opened his mind to the past. Nothing happened for a while until he thought he saw the dead king smile.

~

Nyk and his guard's saw the black mass camped several miles away; they studied them for a while. They took notes of what equipment they brought along and approximately how many made up the army. The enemy brought large structures to batter the walls; other weapons of war were too small to be seen at this distance but would be no less lethal. A quick guess told them they would be outnumbered at least four to one and, coupled with Mahn possessing the Source of Darkness, their outcome seemed rather bleak.

"We are going to have our hands full," muttered the prince eyeing the vast gathering.

They had prepared a multitude of defenses including digging traps on the plains, readying vats of oil, and stringing razor sharp wire along the least defensible sections of the wall. Mahn had plenty of soldiers to break through the city's defenses. How long could they hold out until he did? The well-seasoned veterans could easily keep pace with their vastly outnumbered foes, but not with the demons and the Source of Darkness. They would fight well but without an edge of their own could not hold out for very long… maybe a few days at best.

"I count about a half dozen catapults and rammers," his captain informed him.

"Our walls can only take so much pounding before the stones begin to crack and splinter," stated Nyk ordering them back to the city.

Unfortunately, not even the mountains could hold out forever against such an assault. They would have to destroy or at the very least disable those machines before they could be used, a task requiring a great deal of courage. He tried to envision where they would place those things for maximum efficiency. Their range would depend upon what they intended to hurl at them: something large enough, he surmised, to inflict the greatest damage. They could set them up from any direction or they could concentrate on a specific area, heaving stones against the city walls until they weakened and finally gave way. That would be his course of action. Even if the enemy only managed to undermine the structure, they could then turn to the rammers and create a large enough rift in Bystyn's walls to let Mahn's minions pour through.

"They don't seem to be in any hurry," noted his captain.

No, thought Nyk, *of course they aren't, because Mahn has Ramira. If an entire army was under his control what made them think she could withstand his manipulations?*

Nyk did not like the fear beginning to gnaw at his heart; he carefully concealed it from the others. The last thing they needed was to see him lose faith in this all-important campaign. They rode on, Nyk glancing more than once over his shoulder while disguising his uneasiness behind a stoic countenance.

~

Ramira rose to her feet and looked around. Nothing except silence greeted her. She felt the things watching her from within the shadows. The Kreetch's nervous scurrying becoming more noticeable whenever she approached the staircases. She stopped at the nearest one and craned her neck upward, but it ended in blackness. She repeated her action on several more, all with the same results. She recognized her surroundings: Danyl rescued her from this place when she battled the Kreetch poison. This time he could not save her…or could he?

Ramira closed her eyes and recalled the last time she and Danyl were together. Their spirits had intertwined and soared to the top of a pale blue mountain. A shimmering silver mist shielded them from the world. The image began to fray and shred, the bits and pieces blown away by a foul wind. Mahn violated her sanctuary, yanking her back to reality with a hatred that made her cringe. The visions he filled her with reeked of despair. A city died beneath a conflagration; people seeking to escape were cut down by her own hand, children desperately clawed at her legs begging for a scrap of food. Ghastly faces of people sick with the worst diseases hovered in front of her. All eyes stared accusingly at her. The vilest of them all was the death of Jack and Ida. She slew them, denying the Master of Evil. She had slit their throats, slipping in their blood as she struggled to rise; her eyes brimmed with tears of anguish and remorse. The demons had nearly torn them apart, but had left the most terrible job of all to her. The task that would haunt her for the rest of her life. Even now, tears slid down her cheeks as she remembered the warmth and compassion they radiated, teardrops Mahn ridiculed. His glacial chuckle filled the cavern. The black cloaked figure emerged into the peculiar light.

"You!" she hissed with loathing.

"You betrayed your entire city, yet you let two insignificant lives trouble you? How absolutely delightful," he laughed.

"I did no such thing!"

"Quite the contrary, Ceraphine…"

…The filtered sunlight warmed her oiled and perfumed skin. Handmaidens waved plumed fans to cool her; a servant adjusted the awning on the balcony on which she stood. She scowled down upon those toiling in the street. Their skeletal forms strained with the burdens they carried but none dared look up at her. She watched unemotionally as a woman went down under the weight of her crude basket. One of the overseers immediately began to whip her, shredding her brown garments even further until only strips remained. This woman, however, did look up and for a moment, her brown eyes locked onto Ramira's amethyst ones. She glared back down for a moment then nodded to the overseer who proceeded to take the woman out of her earthly misery…

"No!" Ramira shrieked, "I would never allow that to happen!"

"You sensed the other magic and sought to ally yourself with it even though it cost your people their souls. I must confess I find that to be quite stimulating. That would make you and I the same, don't you think?"

"I am not like you!"

"You have darkened the Source of Darkness for me and, when the time comes, you will remain inside of me forever, sharing all that I will do. By the way, did you know your power obliterated everyone on the plains?"

Ramira took a step back and shook her head.

"I see you didn't."

Mahn slipped back into the shadows, leaving a stunned and bereaved Ramira alone.

She could not have killed them! She had been aiming her might away from them. He was lying so she would lose her will, leaving the Source of Darkness unguarded and vulnerable. Her steadfast conviction and stubbornness erased his words from her mind. If she only knew what color the fire had been. She stood tall and proud willing the Source of Darkness to stir within her, but careful not to let Mahn sense its presence. Closing her eyes, flew down inside of herself. He was watching her but could not see what she was doing. So she hoped. Ramira drifted farther and farther down until the sensations crowding her prison receded into the distance and left her truly alone.

There were no ghosts or nightmares here for they shunned that which she sought. She sensed a low thrumming sound and followed it as it guided her even deeper inside, revealing a pale glow. She angled toward it, the light growing brighter as she faced the brilliant core floating in the darkness. Pulsing with a deep lavender light, the Source of Darkness hovered before her as if waiting for her command. Ramira reached out with trembling hands and touched it with the tip of her fingers. She was surprised such a little thing could be so powerful. Ramira was about to coax it into her upturned hand when it suddenly sped away. It was time to go. She noticed another shimmering form. It was small, nearly lost in the darkness, but it burned with its own power. Ramira stared at it with wonder then instant devotion, the tiny seed bringing joy and strength to her very soul.

~

Zada smiled at Cricket as they joined the king for the evening meal. She was pleased that the young girl had recovered from her perilous journey. Sophie and Anci also attended and it seemed as if the two girls would become fast friends. Cricket had been bereft of such friendships and clearly enjoyed being with someone her own age. Danyl and Karolauren entered the dining hall and took their seats just as the servers began to bring out platters of food. Nyk, Allad, and a few others wanted to decline dinner but the king, sensing there might not be too many shared meals, would not accept their refusals. There would be plenty of time to continue preparations for the attack later. There was some small talk while they ate but it was mostly silent as each thought about what they were to face. The meal ended and they retired to an adjoining sitting room where they shared glasses of wine and ale.

"Danyl tells me you have an interesting little bauble, Cricket," said Zada as she broke the silence. "May I see it?"

Cricket reached into her pouch, pulled out the blue stone, and handed it to the Herkah. Zada stared into the stone, raising an eyebrow at how closely it resembled the beads on the bracelet. She held the smoothly polished egg-shaped stone up to the lamplight. Deep blue swirls curled slowly within its lustrous surface, like an early morning mist in the middle of summer. What sort of memory could it house? Zada handed it back to the young girl.

"The army is encamped a day and a half from the city, Father," said Styph. "They seem to be waiting for their leader to arrive."

"I doubt that will take too much longer but I believe they will attack before he gets here," stated Seven.

"Inflict as much damage as possible?" asked Nyk.

"Yes," replied Seven.

"Then when we are dazed and battered by his army he'll…sorry, Danyl, he'll finish the task with Ramira," said Styph.

Danyl remained distracted and apart from the group, staring beyond the darkness of the balcony window and the snow falling on the city. It would, he guessed, be over within the week. They would pick up the pieces of their lives and go on or die. He rested his forehead against the cold glass, its frigid touch soothing his overheated skin. Ramira's words echoed in his mind: *When this is all over can the two of us go away together?*

Yes, we can and we will, Ramira, I pledge to you here and now, that nothing and no one will stop us.

He closed his eyes and blocked out everything except her face, willing her to hear his silent words that originated from his heart. He didn't care that each of them bore their respective powers nor that their possible annihilation might be only days away. He concentrated on what they had vowed to one another and sent that conviction west, trusting she would somehow hear his declaration. He slowly opened his eyes, the whites gone and replaced by a brilliant emerald hue. They stared unblinkingly into the darkness as a vague shape began to materialize outside the window. The haze developed into a faint outline as it drew closer. Then, her face hovered just beyond the glass. *Tell me how I can help you*, he begged of the fluctuating image.

His heart beat wildly in his chest; the only thing he wanted to do was reach out and grab her even if the likeness was composed of memories and desires. She came closer, placing her spectral hands against the window and prompting him to do the same. He stared into her eyes, willing her with all his might to take shape and return to her flesh and blood form. He gazed into her shifting features; a tear slid down his cheek at the resolute conviction on her face. She had chosen her fate not upon the plains but on the night in the cave when she had pulled him and the Green Might to safety. No matter what was to occur she was willing to challenge it with every ounce of her being. She began to dissolve into a million sparks, leaving him staring into the snowy night once more. His breath condensed on the window, obscuring the night but not the face permanently etched into his mind and heart. He removed his hand from the glass and rejoined his companions.

~

Ramira felt a cherished sensation touch her, much to the dismay of Mahn, who instantly roared to life from somewhere within the shadows. She ignored his objections and threats, focusing instead on the unexpected feeling flooding through her. She followed its gossamer connection to a place far away from this terrible place. The tether extended out from this horrid abyss, pulling her through the frigid night past stars resembling streaks of light and over the dark land. She flew through time and space until a vast shape even darker than the night loomed ahead of her. Then a large window appeared, the light filtering out into the snowy night illuminating the terrace and outlining a lone figure with his head pressed against the glass. Danyl. She floated closer then reached out to him. He wanted to help her but there was nothing he could do right now. She placed her hands against the glass then smiled as he pressed his against hers. She had so much to tell him but what traveled to Bystyn was not composed of flesh and blood and could therefore not speak.

Infuriated, Mahn shattered the connection and yanked her back to her dungeon. He violently rammed her into the foul depths of his cloak amid the tortured souls he had devoured over the eons. They pulled and clawed at her from every direction, some beseechingly, others out of sheer hatred. She brought her hands to her ears to block them out. The air was fetid and heavy; it was like having her face pushed into a vat of rotting meat. As if those horrible things were not enough, he began to assault her mind with more images of the death and destruction he claimed she had caused. The cacophonous screams of the things around her compelled her to do the only thing that would keep her sane. She disappeared into herself and took comfort in the radiant silver sparkle next to the Source of Darkness. She curled up with her unborn child and waited to be released from the bowels of Mahn's malice.

Time seemed to stand still for her as she endured the constant battering from both Mahn and the loathsome things assaulting her. The evil forces surrounding her left her unable to wield the Source of Darkness. Mahn's arrogant plan to wrest it from her in front of Bystyn would be a horrifying spectacle and she shuddered to think what effect it would have on the allies. The Source of Darkness, like a hooded and tethered hawk, would be in full control by its master. Ironically enough, Mahn was powerless to seize the dark power even though she was deep within his foul robes. Perhaps he just bided his time. She brought her knees to her chest in thought. In essence, Mahn already housed the Source of Darkness since it now resided deep within him. He still had to retrieve it from within her. She had to delve deep inside to secure it. How would he seize it? She would not willingly cede the power to him and the nearly constant barrage of horrors he inflicted upon her could not dislodge it, either. The Source of Darkness beckoned like a gold vein deep within a mine, a tunnel he would have to lower himself into to obtain it. The notion of his despicable presence inside of her turned her stomach. Just the mere thought of him ravaging her on his way to securing the Source... She smiled, for the answer manifested itself before her. The only problems were how to convey her solution to the others and how to coerce Danyl into fulfilling his part in the Mahn's destruction.

NINE

The first skirmish began early the next morning. A large contingent of the enemy a mile west of the city beset nearly a hundred horsemen. The battle was brief and violent with major losses to Mahn's men. Those from Bystyn had fewer casualties as they repelled the demon-prodded army. They were able to retrieve their dead and dying, bringing them back to the city before rounding up fresh men and horses and returning to the same area. They battled twice more before Mahn's army simply retreated from the conflict. Things remained quiet until dusk when another wave of attackers confronted the horsemen, fought briefly, then withdrew once more.

Nyk watched as they pulled back, their hit and run tactics serving no other purpose than to test the allies or distract them. The latter thought prompted him to send a patrol both north and south of their present position with strict orders to report anything unusual. Gard took the northern route; Seven headed south.

The prince spat upon the bloodstained snow keeping a watchful eye on the western horizon, waiting for signs of another assault. Nothing moved except the cold wind.

Seven watched the shapes move through the woods bordering the plains- they were spreading out along the line of trees. The enemy wound its way east without bothering to conceal themselves. Their brazen disregard for the patrols paralleling their advancement confirmed that Mahn planned to sacrifice any and all of his men to take Bystyn. The enemy used the brief skirmishes to draw their attention away from Mahn's plan to surround the city. Seven surmised Gard was witnessing the same thing a few miles to the north. Isolated from any help, the army would converge upon the city like some giant noose and strangle it at his leisure. Their only course of action would be to maintain a buffer zone around Bystyn, keeping them at bay for as long as possible before the inevitable retreat behind its gray walls became necessary. Help at that point, if they were fortunate enough to receive any, would be futile. The situation then would be dire indeed. He sent a messenger back to Nyk with the information and continued his vigil.

Gard's thoughts mirrored those of the dwarf as the vague shadows spread eastward through his home. The Khadry felt the bile rise into his throat. He could well imagine what they were doing to the once-bountiful forest. All for one woman with a magic as evil as Mahn's. Gard seemed to be the only one who thought her existence was a bane to them all. He had kept silent during the meetings but the hatred building up inside became more difficult to conceal. If Mahn succeeded in destroying everything using Ramira's power and he survived, he would hunt her down and kill her. Indeed, if given a chance now he would do the same, regardless of the cost to his own life. Or soul, for that matter. Her evil, he determined, was enshrouded in a deceitful beauty that had charmed most of whom she had come into contact with. Was he the only one who had somehow managed to avoid the spell she had cast on the others? Danyl's deep affection for her worried him the most because he knew the prince would protect her with his very life. Those thoughts turned the Khadry's face dark with unease. He pushed the vehemence he felt for Ramira into the back of his mind, focusing instead on the danger all around them. His plans for her would have to wait. He would continue to stand by the others, for to do otherwise would mean they would all be lost. He, too, sent a courier to the prince and waited for a reply.

~

Nyk and a handful of others waited for darkness then slipped away from the city riding south toward the fringes of the enemy camp. Snow began to fall. The weather would allow them to remain hooded without causing any undue suspicion. They had smeared their faces with grime and dressed in well-worn homespun clothing. They were indistinguishable in the night from their foes. Their mounts wore bridles, blankets, and saddles taken from enemy horses that had fallen in battle on the plains surrounding the city. The prince decided the best course of action would be to ride directly into the camp along its edges, then casually merge with their adversaries. There would be precious little time to wreak as much havoc as possible before retreat became a necessity. It was a dangerous plan, but they had to destroy at least a few of the machines. Nyk's concern revolved around the demons. Mahn would surely have sprinkled them amongst his men making their task even more daunting. Allad had insisted he go with them but Nyk refused. The Herkah conceded, and then offered each of them one of Zada's knives. Nyk wished Allad were riding by his side; he greatly respected his fighting capabilities.

The elves took several deep breaths to steady their nerves as they reached the enemy camp then split up into pairs. Nyk and his captain rode their horses as far into the camp as they could, loosely securing their reins before walking aimlessly amid the shadows toward the nearest hurling machine. The captain hunkered down beside the guard while Nyk disappeared into the machines silhouette, nimbly climbing up along the crossbars until he reached its apex. The prince remained absolutely still for several moments then reached into his cloak and pulled out his knife. Ropes as thick as his arm held the machine together. He had to slice through enough of the fibers to keep the machine from falling apart during transport yet render it useless during the first volley. He sawed through them, cutting deep enough to render the machine useless. He replaced his knife and descended the structure. One down. He resumed his listless state as he and his captain walked to the next apparatus.

They had covered half the distance when a peculiar feeling touched him, one he had experienced before. It wormed its way into his stomach: demon. It would be hard to recognize by sight. Nyk and his captain sat down beside one of the fires, staring into the flames while stretching their senses to their limits. They could smell the sweat on the unwashed bodies and hear the enemy coughing and sniffling. A quick, piercing cry off in the distance made him freeze in alarm but the camp did not erupt in chaos.

The unnatural feeling subsided and the elves continued to their next target. The captain again sat beside the guard while Nyk scampered up the tower to cut the ropes. He was about to descend when a large contingent of soldiers approached with drawn weapons. The brief shriek he had heard in the distance echoed within his mind. Nyk watched a group advance from out of the darkness and pressed his body against the beam. His captain followed the guard's response, scrambling away like some tormented animal and lifting his arm up in mock defense. The gang halted a few yards away from the catapult. All but one of the soldiers dispersed; the remaining one stood completely still as if gauging his surroundings. Nyk's eyes narrowed for he knew what it was.

The hooded figure slowly craned its neck first right then left until it focused on the guard and the captain. To his credit, the disguised elf kept calm. The black form advanced upon him forcing the elf to crawl backward until the massive tower blocked any further retreat. Nyk watched helplessly as the demon scrutinized the elf. It surged forward, grabbed the captain by the neck, and lifted him high into the air. The fiend pulled him closer and yanked the hood back exposing the captain's features. A hissing sound of satisfaction escaped the dark cowl as it crushed the life out of the elf. The captain was not about to die without a fight. His charge lay concealed in the darkness above and he was not about to let this creature live to take him. He fumbled with his scabbard then gathered all of his remaining strength to push Zada's blade into the Vox. Nyk's face drained of blood as his captain jerked several times then went limp in the enraged demons hand. The Herkah blade had hurt, but not killed, the Vox. It dropped the dead elf and began clawing at its wound while wheezing and hissing in pain. Two more screams exploded into the night leaving Nyk with the feeling he was soon going to be on his own…if he survived.

A vile wind blasted through the camp, the air so fetid it almost knocked Nyk off the beam. His eyes watered and the morbid cries of the souls imprisoned within Mahn's hatred filled his ears. The frigid air bit into his flesh numbing his hold on the beam, his fingers gripping not wood but a slab of ice. Nyk gritted his teeth, watching as the black gust encircled the distressed Vox and whisked it away. Sweat poured down his face as sought to regain his composure. That was as close as he ever wanted to come to the demon. It was time to leave; the extra guards posted around the machine and undoubtedly the other towers posed a problem. He desperately needed some sort of distraction. He checked the area as much as the darkness allowed looking for anything that would give him those precious few moments to escape. The tree line loomed in the blackness a short sprint away to his right, taunting him with its nearness. It might just as well have been on the other side of the earth. He waited for a while and slowly realized he was probably the only one still alive. He was on his own. The sentries faced outward, their attention on the woods and brush around them and not on the catapult. He could clamber down without alerting them, and then time his move to join them in their sentry duty. He slithered down the crossbars keeping to the shadows, his perfect timing allowing him to join the pacing guards. He participated for a while then indicated he needed to relieve himself, then disappeared into the bushes before they had a chance to reply. He hastened to his horse, jumped into the saddle then heading back to the city. Two other riders materialized from out of the night. At first Nyk drew his weapon in anticipation of a fight then recognized his men. He made them cut themselves with the Herkah blades to make sure they were not demon-infested before racing back to the city.

~

They met with the others discussing what they had seen and heard in the camp. They had managed to tamper with five of the towers leaving seven still functioning. The prince reported on the physical and mental makeup of the enemy and on the fetid mist that came to get the wounded Vox.

"They are swinging up and around us," reported the prince. "My guess is that Mahn is on his way and has ordered them to assume their attack positions."

"I agree," stated Gard, "they are using the forests to the north and south to hide their men hoping to draw us into the trees to fight. That would be a perfect way to increase their demon count."

"They are going to have to get close enough to use their hurling devices, which will be well guarded. Attacking or disabling them will be quite a challenge if we choose to do so," added Seven.

"I think they have learned their lesson," stated Nyk.

"How many of the traps have been set?" asked Alyxandyr.

"Several," replied Mason unrolling a map of the area. "There are three along the forest to the west and north," his finger traced their locations. "Ditches have been dug along these two lines just south of the edge. If they decide to bring any heavy equipment or come by horseback, they will find themselves several feet down; the steep sides will impede their ability to escape."

"We also dug channels that can be filled with oil and lit in crossing patterns all along the plain. Thankfully, the snow has hidden them but I don't think it will hinder the incendiary nature of the oil. We could do little in the south but we did manage to set a few traps to the east."

Alyxandyr absently tapped the map then looked up as Zada joined them, her face haggard and her shoulders stooped.

"How are you feeling?" he asked her as she sat down beside Danyl.

"Fine," she replied with little conviction.

She listened while he updated her, taking deep breaths as she braced herself for another round of images beginning to build inside her mind. The blank look on her face alerted the others; they became silent as the Herkah began to receive more disturbing visions...

There was chaos all around her, the souls screaming in this netherworld agitated by her presence. She could smell their rank odors and feel their ghostly forms as they crowded around her. Zada guessed Ramira was somewhere deep within that obscene darkness. How she was able to withstand those horrors was beyond her comprehension. Zada was on the fringes of this appalling maelstrom and would have to break the contact soon. She had only a few moments and took a chance by sending a message to Ramira, one she more than likely would never receive. To her complete surprise, she acquired one from Ramira, the lightning-fast vision initially confusing until she broke the connection…

Zada sat utterly still while Ramira's feeble thought took hold within her mind, grateful that there wasn't a sound in the room. The fading vision Ramira sent showed a mighty tree sprouting from the trough of a snow-white dune, fully developing in seconds before her eyes. Its sturdy roots disappeared down into the sand, snaking outward and into the dunes around it. Puddles of blood surrounded the roots wherever they penetrated the sand. The bright red fluid trickled away from the tree like crimson tears. A great canopy of leaves blotted out the sun. Zada smiled tiredly.

"Zada?" Allad softly brought her back to the chamber.

The nomad nodded to her mate then reached out for his hand. His touch had always soothed her even after the worst vision and this one, although filled with hope, was no less taxing to her. Zada sat down in front of the fireplace to chase the chill from her bones. She gazed at the flames, holding her hands out to absorb the heat. A movement to her right caught her attention. It was the specter of the brown woman.

Tell me about Ramira.

Not here.

The ghost dissipated before her eyes. Zada's heart constricted at the sadness in the other's brown eyes. The spirit clearly loved Ramira, accepting of her part in the scheme of things but still afraid for her. They all were but this long dead woman continued to haunt the land, refusing to rest until Ramira was safe. Zada doubted the brown woman was her mother although that didn't stem the emotions keeping this shade in the present.

It occurred to Zada that Ramira was not the only one for whom the brown woman was concerned. If the living failed the dead, she would never achieve an eternal peace. Zada was better able to 'see' the ancient spirit because of her inner sight and the fact that her roots were inextricably bound with this distant ancestor. Her eternal destiny hinged upon their success in destroying the evil because the dead were powerless to confront and vanquish Mahn.

That fate rested on two shoulders and the strength and courage of the mortals. Ramira had only hampered Mahn's plan centuries ago when she disappeared; the battle was destined to take place in another time. Evil thoughts and deeds never disappeared but regrouped to arise once more. They always found a host, nurturing and preparing its minions to perform wholesale destruction without any regard for anyone or anything. There were plenty of weak and empty-headed marks for it to home in on. The best individuals to defile were those already corrupted: the greedy and power hungry. Its insatiable appetite to inflict death and misery was devoid of mercy and conscience. She stared at Alyxandyr and wondered whom he would lose in the coming days. Zada looked at the rest in turn for they, too, would lose friends and family. And herself? Whom would she lose? What would remain when it was all over? Would evil rule the devastated land or would the allies live? Her gaze returned to the fire. She fervently prayed she was not seeing Bystyn's future within the orange flames, as they fed off the wood cradled upon the grate. One of the logs popped and fell, sending embers out onto the slate floor near her feet. The image Ramira had sent to her burned in her mind, most notably the immense tree squeezing the blood out of the desert.

~

They stood within the watchtower looking west upon the black plague spreading out as far as the eye could see. The same scene played itself out to the south and along the foothills of the mountains to the north. There were a few pockets of the enemy in the east, too. The adversaries swarming along the forest to the south could easily ride out to prohibit any messenger sent to alert the remainder of the dwarves at Evan's Peak. Seven rubbed his chin while Gard stared at Mahn's forces with crossed arms; his keen eyes absorbed every detail before them. They watched with a sense of fascinated horror as the rear of the army began to part as if a gigantic pair of hands had pushed them aside.

A knot of riders rode down the middle, the enemy pouring back into the breach left in the wake of the black group heading toward the city: Mahn. The time was at hand. He was bringing his prize to the gates where he would tear the Source of Darkness from Ramira and use it to obliterate them all. The sight of him wending his way through his army of demons did not shatter the resolve of those who witnessed his entrance.

"Well," Seven watched the dramatic approach, "we all know what his presence means."

"Do you think Ramira is on one of the horses beside him?" asked Gard as he too, measured the effect Mahn's appearance had on the black host spread around him. One true arrow could end her life and Mahn's ability to take the magic. He noted there were no cheers or even one word spoken as the demon passed through his army. They remained in place, their features blank and their armed hands hanging limply at their sides.

"I doubt he would take that chance, Gard. My guess is she is contained within his robes," replied Mason.

Mahn halted near the middle of his forces, the riders at his side remaining for a few moments before riding off. He stared at those gathered on the battlements. His army was so densely packed few could move about freely. They stood shoulder to shoulder garbed in everything from leather to homespun, some with shields but most with nothing more than a sword. There were legions of archers and phalanxes of spears occupying the forefront; groups of cavalry rode at the ready along the sides. The lack of armor was prevalent throughout the ranks. Their lives were meaningless to Mahn, shells of flesh and blood whose only purpose was to wear down the allies. The blank features of the thousands were the most frightening of all. They had no concept about what was happening to them and it was debatable whether they even realized where they were. Their minds and bodies were no longer their own and they would endure whatever Mahn ordered them to do.

"Where could he have gotten all of these people from?" asked Styph.

"Many lived in Kepracarn and don't forget the towns and villages scattered throughout the land," stated Alyxandyr. The king noted their varied attire and recognized how busy Mahn had been conscripting people from the south, Kepracarn, and places he could not identify. His recruitment had been indiscriminate.

"Are they all inhabited by demons?" asked Mason.

"No, I don't think so," replied Allad. "They have been exploited by him and could return to normal once he is defeated, that I've seen before. See there," he pointed to small groups of figures moving about in a jerky sort of way. "Those are Kreetch and over there," he directed their attention along the sides of the army, "are Radir." He surveyed the groups of foot soldiers, horsemen, and those specializing in swift attacks and retreats.

"And the Vox?" asked Nyk looking around for the elusive demons.

"They have already been dispatched to target Herkahs, I assume," replied the nomad in low tones trying to pinpoint the vile demons. At this point, they would be easy enough to distinguish amongst the rest of the army but the problems would begin once they managed to infiltrate into the allies' ranks. One Herkah/Demon could cause a great deal of damage amongst his people and the allies. His face darkened at the thought of a Vox within the gates, freely feeding upon the nomads at will until fear and terror crushed those who so courageously battled to defeat Mahn. Their vigilance, therefore, must increase tenfold to avoid such a devastating scenario and it was up to the Herkahs to insure that didn't happen.

"Wonderful," said the king, sarcastically.

Danyl stared at a knot of figures toward the middle of the army, noting how unaffected they were by everything around them yet studying their surroundings nonetheless. He sensed Mahn there; Ramira would be with him. She had managed to elude him for a thousand years and saved countless generations, yet the confrontation was now. Why now? What was it about this place and time that prompted such a challenge? What pieces fell into place and would they be beneficial to them or to the enemy? He sighed and pulled his cloak tighter for the day was bright but the sun provided no heat. Winter had claimed the land.

"Can you 'see' her, Zada?" he asked the nomad who stood beside him.

"She is there but I cannot see her."

"They are starting to move forward," said Nyk.

He and several others descended the stone steps and jumped onto their horses. Whether they were fully prepared to meet the horde or not the time to defend was at hand. Every member had a specific duty to fulfill and, although many wanted to join the impending battle, they remained at their designated stations.

The gates opened and several hundred riders rode out into the early morning light to join in the battle. They ignored the fact that nearly twice as many of the enemy awaited them. Nyk and Allad rode directly west while Gard led a contingent slightly northward. Seven and Styph headed south toward the trees. Alyxandyr watched with Clare, Danyl, and Zada; their minds assimilated every detail on the plains. They looked for weaknesses and possible strategies they could use during the confrontation. Eliminating the Radir and the Kreetch would give them an edge but the stamina needed to fulfill that task would leave them vulnerable to the mortals under Mahn's control. Allad had assigned Herkahs to each of the groups. They were to confront the demons using training much better suited to defeating them. That also gave Mahn a chance to procure more Vox if they were unsuccessful. Their choices were limited. The nomads were well aware of the fact that more than one of them would succumb to the demon and fight against their kin and friends.

Few of those standing against the demons had witnessed their terrible wrath. The Herkahs prepared them as best as they could. Zada desperately wished she could supply each member of the allies with a blade to counteract the poison, saving many who would succumb to the demons' venom and join that horrible brotherhood.

They watched the towers of destruction move closer to the

city. The robust horses strained under the immense weight. The machines creaked and groaned, inching forward as the soggy ground sucked at the huge wheels. The snow-covered earth only delayed the inevitable. The archers awaited the signal to rain a volley of arrows into the animals once they were within range, a futile endeavor considering once the horses were within range so would the towers. They looked down at the men dispersed below them, warriors waiting for the giant wooden devices to be set into place. Part of Mahn's cavalry rode toward the allies but none of the foot soldiers followed suit. They remained in place as if cast in stone. Their time was not yet at hand.

The wait turned into hours; the enemy took their time in setting up their implements of destruction. The first volley of rocks were hurled at the city near mid-morning, falling shy of the walls but not of the riders. The crash initially spooked the horses but the horsemen regained control and repositioned themselves as another barrage landed around them. A large contingent of demon-possessed men followed in its wake, their silent throats and vacant eyes devoid of the normal emotions that drove a warrior into battle. Mahn's army fought not for revenge, protection of their lands or for spoils. They had neither goal nor choice in the matter. Those anticipating their arrival stared at the eerie advance then toward their leaders. Allad, Seven, and the others were equally perplexed as they studied the advancing units. It was time. The horsemen kicked their mounts and rode forward to meet the enemy, the violent encounter taking place about a half mile from the gray walls of Bystyn. The fight for their lives and souls had begun.

The furious battle lasted for nearly an hour; the clashing of sword against shield punctuated by the screams of the dying. Rocks whistled overhead. Pieces of the shattered rocks cut into exposed flesh; the larger fragments crushed the unlucky soldier. A second set of catapults was being set up behind the first; their trajectories aimed at the groups of fighters on the plain. Mahn was going to smash into both sides heedless of the deaths of his own men. The king signaled for the red flag to be hoisted over the parapets, preferring retreat to watching his men being dying beneath the debris. The soldiers and horsemen did not notice it for several minutes, minutes that cost many lives. The elves and their comrades extricated themselves from the fighting and retreated back to the city. Oddly enough, however, Mahn's army did not follow them, withdrawing instead back to the main group. Mahn wanted this bloodbath to continue for as long as possible, playing with them like a cat with a mouse trapped between its paws. When the final warrior entered the gates, the defenders slammed them shut.

The fighter's hearts were heavy with bitterness and sorrow. They could do nothing for the dead and dying littering the plains around them. They grieved for their fallen comrades and vowed to seek retribution against the demon. If Mahn hoped to demoralize the protectors of the city by inflicting such horrific injuries, he was sadly mistaken. The newfound resolve springing forth from their souls was greater than any evil he could heap upon them. The light burning in their eyes promised as much. They silently endured the stitches and salve, knowing they would need more attention after the next battle. The physicians tended to the wounded while the Herkahs kept a close eye on them. The nomads slew a half dozen of their comrades in arms; their normally dispassionate faces were filled with emotion as they carried out their unenviable duty. Some of the witnesses rubbed the backs of their necks; others swallowed hard and took a step backward as the possessed bodies writhed in agony then became still. When the grim task was finished, the warriors exchanged unspoken vows to seek revenge upon Mahn and his minions.

Seven, Nyk, and Gard stood on the parapet with the others pointing out a host of possible counterattacks. They ignored the Healers attending to their injuries. The three brushed them off ordering them to care for those who were in dire need of aid as they continued to collaborate on the strategies. The catapults were becoming a problem. Mahn could press forward until the devices smashed into the walls of the city. He chose not to do so creating a momentary stalemate upon the plains. This would not last. With every skirmish, fewer defenders lived to withdraw into the city. Nyk's earlier sortie, although successful, had made little impact on the amount of damage the remainder of the catapults delivered. Barring a miracle, they would have to endure the aerial assaults.

Danyl stared hard at the scene before him, knowing he held the Green Might, a power that could lay waste to the machines if only he could let it rip from his body. He sensed the power swirling within, but try as he might, it would not fly forth. He could cause so much destruction with it, saving all of these good people. He glanced at Zada and immediately looked away.

"It will come when it deems the time to be right," she whispered to him.

"So many will die needlessly in the meantime."

"I know, Danyl, but you have to remember the magic responds to things no one can understand…just like it did when you saved Ramira's soul after she was poisoned by the Kreetch. It came and accomplished its goal then and it will do so again."

"It's so hard to just stand here and do nothing, watching and waiting as the slaughter goes on."

"Have faith, Danyl."

Faith. The word stuck in the elf's mind like a painful barb, taunting him as he glanced from injured elf to dying Khadry. Their courage and determination were steeped in the faith they held for each other and in the belief that the elven magic would save them. Danyl held up his hands and stared with disgust at what would not burst forth. For a brief moment, an image of his blood covered hands dripping into a pool at his feet filled his mind. Each droplet fell with such force it splattered his face. He recoiled at the contact, cringing as the droplets ran down his cheeks and mingled with his tears. The sound they made as they fell echoed the drip dripping he had heard in the maze. Was that the meaning of the labyrinth? Would he remain incapable or unfit to wield the might locked away in the maze while the sound of death trickled down into his stone prison? The vision dissolved away leaving him standing beneath the suns cold glare, oblivious of Zada watching the darkness settle upon his face.

~

Ramira stirred from her temporary haven; she sensed that most of the souls were elsewhere. She left her sanctuary, rising to consciousness and probing her black prison to insure she was indeed alone. The silence increased her wariness as she checked the darkness in which she was restricted. She suddenly sensed Mahn. He immediately wrested her from her foul confines, the violence with which he extracted her equal to the impact of the blinding daylight and noise. She shielded her eyes but could not do the same for her ears as the furious sounds of battle assaulted them. Her senses, accustomed to the gloomy prison in which she had been isolated, overwhelmed her. She toppled toward the blood and mud encased ground. She felt a vise-like grip reach out and grab her by the back of her dress. She saw the horror upon the snow-covered plains surrounding Bystyn. The terrible carnage stole her breath away and brought tears to her eyes.

Debris crashed down upon the plains, smashing into friend and foe alike. The sounds of metal clashing against metal and the screams of men and horses filled the air. The black army surged forward. She looked over her shoulder and saw another wave waiting their turn to fight those who valiantly strove to protect Bystyn. She blanched as Mahn's forces tore the dead and dying into shreds, their companions unable to stop them. Ramira noted the bitterness, determination, and grief on their bloodstained features as they clashed with the enemy. Hatred rose inside her as she glared at the black cloaked shape sitting atop his horse behind her. She peered up into his cowl and saw only a vague mist, one even darker than his garb. She reached back to thrust her hand into that horrible void but his gloved hand caught it. His grip squeezed her wrist until she thought her bones would break.

"In due time you will be reaching for your friends," he hissed.

"I will not relinquish my power to you!"

"Of course you will…"

"*Never!*" she shrieked, her tone so venomous the Vox turned to see what transpired behind them.

Their disinterested looks returned to the battle at hand and, without a word, they rode away. Ramira watched as they split into pairs, each of the three teams heading in different directions.

She knew where they were going: they were hunting for Herkahs. Ramira fumed as she watched the conscripted army kill the elves and their comrades as well as each other. The catapults indiscriminately flung their deadly cargo into the midst of all those battling on the plains. She vowed to put a stop to the carnage unfolding before her. Ramira began to summon forth the Source of Darkness.

Mahn immediately recognized what she was doing and assailed her with vicious images to stop her. They were so intense he could not have inflicted greater damage had he pummeled her with his gloved fists. Her eyes went wide but she managed to thwart the visions and proceeded to gather the power within her once more. The images were losing their effect, compelling Mahn to squeeze her innards in a desperate attempt to regain control. His fierce retaliation was so swift she could feel the blood trickle down her chin as the standoff between the two continued: she with the Source of Darkness and he with his iron will. She would not give an inch of ground. Sensing her stubborn determination, he commanded the evil souls to torment her once more.

This time she did not hide within herself. She flung the Source of Darkness at the horrible shades, incinerating one soul after another. Mahn hissed with pain and rage as wayward bits of the power struck him. He brought his fist down across her face and sent her into unconsciousness. The Master of Evil glared down at her with a mixture of hatred and fear, sentiments hidden deep within his cowl. Her ability to control the Source of Darkness disturbed him; his growing inability to restrain her was becoming problematic. How long would he be capable of suppressing her with brutality before that, too, became ineffectual? For the first time since he snatched Ramira from the safety of this accursed city, doubt began to creep into his mind. Time was no longer a luxury.

~

Zada watched the sudden eruption occurring in the midst of the army and suddenly smiled. Mahn had lost control over

Ramira. He had made the mistake of allowing her to see the bloodshed on the field, expecting her to be too stunned to do anything about it. He had also not anticipated her being able to handle the Source of Darkness. Ramira would not go quietly and that gave the Herkah a certain sense of hope, even after she watched him strike her into senselessness. Ramira's sense of duty and loyalty clearly lay with the Bystynians.

"Why the smile, Zada?" asked Danyl.

"It seems as if Ramira has seen the carnage on the plains and is trying to use her dark power to stop it."

"Can she do that?" he asked.

"I'm not sure but she certainly has given Mahn something to think about."

"Wouldn't he be able to take the power from her if she brandishes it?"

"No, son. As long as she wields it, he is at her mercy. The bearer controls it."

"Then why take the chance? Why not take it from her before she annihilates him?"

The elf stared hard at the knot of darkness though he was unable to pinpoint Ramira. Her vow to keep harm from descending upon the city echoed in his mind. A wry grin lit up his face for he was well aware of how trying she could be once she made up her mind.

"Think of it as hunting with a hawk, Danyl. The bird of prey is cunning with sharp claws and a beak capable of ripping your flesh to shreds. It only becomes submissive when you place a hood over its head."

"Mahn can't get the hood over her eyes, can he?" he spoke almost as if to himself, his gaze never shifting from the black group across the plains. The demon had her within his grasp; the desired power was at his fingertips. Her obvious success in eluding him over time was not anywhere near as frustrating as her refusal to cooperate. *Well done, my love.*

"Danyl," the nomad's firm voice forced the elf to focus on every word she spoke.

"I had brief contact with Ramira yesterday. She showed me a

huge tree beginning from seed then growing tall and sturdy from the desert sands. You, I am convinced, represent that tree and she the white sands. I don't know how that will be achieved but your powers are to unite somehow and defeat Mahn."

Zada searched his face and found only despair. His demeanor darkened at the knowledge she gave him and further eroded his conviction. His inability to summon forth the power was steering him farther away from the sacred trust imparted unto him. His doubts manifested themselves in subtle ways: the nervous rubbing of his thumb and forefinger together and the inability to make eye contact. The Green Might burned like fire through his body yet it refused to be set free. Not yet, anyway.

"What if the Green Might has other plans?"

"You are trying too hard," she replied, her words echoes of what he had heard in the great hall.

Calm resumed around Mahn. He had managed to suppress Ramira's rebellion. His mind drifted back to the vision she had sent Zada and wondered how they were supposed to combine their powers to defeat Mahn. Would the Green Might cede to such a fusion? He had to trust Ramira's insight, though, for she was in a position to see and know what they could not. She had told him she would do everything in her power to keep from ravaging any of them. He believed her even though others, he suspected, did not. He glanced at Gard; the Khadry not bothering to hide his resentment. He had vocalized his distrust on more than one occasion and Danyl could not really blame Gard for feeling that way.

The Khadry had lived in relative comfort within the forest until Ramira came, followed by the menace that had destroyed their homes. All of this was happening because of her, but she, like all of them, was at the mercy of an evil that would never rest until it had the Source of Darkness. This confrontation could have happened a thousand years ago but it transpired now. They had no choice but to defy it or perish. As distasteful as Cooper was, he had lost his entire city while countless other villages perished under Mahn's relentless pursuit of the dark magic. The king deserved a great deal of misery for his recklessness but the price he now paid was unjustified. His city was his soul, his reason for being and to be bereft of it, especially under such circumstances, had to affect even his cold heart. The destruction and sorrow would continue unless Mahn was stopped here before Bystyn fell as well. Danyl filled his lungs then exhaled, his breath concealing the terrible scene below.

~

Cooper stared out the barred windows, the battle sounds detected even through the thick walls. He had been largely ignored, which allowed him a great deal of time to plot his life after the fall of Bystyn. He had to find a way back to Kepracarn and unearth his hidden treasure trove to buy…to buy what? There wouldn't be anyone left in the land. He would become like a rat slinking from cave to deserted village searching for food. He'd always be looking over his shoulder for the inevitable fate to come crashing down on him. There would be no one left to hate! There would be nothing to enjoy either, like women or fine wines or those delicious little songbirds marinated in spicy oils. No more elves or dwarves…not even a stinking desert insect! Cooper's face abruptly lost all color. Those whom he hated and had betrayed would be stalking him, never giving him a moment's reprieve. His dry lips twitched as he imagined Allad trailing him from one end of the land to the other, at no time tiring in his pursuit to turn him into one of the lesser demons. The Herkah would torment him for all eternity. He scratched at the stubble on his chin, rethinking his escape plans.

He knew the only reason Mahn let him go was to do more than bring information to the elves; he had brought something with him to aid Mahn from within the city.

"Hmm. Allad killed the horse and I carried nothing from Mahn with me…what in the Four Corners does he want me to do?"

Cooper slapped his forehead as the truth began to manifest itself in his mind. Mahn depended on Cooper's duplicity to perform certain deeds, which would simplify the demolition of the city. Mahn wanted Cooper to kill all of those whom he hated and what better weapon than the king who had always lusted for what his enemies possessed? Slay the leaders of those gathered here and seek revenge upon the despised Herkahs, starting with Allad, the most detested of all.

The king would harbor no regrets in performing such tasks and indeed had looked forward to such an opportunity for a long time. Things were different now because those he had scorned the most were also the only ones who could save his skin. The only problem was he had to tell them about his revelation. Their response, he was sure, was to post more guards and tighter bolts on the door. No, he had to devise a plan to get free. The Herkah guards would not listen to him; neither would the few others who had any contact with him. His own reaction to such words would be to execute the messenger. Rulers rarely survived if they did otherwise. What would they say or do after he revealed this information? That he would lend them his sword to fight for their survival? He laughed at his own thoughts so he could well imagine how they would react. He had to try nonetheless. He banged on the door waiting for the small panel at eye level to slide open.

Unblinking black eyes stared at him. "Speak."

"I need to see the elven king or Zada. It's very important."

The nomad slammed the trapdoor shut. Cooper did not hear any footsteps in the hall. He sighed. Cooper sat and waited, his thumbs drawing nervous circles around each other as the minutes ticked by. The wait seemed like hours but finally he heard the lock snap open. Danyl, flanked by two Herkahs, walked in. The prince studied the king for several long moments before Cooper could speak.

"This may sound contradictory, Danyl, but I think I've figured out why I was sent here," he began hesitantly, not expecting the elf to believe a single word he was about to say.

"You? Contradictory?" Danyl was in no mood for Cooper's games, the acerbic tone in his voice conveying that thought to the king.

"Yes," he ignored the sarcasm and continued. "Mahn expected me to...well, kill you."

The Herkahs immediately surged forward held back only by Danyl's raised hand.

"What is your point?"

"Look, Danyl, I don't want to end up as some filthy demon any more than you do, so let me help in the fight against Mahn."

"You first tell me that you were sent to kill us then you have the audacity to ask for a sword and be allowed to roam freely in our midst?"

"Well…yes."

"Why should we trust you not to carry out your assigned task?"

"Because if I do that then I'm a dead man and I am not yet ready to depart this world!"

"Mahn would have expected you to be isolated, locked up, and well-guarded. Where did you get the idea you'd have access to my father, Zada, and the rest?" demanded Danyl.

"Because my innermost feelings toward you are…were his most potent weapons."

"Mahn judged you well."

"I've lost my city, my people, my riches and I could be turned into one of those repulsive creatures. All I am asking is that you give me a chance to at least put up a fight and save what shards of my life there are left!"

"You are Mahn's puppet, Cooper."

Danyl's accusatory glare only intensified the powerful emotions surging through Cooper. The king's volatility smoldered then burst into life. Cooper had had enough and rushed forward not to harm the elf but to drive his point home. The Herkahs immediately placed themselves between the prince and the king with weapons drawn.

"I will not bow down to him or anyone else!"

Cooper was livid. He despised being exploited and not taken seriously by anyone, including his enemies. His defiance had turned him into the perfect pawn for Mahn. Cooper was absolutely in control of his own soul, the rage radiating from his body borne of the indignity caused by Mahn.

Danyl stared at Cooper's clenched jaw and the veins straining

327

along his neck and face. The king's emotions were raw, unfettered even within this prison. Mahn singled out Cooper because of his deceit, a trait the relied upon to complete his plans. What Mahn failed to anticipate was that Cooper despised him. Cooper chose life and that meant aligning himself with those that fought from the city. What was murky was how much influence Mahn held over the king. The decision was not his to make.

"I will speak with the others," he stated curtly and left.

Cooper stood in place for a long time with fists clenched and eyes boring into the thick oaken door. He had done his best to persuade the elves to set him free but that did nothing to quell the nervousness in his stomach. What if this was also part of Mahn's plan? Was he thwarting his intentions or merely helping them to fruition? Doubt gnawed at him for the first time since arriving in the city, leaving him strangely exposed and completely unsure of what to do. His hands unclenched as he dropped into a nearby chair, his fixed gaze never wavering from the door.

~

"What the devil is he up to now!" barked the king. The last thing he needed was an added distraction. Alyxandyr never lost the scowl on his face while listening to his son recount Cooper's words.

"I don't know, Father, but he did seem genuine when he revealed that information to me," finished Danyl.

"He wants us to know he was sent here to kill us and by the same token he wants us to free then arm him so he can help? I don't like that at all," stated Styph gathering his weapons together to return to the fight on the plains. His father, Zada, and the others would have to make that decision but he could not help but insert his thoughts before he rejoined his comrades. The crown prince was not about to battle death and worse only to find the leaders murdered from within the walls. He stopped at the bottom of the staircase and looked up first at his father then at Zada before disappearing around the corner.

The Herkahs eyes lingered for a few moments where the prince had just stood. It would be a perfect coup for Mahn to slay them within the protection of the city's walls while their warriors died outside of them. What Styph overlooked was the fact that Cooper, as blameworthy as he was, had had no choice from the moment Mahn arrived at his gate.

"Styph is right, Alyxandyr, but Cooper has lost much and, like us, stands to lose more," Zada said.

"Are you suggesting we take such a chance and free him?" asked the king, unsure why the Herkah of all those gathered held any compassion for him. After all, Cooper had made it a point to hunt the nomads in an almost sporting-like fashion. She had every right to wish him dead.

"I'm saying that Cooper has not been tainted by any demon and is therefore making his own choices."

"One more sword will not turn this tide," he said quietly watching more and more of their people fall lifeless from their saddles while they valiantly fought against the enemy.

"Perhaps he is not meant to take his place on the field for fate has always set forth strange assignments."

"Do you think it is fate that will have you die by his weapon?"

"There is a reason for everything, Alyxandyr. I do not think he will slay me. You forget that Cooper's only motive to ally with us is to resume the life he once led. If that means standing by my side then he will tolerate that." Zada was sure of her words even though Alyxandyr's suspicions remained palpable.

"For now."

"Yes, for now. You disregard one very crucial fact, Alyxandyr," she said softly. "You can apply many safeguards but there is always something you cannot foresee. Mahn knew what kind of person Cooper is but couldn't predict that Cooper could develop a conscience, as thin as the meaning of that word is in his case."

"You think he has his own peculiar destiny linked up with ours?"

"I do."

Alyxandyr did not want to be bothered with Cooper right now. The fierce clashes occurring below them had resulted in many senseless deaths on both sides. Such a waste of life disturbed the elven king. Zada had every right to insist on an increase in guards around the king yet the Herkah gave no such indication. Alyxandyr studied her strained features looking for any evidence of fear or doubt. He saw only certainty. They had trusted her counsel from the moment she arrived and there was no reason not to do so now. After quickly conferring with Clare and Gard, Alyxandyr reluctantly ordered his release. Cooper's freedom- and life- ended the second he made even the most innocent of false movements.

"Zada…have you sensed the elven power yet?" he asked. The elf king's tired expression appealed to her for any measure of hope.

"It is nearer than you think," she replied.

"Do you suppose it could be conjured up to help us?" he asked, unaware that Danyl had been trying to do just that from the moment he found out he housed it.

"It, like Cooper, has its own part in all of this," she replied softly, offering Danyl a slight smile of encouragement.

It did nothing to assuage his sense of helplessness, compelling him to avert his eyes from all those standing around him. Alyxandyr's next words stabbed at his heart. Danyl gripped the balustrade tightly and squeezed his eyes shut.

"We could sure use it about now," he spoke so quietly they could barely hear him. The despondency in his voice was for the dead and dying that littered the snow-covered plains. The king knew the horror would worsen until the respective bearers wielded the Source of Darkness and the Green Might.

Alyxandyr was convinced the Source of Darkness and the elven magic were opposites and would be brandished against each other. He wanted to gain as much edge in the conflict as he could before that happened. It certainly was not due to the lack of courageous actions by the warriors battling for their future. What did he really know about Ramira? He assumed Mahn would be victorious in taking the dark magic away from her. He kept these thoughts to himself because to air them would only cause pain and resentment, especially for his son who loved Ramira very much.

Alyxandyr looked upon Danyl's face and saw a great weight within it that seemed to spread out to his shoulders. It suddenly occurred to him that the heaviness that forced his body to stoop was not just about the loss of the girl but of something else. He peered into Danyl's eyes and saw something unexpected within them. He was about to speak when Danyl's eyes pulsed with an emerald light. It was then that the king, standing there shocked and speechless, understood.

Zada saw the same thing but did not register the same astonishment. She felt a sense of awe at what was taking place beside her.

Danyl felt a sudden surge of power as it reacted to something on the field. He looked toward Mahn. The black power incited the Green Might. The elven magic began to burn through his veins scorching muscle, sinew, bone, and blood. It raced to his eyes, enveloping everything in an emerald mist then slowly cooled until it felt like ice in his veins. He shivered beneath its touch then held his breath when Mahn's mocking voice filled his mind.

Do not fret for her for she is nothing short of my kin.

You lie!

Think about it, Bearer, for how else could she survive fighting the Vox and the other demons?

You will not convince me, Mahn.

Do you know what the Source of Darkness actually is? It is composed of all things dark and horrible.

That is what you are.

And what she is.

No.

Her memories were so tainted by her evil acts her mind had to suppress them or go mad.

So you say.

Break some more of the beads and find out for yourself...

Mahn released him from the mental hold. Danyl glanced over at Zada who conversed with his father. She had not been privy to their conversation. Mahn knew who bore the Green Might. Did he do so to toy with him or was Mahn worried that Danyl and his power could overwhelm him? Was he therefore planting seeds of doubt and despair into his mind to hinder such an encounter? Perhaps Mahn thought Danyl to be weak and preyed on that flaw to gain an edge? He felt the fire burn brighter and more intensely in response to the echoes of the demon's words. Mahn knew about the bracelet…what exactly happened after breaking the beads? Did those actions send a signal to Mahn? Had he somehow planted that trinket for that specific purpose?

"Danyl…" Zada began but he held up his hand to both her and his father.

"He knows, Zada, and now, Father, so do you. I house the Green Might and no, I cannot wield it right now."

"Your eyes have not yet changed, Danyl," Zada reminded him. "They appear just as they did the night you pulled Ramira from Mahn."

Danyl realized the power still thrummed within his veins and wondered why it did not seep away as it normally did. He raised his hand and concentrated on the flow of power as it coursed down his arm and into his fingers. The residual tingling and burning made his skin itch. The magic formally manifested itself to his flesh and bones.

"Why would he contact me, Zada?"

"Intimidation, I assume."

"It's not going to work," he replied, the depth of his commitment shining from within his eyes.

"Why didn't you tell me about this when you first learned you had the Green Might?" the king charged. He was very upset, wondering how different things could be now if his son had wielded the magic. He glanced over at a motionless and ever-present Lance, the captain watching from a short distance away. He had known about Ramira from the start and several other 'secrets'. It would not surprise him if he had been privy to this one, too.

"We believed the fewer who knew the more of a surprise it would be." Some 'surprise': Mahn already knew he housed it. "And obviously of my inability to use it."

"Is that changing now?" snapped Alyxandyr.

"Yes. Father? I apologize for not informing you but that was a decision we thought would be the best one."

"I do not agree but I would appreciate being informed of any other bit of information that you might have." The statement allowed them a chance to confess but neither Zada nor Danyl had anything to add.

They stood together, their woolen cloaks unable to keep out the winter chill. The afternoon sun cast long shadows, turning the macabre scene before them even more ghastly. The wind blowing from the west brought the cries of dying men. It was redolent with the smell of death, which washed over those standing on the parapets. Alyxandyr ordered replacements for the men on the plains so they could eat and rest for a while. A fresh group of fighters rode out from the city but instead of replacing their exhausted comrades they fought by their sides. Sensing their weariness, the black plague surged forward, pressing hard to push the allies closer to the walls. They drove forward but the valiant efforts of the allies kept the enemy from gaining too much ground.

Finally, the sun began to set and the combat began to diminish. Alyxandyr sent out fresh forces to patrol the area around the city while those that had fought long and hard came in for food, rest, and treatment. He, Clare, and Zada listened to their reports. The elven king watched the stragglers enter beneath the gates, their heroic efforts to destroy the enemy coming at a high price. They had killed many but the sheer number of foes replacing the dead made it seem as if none had perished. If they continued to lose men at this rate, they would be in serious trouble within two or three days.

~

Cooper heard the lock snap open and jumped to his feet as four Herkahs entered the room. Ramsat, the group leader pointed to the door. Cooper had wholeheartedly agreed to the stipulations Alyxandyr set forth. He was going to be able to see what was transpiring outside the city walls. He entered the dining hall and seated himself at the end of the table. The Herkah guards planted themselves within a few feet of him, their unassuming stances belying their readiness.

"I appreciate your trust," he said to them, then offered them a little bow.

"Trust has nothing to do with it although I am surprised by your advocate," the elven king said.

"Who..." he began to ask then locked eyes with Zada.

Allad glared at him from beside her. Although the Herkah guards stood at his shoulders, Allad's gaze warned him he would reach his throat first if he made any move toward his mate or anyone else seated at the table.

Cooper could not hide his incredulity and nodded in thanks. He did not meet Allad's eyes. Zada's mate was the best warrior in the land; Mahn coveted him. Even after all of the fighting, there were few wounds on his body and he seemed as fresh and strong as ever. Nyk and Gard appeared a bit worse for wear but still capable of fighting. The unflappable Seven moved about with ease though he had a head wound and bandages poking out from beneath both of his sleeves.

There was little conversation during the meal; the short time they shared afterward spent more in contemplation than conversation. Everyone was very concerned as to what the next sunrise would bring. At what point would Mahn determine they suffered enough before he ripped the Source of Darkness from Ramira and completed his task? Cooper looked from one to the other: no one showed signs of defeat.

"There is a large contingent of Vox and Radir just south of the edge of the forest," Allad stated accepting a small glass of Sevens concoction, "I'm not sure what they are planning but I do think we should find out."

"The perfect trap," said Mason his steel gray eyes locking onto his brother.

Cooper subtly flinched beneath his gaze, for Mason would not think twice about killing him if the need arose. Mason was just as adept with a weapon as anyone else was.

"Mahn would not risk so many Vox in one area without a

reason and that is incentive enough to hazard a look," replied Allad.

Cooper began to squirm in his seat in response to a vague yet familiar sensation creeping up inside of him. He could not quite pinpoint what it was, only that it made him tense and uneasy. He took a deep breath and ignored the feeling.

"I'd sleep better if you took more elves and dwarves than nomads, Allad, just in case it is a trap," suggested the elven king.

"I agree," said Seven. "Perhaps King Cooper might like to travel with you?"

"I spent a year with those miserable things," muttered Cooper. "I don't think another day will matter much." He kept his eyes averted to avoid anyone seeing the unpleasant thoughts running through his mind. The idea of being near those monsters again sent the bile up into his throat.

"I believe you should stay here," stated Styph, "that way one of us will have the pleasure of killing you when you finally act on your orders from Mahn." Styph's undisguised mistrust silenced the room. Cooper may have dined with them but that did not mean he was accepted.

"I have no orders, Prince Styph," he countered glaring at the crown prince.

"That's enough," said the king scowling at his son.

"We have a great deal to plan, Alyx," said Allad as he rose from his chair, "and the sooner we start the better. Nyk?"

The prince joined him and the three of them left the room. Alyssa, Seven, and Clare followed not too long afterward leaving Danyl, Mason, Alyxandyr, and Cooper alone in the room.

Alyssa took control of the city making sure those within were properly cared for. She discarded the silks for tunic and trousers and made her presence felt in every corner of the city. She no longer fretted over trivial details, concentrating instead on the basic needs of several races. Alyssa, like her brothers, could rule if something befell their father.

"Mahn would like nothing more than for Allad to become one of the Vox," stated Cooper staring into his goblet of wine.

"You believe it is an ambush, Brother?" Mason asked with a

modicum of skepticism.

"Don't you?"

"Perhaps," replied the First Advisor while scrutinizing his brother.

Mason knew, as did Cooper, that he could have ruled Kepracarn. Mason chose to extricate himself from his birthplace, ending up as the elven king's friend and counsel. Thinking back on his decision all those years ago, he wondered how different their present situation would be had he chosen to stay. His relations with the elves would have been warmer and Mason would certainly not have hunted the Herkahs. The First Advisor realized he would have made a better king than Cooper but fate had determined his purpose lay in Bystyn.

"What will you do when this is all over, Cooper?" asked Alyxandyr.

"What indeed? If my city still stands and there are enough people left I'll start over, now won't I?"

"And if that is not what awaits you?"

Cooper had thought about that, too, but everything was out of his grasp until the final battle was decided. He thought about Antama. His lips pulled back into a snarl for she had been the one to coerce him into following the stranger who turned out to be Mahn. He doubted he could have avoided the inevitable but her alliance with the demon still made his stomach turn. He knew she was out there somewhere on the plains and vowed he would find then tear her apart.

"Whom do you hate so much to make your face contort with such loathing, Brother?"

"Antama. I will not rest until my hands are around her throat."

"You may get your chance, Cooper," Mason's deep tones filled the silent room.

Yes, I will.

~

Zada handed Allad a glass of wine when he returned to their room later that evening. They had noted a number of good changes in their companions. The Herkahs knew everyone would step into their roles with a gritty resolve that would not easily crumble beneath adversity. They sat down in front of the fire, their arms around each other, as they absorbed the rare moment alone. Their souls drew strength and courage from each other as they realized this might be their last night together. They let go of everything but each other as they stared into the fire. They rose after a while and sought solace in each other's embrace, a scene that was repeated in Seven and Clare's room.

~

Danyl stood on the balcony; the Green Might kept him warm. He could feel it building and shifting within him; his breath was tinted green. He felt strangely calm even though his heart ached for Ramira and all of those who would face the severe challenges in the days ahead. He closed his eyes and waited for the maze to reappear with the truth he could not understand.

It did not emerge this time, although he could hear the dripping echoing in the back of his mind and the dank smell permeating the corridor. Then another scent began to seep in. He could discern spices and unearthly flowers that bloomed only by the full moon. He knew that perfume all too well. The elf smiled at the memory. They were together and nothing was going to ever separate them. The magic swelled briefly as if confirming his thoughts- for a fleeting moment, they were both in accord.

~

The Herkah guards left the barracks and headed toward the castle to relieve the pair guarding Cooper. They walked along the path between the soldiers' quarters and the residences. No lights shone from the windows; no sounds filled the darkness. The sentries were absent. The pair stared at the looming archway, the gloom beneath the walkway uninviting. Movement to their right and rustling from the left startled them. They withdrew their weapons then scanned the area. A shadow detached itself from between two buildings, the sense of danger clinging to the form as it neared them. The Herkahs spun around and pressed their backs against each other as their exhalations floated over their heads.

"Kee-yat!" one of the nomads swore.

A silhouette detached itself from the surrounding gloom and launched itself at the Herkahs. The nomads raised their weapons to block the attack then cringed as the Vox exposed itself. The Herkah/demon rammed the hafts of its knives into the sides of their heads. The stunned nomads collapsed at the demon's feet without a sound. The Herkah/Vox dragged their bodies beneath the archway, their muffled screams echoed off the stone archway.

The Vox walked up the stairs to Cooper's room, the elves too busy to pay him much heed. He stopped in front of the Herkah.

"Where is Ramsat? You know better than to walk this place alone."

"He was detained."

The guard stared at the wheezing Vox, his blood abruptly running like ice through his veins. He opened his mouth to shout a warning when the demon seized him by the throat and hauled him into an unused hallway.

~

Cooper shifted in his bed, that peculiar crawling sensation keeping him awake. He tossed and turned several times scratching at the imaginary itch that would not go away. Frustrated, he rose and poured himself a glass of wine, looking around the room for the annoying insects invading his slumber. His tired mind tried to tell him something but the only thing he wanted to do was lay his head on the pillow and close his eyes.

"I thought those damn elves would at least be able to keep the vermin out," he muttered with distaste then drained his goblet and headed back to bed and a fitful sleep.

TEN

Karolauren looked up as the sound of books toppling from somewhere in the back of the library caught his attention. He cursed at the carelessness of the scribe who had placed them on the shelf then rose to investigate the sound. He walked past rows of bookcases and saw nothing. He was beginning to think he had imagined the noise when he noticed the fallen stack at the far end of the last row. Still muttering, he headed for them. He squatted beside the fallen clutter when he caught a movement out of the corner of his eyes. The ancient elf was too slow to keep the blades from slicing across his throat. The shadow stood over the body, the knives slick with the Historian's blood as it dripped onto the stone floor. The dark shape followed the hall to the back of the library where it forced open the massive doors. It grabbed a torch before entering the room. It scanned the chamber then removed the bottle of Queen's Blood before leaving the Historian's realm.

A silence descended upon the chamber as if the histories mourned the loss of the one who had so lovingly cared for them. Karolauren's blood seeped away from his body and followed the grooves in between the stones until it reached the fallen pile of books. It then wended around them as if the dead elf embraced his treasures for the last time, touching that which had driven his spirit for so many years. His fingers twitched once then the sparkle in his blue eyes went out.

~

Allad and Nyk headed toward the Vox; Styph and Gard led a large contingent west while Seven headed back south to contend with the enemy that massed near the Ahltyn. Danyl had ordered Lance to accompany Gard and his brother but the captain was reluctant to take up a position between the two princes. Lance hesitated, for the command Danyl gave him went against his training and oath. It was hard for Danyl to explain to Lance that the magic surging within him effectively made Lance's capabilities obsolete.

"Danyl," his tone bordered on defiance, "my place is beside you."

"I know, my friend, but you must trust me and go with them."

Lance looked into Danyl's eyes and noted the secret he strove to keep. The captain's demeanor veiled the information he processed; his conclusion saddened him. His thoughts centered on his lifelong friend and the burden that weighed down upon Danyl's shoulders. It made perfect sense: Ramira housed the dark magic while he harbored the elven magic.

"You have a new captain to protect you," he said after a long pause.

"There will always be only one captain, Lance."

Danyl placed his hand on his friends' shoulder then nodded for him to join the princes. The elf disappeared after a few seconds and then linked up with his new charges. Danyl watched them head out the gates.

~

Cooper, still plagued by that nagging feeling, remained in the castle with Zada and Alyssa. The Herkah guard scrutinized his every move. This annoyed Cooper for he was not a threat to any of them, at least under these circumstances. He checked his tongue then cast a sly glance at the unsuspecting princess. Zada broke into his lustful reverie.

"I would think that would be the least of your worries," she reprimanded him.

"What...?" he stuttered as the Herkahs intense stare locked onto him like a razor sharp steel trap. Alyssa looked over at them; Cooper hid his lecherous expression. Now was not the time to fantasize about the elf princess.

"What did he do?" demanded Alyssa.

The fire in her eyes made the king smile. Her spirited energy was nearly as exciting as her beauty.

"You should be more careful or you will find yourself back

in your chambers," the nomad's words were laced with a sharp warning.

~

Alyxandyr and Danyl positioned themselves on the battlements for a clear view of the impending battle. He looked over at his son and realized how much he of all of his children resembled his mother. He remembered that although she never favored one child over another, she did regard Danyl with something he could never identify. The queen had been a direct descendant of the first king; Alyxandyr deduced that Danyl had acquired the Green Might through her. Anjya probably knew all along. She never mentioned anything to him and apparently believed, as Danyl and Zada did, the fewer who knew the better. Either that or the knowledge would somehow change Danyl.

He spotted Allad and Nyk heading north and silently wished them well, his anxiety for their welfare chiseled into his face. What they rode off to face was almost as perilous as Mahn. Alyxandyr felt a knot form in his mid-section and it took all of his will not to shout out for them to turn back. He had to believe, just as they did, that the only way to fulfill their destinies was to face the unknown. Allad's and Nyk's destinies waited for them on the plains.

~

Nyk and Allad rode quietly side-by-side. They could sense the Vox even from this distance and the anticipation grew into apprehension. Zada had provided them each with a poisoned blade but that did not ease the tension in their chests. They faced a foe resembling the only Herkah in the group, the one all of them had grown to respect.

Nyk glanced over at his friend remembering the first time they had met. Allad had saved his life and the souls of his men out on the Broken Plain. Allad's and Zada's guidance had opened his eyes to himself. He understood the Herkahs and a part of him wished he could roam the Great White Desert with them. He had yet to repay Allad and vowed to protect the nomad with his life.

Allad turned his head and met the prince's gaze; his features were calm and sure. They urged their horses to run closer together then reached out to grasp each other's hands. The contact sent a surge of energy from one to the other and to their men riding behind them. Killing the Vox would not be an easy task and many that now rode toward the fiends would not return. They reined in their horses about a hundred yards from the knot of evil and studied their enemy. The Vox tarried, speaking amongst each other and occasionally pointing at the intruders. Allad narrowed his eyes at the overt communication then scanned the area around them for a trap.

"Something is amiss," stated the nomad.

"I agree, Allad."

The demons finally turned their attention to the allies. Their dead stares were focused on Allad. He felt a chill run up his spine and knew this was indeed an ambush. They would have to retreat and rethink their strategy. The Vox had other plans and headed for the elves and the lone Herkah, mounted their demon steeds and raced toward Nyk and the others. They wanted Allad; the prince was an added bonus.

Nyk ordered an instantaneous retreat. They kicked their horses and dashed back the way they had come. The demons caught up to them before they had traveled halfway back to Bystyn. The group hoped they could get close enough to the city where reinforcements might come to their aid. The Vox, however, had other plans. They fanned out and cut off their escape. With Bystyn looming before them, the noose was set and their way to safety cut off.

They jumped off their horses, Nyk barking orders at his men as they formed a tight circle facing outward. The Vox advanced slowly, deliberately allowing the prince a few precious moments to gauge his men. Pride flooded his features as his men stood tall and resolute against the evil that should have made them cower. They drew their weapons, bracing for the horror that was about to descend upon them. No one flinched as the demons advanced. The elves cut and slashed at the demons wounding the bodies but not the monsters thriving within. The Vox, in turn, hacked and killed their way through them to get Allad. Three Vox stepped over the bodies, disregarding the three Vox Nyk and Allad had slain.

Allad managed a look of praise for the elf prince. He fought the demons as if he had been born a Herkah. With the elven guard dead around them, Nyk and Allad prepared themselves for death. The elf and the Herkah pressed their backs together. They pulled out the small knives with one hand and clutched their swords in the other. Elf and Herkah were primed to deny Mahn two extremely desirable bodies.

~

"Sweet Mercy!" whispered Alyxandyr, his knuckles white as he grasped the edge of the parapets. His son and Allad were on the brink of their mortal lives, the black chasm on which they teetered crumbling beneath their feet. The king could not breathe or move so transfixed was he by the distressing sight.

"We should have listened to Cooper," stated Mason as he watched the carnage beside the king.

"They wanted Allad all along," muttered Danyl. He knew that Allad and Zada would be as much of a jewel in his crown as Ramira. There was room for one more gem: himself.

Styph rallied his men and rode hard to get to his brother and the nomad. Those watching on the battlements screamed for them to stop, for they, too, would meet the same fate. Styph could not hear them nor did he look up at the flag ordering them to pull back. Danyl pleaded with the power, begging it to rise up so he could help his brother and the others. It refused his appeals. The elf felt the bile rise in his throat. He had the power but not the resolve to brandish it and that was more painful than watching the carnage near the trees.

~

Zada and Clare had not seen the Historian all morning and decided to pay him a quick visit. They entered the vast chamber and found it empty and cold. Pages of a book flapped near an open window. Clare closed the book and placed it on the

Historian's desk. Karolauren would not allow the cold winter wind to penetrate the library.

The two women unsheathed their blades and began to search the library. They guarded each other's backs as they made their way past the rows of bookcases, nervously licking their lips and gripping their hilts tightly. They squared around toward a noise in the front of the room, remaining immobile for several long moments before resuming their search. They stopped at the end of the rows and inhaled sharply. Karolauren lay in a bloody heap amongst a pile of scattered books. They could not believe anyone would harm the old elf. Clare kept watch as Zada crouched beside the Historian. She pushed back the blood soaked strands of white then flinched at what she saw.

"Zada?"

"The strokes are from a Herkah blade," she could barely speak above a whisper.

"But..." she protested.

"I know, Clare. There is a Vox in the castle and we have to find it." Zada caressed Karolauren's lifeless cheek then closed his eyes. She whispered a Herkah prayer to him then rose to her feet.

They left Karolauren where he had fallen and headed back out into the hallway, their hearts grieving for the gentle soul. They emerged into the main entrance. Clare called over one of the elven guards while Zada scribbled a note to the king. She sealed it and ordered the elf to take it to the king immediately.

"How many Herkahs have access to the castle, Zada?"

"There were six, Clare. Me, Allad, and the four guards assigned to Cooper."

"One of the guards..."

"So it seems. Do we wait or do we lure them down here?"

"I take it you are as capable with those blades as Allad?" asked Clare gripping her weapon.

"I am not as fragile as some suppose."

"That thought never crossed my mind, Zada."

"We'll give Alyxandyr a few minutes then we'll go upstairs..." Zada began then spotted Cricket and Anci heading

344

for the stairs.

Cooper and his escort walked toward the girls from the opposite direction. The girls took one look at their faces and froze. Clare urged them to run downstairs and out the door as the five men began to make their way down. Zada studied each of the nomads very carefully as they approached. It occurred to her that it was highly doubtful that only one of the Herkah guards was a Vox. Initially, perhaps, that was true but it would be a simple thing for one to take the remaining three bodies. If that were the case then they were in very dire straits. Two women, a handful of elves, and Cooper were no match for them regardless of their skills. She glanced at the king who finally realized what that odd feeling was and he, much to his credit, kept calm and alert.

Cooper's complacency within Alyxandyr's protection did not stem the feeling but had dulled his awareness of its origin. The result of his ignorance now threatened them all. Cooper silently blasted his stupidity hoping they would all emerge unscathed from this desperate predicament.

Zada barked out several words in the Herkah tongue and watched all four react without stopping. They continued their approach; their fixed stares bored into her.

Clare heard her curse under her breath, and it was then that she realized that all four of the Herkahs were possessed by Vox.

"Sweet Mercy," she muttered as death advanced toward them. Clare took a deep breath to help steel her resolve for flight was not an option. Clare prayed that Zada's message would reach Alyxandyr in time. Every second counted. Staying alive would be a monumental task at the very least.

~

Nyk and Allad brought the blades to their throats, the demons only a dozen paces away from them. Their time, it seemed, was nearly through. Their backs touched; they shared a peculiar comfort from that contact. Facing certain death together made the inevitable less lonely and frightening. They were both proud and honored to die together.

"I am a better man for having known you and your people," said Allad, his voice clear and strong as he faced his last moments on earth.

"As am I, Allad," replied Nyk. The elf could feel Allad's muscles bunching against his back; the heat from his body radiated through the heavy woolen tunic. They lightly bumped skulls and pressed the knives into their throats. They strained to break the skin on their necks. They dropped their swords and added a second hand to the hilt. The result was the same.

"Nyk!"

"Allad...what..." He and the nomad sank every ounce of strength into their mortal task but the edge refused to budge. The more energy they applied to their weapons the more resistance they encountered. Panic began to take hold as the Vox loomed over them; the demons' bodies blotted out the ineffectual sun.

Allad faced his worst nightmare with uncertainty; his only way out of this terrible predicament was impeded by the will of his enemy. He was afraid for those whom he loved. The Herkah spurned the idea of just sitting there waiting for the Vox to take him and the elf.

"Nyk?"

"Yes?"

"We need another strategy."

"I'm open to ideas," panted the elf.

"What if we..."

Allad never finished his sentence. Two of the Vox yanked them to their feet and grabbed the wrists holding Zada's knives. They squeezed them until the daggers fell from their lifeless fingers. Allad and Nyk tried to bring up their other weapons but the third Vox quickly disarmed them. The Vox held their prizes up in the air and began to immerse themselves into the elf and the Herkah.

Allad felt its icy breath envelope him, the hissing streaming into his ears and permeating his mind. He stared at the face distorted by the evil parasite living within, recognizing the nomad named Bahnal who had been lost two years ago. Bahnal's hand reached up to his face, grabbed Allads locked jaw with an

346

iron grip, and forced his mouth open. The nomad began to breathe heavily, loathing the creature that was about to violate him in the worst possible way. The Vox turned toward one side allowing Allad to see what was happening to Nyk. His distended features brimmed with repugnance and agony as the Vox poured itself into him. The tendons and ligaments around his face and neck nearly burst through his skin; tears streamed from his wide eyes as the repulsive monster oozed into him.

Bahnal's subjugated features replaced the elf's tormented countenance. Allad flinched as the Vox closed the distance between them and opened his mouth, helplessly watching as the Vox vomited his essence into him. The sickly yellow haze appeared as polished as a finely honed blade one moment then flared like fire the next. It flowed into his mouth and down his throat, slicing and searing everything in its path. Allad jerked and twitched, gagging on the foul taste as it spread outward from his torso to his limbs. It pierced his organs and burrowed into his muscles then seized the core of his being. It settled upon everything except his mind like some loathsome blanket. The malignancy began to swell up into his head, rounded up his spirit and slammed it against the back of his skull. The appalling mist formed a net around his soul, keeping it imprisoned but permitting it to witness the horrors it would unleash. Allad's spirit would not cede quite so easily. He rose up and retaliated against the Vox with such intensity the demon lost control of his soul. Allad's will was greater than the Vox's and he began to drive the demon from his body. The repulsive monster had never encountered such determination before and only Mahn's interference kept Allad from prevailing. The Herkah had no choice but to relent beneath the overpowering black might batter him from without. Allad ceased his uprising and returned to his prison, a single tear running down his once proud face.

~

Styph watched with dread as Allad and Nyk rose amongst the other demons gathered around them. They were too late to help: to attempt a rescue now would mean adding their bodies to that terrible group. He gestured for them to break off the attack and head back to the fighting, his heart and mind numbed by the loss of his brother and the nomad. He searched the parapets and, to his dismay, saw his father staring at Nyk and Allad. Danyl's unmoving form stood near the king. Where was that damn elven magic? It could have saved them! It could save them all!

Fury rose from the depths of Styph's soul, prompting him to spur his mount on. He needed to release his frustration. Styph neared a cluster of enemies, raised his sword high into the cloudless air, and roared with rage. They thrust themselves into their foe. Their ferocity became infectious and soon the outnumbered allies began to push back Mahn's army. Each of the races shouted their own particular war cries, sharing the words until elf praised Herkah and dwarf celebrated the Khadry. The words drifted back and forth across the blood and mud-covered snow, then back to the city where those upon the battlements heard them. They called back down to them, encouraging them with shouts and raised fists. The momentum shifted and the allies, filled with a renewed sense of strength and courage, rallied against the dark force that threatened their very existence.

~

Alyxandyr's heart stopped beating as the hated demons took his son and Allad. The king could not breathe nor blink; his gaze was transfixed on the horrifying scene on the plain. He turned and glared at Danyl. He looked back at the Vox as they disappeared into the trees, their indifference ridiculing those that watched. Riveted in place by the awful memory, Alyxandyr ignored the soldier who desperately sought his attention. The elf yanked on his arm repeatedly.

"My Lord!" shouted the messenger then pressed the note into the king's hand.

The king's face turned pale as he read the note; he barked several orders then raced down the stairs. A contingent of Herkahs and elves followed right behind him. He shoved his anguish into the back of his mind as this new and greater danger took precedence. He grabbed Danyl by the arm; the group jumped onto waiting horses and sped up the main avenue to the castle. People scurried away from the fast-moving group, watching with trepidation as their king accelerated up the avenue. The Vox had taken his son and friend but they would not have Zada and Clare.

~

A half dozen of the royal guards formed a protective circle around Clare and Zada as the Herkah/demons advanced. The nomad watched as Cooper, forgotten by the demons, slipped down the hall and out of sight. He had, apparently, succeeded in executing Mahn's assignment and left them to their fates. Her eyes lingered for a moment at the spot where he had disappeared before focusing on the urgency at hand.

"Coward," hissed Clare as she surged forward and joined the elven guard in combat.

The Vox were fierce fighters; their skills borrowed by the bodies and souls of those they occupied. Clare's determination, the elven guards' resolve, and Zada's own abilities, however, did not allow for an easy victory for the Vox. The elves managed to kill one as did Clare but the cost had been all but one of the guard; the injuries Clare had sustained were beginning to sap her strength. The last elf went down leaving two unharmed Vox facing one injured and one exhausted woman. The odds were against them and, as each Vox rushed forward, a blur materialized from behind the one seeking Clare. The unsuspecting demon fell to the ground a second or two after his head; his companion hissed with hatred at Cooper. The king did not shrink back. He raised his weapon in defiance, the cold determination blazing from his eyes eliciting a slight smile on Zada's face. The Vox, however, would deal with him later for his main quarry was Herkah standing a few paces away.

It lunged at her then parried the strike Cooper swung at him. The king attacked several times and only a ringing blow to the head dazed him long enough for the Vox to concentrate on his prey. It surged forward, overwhelming the Herkah with lightning fast strokes. Zada warded them off while retreating one step at a time. Clare endeavored to rise and help her friend but her wounds betrayed her, stealing what little energy she had left. All she could do was watch in horror as the Vox systematically overpowered Zada. The Vox pinned her against the wall next to the massive castle doors.

"Cooper!" shrieked Clare as the king labored to his feet.

He swayed unsteadily as he took a step in Zada's direction. He wanted nothing more than to slay the demon. He tried to distract the Vox by shouting and cursing at it. The Vox ignored him, the prize seconds away from being in his possession. Cooper lurched forward and fell painfully onto his knees. He staggered to his feet shaking his head to keep the room from spinning. He dashed toward the Vox, slipping on the bloody floor and falling in a heap upon a dead elf. He panted and fought the urge to retch. *Can't...let it...have her!* His mind demanded that his body rise and defend Zada but it was not to be.

"*Zada!*" he shouted, his blood-laced spittle spraying the dead around him.

The Vox brought its dagger up just as the king and the others burst through the entrance, crushing both combatants between the door and the wall. The heavy oaken portal hid what transpired behind it; the ensuing silence was deafening to those who waited for it to close. They could do nothing but stare in dread at the gruesome scene before them. Clare slouched on the floor amid the bodies of the elves and three Herkahs while Cooper, sword in hand, bent over her. Their unblinking eyes focused on the closing door; the creaking noise it made grated their nerves. The door closed with a thud revealing Zada and the Vox up against the wall, locked in a hideous embrace. The Vox glared down at her; their bodies concealed their hands. Zada stepped back haltingly; her rigid body quivered. The nomads' dagger penetrated the demon's heart.

Zada shuddered with revulsion as the damned darkness came to claim her soul. Her strength nearly gone, she reached into her tunic to retrieve the only thing that would save her from that terrible fate. The message she had sent the elven king would not bring help in time, and neither Clare nor Cooper was able to come to her rescue. They had all fought valiantly, even the king, and she rued the fact that the evil would consume them as well. She had to use the small blade on the Vox to avert that disaster. The Vox was upon her; she shivered as the evil gushed over her. It filled her nose and throat; it poured down inside her then radiated into every fiber of her being. The need to spew out the abominable sensation overwhelmed her. The Vox was not yet ready to inhabit her for it wanted to inflict her spirit with one final blow: it revealed what had befallen Allad and Nyk. She converted the anguish lifting up from her soul into a weapon the Vox had not anticipated. She drew strength and courage from her loss and was determined not to spend an eternity with Allad in a place devoid of love. She gritted her teeth, centered her hatred and self-preservation into the blade and thrust it into the Vox's chest. The demon grabbed her by the throat and began to squeeze the life out of her. Her eyes watered; she struggled to breathe. Zada began to lose consciousness until the sudden impact of something slamming against her back pushed her against the demon. The impact plunged the knife through the Vox's body.

~

"Zada?" Clare called out to her in a shaky voice.

"No!" Cooper held his hand up as the elven king began to move toward the Herkah. "We have to make sure she has not been affected by the demon!"

Danyl understood Cooper's fears but ignored him and walked up to Zada. He lifted her chin with his fingers; her skin was hot and sweaty. Did the Vox poison her before she killed him?

"I know…what they did to…Nyk and Allad," her voice was barely a whisper. "It showed me…for spite…"

Tears flowed down her cheeks; she collapsed against him. He collected her in his arms and carried her to a chair while the king, his grief as fresh as Zada's, approached the dwarf queen.

"How are you faring, Clare?" he asked squatting down next to her and inspected her injuries.

"I will heal but…"

"But what?" asked Danyl, the unspoken knowledge leaving him with a hollow feeling. What else did the Vox do?

"They killed Karolauren," Clare said.

"They did what?" Alyxandyr's eyes went wide with disbelief as the news sank in.

"We found him…in the library…that's how we knew the Vox were in the castle."

"You will have to tell the others about Nyk and Allad," said Cooper. H pressed his palm against a deep cut on his forehead. His wounds were insignificant compared to their dilemma.

"Yes, I know," said the king. "Danyl, pass on the news."

They had lost Allad and Nyk; Zada narrowly escaped that same terrible fate. Cooper and Clare survived yet could just as easily have become members of that dark brotherhood. The elven king looked at Cooper; the king's face was smeared with blood and his eyes were devoid of their trademark arrogance. Cooper exhaled with relief as Zada regained her composure. Alyxandyr left Clare and stuck his hand out to help Cooper to his feet, checking the gash on his forehead.

"You'll barely notice it when it heals," stated Alyxandyr. He held Coopers baffled gaze for a moment, then subtly nodded at him.

Danyl crouched beside the Vox who lay by the door. He reached into the dead Herkahs pocket and pulled out the round bundle that had caught his attention. The prince removed the cloth and held the bottle of Nefret up for the others to see then walked over to Zada.

"I believe this belongs to you."

~

Ramira fumed and shrieked at Mahn; he assailed her with everything in his power whenever she attempted to wield the Source of Darkness. She was extremely difficult to restrain and there were times that he thought he was losing control of her. It was almost time anyway, and soon she would be nothing more than one of the thousands of souls existing within his tormented domain.

Nyk and Allad were worse than dead and all because of her. So many slain because of what she housed. How could she ever face any of them again? She could feel the Source of Darkness react to her rage; it rose from the depths of her soul like some phantom whirlwind seeking to destroy what caused so much misery. She could have helped them just as she helped Danyl and the others that day on the plains. She had to cling to those things that offered hope. Mahn sent his best to acquire those bodies and had failed because Zada, Clare, the elven guard, and even Cooper rose above their fear and defeated the Vox. What had she done that could be even remotely comparable with their courage?

Come, Ceraphine, leave your petty musings behind and greet your friends...

Mahn deposited her onto the plains to stand before the vacant eyed Herkah and elf. He hissed with pleasure as she mourned for them. Both Vox struggled to control their resolute spirits. Ramira saw that these two, like Horemb, would never fully relinquish themselves to the demons that invaded their bodies. She fingered her blades, her desire to set them free the only thought in her mind. She moved with incredible speed, managing to catch Mahn completely off guard as she lunged forward and slew Nyk. He fell in a heap, the fleeting look of gratitude radiating from his soul negating the gaping wound across his throat. Allad's spirit came to life within its prison. He tried to manipulate the Vox into position so that she could grant him the same end. The demon grappled with its host, losing ground until Mahn interfered. His gloved fist came crashing down on her cheek; she immediately collapsed to the ground.

Mahn was beside himself with anger. She had denied him the elf and would have stolen one of his greatest prizes had it not been for his supreme overconfidence. He could not take the knives from her nor could the demons, for their touch was an anathema to them. The dangers she posed became evident, compelling Mahn to hasten his plans. He glared at another hooded and cloaked figure standing by his side. It lifted its head until a woman's ultra-pale face with crimson eyes became visible. His spirit bored into her with such vehemence that her body trembled but her features never exhibited anything but apathy. The High Priestess had made a terrible pact with Mahn a thousand years ago and he was determined to extract a severe payment for her past failure. Her tainted soul shared the body of another corrupt individual, one craving the same chaos he intended to inflict upon the land. The High Priestess' desire for glory beneath Mahn's black rule paled beside that of Antama, who dominated the host body. Ina, weakened by her failure centuries ago and no longer protected by Mahn, would be no match for her. The hiss of spite scattered his timid minions and prompted the woman to carry out her assignment. She walked away, disappearing within a knot of fighters as they turned to confront a band of elves.

~

Father and son stood next to each other upon the ramparts, the setting sun accentuating their pale faces. They watched their enemies start their fires and knew there would be no rest tonight. They had lost so many good men and women. Reason told them the enemy would attempt to gain access to the city and terrorize it from within. Alyxandyr hoped his son could find some way of wielding the Green Might. He could not even begin to imagine what his son was going through while the power surged within him. The king looked up to accept a message from an exhausted and bloodstained dwarf, who turned back to continue to fight.

"What does it say?" asked Danyl.

"All of the units are being forced to retreat. At this hour, Seven, Gard, and Styph still live."

"Mahn will come to the gates tomorrow."

"How do you know that?"

"I feel it," he replied then left his father.

~

Styph met up with Seven just inside the barracks after sunset. Their filthy and sodden clothes hung limply from their bodies. Alyxandyr had sent out the last fresh group of soldiers to relieve them.

"We lost Nyk and Allad today...they were taken by Vox," Styph sadly informed the dwarf king as they stripped off their armor and accepted mugs of tea.

"I heard. Zada and Clare also had their hands full," replied the king as he sat down on the makeshift table across from the prince. He stared at his clasped hands, disregarding the dirt and blood he thought could never be washed away, and then closed his eyes. He thought of Allad and Nyk and gripped his hands more tightly together, the pain of losing them ripping into his heart. They ate stew and fresh bread without tasting them and washed them down with hot tea.

"They managed to get into the city and who knows how many more of them are lurking about. We've lost so many, Seven, and I doubt we can protect the city if we lose even a fraction of that tomorrow."

"Where is the elven magic, Styph? Why isn't someone brandishing it in our defense?"

"I wish I knew, Seven. It falls onto our shoulders to buy as much time as possible until that happens." Time, the prince realized, that was nearly expired.

"And Ramira? When will he drive the stake into our hearts with her?"

Many had died on both sides because of the magic she housed. Neither Styph nor Seven placed any blame on her, for she was a pawn just as they were. That she was able to keep the Source of Darkness out of Mahn's grasp was nothing short of a miracle. They looked up as Gard joined them, the Khadrys face as fatigued as their own. Styph updated him on what had occurred during the course of the day.

"Losing those two does not bode well for us," Gard remarked around a mouthful of food.

"Zada and Clare, with some help from Cooper of all people, were able to kill four Vox - Vox that had been assigned to guard Cooper," Styph told him.

"How in the Four Corners of the land did four Vox accomplish that feat?" asked the Khadry.

"We don't know, which leads us to believe other demons may

already be in the city."

"Wonderful. And what of Cooper? Did he atone for all his sins by saving them or are you still considering him a tool of the darkness?"

"He could just as easily have killed them without anyone knowing, Gard," Styph pointed out.

"Which means they weren't his only prey?"

"Zada and Clare would certainly have been worthy trophies," corrected Seven.

"That is not what I meant, Seven. I meant there is something else he seeks either to gain or to destroy."

"The elven magic."

"Exactly," said Gard using the end of the bread to sop up the rest of the stew.

"Zada said that Mahn could take it once he had the Source of Darkness."

Seven looked into his mug of tea. The faint candlelight reflecting off its dark surface reminded him of the moonlight shining on the river by his home. If he could just sit at the top step leading into the Hall with a pipe in one hand and a glass of his…he forced the foolish thought from his head.

"Well, whoever it is," said Styph as he stretched out and tried to rest his weary bones, "he or she had better wield it or there won't be anything left to save."

Gard was silent; his ire was focused on Ramira, the reason all these people were dying in the first place. And what of the elven magic? Where was it and why hadn't anyone used it yet? How many more would be slain before it surfaced? He sighed and extended his aching arms and legs as he, too sought a few minutes of rest.

ELEVEN

Zada lay curled up on her bed and stared out into the dismal morning with red-rimmed eyes. She sniffed and reached out for the empty pillow beside her, gently caressing the place Allad's head had once rested. She tiredly got to her feet and dressed. She stuck her hands in her pocket and felt the bracelet wrap itself around her fingers as if it demanded her attention. She took it out and gazed at it. The tiny beads gleamed dully in the light.

"Well, Zada," she took a deep breath and collected her scattered emotions, "you can't help Allad or anyone else by sequestering yourself in this room."

She answered the knock at her door, graciously accepting the tray of food the elf brought her. She sipped her tea, feeling the hot liquid warm her cold body.

The Herkah rose and armed herself, sliding blade after blade into small scabbards on her arms, legs, and around her waist. She gained a sense of purpose with every click of a knife snapping into place.

She stood in front of the floor length mirror and smoothed out her garments, gauging her worthiness when her sight became active. She looked beyond her reflection at the nebulous haze beginning to coalesce behind her. It formed the brown woman, who drifted over and enveloped her with heartfelt sympathy. She gratefully accepted Oma's ethereal embrace, the brown woman's warmth and caring soothing her broken heart. Zada's inner sight began to open allowing the cold air of the in-between world to stir her clothing. She would be withdrawing from her chamber, but not through the door leading to the hall.

Time is growing short, child. Do you have the strength for the journey?

"Yes."

Are you afraid, child?

"No."

Good. Do not attempt to make any contact or interfere with what you are about to see. These things happened long ago. If you try to communicate you will leave your world forever and exist in a place that is somewhere in between.

"I understand."

You will experience everything, child, but will remain unseen...

Zada took Oma's extended hand and felt her entire being dissolve into glittering dust. She was aware of every single one of the sparkling motes and of Oma's essence that merged with hers. Her room turned grainy then disappeared into a smoky haze. Zada's world became muffled then silent. Her body lifted up then was pulled in an unknown direction. The air was cold; the dizzying impression of speeding through time was as numbing as the frigid surroundings. Zada could not tell if they hurtled past points of light or if the lights dashed past them. The Herkahs nervousness began to manifest itself but she held fast to her trust in Oma. They continued to speed into the distant past through this eerie corridor. The nomad was frightened. She had begun the journey and there was no turning back. Nor did she want to. Time seemed to stand still and the blackness continued to roil around her as she hastened on, her anxiety and curiosity growing the farther she went.

The corridor finally began to lighten, turning first dirty gray then into a creamy shade before exploding into bright white. The sudden cessation of movement and the blinding light combined with the extreme heat paralyzed her. She began to falter, losing her bearings and, more importantly, herself in this strange place. Oma squeezed her hand reassuringly and waited for Zada to settle down. The Herkah relied on all of her other senses as her sight gradually began to clear. Waves of cool air touched her hot skin; the unmistakable scent of incense filled her nose. She heard scuffing sounds and people talking and the feel of cloth as they brushed past her. Hooves pounded on stone and somewhere off to her right was the sound of a child screaming over its mother's admonishment. Her feet were uneven and she cautiously pushed the higher of the two forward. She stubbed her toe. Zada's vision began to clear; the scene stole her breath away.

She stared upward trying to absorb the magnitude of what towered before her. Massive columns shouldering monumental stones fronted a structure. The colonnade continued through the middle of the huge building, disappearing into the darkness that seemed to stretch forever. The sides flanking the gallery were enclosed; the stone was carved with gigantic images of battles and people on thrones. Oma nodded to the huge entrance, catching a stumbling Zada as the Herkah craned her neck to absorb the awesome sight before her.

Zada marveled at the brilliant images painted all along the pillars. There were birds flying over and landing on a reed-enclosed river so blue that she reached out to dip her fingers in its cooling water. A tall, white crane watched her walk by, its painted beak longer than a lance. She furrowed her brow at a column filled with peculiar black symbols neatly divided by deeply incised panels.

Zada finally took notice of the people walking past her. The men wore white linen kilts; the women donned flowing gowns of the same material. Their oiled nut-brown skin was a perfect contrast to the snowy fabric. Both men and women shaved their heads; some wore braided wigs bearing gold sheaths at the tip of the plaits. They accentuated their costumes with gold bracelets, earrings, and rings. Each piece was marked with the same strange characters Zada had noted on Ramira's blades. The shade of the brown woman penetrated through her awe and reminded her that this was no time for sightseeing.

"Where are we, Oma?"

Welcome to your roots, child…

Dar-Ahnet strode through the palace as if she were already Ceraphine. All those she passed bowed low to her. Her head remained erect as she cast disdainful looks down at the backs of the servants' perspiring skulls. Her perfumed skin glistened with oils; the pure white linens covering her slender limbs were so finely woven they were nearly transparent. Jewelry crafted of the finest gold and encrusted with brilliant gems glittered upon her dark skin. Her lovely features suffered beneath her arrogance and contempt.

The ruling Ceraphine's decline into death was taking longer than Dar-Ahnet had anticipated. Her mother's refusal to die would not put a wrinkle in her plans. Dar-Ahnet fingered the vial hanging from a chain around her neck as she entered the Ceraphine's chambers. She dismissed everyone except for the High Priestess, Ina. The woman, clad in red robes, inclined her head in greeting then joined Dar-Ahnet beside the bed. The Ceraphine lay in a semi-lucid state, her face pale and a silken sheet covering her gaunt body. The High Priestess grabbed the woman's jaw and forced it open then waited for Dar-Ahnet to pour the liquid down her throat. Dar-Ahnet drained the small bottle and watched as Ina closed her mouth to prevent the Ceraphine from spitting out the bitter liquid. She convulsed and clawed at the air around her, her face turning first crimson then purple before becoming wan once more. The Ceraphine twitched twice more then lay still.

"We've managed to gain an extra week, Ina. Go and prepare the Blood Prophecy. I'll meet you in a little while."

Dar-Ahnet stared down at her mother's lifeless body, the feel of the crown already heavy on her head. She crossed her arms and closed her eyes, her hands grasping an imaginary gold flail and crook. She heard the roar of the crowd as they chanted her name repeatedly, immediately silencing them with a wave of her hand. She had so many changes to make, starting with the demise of her siblings. She planned to invade the Water Dwellers in the far south and go after the strangers heading east. All of this was possible because she housed the greatest power in the land. Ina had told her so.

The leader of the strangers, according to the High Priestess, teemed with power, a might she intended to assimilate with her own. The main obstacle to her objectives was now dead and soon anyone else with rights to the crown would meet the same fate. She and sneered at the dead Ceraphine.

~

Dar-Ahnet strolled out of the Ceraphine's rooms, following the endless corridors leading down into the bowels of the palace. The beautifully painted limestone blocks found in the upper rooms became giant cubes of unfinished stone at the foundation. The fit between the stones was perfect, and not even a sheaf of paper could fit in the gap. Torches jammed in wall brackets provided the only light; smoke from the oil soaked tops blackened the wall around them. The brands near the airshafts flickered, casting eerie shadows along the angular walls. Dar-Ahnet brought the edges of her gown up across her nose and mouth to filter out the heavy incense confined to these dank depths. She sniffed and wiped away the tears trickling down her cheek, anxious to cleanse the musty taste from her mouth.

She descended the last few steps and saw the massive doors at the end of the dim gallery; their hinges were as long as a man's arm and the iron rings wide enough for her to slip her entire body through. Two hooded priestesses effortlessly pulled open the portals, bowing as she walked past them into the immense chamber. It was empty except for a large altar surrounded by stands bearing torches.

"I've come to see the blood, Ina."

"You will see it, Dar-Ahnet," she replied in a low and flat voice.

She clapped her hands and summoned two vacant-eyed priestesses bearing a chalice of silver encrusted with sapphires and diamonds. They handed it to her, averting their eyes as they backed out of the room. Ina poured the thick blood mixed onto the corner of the altar and watched it flow down the main channel. The mixture zigzagged over ancient symbols. It seeped this way and that until it finally drizzled off the end into a waiting vessel. The High Priestess took the urn and lifted high over her head then looked at the pattern on the altar.

"What...?" Blood filled every furrow and continued to ooze out onto her feet from the spout that had fed the urn. It overflowed the grooves, cascading over the sides at an alarming rate. It lapped up against her ankles then her knees like some ghastly red tide rushing in to drown everything in its path. It whirled around her waist, climbing steadily upward to her shoulders and finally filled her mouth. Ina dropped the urn, the echo of shattering pottery breaking the hold the image had over her. She wiped away the sweat with trembling fingers, her lungs aching for lack of air. Ina dared to look at the altar top and the blade-like imprint created of blood.

"Is something wrong?" demanded Dar-Ahnet.

"Ah, no, Dar-Ahnet, the reading is quite clear."

"What does it say!" snapped the other impatiently.

"You will be Ceraphine."

"That is all? I came down into this place for four words?"

"They are important words, Dar-Ahnet," she replied with the utmost of reverence, her black eyes staring at the trail on the stone.

Dar-Ahnet turned and left, the trek down to this loathsome chamber hardly worth hearing the report she had already surmised years before.

When the massive stone doors swung shut, Ina cursed everything under her breath. She had chosen poorly, applying her dark secrets and energies on the one that did not house the Source of Darkness. What had she overlooked? What hint or clue had she ignored? What could she do now to correct her mistake? He was to awaken soon and would not be overjoyed at her error.

The High Priestess had ten to select from and Dar-Ahnet seemed the most logical of the choices. Who held the power? She had less than a week to rectify her mistake for once the strangers passed by it would be too late. She had already awakened Mahn and he expected the Source of Darkness at the apex of the next full moon. It was then that she was to sacrifice the bearer and allow him to take the power. He would not know of her mistake until then but she was not about to waste any time amending it. Her failure, she knew all too well, would be punishable in ways she did not even want to imagine.

She paced back and forth, willing each of the Ceraphine's offspring into her mind then eliminating the least capable of them until four remained. The only sure way to know was to perform this very ritual with each member present. Dar-Ahnet would find out and attempt to prevent her from carrying out her task, killing her siblings before she could even read the blood. She had to get all four into this inner sanctum at once, a difficult challenge indeed. She needed an excuse, a very good one. Even the High Priestess was expected to justify her actions.

Ina left the damp chamber behind and walked steadily upward; daylight made her squint. She stopped as one of the four family members she had decided upon turned the corner in front of her. This child frightened her for reasons she could not explain, and was the only one who dared to show her contempt openly. The High Priestess bowed to her; the fear and hatred for this woman was barely kept in check.

"Why are you out of your snake pit during the day?" she demanded, not bothering to conceal her loathing for the High Priestess.

"Many pardons, Dar-Ramira, but I have important business to attend to."

"Whose mind are you intent on poisoning now?"

"Please, Dar-Ramira, my entire life is devoted to your family and the city," her words prostrated themselves in front of Dar-Ramira.

"Then why have you spent so much time at the black well?"

Ramira flexed her fingers, the desire to wrap them around Ina's neck overwhelming. The High Priestess quickly glanced at them and took a step backward, swallowing hard at the remorselessness radiating from Ramira's eyes.

The black well was located north and slightly west of the city at the northern edge of the trees paralleling the mountain range to the east. It rested upon ground that had long ago ceased to sustain growing things. It reverted to a swampy place surrounded by a foul yellowish mist the sun could not penetrate.

"You must be misinformed, Dar-Ramira, for that place is forbidden…"

"My eyes do not deceive me."

"In truth," the High Priestess began as she sought to extricate

363

herself from Dar-Ramira, "I needed a specific kind of root that grows only near its border."

"Really?"

"Yes," she replied, kowtowing to her with clasped hands. *My work will be so much more arduous if you are the one. Although the pleasure your terrible death will bring me will make it all worthwhile.*

Dar-Ramira said nothing. She continued down the corridor knowing there was only one reason the High Priestess would go to the black well: to trifle with the evil imprisoned there. The High Priestess was determined enough to toy with something that was beyond her comprehension and power. Dar-Ramira was just as resolute to keep that from happening. The High Priestess was responsible for making the Ceraphine lose sight of her duties and then subverted Dar-Ahnet to believe she was going to be the next queen. The palace sycophants would follow whoever sat on the throne. They latched themselves onto the High Priestess thinking she would be the one to propel them to higher positions. The dangerous games being played within the palace prompted her to seek companionship outside the polished limestone walls, yet duty compelled her to observe and, if necessary, to intervene. She had accepted that responsibility from Imhap, Horemb, and Oma without question.

~

Dar-Ramira abandoned the cool confines of the massive structure and stepped out beneath the searing sun. She adjusted her head covering as she descended the wide staircase leading to the thoroughfare lined with statues and fountains. Trees, flowers, and shrubs clustered around those life-giving waters as they braved the hot breath of the desert and the blistering sun slipping into the west. She headed for the crowded section of the city that housed all those who toiled for the palace. They rested their bones inside their Spartan mud homes. The delineation between the two was immediate, made even more so by the thick wall separating the two classes. The side facing the palace displayed richly painted scenes heralding the Ceraphine's achievements;

the other was composed of adobe bricks partially covered with crumbling plaster. The narrow alleyways abounded with wares, food, weaponry, and other goods including the carts that zigzagged between people and animals. Barking dogs and clucking chickens mingled with the bickering merchants. She passed by clay jugs filled with wine, baskets of fruit, and vegetables. Marinated meats on long sticks simmered over open pits and aromatic spices clung to one's clothing. Life continued as it had for centuries. They labored until their bodies gave out yet never shared in the bounty they reaped. Ina, through Dar-Ahnet, would make their lives impossible. Dressed in loose trousers and tunic with her hair hidden under a head covering, she passed unnoticed through the constricted streets. She took several twists and turns before ending up in front of a nondescript house deep within the packed quarter.

"Oma?" She smiled as the brown woman beckoned her into the small kitchen.

"Good evening, My Sweet," she said hugging Ramira. Her work-hardened fingers reached up to push a few red-gold strands of hair back as she studied Ramira's tense expression.

"I need to speak with you."

Ramira helped herself to a plate of honey and date treats the other had placed on the table. She lifted the delicacy to her lips but the bile still burning in her throat from the encounter with Ina took her appetite away. She placed it on the tray then folded her hands on the table.

"Go on, child," Oma urged, wiping her hands on her apron. A bad feeling began to gnaw at her as she looked at the crimson staining Ramira's cheeks and fire blazing in her eyes.

"I think the High Priestess is trying to awaken what is imprisoned in the black well."

"Yes," sighed Oma, "I thought she might."

"What are we going to do? No one else in the palace cares or is aware of her plan and I don't know how far she has gone to resurrect it."

"If she has already been there then I believe it is already astir, child. That means she has focused on the Source of Darkness, which it needs to become as powerful as it once was." Oma spoke very slowly.

"What are you talking about, Oma?"

Oma knew this day would come. She took Ramira's hands into hers and gazed with love at the woman she had helped bring up. Memories of the little girl curled up in her lap filled her mind. How many times had she held and rocked her, humming a tune until she drifted off to sleep? How often had she dabbed at the scrapes and bumps on her elbows and knees? Ramira had sought to escape the dishonesty prevalent within the palace and, fortunately for them all, she chose to go to Oma. The brown woman had been present at her birth, cradling her in her arms the moment her mother released her into the world. Oma had continued to hold and coo to her even after the birthing chamber emptied out. Everyone except the three who had accepted the Lady of the Sands' daunting behest ignored the newborn girl. Now the grown woman before her would learn of the truth hidden from her since she was born.

A low, melancholy sound traveled throughout the city silencing everything in its wake. Birds took flight from rooftops and dogs whined. Vendors and buyers stood motionless, the former with their hand out to accept pieces of silver for the wares the latter clutched against their chest. People looked from one to the other, their faces registering both mourning and apprehension. The Thebans resumed their activities, their voices, when they spoke, were hushed. They glanced about nervously; mothers called to their children and men took deep, tense breaths.

Oma closed her eyes as the horns' echoes faded. She looked over at Ramira to gauge how she took the news of her mother's death. Ramira stared past the wall and toward the palace, her features cold and unforgiving. Oma felt a shiver run up her spine and the warmth leave her limbs.

The Ceraphine had been wasting away for weeks now; Dar-Ahnet handled the palace affairs. The High Priestess, initially a shadowy form behind the throne, became more active in the day-to-day activities. The trips to the black well and the Ceraphine's death did not bode well for Thebes or her people. Ina was under the assumption that Dar-Ahnet held the power and would, through her, advance her own objectives. Her miscalculations would, with any luck, buy them some time.

"Ramira," the words were thick in the woman's throat. She had kept this information from her fearing the day when she would have to explain the dark truth to someone she had grown to love as her own child. "You house the Source of Darkness."

"Me?"

"Yes, My Sweet, you."

"Why didn't you ever tell me about this before?" Ramira just sat there, her fingers nervously plucking at her sleeves. Ina's image formed in her mind, the corners of her mouth turned down; her hands flexed around invisible knives.

"Because we thought that you'd be better protected if you didn't know and..."

"And what?"

"We hoped that the disposition of the bearer would keep the Source of Darkness in check. Imhap, Horemb, and I decided to interact with you on every level to avoid, we hoped, you being corrupted by the dark power."

The Lady of the Sands had called to Oma, guiding her to the dais in the desert where she revealed the bearer of the Source of Darkness. The Lady had presented Oma with an alternative, one that might keep the power from falling into the wrong hands. The Lady believed that with the right training, discipline, and emotional involvement, Ramira's spirit would be able to withstand the Source of Darkness' influence and keep its evil intentions in control. There were no guarantees or assurances they would have any success. Oma and the others accepted the daunting challenge.

"Are you saying that the Source of Darkness is evil, Oma?"

"Yes, child, it is, but you are not and that eases my apprehensions. We are not worried that it resides in you for we believe you will not use it to destroy, whereas if it dwelled in anyone else..." She could not finish for the very thought of Dar-Ahnet housing the power was frightening indeed. Her lack of insight would allow Ina and the demon to wrest it from her, then

367

brandish the power to smite everything in their path.

Oma could only watch as Ramira gazed down at her hands as if she were waiting for the power to spring forth from them. Her lovely features rippled with awe then dread; her simple appeals for help heartbreaking to the other woman. The lack of interest in Ramira by the court all these years determined whether the course they chose was the right one. Desperation had driven the three to confront the Source of Darkness, the initial fear of doing so quieted but never completely lost over the years.

"What do I do now?" she asked in a small voice.

"Continue to behave as you have and do not tell anyone that you have it," warned Oma. "If the High Priestess begins to suspect you might be the bearer you must take any and all precautions to insure she does not acquire it."

Horemb's part in tutoring her with the blades was an essential ingredient in preparing Ramira. She had learned her lessons well and would need them the not too distant future.

"Oma?"

"Yes, child?" Oma placed her arms around the now grown woman. She held her tightly and kissed her forehead while fighting her own tears.

"Things are going to change now, aren't they?" she asked, her voice quaking.

"Yes, My Sweet, they are." Oma spun the bracelet on Ramira's wrist.

~

Dar-Ramira returned to the palace, entering the royal wing just as Dar-Ahnet and her perfumed entourage exited her rooms. The looks the two women exchanged were anything but cordial. Dar-Ahnet dismissed her retinue and faced an unemotional Ramira.

"I will be Ceraphine," she hissed at Ramira. "The first command I will give is to have your head presented to me on a platter of woven reeds."

Ramira ignored the insult, inwardly preferring a tray of rush to one composed of gold and precious gems. Ahnet discerned as much, which angered her even more.

"Thank you for the warning," Ramira replied, the desire to slay her half-sister creeping into her mind. "I'm curious, Ahnet, what honors will you bestow upon Mother during her entombment?"

"She will be given the proper respects then placed in her crypt within a few days."

"You are foregoing the customary month of mourning?"

"The High Priestess Ina has seen dark days ahead and has counseled me to expedite the services."

"The two of you can't wait to establish your plans, can you?"

Ahnet stared at her half-sister, her features darkening with every passing second. Ramira pretended not to care for the mantle of power. The moment Thebes' crown rested upon her head, her half-sister would plot to take it away from her. Her nonchalance failed to mask the conspiracy already hatching within her black breast. Ahnet would foil Ramira's plans before she had the chance to act. The eternal night would claim her other siblings, but Ramira would be much more difficult to kill. She and Ina had already discussed possible methods of murdering her. The High Priestess, probably Ramira's greatest adversary and most hated of all people, wanted that assignment, one Ahnet was loathe to give up. Dar-Ahnet would grant Ina that honor with the stipulation she was able to witness the assassination. *I will throw a festival on that day celebrating your death by re-enacting it!*

"I understand you have taken a great deal of interest in the trespassers," the silken words oozed from her mouth as she watched Ramira's reaction.

"I am merely curious," she responded, refusing to fall into Ahnet's trap. Ramira openly accompanied the scouts assigned to tracking the strangers' progress as they made their way east along the southern boundaries. Her nighttime excursions to study them on her own, however, remained unnoticed. Subtle undertones of aggression against the outsiders permeated the air. Ramira had seen nothing from the group indicating an invasion, leaving her to wonder why the High Priestess focused her attention on them.

369

"Perhaps we can capture a few and allow them to entertain us."

"Maybe you and the High Priestess could prod them with your forked tongues."

"How dare you!"

"I dare, Ahnet, but you do not have the stomach to play that game; you leave your dirty deeds to others."

"I could have you executed for uttering such insults!" she shrieked.

"My point exactly," retorted Ramira, who turned her back and walked away.

"I did not dismiss you!" proclaimed Dar-Ahnet.

"I didn't ask for permission," Ramira muttered to herself as she disappeared around the corner.

Ramira changed into traveling clothes then packed a small bag; she disregarded the luxuries that surrounded her. Beautifully carved boxes of fragrant woods held the finest of linens while equally elegant stands held perfumes, aromatic oils, and a variety of cosmetics. Lush river scenes decorated the walls. Ducks flew in between reeds and over fish swimming in sparkling waters; pure white blossoms floated upon emerald lily pads. She ignored the canopied bed; its silken sheets and soft blankets were as appealing as a bed of nails to her. The statues and busts and other fine pieces that filled her chambers meant nothing to her. She turned her back on the opulence and sneaked out of the palace through a maze of hidden corridors. Ramira exited the vast complex via the garden to the east then headed out to find the strangers.

Ramira rode south and west, keeping to the brush and trees as she watched for the large group of travelers making their way along the edges of Thebes' lands. Her curiosity and something she could not quite identify drew her on; the revelation of the Source of Darkness' location reverberated through her mind. If Oma knew then so did Imhap and Horemb. Her entire life had revolved around these three individuals and even knowing what she housed had not lessened their affections. She swore she would do everything in her power to keep them safe, regardless of the cost. Imhap had encouraged her to glimpse the strangers as they passed by, heightening her curiosity with bits and pieces of information. They were heading for some unknown destination, the keen interest shared by Dar-Ahnet and the High Priestess in them not lost on Ramira. Ahnet's and Ina's malevolent intentions were something Ramira was not going to allow.

She spotted their trail about an hour later. Ramira pursued the travelers for several miles as they wound their way eastward. They would be near the line of trees running perpendicular to the mountain range. She cleared a little rise and saw the end of the undulating line of wayfarers in the distance. Her inquisitiveness and excitement grew as she tried to imagine what the outsiders looked like. Would they be dark or fair? Thin? Heavy-set? Learned? What language would they speak? Would they be friendly or hostile? She tracked them within the concealment of the trees well into the early evening, thankful when they finally decided to stop for the night. Ramira dismounted and rubbed her sore muscles; her eyes never wavered from the scene below her.

Dusk camouflaged many of their details but that did not discourage her from inching closer to their camp. She moved soundlessly down the rounded hill and hid herself in the last series of brush and trees near the base of the hillock. Some of the travelers tended to their horses while others checked the wagons for wear and tear. The campfires sprouting up in the darkness cast a soft light on the figures sitting around them. She guessed there were at least several hundred encamped below then wondered if more were bringing up the vanguard. One of the strangers caught her attention as he moved from campfire to campfire, speaking with nearly everyone as he made his way through the encampment. He would lend a hand when needed, and then proceed to the next group huddled around the flames. She watched as he walked well beyond the edge of the camp and placed his hands on his hips, the full moon eliciting an almost unearthly glow about him. Ahnet's words of capturing some of the strangers echoed in her mind. Ramira could well imagine what horrors Ina would inflict upon them if that happened. She estimated the group would be beyond Thebes' borders by daybreak. How far had Ina's preparations progressed to capture some of them? Should she warn the strangers or take the chance they would be gone before anything happened?

Ramira watched the man turn around and slowly make his way back into camp while studying the dark land around him. His gaze seemed to linger in her direction, prompting her ease back into the darkness.

She decided to convey a warning; if nothing else, she would at least appease her curiosity. She rose to her feet and brushed off the dirt and leaves stuck to her clothing. Ramira searched in vain for the man. He couldn't have gone too far; perhaps he had stepped beyond the firelight into the darkness. She watched the far edge of the camp for several long moments before spotting him looping around and heading in her direction.

She remained rooted in place, her feet unwilling to carry her toward the outsider. A slight rustling sound behind her urged her to crouch down. Ramira held her breath; she strained her senses but could not detect any movement around her. She breathed a sigh of relief when someone grabbed her from behind. She felt a peculiar stirring react to his presence. Unafraid and strangely calm, she turned and faced him.

The full moon cast its silver light upon his features. It illuminated his elegantly arched brows and ears; his handsome face radiated strength and curiosity. The unabashed scrutiny was mutual. Silence claimed the hillock as their gazes met and held. She sensed a current running from him through the contact on her wrist, one burrowing into her flesh then vanishing down into the depths of her soul. It spiraled downward like some mighty bird of prey and she swore she felt the tips of its extensive wings brushing against the sides of her existence. Then, as if spotting its quarry, it swooped down to a specific point within her, folding back its great wings as it dove onward. She suddenly realized what that target was and immediately broke the connection. She took several steps backward until his intense gaze riveted her to the ground.

"Who are you?"

"I...I have come to warn you," she replied, her voice

suddenly very faint.

"From what?"

"You cannot stay here for there are those whose interest in you is far from civil."

"From that city?" He pointed toward her home. Patrols had informed him of its presence long before they traversed its southern perimeter. He had had the opportunity to send an emissary there but something advised him to forgo that plan. This woman seemed to corroborate his decision.

"Yes. The city is called Thebes and it is about to receive a most unpleasant visitor, one that you don't want to be near."

"I sensed an evil as we passed by. We need to restock our provisions and have many repairs to make on our wagons before we can continue."

"You must go...tonight...now."

She turned to leave but he grabbed her wrist. She escaped and withdrew into the shadows. Ramira heard him running after her but she managed to jump on her horse and ride away before he had the chance to catch up.

He stood in the darkness watching the night devour the dark shape. He had sensed an odd emanation from her, one he did not recognize yet respected nonetheless. He sighed and returned to camp, her forewarning resonating in his mind.

~

The High Priestess had surreptitiously tested Ahnet's siblings, yet none of them exhibited even the faintest hint of the Source of Darkness. She became concerned, for she had to complete the final spell tonight to free Mahn. He was already loose in the land but needed the dark power to complete his transformation from phantom to utter power wielder. The red woman was in a dilemma. She could do nothing to prevent him from coming to Thebes nor could she turn to anyone else to help her destroy him. If she could locate the Source of Darkness then perhaps she could brandish it and defeat Mahn. Who was left?

The High Priestess cringed when she realized who the bearer was; it could not have been a more hated enemy. Ramira. Ina realized Ramira was her most formidable foe, one that was even more relentless with her hatred than the evil she had aroused in the swamp. She would be difficult to trick and it would be nearly impossible to extract the Source of Darkness from her if she knew she carried it…but if she didn't know, then Ina's task was that much easier. Who would know of its existence other than herself?

The red woman thought long and hard about who else would be aware of the dark power. It occurred to her that Ramira spent little time at the palace. She preferred living amongst the residents of the city. One of the houses she frequented belonged to a woman named Oma. Ina tapped her thin lips with a gaunt finger, her eyes half closed as she analyzed what she knew about the woman. The jeweler's widow lived alone and had been present at Ramira's birth, taking care of the child within the palace until Ramira was old enough to walk. Oma had never done anything out of the ordinary; she cared for Ramira according to the rules set within the royal residence.

"Why you? Who chose you, a member of the lower class, as guardian to a royal child?"

The High Priestess scowled for the one person who could answer her question lay cold and stiff in her chamber. The Ceraphine must have selected Oma to watch over Ramira…or did she? Two others also interacted with Ramira: Imhap the Vizier and Horemb the General of the Army. She shook her head for they were responsible to teach all of the Ceraphine's children. Imhap educated them and Horemb taught them fighting techniques.

Ina walked over to the altar, the memory of drowning in blood still fresh in her mind. She stared at the hundreds of small channels making up the maze on the altar top for so long they began to shift and change before her eyes. The edges of the grooves began to blur; their borders became rounded then flattened out. It began to ripple and flow, like a tiny lake, complete with shadowy reflections along its 'shore'. She reached out a trembling hand and hesitantly dipped her finger into the black water. She immediately recoiled for the water burned and froze her. She wanted to massage the life back into her finger but the blistering pain stopped her. She lifted it up and eyed the frostbitten digit bearing multiple welts. They gradually disappeared leaving her finger as before. Was this an omen?

Whether Oma and the others were innocent or not was no longer an issue. She had to find out what, if anything, they knew, regardless of the consequences. He would soon sweep across the desert and into Thebes taking what she had promised him. The result of her failure to deliver her end of the bargain would be dire indeed.

~

The High Priestess hurried to her chambers, changed into simple clothes, and headed out. She blended perfectly with the denizens who carried out their arduous chores to keep the city and, more importantly, the royalty, comfortable and wealthy. She made her way through the crowded streets taking several twists and turns before ending up in front of Oma's home. She knocked on her door.

Oma recognized her but admitted her anyway and ignored the sick feeling beginning to grow in her stomach.

"What do you want?"

"What have you told Ramira about the Source of Darkness?" demanded the High Priestess.

"You haven't found it, have you?" Oma crossed her arms in defiance; her usual gentleness was replaced with an air of utter control. She stared hard at the High Priestess regardless of the hatred blazing from the other's eyes.

"Does she know she houses it?" The High Priestess hissed while trying to hide her growing fear of the woman who began to loom over her.

Oma remained silent while watching Ina's face take on a crimson cast. Beads of perspiration formed on her forehead and trickled down her sharp cheekbones.

"What will you tell him when he comes, Ina?"

"What?"

"How will he react when he finds out that you are incompetent?"

"Ramira has it...doesn't she?" snarled the High Priestess while fumbling within the folds of her clothing.

"Ramira has many things."

"I know of one thing she will no longer have."

The High Priestess pulled out a dagger and buried it in Oma's chest. The brown woman's gaze never left Ina's, even as she fell in a heap to the floor. The red woman rested one knee on the floor; her features were unrepentant as Oma lay dying before her. Blood dribbled from the corner of Oma's mouth. She reached out and grabbed Ina's thin wrist with a strength that surprised even the High Priestess. Oma's breathing became ragged but she did not relinquish her hold on Ina. The High Priestess tried to extricate herself from the brown woman's powerful grip.

"Hurry up woman- I have things to do!"

"You...have already...failed..."

Oma winced as the High Priestess brought the blade across her throat then ripped her hand free of the dead woman grasp. She rose to her feet and glared down at Oma, contempt and a hint of fear crowding her countenance.

"I have not failed."

She headed back to the palace, the searing rays of the sun unable to penetrate the gloom in her soul. Her black clothing obscured Oma's blood but it could do nothing to ward off the growing truth of her words. She had not failed but simply miscalculated her plans. She had plenty of time to rectify her mistake; two more individuals could help her. Ina took a left at the corridor beyond the entrance to the palace, ignoring the stately columns and open-air rooms beneath them. She disregarded the scribes with shaven heads and writing surfaces placed across their crossed legs. They dipped their reed styluses into wells of black ink, entering information onto sheets of paper from the lists handed to them. She walked on and entered the plant-enclosed courtyard at the end of the hall where she found a skinny little man sitting in front of a fountain. He stood up in one fluid motion and offered her a polite bow; his black eyes were devoid of emotion as they scrutinized her garb.

"My presence doesn't seem to surprise you, Imhap."

"Neither does the Ceraphine's passing."

"She was quite ill."

"And so are the tidings you bear, yes?"

"Where is Ramira?"

"She is not scheduled for any teaching at this time."

"Where is she?"

Imhap folded his hands in front of him, his fingers clutching a sheaf of documents. He had observed Ina taking Ahnet under her wing, indulging and training her from the moment she was born. The young girl had been corrupted over time, growing up on the bitterness and arrogance that Ina had disguised as tutelage.

Ramira was a willing student for him, ravenously devouring everything he had taught her. She memorized the maps and histories and paid special attention to the races living around Thebes. The Ceraphine was dead and the High Priestess wore common clothing flecked with blood. The self-proclaimed Ceraphine was an intelligent, albeit self-centered woman who was about to plunge Thebes into darkness with the help of the High Priestess.

"I do not know."

"Guess!"

"My guess is that she is beyond your influence and control."

Ina muttered unintelligible words under her breath as the little man calmly frustrated her attempts to gain information. He mocked her without appearing disrespectful; he made her feel insignificant and worthless. Malice rushed through her at lightning speed, carried on the beginnings of panic. Her constricting chest muscles squeezed at her lungs and her stomach pumped bile into her throat.

"Damn you!"

Imhap stood motionless as the blood spurted from his throat down his wiry chest and followed the contours of his arms onto the papers. He never raised his arms in defense nor tried to run from the knife-wielding High Priestess, which infuriated her even more. She glared at his crumpled body, gasping for air as her options dwindled down to one man. She did not relish confronting the mighty Horemb.

~

The unseen witnesses followed the course of events. Zada's hand covered her mouth during all the incidents, especially the murders of Oma and Imhap. The spirit of the brown woman wiped the tear running down Zada's cheek then gently patted her hand. Oma inclined her head to the dead Vizier and closed her eyes as if in prayer. She remained that way for several long moments, and then took a deep breath to face the next series of circumstances.

This was the easy part.

"Easy? Oma, how can you say such a thing?"

Because it is the truth.

"Sweet Mercy! She murdered you and Imhap!"

It gets worse, child. Come.

Oma directed her to the exercise grounds behind the palace where soldiers practiced beneath the mid-morning sun. Groups of well-muscled men in loincloths sparred with swords, lances, axes, and other weapons under the command of one man standing well above them all. His legs were like oak trees and his solid body seemed chiseled out of a single slab of granite. His arms bristled with muscles. Horemb's glittering eyes caught every movement from every man without ever moving his head.

"Falit! Keep your sword up or he will cut you into pieces! Sentet, what have I taught you about gripping your hilt? Vesna! Rest the back of your shield against your forearm and upper arm or it will completely break apart with your enemy's first strike!"

Horemb walked into the midst of the gangs who moved back respectfully, listening to everything he said or did. He moved Sentet's fingers along the haft of his sword for a better hold then scrutinized Sentet as he manipulated the blade in the air in front of him. He repositioned Vesnet's shield, nodding as the man deflected blows from another man without the discomfort he showed before.

The High Priestess glared at Horemb from behind a succulent bush full of pale pink blossoms. Ina could not simply walk up to the general and challenge him as she had the others. He would be as unwilling to reveal what he knew as Oma and Imhap had been. She crossed her arms and bit her thin bottom lip. She needed an appropriate punishment for him, one that would haunt him for eternity. She nodded to herself as she remembered the special demons that would accompany Mahn from his morass. These demons thrived on the physical capabilities that defined Horemb. She grinned wickedly then frowned. Why hadn't she thought of that before killing Oma and Imhap? Well, she was not about to let this opportunity pass her by. She scanned the practice yard and spotted Horemb's water jug. She grabbed a pail and worked her way along the edges of the training field filling up the containers. She may be the High Priestess but she had no privileges to be on the field. She shuddered to think what Horemb would do if he caught her. Ina finally approached Horemb's jug and added a few drops of a pale blue liquid along with the water. She held her breath and then casually strode back to the well and replaced the pail. She returned to her vantage point and waited.

Horemb finally ended the exercises late in the afternoon; a sweat drenched High Priestess glowered at him from behind her concealment. Ina used a sodden corner of her head covering to wipe away the perspiration, watching intently as the general neared his water and dipped the ladle into the opening. He lifted up to his lips; the High Priestess leaned forward without breathing. She scowled as Sentet marched up to him and engaged him in conversation, the dipper forgotten. Horemb dropped the scoop back into the vessel and held up his hand showing the novice an imaginary grip that Sentet copied. The general nodded with approval, slapped the young man on his shoulders then raised the dipper to his lips. He tilted his head back and emptied out the scoop. The High Priestess smirked as he dipped it into the water for more. *Easy Horemb...I want you awake so you can appreciate my little surprise.*

Horemb picked up his gear and walked toward the building near Ina, his initial steps steady until he reached the bush where she hid. He stopped, wiping away the perspiration suddenly pouring down his face. He began to stagger and dropped his equipment. He barely made it to the stone bench just feet away from the red woman. Ina scanned the area to make sure they were alone and then joined the ailing general.

"My Lord does not feel well?"

Horemb noted her casual attire and the hood framing her gaunt face. She was out of her temple during the daylight hours and sat fearlessly beside one of her adversaries. The feigned look of concern awkwardly twisted her features. He could recoiled from the arm she placed around his burly shoulders, its cold touch induced gooseflesh even beneath the hot sun. She sneered at him as he tried to lift his hands to crush the life out of her, the effort unleashed nothing more than a torrent of sweat.

"You foul and purposeless fiend…"

"You flatter me, Horemb."

"I'll…kill…you…"

"You've had plenty of chances," she leaned over and kissed him on the lips.

He mustered up enough spit to wash away some of the repulsive aftertaste clinging to his mouth. It dribbled down his chin and dripped onto his glistening chest. Hatred formed a knot in his chest and radiated outward. It strengthened every fiber of his being until every muscle strained against his skin. Ina's eyes went wide; she shrank back and fumbled for her knife as Horemb labored to stand. He managed to gain his feet and grabbed a handful of her hair, which he ripped out as he tumbled forward. She yelped with pain then kicked the sweating man panting on the ground before her.

The High Priestess tied a rope around his ankles then hoisted him up into the back of a cart, carefully concealing the unconscious general with an old blanket. No one paid any attention to the spare figure on the rickety wagon being pulled down the main avenue by a limping old horse. The dray creaked and rumbled unevenly over the stone boulevard, every bump dislodging rusting nails or pieces of planking. Ina prayed that the wheeled crate would hold together long enough to get her to her destination.

The setting sun cast long shadows by the time she reached the main gate. She yanked on the reins then smacked them down on the horse's hindquarters, urging it in a northwesterly direction toward the mountains. The hot winds pressed down upon the sands then rose again as the cold night air began to seep across the desert. Sand devils erupted at will, the swirling sands towering into the star encrusted heavens or barely reaching her knees. They emitted high-pitched whooshing sounds as the fine grains brushed against each other in their frenzied dance. They became less frequent the further she ventured from the desert; the mountains were an imposing wall the winds could not penetrate.

The changes in her surroundings marked her entry into the demon's domain. A sickly yellow mist swelled in front of her, obscuring everything around it. The air grew foul; the ground to either side became more viscous the closer she came to the edge of his dominion. Twisted skeletal trees loomed on either side of her, their tortured roots trapped in a quagmire that belched up gasses. The slurping noises it made while reabsorbing its own waste made even Ina queasy. The air was thick and heavy. It pressed down with such palpable weight it threatened to break every bone in her body. Her neck and shoulder muscles ached as they fought the pressure and kept the terrified horse from bolting into the marsh. She had numbed its senses with potent herbs, but even the strongest potion could not completely buffer it from the evil lurking within the swamp. Her previous trips had been difficult; now that he was about to rise and assume his full power it became nearly impossible. She glanced over her shoulder and watched the fog swirl. She pulled on the reins and stopped the wagon. She took several deep breaths to calm herself enough to be able to convince him that everything was proceeding as planned. The wait was interminable; the mist clung to her exposed skin like leeches seeking blood. Brushing them away, she knew from experience, worsened the situation. Once broken, the beads formed an icy layer that seeped into your soul. That mistake forced her to spend days beneath a mountain of blankets and even the searing noonday sun could not penetrate the malaise. She shivered at the memory then froze as a deadly silence settled down upon the marsh.

A shape materialized within the fetid mist; its shifting form human one moment then massive without delineation the next. It ambled toward her and stopped. The soupy haze veiled something she was glad she could not discern.

"What have you brought me?" he hissed.

"My Lord needs warriors," she bowed low to him. "I, your humble servant, thought this one might be adequate enough to fulfill that role."

"Indeed."

Mahn parted the mist; the High Priestess cringed. The undefined specter moved forward and brushed against her, its touch burning her skin. She fidgeted with her cloak, backing away from the shape hovering over the prone Horemb. The Theban general stared up at the monstrosity filling his entire vision. Mahn opened his nebulous robes and formed a tent around him and Horemb. The demon's head tilted back, his lengthy arms elevating until they seemed to scrape against the night sky. He shoved an indistinct shape into the general; his movement was lightning fast and filled with a depraved glee. Horemb convulsed; his back arched until Ina thought he would snap in half. Mahn violated the general for several long minutes then departed his body as abruptly as he had invaded it. The High Priestess stared at Horemb's lifeless form. Her brows wrinkled together while her fingers knotted her garment. She dared to look over at Mahn who stood unmoving several paces away. Did she lug Horemb here only to have Mahn kill him? She opened her mouth to speak then jumped as the general's eyes snapped open; he stood erect as if yanked to his feet like a puppet.

Mahn walked around the partially suspended man, nodding with approval as he looked at him from head to toe. The demon tore a strip of cloth from his robe, wrapped it around his hands, and pulled tightly on it. The cracking noise it made sounded like thunder, which reverberated through the swamp. Unseen things scattered into the mist. He placed the piece over Horemb's shoulder and stepped back, whispering words under his breath while waving his hand to the subtle cadence. The section of fabric began to expand, leaving Horemb clothed in black within moments. Mahn reached over to the man and flipped a black cowl over his head, blocking out the hatred burning from Horemb's eyes. *I will have an entire army composed of creatures like you!*

"You have done well. How goes the preparation for the Source of Darkness?"

"Everything is on schedule, my Lord."

"Good." Mahn turned without another word and disappeared back into the haze, taking his new prize with him.

"Yes, my Lord," she replied bowing low. The High Priestess headed back to Thebes. The breath she exhaled seemed to last all the way back.

~

The passing miles increased the distance between Ramira and the newcomers, but did not decrease the sensations still flowing freely through her mind. His appearance and the electricity that emanated from him captivated her. She rued the fact she would never be able to learn anything about them. They would face enough trials and tribulations on their journey without having the added pressure of contending with Thebes' problems. She had her own worries to contend with when she returned to the city. The sun was just painting the morning sky when she re-entered the city and stole back into the palace; she increased her vigilance due to Ahnet's very real threat. Ramira disappeared into her rooms after checking every corner for signs of an assassin.

Ramira bathed, dressed, and then headed down the brightly painted stone corridor. She suddenly doubled over in pain and dropped to the floor gasping for air. She looked around but found herself alone. Ramira crawled over to the wall and used it for support as she rose unsteadily to her feet. A white-hot fire burst deep inside of her. She continued to wheeze as the hallway began to spin; it took all of her will to keep from fainting.

A sensation began to flow through her, drawing her down into the bowels of the palace. She walked on in an almost trance-like state, the sounds of the living slowly diminishing as she disappeared down into the deepest section of the palace. Her bare feet did not feel the cold of the stone floor nor did she gag on the pungent incense hanging heavily in the darkness. She forced open the massive doors shutting out the world from the High Priestess' lair. Ina stood at one end of the altar, her arms overhead. Ramira interrupted her in mid incantation, the look on Ina's face bordering on panic. Fully in control again, Ramira noticed the thick, incense-infused blood oozing down the top of the altar toward a pair of black daggers. The viscous liquid began to turn black and effervesce the closer it coursed to the blades. Soon tendrils of steam lifted up from the altar. The sounds of moaning and shrieking echoed somewhere far off in the distance. The torches began to flicker; the flames undulating wildly then turning bright red. Ramira had no idea what the blades were for but everything the wicked woman in red did revolved around evil. The spell Ina was casting over the knives wormed itself into Ramira's mid-section and stimulated the pain that had brought her here. Ramira ignored the discomfort and closed the distance between herself and the daggers. The High Priestess spoke faster, trying to hurry the process along before Ramira could react, but her victim had other plans. The daggers were key to extracting the Source of Darkness and would be of little use if they were not fully saturated with the potion. Ina's voice began to falter; her hands shook. Ramira was within an arm's length of her.

Ramira reached out and snatched the blades from the altar before the concoction defiled them. The hilts felt cold yet oddly revitalizing at the same time. Something began to surge through her hands and up her arms until the feeling inundated her entire being. It also ignited the Source of Darkness. The power sprang to life within her and coursed through her veins like liquid fire.

The High Priestess shrieked in denial and raced around the altar to take back the blades. Failure meant having to face Mahn and she had little time before he arrived. She labored to keep the hysteria at bay as the potion neared the end of the altar top. She took a step toward Ramira then shrank back when Ramira brought the blades up. The chamber became deathly still. Plop. The High Priestesses' face started losing what little color it had. Drip-drip. Ina cringed as the solution poured into the stone vessel at the end of the altar. Panic sent its roots deep into her black soul.

"What have you done? Let me finish or he'll kill me!" she

screamed while lunging for the knives.

"*I* will slay you, but first you will tell me what you did!"

"He is the Lord and Master and will take what you have, then rip the power from the strangers," she screamed.

"When?"

"Tonight," she replied, her eyes riveted on the knives in Ramira's hands.

Ramira held the implements of her own death. The reason behind their creation should have appalled her, yet she gripped the hilts more tightly instead. A strange connection began to form between flesh and metal, one that brought on an odd sense of confidence within her. Her mentors had instilled that same conviction into her, placing their trust in her ability to draw from the lessons she had learned from them. Failure was always a factor. Ramira had had little time to think about the Source of Darkness or its reason for existing within her, relying instead on her instincts and training. Killing Ina became a priority, one emanating from within her glittering eyes as they stared into the High Priestess' black ones. Ina stood her ground; afraid yet driven by the thought of what the demon would do to her if she faltered. The red woman was running out of time, but then again, so was Ramira.

The High Priestess was being uncharacteristically open in providing her with this information, turning suspicion into caution. Ramira walked around the altar forcing the red woman to follow suit; she searched the dark shadows permeating the vast chamber. They were alone, yet that did not alleviate the sense of foreboding in her mind. The red woman was stalling her and Ramira knew she had to leave or fall prey to her schemes.

"You have betrayed your people and now you are on the threshold of doing the same to the demon. How very fitting."

Ramira's dark tones seemed at home within the dismal chamber as they reverberated off the ancient walls. The hatred she felt for the red woman radiated from her face and burned into Ina's corrupt soul. Ramira had not forgotten the High Priestess' treachery as she spun the ceremonial daggers in her hands.

Ina's face drained of blood, her fingers twitched nervously.

A sense of desperation burned in her breast as she sought to delay Ramira's departure and save herself from Mahn's wrath.

"I care nothing for anyone, least of all a group of vagabonds! Give me the knives, Ramira."

"I think not. You will undo the bargain you made with Mahn."

"It's too late! He will come no matter what you do and will take what you house!"

Ramira glared at the traitorous woman who began to close the distance between them. The loathsome bargain the High Priestess made with Mahn was about to reach fruition. The only thing lacking was the Source of Darkness. The power Ina sought would claim most of her people's lives, but the strangers had a chance to survive. When she was finished here, she would find a way to help at least some of the Thebans escape.

The High Priestess gathered the last shreds of courage and stood in front of Ramira. She licked her dry lips and discreetly slipped her hands inside her blood red gown. She never had an opportunity to pluck out her knife.

"No you don't," snarled Ramira.

She slashed the High Priestess' throat. Ina crumpled to the ground, twitched several times then lay still.

Ramira stared at the dead woman and then left the chamber. She extinguished every torch along the way, fighting the urge to wield the Source of Darkness and bury the evil lair beneath tons of rock and debris. She was sure that, deprived of his prize, the demon would destroy it. Mahn would rise from his sulphurous realm tonight, leaving her precious few hours to help those who could escape.

She headed to Oma's home. People scattered away in terror from her as she walked down the street. The High Priestess' bloodstained her clothing and skin; her eyes glittered fury. She entered the home, her foot bumping into something on the floor. She looked down and felt every ounce of strength flow from her body.

Ramira dropped to her knees beside the corpse. Her eyes filled with tears. She held Oma in her arms, rocking her just as the brown woman had done to her since the day she was born. Her silent grief spilled over the body in huge waves nearly cleansing it of the blood that had begun to dry. The tears finally abated and Ramira leaned forward and kissed Oma on the forehead. She hugged Oma's body then gently lay the woman on the floor. Ramira let out a moan that carried to every corner of the city. It resonated with an anguish steeped in the loss of a loved one but was carried on the wings of vengeance. The entire city trembled beneath the onslaught of those fierce emotions. Ramira knew this same fate had befallen Imhap and Horemb, and she would avenge their deaths in ways that would make even Mahn cower. There were only three people in her life that meant anything to her and now they were all dead.

The sun began its descent as she emerged from Oma's home, blood soaked and raging with fury. Veins and tendons stood out along her neck and face as she struggled to control her feelings. The High Priestess had doomed Thebes by making her evil pact with Mahn; Ramira could at best reduce the damage that bargain had caused. She had to try to take advantage of Mahn's temporary ignorance. She could not afford to make any mistakes. Ramira forced the chaotic eddies of emotion into a corner of her mind then seized the nearest horse. She sped out through the main gates.

Ramira noticed a yellowish glow that punctuated the impending darkness in the northwest. Time was running out. She had to make sure the strangers had heeded her warning and forced her horse to sprint to the last place she had seen them. The ride seemed to take forever. Ramira's mind whirled, conjuring up their death and destruction. The vision became sharper with each passing mile until she returned to the knoll from where she had first observed them. To her relief the wagons and tents were gone, the trampled grasses marked their progress through the verdant plains heading east. Ramira hung her head, the tears ran down her cheeks as she looked back toward the yellow haze. It had intensified and served as a beacon to call her back to complete her duties. She wiped away the teardrops and turned to remount her horse when a shadow detached itself from the darkness.

"What is going on?" he demanded grabbing her wrist to keep her from fleeing.

"You should not be here…your people…"

"They are gone many hours," he stated. "What is that?"

His tone cut through her uncertainty, its strength shored up her crumbling resolve as they watched the unhealthy light spread to the outer walls.

"Death," she replied in a small voice. She was too late and too far away to help. She had failed.

"I sense its evil," he admitted.

Ramira jerked her arm then jumped on her horse to race back to Thebes.

"Wait!"

Despondency clawed at her soul as she dashed back to the city in a foolhardy attempt to do something…anything to stop Mahn. Her breath stuck in her throat as the sickly luminescence plunged into the palace where it would discover the truth. She kicked the animal's sides, disregarding the foam spreading from its mouth, down its neck, and across her legs. Its ragged exhalations kept time with its pounding hooves but Ramira refused to relent to its exhaustion. She heard the stranger pursuing her, cursing under her breath for the very thing she did not want was for him to be near the ill-fated city. She shouted back at him, begging him to turn away, but the stranger only followed her with more determination. He finally caught up to her and seized the reins and kept her from heading to her death. He forced her off her horse and was about to reproach her when a sound filled their ears. The noise sounded like bones being broken as the demon shattered the city.

The devastation began in the palace, the destruction continuing unabated as Mahn followed the main avenue south to the main entrance. His enormous smoldering shadow demolished and consumed everything in his path; he ground stones into dust. Fire exploded everywhere; the faint screams of the dying reached their ears. Mahn shattered the gates with one tremendous burst of power, its pieces rained down even upon the pair watching with dread. Spooked, the horses disappeared into the night stranding

Ramira and the stranger. Ramira knew Mahn had found the High Priestess. She had inadvertently done Ina a favor by slaying her. Ramira tried to rise and retrieve her mount but his strong hands pulled her down into the concealment of a nearby ditch. The inferno extended into the heavens as they fed upon the carcass of the burning city. It spread quickly, engulfing everything in its path as it feasted on wood, oils, canopies, and, worst of all, human flesh. The intense heat carried that horrible smell to the pair hiding in the darkness. The hatred, borne upon a foul wind, rushed toward them, stilling her protests as she clutched the stranger's hand in fear. Mahn, she was sure, was about to find them.

~

Mahn swooped down into the bowels of the palace anticipating the feast he was about to enjoy. Once he had sated himself with the Source of Darkness, he would hunt down the other power that existed in the land. The souls imprisoned within him felt his excitement. Soon countless others would join them in their realm of darkness. They looked forward to the new arrivals; they would torment them just as they had been when they first entered this appalling black kingdom.

He flew through the unlit corridors and reached the huge stone doors separating him from his prize. They were ajar. He paused; the empty silence and lack of burning incense was not what he had expected. He forced the doors open and stared dispassionately at the slain body of the red woman. He glared at the altar and watched the last of the liquid dripping into the carved bowl. The daggers were gone.

"You will not escape through death for I command you to rise…rise and face your Master!"

The red woman began to twitch then rose to her feet in jerky movements, her wide-open eyes were filled with fear. He had called her back from the only place she could hide. She began to change, the human emotions surging through her cold soul replaced with the need to serve the demon.

"Where is it?" he hissed.

"She escaped...she went to warn the strangers..."

"You managed to deny me *both* prizes?"

He fumed with such intensity that the walls shook. Mahn, the High Priestess firmly in his grasp, rushed up the stone corridor. His passing scorched even the impenetrable granite walls of the hallway as he hurried to salvage his plans. Mahn refused to abandon his scheme even if it meant laying waste to everything within his reach. He exploded out of the palace, the cacophonous cries of the imprisoned souls wailing in accompaniment to his own thunderous rage. He landed at the base of the great staircase into the palace, the High Priestess dangling limply from his black gloved hand. He searched for the Source of Darkness.

He deposited her unceremoniously upon the sands then prepared himself to destroy the city. He sent mighty pulses of black power into everything heedless of the falling debris raining down all around him. Obelisks cracked and collapsed down upon themselves; mighty facades built centuries ago crumbled onto the streets. Well-tended trees and shrubs burst into flame as did the pennants hanging from the poles both inside and outside the city. The ground shook, sending what barely remained erect into the street. Great billows of dust rose up and mixed with the smoke, obscuring the entire city and most of the evening sky. When it finally cleared, the devastation Mahn wreaked could not have been more complete. The great buildings and outer walls of the city lay in smoking ruins while every living creature succumbed to his power. Except for the occasional cracking of stone or the popping of fire, there was total silence. He could not sense the Source within the city so turned his vengeance onto the plains on the other side of the mountain. Mahn roared over the peaks as if they were no bigger than anthills, sending his fury into the trees and brush as he passed over them. He burned everything in sight, filled the plains with his venom. The poison leached into the soil until it could no longer sustain a single living thing.

Still he was not satisfied; he knew the others had succeeded in moving just beyond his power and they, for now, were out of his reach. He turned his attention back to the city where he continued to search for the ultimate reward.

Thebes was no more, child...

~

The gray mist closed in on Zada, mercifully concealing the horror she witnessed. She returned to the present, the journey into her past leaving her reeling with emotions and many questions. Oma had shown her the demise of the city from where the Herkahs hailed. She had revealed that it was the Lady of the Sands who bestowed the inner sight upon her. The stone pavilion marked her realm and it was here where she judged the Herkah leaders worth. How far did the Lady's power and influence extend? Zada suddenly remembered that 'other' sensation she had experienced, the one that stayed just beyond her sight. Was the Lady watching from a great distance?

What of Ramira? How did she end up housing the Source of Darkness? Oma had shown her the deception by the High Priestess but not why Ramira housed it. Was it passed on through the generations like the Green Might or was it somehow infused into her? If the latter, then, when? Just prior to the High Priestess' betrayal? At birth? Where would it go when Ramira died?

Zada's exhaustion sapped her strength. The strain of the past few months culminated in the journey back to her roots. She was sure Oma wanted her to discern something her tired mind could not quite grasp. All she wanted to do was sleep. Zada collapsed on her bed; her last thought before falling into a deep sleep was of Allad...

TWELVE

The prince tried to rest but the power vibrating within him would not let him. He tossed and turned but the magic grew more insistent. It first heightened then dulled his senses until all he could do to keep still was to clutch his blankets. He got up and poured himself a glass of wine, his shaking hand threatening to spill the contents all over the floor. He took a sip then walked out onto the balcony. The cold night air washed over his heated body and chased away the frustration gathering in his soul. He went back inside and sat in front of the fire, staring into the flames until the flickering orange glow disappeared and left him within the maze once more...

The corridor was as before complete with locked doors and the dripping sounds echoing hollowly in the distance. He glanced upward and saw the infinite blackness stretching far away over his head. He looked down both ends of the hall. He cocked his head to the side pondering the meaning of the doors. They were of wood and as ancient as this place. He approached the nearest door and gently pushed against it; he tried to pry it open without any success. He lifted his hand and knocked. Did he really expect someone to open it from the other side? The rapping, however, echoed beyond the door.

He sighed then felt the Green Might begin to twist as if in response to something. Danyl began to smile for the key to unlocking this maze was the power. He let go of it, allowing it to explore the surroundings without hindering it with his doubt and frustration. To his amazement, the magic began to shift and change. It altered his psyche in the process as it tentatively, and then with greater certainty challenged the portals by slipping underneath and taking him with it.

Danyl looked upon the dwarf king, the Khadry, and his

brother as they slept fitfully within the barracks. Their bloodied and filthy clothing spoke volumes of their tireless efforts. While he stood upon the parapets, these brave warriors battled with every ounce of their abilities. The Green Might remained inert within him. Now, as the power began to settle within him, he understood wielding a weapon of steel was not his destiny.

Gard woke first and stretched, never acknowledging Danyl who stood only a few paces away. The Khadry's breath was visible as he sought to warm himself with a mug of tea. Danyl tried to speak to him, but no words came out nor did any breath materialize before him. Was his shade gazing down upon his companions? He reached out to touch the Khadry but his hand disappeared right through the other's chest.

What...?

Danyl stared in shock at the scene before him. Warriors who had died on the plains outside the city walls filed past him as if they had returned to eat and rest before heading out once more. Elves, Khadry, Dwarf and Herkah moved silently by, their hands and quivers empty. Danyl's brow knitted in quiet grief as each ghost nodded at him. He had failed them yet none accused him of causing their deaths. He stood there mouth agape as so many spirits passed by until his gaze fell upon Nyk. A sob lodged in Danyl's throat as Nyk halted in front of him, the urge to hug his brother was overwhelming. He had escaped the ravages of the Vox because Ramira had severed that horrible bond, but she could do nothing for his bruised soul. The Vox's touch would stay with Nyk for eternity. His eyes reflected the repugnance he felt for that brief merging yet they also radiated a sense of concern for those still defiled by the demons, especially Allad. Nyk lifted his hand and placed it against Danyl's heart. Love, gratitude, and that powerful connection that exists between siblings surged from Nyk into Danyl. The intensity brought the younger brother to his knees. Tears formed in his eyes as he grieved for Nyk, his shaking hand reaching up to touch the spectral one resting on his chest. The Green Might flared and erased the last vestiges of the Vox's contact, leaving Nyk completely free of its corruption. Nyk offered him a sad smile. It was time for Nyk to go. The dead prince followed the other apparitions as they disappeared into the darkness. All Danyl could do was stare after them. If he were dead then why was he not following them? If he were alive then why could he not touch Gard? Was he somewhere in-between? Danyl raised his hand to his face: it was fully enveloped in an emerald mist. The Green Might was fully awake and began to saturate his form, the reason he was able to exist in this in-between place.

The door slammed shut leaving him standing within the corridor once more. He ignored the doors showing the living and dead in one place, a place that he did not want to revisit. Why had the magic allowed so many to die before it completely awakened? He glanced down both sides of the corridor then upward. Darkness greeted him. It dared Danyl to probe its obscurity, mocking his doubt and trepidation. The memory of his brother's touch and the hope in his eyes materialized briefly in Danyl's mind, reminding him time was running out. He gathered his courage and positioned himself as close to the center of the corridor as possible. He took a deep breath and willed the Green Might upward into the daunting blackness...

~

Zada woke with a start, the sudden ignition of power exploding into her inner sight. She gasped for air and shielded her eyes as waves of energy pummeled her mind. The might felt like insects crawling across her skin. The prickling sensation surged through her mind and out her body. The floor shook; bottles and books vibrated off shelves and tables. She clung to the bedpost until the jolting peaked then subsided. For a brief moment all was still. Then a massive thunderclap exploded throughout the city.

She smiled and walked out of her chamber, the hallways filled with people who sought an answer to the explosion. She passed by a window and noted that the sun would soon rise and the fighting and dying would begin anew. This day, however, would be different. She took a deep breath and stared at the gold, lavender, and pale pink pastel hues tinting the horizon.

~

The elf prince surged upward, his body shifting with the Green Might as it swelled toward the heavens. The Green Might felt like a snake slithering through his body. It encircled his heart then dove toward his awaiting soul. He held his breath as it hovered over his spirit, sensing the souls of those who had wielded it in the past. Some had wilted beneath its potency while others gained strength from it. All had endured its intense scrutiny. He could not shake the feeling that they now watched his reaction to the power.

He released all of his apprehensions and emotions to make room for it. He could not abandon one thing: love. He needed to cling to the love of his family, friends, and all those who inhabited the city and, most of all, to Ramira.

Let go of it all.

"I can't."

You must or the metamorphosis will not be complete.

"No…"

What kind of person would he be if he relinquished all that he was? Would he be lost forever? The magic became insistent; he could not turn back. Not fulfilling the transformation would be disastrous because Mahn could seize it. Danyl cast aside everything that bound him to the world. The effect was immediate.

The Green Might incinerated his memories until he became nothing more than an empty vessel. Then, when it had completely expunged all that he was, it began to pour back into him. The magic rushed into him until the elf thought he would drown. He remained as calm as he could, allowing it to wash over and through him. Then and only then did it finally stop.

He waited for its command but none was forthcoming. The elf realized he was on his own.

Danyl opened his eyes and found himself standing in the great hall in front of the tapestry. The prince sensed the souls within the hall but they were silent. It was only fitting he should stand before them brimming with the power they had brought from their original home. The prince knelt down in the middle of the hall, placed his crossed arms over his chest, and bowed to his ancestors. They emerged one by one from their places of honor to stand around him in a circle. The last to approach were the first king and a beautiful woman clad in a flowing blue gown.

"My Lord...my Queen."

Danyl beheld Alyxandyr the First and his own beloved mother. The kings piercing green eyes bored into him while his mother's benevolent gaze soothed his racing heart. Instead of uttering a single word, they descended upon him as one, forming an eerie cocoon around him. He remained motionless even though the unnerving handling by the dead overwhelmed him. He strained to keep still, the beads of perspiration upon his forehead dripping upon the stone floor. When they were satisfied, they all floated back to their displays except for the first king and his mother. They stared down at him for another moment: his eyes filled with anticipation while hers brimmed with love. No matter how difficult the impending battle was to be, Danyl knew he would not face Mahn alone. He rose to his feet and left the hall.

~

Seven, Gard, Styph, and the other soldiers were in the process of dressing to face another day when the explosion startled them all. They exchanged perplexed looks then grabbed their weapons. Alyxandyr and Clare met them as they rounded the corner near their horses, their features reflecting the same uncertainties.

"What in the Four Corners was that?" asked Clare as she stopped adjusting Seven's leather breastplate. Her hands clung to the straps in anticipation of another concussion.

"It arose from within the city," said Styph glancing at the buildings for any signs of damage. His first thought was that Mahn and his forces had managed to hurl rocks over the walls but the buildings stood intact.

"I'm going to..."

The elf king did not finish his sentence for he and the others watched a rider enveloped in a green mist gallop up to them. They recognized the rider as he neared them, their incredulous stares tempered only by the feeling of hope they now all shared. Danyl halted a few paces away, dismounted his steed, and stood before them. The hope that the elven power might stem the tide of death renewed their energy to fight.

"You?" was all Seven could muster. He stared at the magic pulsating from the elf. His heart brimmed with pride and the confidence of knowing Danyl would not fail them. The dwarf king looked into Danyl's eyes but the detached look within them forced the dwarf king to drop his gaze.

"Yes, me," he replied in an unemotional tone.

"What will you do now?" his father asked, studying his child who had grown into a man and then into something completely unfamiliar. The king would never have guessed such a moment would arise in his lifetime. Fate chose various individuals for reasons only she knew and mortals had no hand in altering that destiny. His child had become a thing of legend and now stood before them with his own legacy to fulfill.

The sun chased away the shadows; no clouds floated across the sky. This sign heartened those who were already fighting for their lives and for those who were about to join them. Zada arrived and beheld the prince's radiance.

"Nyk is dead, Father."

"No, Danyl, a Vox took him," was Alyxandyr's grief filled reply.

"The Vox had him but no longer," he clarified, the power not allowing him to share in the sorrow. His emotionless reaction drew perplexed stares.

"The only way for Nyk's spirit to be released from the demon would be…" began Gard.

"Ramira. That was what that commotion was all about," Zada finished for him. "She must have tried to help Allad, too, but Mahn…he must have severely punished her."

A part of Gard questioned his harsh judgment of Ramira, the established blame he had placed on her for causing all of this devastation beginning to waver but not disappear. Her merciful act eased but did not erase his intolerance for her existence. Nyk and Allad would not have been taken by Mahn had she not lived in the first place. He found it difficult to let go of the one thing that made sense to him. He flinched as Danyl's cold, hard glance penetrated his thoughts.

"We have to go," said Seven.

It would, they knew, be the last battle: today they would either stand in mournful victory or become a part of the black army pressing toward the city. They said their farewells; the heartfelt embraces rekindled their resolve. Those who remained watched their companions head out to meet their individual destinies.

"Go with them, Lance," ordered Danyl.

Although awed by the prince, the captain stuck his hand out to his lifelong friend and gripped it tightly. Danyl nodded at Lance who turned and followed the others. The burden of their existence depended upon his ability to wield the elven magic. Death and despair would not wait for him to perfect his skill with the power. He would have one chance only.

~

The Source of Darkness responded to the Green Might, flaring in greeting and infuriating Mahn. He pondered what to do with this new adversary. He knew it because he had come so close to extracting it from the other bearer a thousand years ago. It was imperative he take the Source of Darkness soon or the other magic would become too strong for him to overpower. Mahn decided he would allow the decimation of the elves and their allies for a few more hours before drawing forth the dark magic. He would then concentrate on obtaining the other power before obliterating every living thing on the plains. He hissed with satisfaction and imagined himself towering so high in the air that he could plant one foot on each side of the city. He would glare down upon the mortals and squash them with his heel as if they were insects. He would then turn his wrath upon the witch that had hidden the Source of Darkness from him all of these years.

She had managed to make things difficult for him all these

centuries. She thought herself clever by concealing it out in the open. He stood on the brink of total victory while the witch cowered within the silver sands. He would poison everything with his hatred and would leave no living thing in his wake.

He watched the mortals fall beneath each other's weapons while gradually riding closer to the city. The gray walls were pitted by the debris hurled at them. His huge steed had to pick its way over the fallen bodies, but Mahn never looked down. He focused on the figure that had emerged from beneath the gate, a lone rider taking up position on a small rise in front of the city. Mahn sensed that there was something different about this bearer. The magic was the same yet something else thrived within this elf.

Mahn strained to detect who was beneath the simple brown hood, noting nothing more than a patient restraint. He had misread this elven power's influence centuries ago and would not make the same mistake now. Mahn decided to test the bearer.

Do you actually think you can defeat me?

Mahn sent the thought into the rider as swiftly as an arrow, but he remained silent. He assailed him with the same images he had tormented Ramira with and again there was no response. Mahn stared at the unemotional figure, the uncharacteristic response an enigma he would try to deal with in another fashion. He displayed Ramira to him, her face contorted with the pain he inflicted upon her and still the rider appeared not to care.

I will eat the flesh of your father and drink the blood of your friends.

"You will choke on both."

Ah! It has a voice and it sounds as if it belongs to a little boy!

Mahn waited for a reply but none came. Urgency began to grow within him as this magic calmly challenged him from beneath the shadows of the city. He urged his mount on a bit faster, his presence creating a crease through both sides of warriors. He sat up straighter in the saddle, his head tilted arrogantly to one side as he absorbed the fear lifting from the plains like the shimmering heat waves in the desert. He glared at the possessed faces of his army, then over at the determined allies. They hammered away at his army desperately trying not to falter beneath their enemies' blades. He reveled at the panic and horror contorting the faces of the elves and dwarves as they fell beneath his army's swords. Mahn consumed their emotions as if dining at a sumptuous feast. Mahn saved his appetite for the banquets main courses: the Source of Darkness and the Green Might.

~

Each of the companions contemplated what they had seen as they rode out to battle the enemy. They shared their amazement that Danyl housed the Green Might, hoping perhaps now so many would not have to die. They wondered how long he had known that it thrived within him as they neared their opponents and drew their weapons.

Seven and his men returned to the southern portion of the plains, the king remembering the stoic look on the prince's normally emotional face. How much had the magic to do with that? The prince had always been compassionate, quick to lend a hand, and openly showing his feelings toward those whom he cared for the most. He had gazed down upon them with a detached look, as if the power had somehow dulled that which made him Danyl. The dwarf king hoped and prayed today would be the day that the powers engaged each other. So many had died, leaving too few to continue this fighting.

Seven had a great deal of faith in both Danyl and Ramira. After having seen the prince's transformation and Ramira's deep and abiding love for him and her friends, he felt as if Mahn had no chance to defeat them. If they survived, would they be able to gather their feelings for one another and persevere? Seven cast his musings aside as the exhausting battle began once more. The dwarf king and his men hacked at their opponents who thrust themselves upon their blades, heedless of the death the warriors dealt to them. The king brought his sword down nearly cutting a man in half only to find another ready to take his place. Seven wondered how Evans Peak fared and hoped the demons had not reached it. There were few dwarves left to defend his home. It would all be gone if he did not focus on the bloody task and, as he chanced a glance at Danyl sitting unmoving upon his horse, if the prince failed.

~

Styph turned his head and watched Lance catch up to him. The crown prince gratefully accepted Lance's presence for the captain's abilities, heightened by the training he had received from the Herkahs, were formidable indeed. The fact that Danyl no longer needed him spoke volumes about the power he held. Styph realized that he was not one bit envious of his brother. He was sure Danyl did not particularly relish what he housed, but destiny had decreed otherwise. The crown prince gave his brother a lot of credit for handling it as well as he had. The black line grew and swelled stirring the elf into action. He headed for the weakest section of the opposing army and pulled his sword from its scabbard. Lances and swords reflected the sunlight no matter in which direction he looked. Cavalry units broke through the ranks of foot soldiers. Mahn was sending every available body at them. Arrows fired from both sides whizzed by his head forcing him to lay low over his horse's neck. His sweat mingled with the steeds as they surged forward. An arrow lodged itself in the saddle beside his knee and another whistled through his tunic without penetrating his flesh. His luck would not hold out forever and no sooner did that thought cross his mind when a barb imbedded itself in his thigh. Inhaling sharply, he reached down and wrenched it free then pushed the pain into a corner of his mind. The morning sun continued to climb into the bright blue heavens.

They fought hard but the sheer numbers of their opponents began to overwhelm them. It was only be a matter of time before the enemy held the upper hand. Gard, Styph, Seven, and all the others who knew of the Green Might kept looking over at Danyl, but the prince had not moved since posting himself on the rise in front of the city. Why wasn't he wielding the power to stop the slaughter? What was he waiting for?

Seven quickly deduced that the enemy swarming from the

forest was about to overrun them. He called for a retreat. The blackness streaming forth forced them backward to the city and was herding them like cattle toward Styph and Gard. It was clear they would all meet before the sun rose much farther. Those fighting were too exhausted and wounded to shout out any battle cries, grunting instead with the effort of wielding their weapons. Seven bellowed over the noise and ordered his men to sever contact and head for the closest knot of fighters. The dwarf king brought his sword down upon a foes head. His blade sliced through the armor and skull ending up at the base of his shoulders. He pushed his men on, glancing at the unmoving figure watching the battle from atop his horse. *Come on, boy. Do something!*

~

Pale with fear, Alyxandyr and Clare stared down at the waves of friend and foe that began to wash up along the gray walls like some terrible tide. They could no longer stand idly by. They were at a critical juncture where saving themselves from death was a moot point: there would be none to rule if they stayed on top of the battlements. The king shouted orders over his shoulder as he and the queen mustered whoever was capable of lifting sword or longbow to follow them. They left the city and headed for their nearest comrades. Their heart and determination caught on and they succeeded in regaining some of the lost ground. That changed as Mahn urged his army on until the allies were on the defensive once more. Clare and Alyxandyr lost track of one another during the fighting. The blood and mud covering them from head to toe concealed their identities from each other and everyone else around them. They became just two more bodies in a sea of thousands. The enemy fanned out and began to push inward. Those who valiantly fought on the plains knew without question the noose was tightening.

~

Zada searched for any sign of her companions. They were indistinguishable from the masses hacking and chopping away at each other. The elven archers, fearful of hitting their own kin, descended the ramparts and took up their swords. The only people left in the city were the old, infirm, and the children. The nomad ran along the parapets dodging arrows loosened by the enemy while searching for a position where she could see both Danyl and the approaching Mahn. The high demon casually rode closer as if he already tasted victory. His massive steed carried him over the fallen.

She silently implored Danyl to do something, begging him to make use of the power coursing through him, but the prince watched blankly as Mahn advanced. She could sense Ramira within the dark cloak. The Herkah had no way of knowing how powerful the elf had become nor could she tell how weak Ramira was. She could clearly sense the black force straining in Mahn. His enormous cloak billowed insanely as if some monstrous storm raged within its blackness. Ramira was stranded somewhere within that terrible tempest enduring things Zada did not even want begin to imagine.

~

Cooper descended the castle steps armed and ready to join the fighting. He reassuringly touched the small blade strapped near his chest then grabbed the reins of a horse. He kicked its sides and raced toward the gate at the end of the avenue. He was about to pass the intersection when he caught sight of an odd shape keeping to the shadows of the buildings as it moved along the street. It disappeared then reappeared from within shops and storehouses, its movements feral in nature. Cooper reined in his mount fearing more fiends had infiltrated the city. The king had no idea who it was or what it was looking for. He was about to investigate when the shape spotted him. It became motionless and fixated on the king, wanting to approach him yet loath to abandon its purpose for being in the city. The king rode over to it, halting a few feet away.

"Who are you? What are you doing...?"

Cooper glared as the figure pulled back the cowl to reveal a deeply tanned woman with short-cropped hair. A red mist pulsed from where her dark eyes should have been, the haze matching the hatred forever chiseled on her features. Antama. He dismounted, withdrew two daggers and walked toward her. The savage look on his face did nothing to deter her nor did the brutal swings of his blades. She deflected his blows with ease but could do nothing to parry the vehemence attached to every stroke. Cooper used the blunt end of the hilt to pummel her whenever he had a chance, disregarding the slashes she administered in response.

"You fight like a woman," she taunted him.

"You filthy wretch! You will not live to see the end of this day."

"You think to kill me with those ineffectual weapons?"

"No, Antama, but I believe this will suffice."

He feigned to her left, dropped one of the blades and wrenched out Zada's knife. He lunged forward and buried it into her throat, the look of surprise gave him a moment of satisfaction. His expression turned to bewilderment when she pulled it out and tossed it at his feet.

"Is that all you have?" she jeered.

What sort of demon had filtered into her body? Not a Vox or she would at least have appeared distressed. Not a Radir, either, for she remained lucid and focused. What was the red mist inside of her?

Cooper did something Antama did not expect. He smiled at her. The curious response caused her hesitate long enough for the king to raise his sword and bring it down on her neck. Her head fell on the cobblestone street with a heavy thud, rolled several feet then came to rest face up.

"That's what I've got, *my love*."

Cooper spat on her then kicked her head over to her body. He stood over the corpse, the lingering question of what possessed her still occupying his attention. He was about to squat down beside her when the red haze oozed out and floated over the remains. The king took a step back. Not a Vox or Radir but belonging to Mahn...what else could it be? The king's gaze fell on Zada's knife. He picked it up and slashed through the vapor;

the mist burned his skin. The haze separated wherever the Herkah blade touched it but did not react to Zada's blood. It suddenly formed a spear point and shot away toward the gate before Cooper could vex it any further. Cooper watched it cut through the air, fervently hoping it was not seeking another host. He glanced down one last time then mounted up and continued his ride.

~

Zada grasped the edge of the bulwark and stared down into the melee. There was barely enough room to swing a sword and those who fell beneath a blade remained propped up against those who still wielded one. Warriors from both sides tripped over arms and legs; they grabbed at anyone to help break their fall. Soldiers pushed up against the walls of the city disappeared beneath the crush of men.

She turned her attention to Danyl. He brought his hand up and for a moment Zada thought he would release the Green Might. Instead, he reached into his cowl and scratched his face. She refused to watch any longer and took a step toward the riser. Her inner sight clicked on and turned her toward the impending danger. She opened her mouth but no words came out as the red arrow sped in her direction. Her feet merged with the gray stone below her. Zada raised her trembling arms in front of her. The evil cloud passed over the barracks, crossed the alley between and dove straight at her. A choked cry escaped her throat. Zada crossed her arms in front of her and braced for the impact.

The haze was mere inches away from her when a brilliant green bolt enveloped it and ground the red particles into dust. The mist's annihilation broke the hold it had on her. She breathed in deeply trying to regain some measure of control, then rose shakily to her feet and stared at the elf prince. His impenetrable hood pointed her way then turned back to the monstrosity across from him. Zada left the ramparts and headed out of the gate.

~

Mahn finally stopped and dismounted near the southwest

corner of the city. He grunted with displeasure as the bearer denied him the Herkah witch. He was untroubled for he would seize her once he conquered the elf and took his power. There would be no one left to help her then.

Mahn withdrew the control over his army to concentrate on this last task. Individuals then groups withdrew, pushing away the allies as they retreated from the demon standing upon the plain. They looked at each other as if awakened from a long nightmare. They ceased fighting, drawn to watch what was about to unfold. An unnerving silence hovered over the plains.

~

Seven grunted with pain as he tumbled from his horse and landed on his shoulder. Grateful that it was not his sword arm, he rolled to his feet and fought on. Every stroke of his weapon made him wince and soon the aching that began in his shoulder worked its way down into his body. He was growing weary and the small knot of men that remained to challenge the enemy thinned out. He quickly glanced over at the disturbance to his right and saw Mahn about to commence the final stage of this conflict. His attention returned to the struggle at hand and none too soon. He blocked a blow that would have decapitated him. The dwarf managed to jam the others weapon. It struck his wounded shoulder and deflected up against the side of his head. The blow knocked the dwarf to his knees. He looked up at the shadows around him knowing he did not have the strength left to fight. The blood from his head wound ran into his eyes; he struggled to rise but was too dizzy and in pain to succeed. A black silhouette towered over him and redirected a blow meant for his head. It took a second for Seven to recognize who saved him. It was Mason. The First Advisor helped the dwarf king to his feet and protected him as best as he could.

Styph and Lance began to merge with Gard and the remainder of the Khadry's men. The sheer numbers of the enemy forced them to rally around each other much like Nyk and Allad had done the day before. They were about to die together as

406

comrades. The enemy had moved the catapults close enough to hit the solid gray walls and the continuous thudding sounds reverberated around them. Loose debris rained down on them and more than one man dropped to the ground with a gaping hole in his head.

The luxury of looking around to see how the other units were faring had ceased. Most of the morning had been devoted to keeping one's head intact. Except for the warriors in the immediate area, none of the combatants on the plains knew how the others were managing. The only sure thing was that Danyl waited outside the main gate. The enemy swarmed around them and began to slaughter those on the edges as they worked inward to the princes.

"Do you see any place to retreat to?" shouted Styph warding off one blow with his sword while thrusting upward with his dagger at another attacker.

"We're completely surrounded...just like everyone else on the plains!" replied Gard.

Gard then groaned as the flat end of an axe smacked him in the back. He recovered and blocked a blade that would have sliced into Lance's neck.

"What in the Four Corners is Danyl waiting for?" cried the crown prince as he severed the hand of an opponent.

"I think his wait is almost over."

One of the Vox spotted Styph and headed for him, the Herkah/demon's attraction to the prince alerting Lance. The Vox sprang forward, cutting apart all those who were in his way. He launched himself toward the prince; Lance surged forward and pushed Styph into Gard's arms. The two princes watched with horror as the Vox's blade passed completely through the captain's chest and out his back. Lance, however, was not about to die without taking the hated demon with him. With bloodstained and trembling hands, he grabbed the Vox's tunic with one hand and yanked Zada's knife out with the other. With the last of his strength, the captain jammed the blade into the demon's throat. The two of them fell into a heap at the prince's feet. Styph and Gard, fearful of another Vox attack, spun about

407

until their backs touched. They prepared to make a last stand. A brief image of Nyk and Allad filled their minds: they did not intend to meet that same fate.

THIRTEEN

Danyl stared at Mahn and the rigid form he yanked out from within the folds of his cloak. The elf's handsome face was devoid of emotion. The Green Might had destroyed the High Priestess before she had a chance to infect Zada and it now rose to face its ultimate challenge. Mahn relinquished his control over the army and demons to focus his power on the elf. The Radir paused while the Kreetch, confused by their master's sudden abandonment, moved away and converged into a knot of black at the edge of the plain. The Vox lurked amongst the silent horde on the plains. His gaze rested on a still cloaked and hooded Ramira, pushed to the forefront by a smug Mahn standing a few paces behind her.

"The time has come, *boy*," roared Mahn.

"You will not be victorious." Danyl glared at the monster.

"I have already been triumphant, *boy*. Look around you. I will spare the rest if you cede to me."

"Never."

"Never is a very long time, *boy*."

Mahn hissed with satisfaction and ripped off Ramira's cloak. Her blank gaze did not vary as he hoisted her off the ground by the back of her dress, holding her aloft like a shield. If Danyl were to fire his magic at the demon, he would to hit her first. Mahn guessed that would be the last thing he would want to do. Confident that he was safe behind her body, he began to pour himself into Ramira to retrieve the Source of Darkness. The prince stared at Mahn but made no attempt to stop him. The bystanders gasped, for their worst nightmare was about to come true and the only person capable of preventing it stood apathetic upon the field.

~

Ramira felt the vileness burn as it oozed down toward the Source of Darkness. He purposefully raked and clawed his way

409

filling the gashes with his poison. She shuddered and moaned as the venom scalded into her being, refusing to ignite the dark power to protect herself. He inflicted every possible abomination on her as he continued, the residue of his misery preceding him like detestable heralds announcing his arrival. As offensive and obscene as all of this was, she knew she had to endure it for once Mahn was deep within she could trap him allowing Danyl to destroy him. She could not stop him from taking the Source of Darkness, but once he had secured it, there would be little, if any time for the elf to strike. Would he wield his power to annihilate Mahn if it meant killing her? How could he not brandish it when their end was so painfully evident?

Ramira focused on the love of her life and slowly lifted one of her hands to her heart. Her finger marked the place where he should concentrate his fire. She watched him study her as if it were the first time he had beheld her. This response frightened her. What happened to him? Why did he remind her of one of the demons…no! It couldn't be! Please don't let him have been taken by one of the Vox! Panic began to well up deep inside of her, a response that Mahn mistook as a reaction to his intolerable presence. He increased the horrors of his passing, gleefully plunging deeper into her. For a few precious moments, he was oblivious to everything transpiring outside her body.

Ramira watched Zada ride over to Danyl then dismount and walk the last few paces to stand beside him. She wore that same dark look on her face. Mahn was halfway to the dark power. She could endure the horror from within but not the complacent faces without. All of Mahn was now inside, his presence searing every nerve and fiber of her being. He continued to punish her, inflicting as much pain and despair as time allowed. He hovered over the Source of Darkness, the prize just moments away when he noticed the silver sparkle beside it. He leaned over to investigate what this new thing was, instantly recoiling as he identified the bits of green and amethyst mixed in with the silver. He howled with fury and fear then reached past it and grabbed the Source of Darkness.

~

Zada looked over at Danyl, imploring him to use the power. Mahn would only be trapped within her for a short time before he seized the dark magic. The window of opportunity was small and the elf needed to act immediately or there would be no other chance to do so.

"Danyl, use the magic," she beseeched.

Bereft of his emotions and unable to comprehend what the power had done to him, he stood as an image carved of stone. He had wielded the power to save Zada from the red mist, an enemy he could recognize. He saw Ramira point to her heart and the pleading within her eyes, yet he could not raise his hands to administer the fatal blow.

"Danyl…" Zada's voice was filled with panic.

Ramira stiffened while she tried to restrain the monster within, an evil that, by now, would have realized his mistake. Her face reflected the agony of enduring his presence and that she was nearing the end of her limitations. Mahn was seeking his escape. The tremendous effort it took for her to keep that from happening distorted her features and bathed her in perspiration. Her mouth opened but the soundless scream remained stuck in her throat; her face began to turn purple with the effort. Ramira could not hold on much longer.

~

Seven and the others nervously observed the prince do nothing. Gard focused on Ramira, the exertion and pain she endured so the elf could defeat Mahn etched on her face. The Khadry located the elven king, the look of dread on his face mirroring his own. Styph's face was unreadable. Gard could well imagine what this torturous wait was doing to him for he, too, felt as if his fate hung on the brink of a massive cliff that ended in a black well of horror.

~

Time is running out, Danyl!

The prince locked eyes with Ramira and she conveyed all she

411

felt for him, their friends, and all of the people that lived and died upon the plains. She begged him to drive the Green Might into her and end the nightmare before the moment passed.

If you have any love for me and all those who wait, then you will strike me with your might.

"I cannot kill you."

If you do not, the fate you resign us to will be unimaginable.

Danyl took control of the power then unlocked the door that held all of his feelings and emotions. He steeped the magic in his passions making it glitter with a ferocity that blinded even him, then, screaming with dismay at what he was about to do, let the fire fly from his hands. The brilliant bolt of green shrieked across the plains, its sound like a thousand voices crying out in defiance. Those who watched covered their ears and shielded their eyes. The concussion from the emerald blast knocked Zada to the ground, her inner sight a maelstrom of images and colors as it followed the power to its intended target. She gasped for air, as the incredible force seemed to suck the life from her breast.

Ramira watched as the green bolt, a gleaming spear bristling with not death but life approached her in slow motion. Those closest to the hurtling power threw themselves upon the soggy ground while many pushed away from the monstrosity that was about to taste its potency. She felt the fire pierce her flesh, then drive deep into her heart. Its touch was cool and comforting. It washed over her like a cooling rain, leaving her at peace for a brief moment. Then the elven magic changed. It began to expand, the refreshing sensation turning into a blistering heat that scalded her before exploding then trickling down to cut off Mahn's escape. Trapped, he had no choice but to stand and wield the Source of Darkness. The ultimate battle would not take place on the plains outside the city but deep within Ramira, who braced herself as best as she could against the impending clash.

Danyl stood in the center of a glade. Trees and brush surrounded it and he could glimpse white dunes beyond their trunks. A slender birch reached gracefully up into the soft light falling through the canopy onto the ground. His gaze drifted toward a pile of rotting wood that had fallen into a heap. He turned and spotted a vine clinging tenaciously to a tall tree. He could almost hear it grunt with exertion as it sought to reach the top. A hint of white to his left caught his attention: tiny blooms peeked around thick, waxy leaves with the shyness of a small child. Danyl looked down and saw that the ground was composed of sand dotted with thick patches of grass. He noticed a small black ridge poking up through the grains; the curved thorns formed a faint circle beneath the sand. A twig snapped somewhere within the streaming light ahead of him. He stared into the half shadows and haze; the Green Might drained down his arms and into his hands. Danyl's wait was short.

A glittering ball of black screamed toward him from the trees and fell short of its target. The roar of fury following it quickly took on the shape of his adversary. Mahn exploded from the murkiness, firing volley after volley of power at Danyl. The closer he came the more accurate his aim became. Danyl easily deflected the magic, holding his ground as the darkness rushed toward him. The elf sensed he had assimilated the Source of Darkness with his own energy and braced himself for the worst. The two combatants faced off against each other in the center of the glade. One bristled with death while the other blazed with life. It was time to determine which fate would befall the land and her people.

Mahn surged forward blasting the elf with his blackness. The Source of Darkness weighed down his powers as if it were forged of lead. He continuously missed his target regardless of how precisely he directed it. *Stabilize it you fool!* Mahn concentrated on steadying the powers but found them even more unwieldy than before. The elf began to move forward, pummeling him with the Green Might. Mahn was initially able to ward them off but the dark power tugged on his arms making it difficult for him to lift them up. He had to discard it…for the time being, anyway. Mahn released the amethyst power, unconcerned that it lay within easy reach of the elf.

Danyl smiled when Mahn discarded the Source of Darkness. The demon had misjudged not the dark magic but the person who had housed it all these centuries. The elf began his assault, flinging one bolt of emerald after another at the black shape expending all of his energy to prevent the Green Might from consuming him. Great bursts of power incinerated bushes and blew branches off the trees. Mahn sent a mighty blast at Danyl who sidestepped it and watched as the tiny white flowers turned to ash. Another discharge splintered the willowy birch; the agonizing cracking sound it made as it toppled to the ground echoed throughout the dell. The vine wilted beneath the onslaught; it hung limply from the trunk. The gentle light that had illuminated the hollow became lost in the smoke and fire devouring the glen.

Mahn circled around Danyl, absorbing the painful blows as he drove him toward the thorny ridge. The menacing barbs began to twist and bend, pointing toward the elf. Mahn struck the ground behind Danyl, opening up a jagged rift that caught his foot. He stumbled and began to fall backward. The elf rotated to one side and landed inches away from the spines. He rolled away from the black magic Mahn hurled at him, choking on the dust and fine grains of sand stirred up by his movements. They got into his eyes and mouth, and no amount of tears or spit could oust them. He scuttled backward, dodging the blows Mahn rained down on him while never getting a chance to return his own fire. The demon tried to force him toward the crest of spines; the razor sharp points twisted toward Danyl no matter which direction he took. They hungered for his flesh and blood as much as Mahn did. Mahn redoubled his efforts to finish off the elf and take his prizes. The demon hissed with satisfaction as Danyl sought to catch his breath. The prince struck his head on the pile of moldering trunks blocking any further escape. Blood seeped from the gash on his forehead but he could still make out the blurry shape looming in front of him. Mahn clasped his hands together and formed a huge ball of energy then raised his arms high overhead.

You have lost, boy!

Danyl shook his head, ignoring the droplets of blood flying away from his face. He rubbed away some of the sand from his eyes; he squinted and coughed up the fine dust. Mahn menaced him with the black power spinning crazily between his gloved hands, the triumphant set of his shoulders matching the exultation in his hiss. The demon's gloat left the door open for the elf. Danyl clapped his hands together and concentrated all of the Green Might into a gleaming emerald spear. He plunged it into the center of Mahn's hood, holding on as the demon first shivered then began to convulse. Danyl clenched his jaw, every muscle and tendon visible beneath his reddening skin as he labored to keep the contact. Bits of Mahn's power rained down upon him, the droplets feeling like acid as they dripped on his body. He ignored the pain, concentrating instead on the shuddering form above him. Then, without warning, the spear left his grip and propelled Mahn into the middle of the glade. Danyl's chest heaved; his eyes were wide as the demon began to break up into pieces. The fragments started to revolve around the green lance, whirling so fast that they kicked up the debris around it. The elf brought his arms up to protect his face then vaulted for cover behind the fallen trees. He peered through a gap in the trunks and held his breath. The Green Might sent out sizzling currents of power, encompassing the blackness swirling around it. Danyl shielded his eyes from the brilliant elven magic then jumped as the whirling mass exploded with a mighty boom.

The glen was utterly silent. He looked through the break and rose to his feet, leaning on the tree while surveying the area around him. The Green Might spiraled lazily overhead like some bird of prey riding the air currents. Danyl placed his hands behind his head as he looked at the devastation done to Ramira's soul. His arms dropped to his sides and he lowered his head in grief and regret. His blood dripped on the ground. A rustling sound from behind pulled him from his anguish. He turned toward it and stared in disbelief.

Ramira stood just beyond his reach. Her red-gold hair shone like silk and her bronze-hued skin glowed warmly in the soft light that fell once more upon the glade. Her eyes sparkled with love and the smile she bestowed upon him made Danyl forget about every terrible thing that had transpired. His gaze traveled down to the bundle she cradled protectively in her arms. A tiny hand reached out from the blanket and elicited a choked cry of astonishment from the elf. He cocked his head to the side and moved toward them, his fingers extending out when the Green Might slammed into his back and began to yank him away. He fought the elven power with an intensity that made his battle with Mahn seem like nothing more than a skirmish. The Green Might was determined to return him to the land of the living, but Danyl had other ideas. He would rather die here with them than return to the loneliness that awaited him. The elven power desperately clawed at the elf, raking and shredding his essence as it sought to control him. Danyl's substance began to break apart as he strained toward Ramira.

You must go Danyl! You cannot stay here!

I won't leave you!

You must finish your task out on the plains.

Danyl watched Ramira withdraw into the shadows, the sad look of resignation the last thing he saw. He took a deep breath and swayed unsteadily on his feet as the last of his strength ebbed from his body. He had won and lost at the same time. The Green Might swirled around the complacent elf and transferred him out of Ramira's devastated soul.

~

The ferocious energy radiating from Ramira's eyes stunned Zada as the Green Might battled the demon. She could not fathom how Ramira was able to survive what was transpiring within her. The Herkah saw the elven magic tear and rip into the black power as it in turn tried to destroy the other. The elf, however, was not about to relinquish his grip. It began to pulverize Mahn with a retribution that was truly frightening. The demon eventually succumbed to the furious onslaught. She could sense Ramira away from the confrontation, for the woman had done her part and now awaited the outcome just like everyone else on the plains. Rivulets of blood ran from Ramira's nose and mouth and stained the ugly purplish bruises visible on her skin. If she died before Danyl triumphed over the demon then Mahn would be set free with the Source of Darkness to fulfill his dark purpose.

Alyxandyr and Clare clung to each other and stared wide-eyed at the terrible scene. They, too, noted that Ramira's body was on the verge of failing. They glanced over at Danyl, his nebulous form burned brightly with the Green Might; the ground around him smoked as the power scorched it. The king and queen prayed the conflict would soon end, a thought shared by everyone on the plain.

Danyl administered the final blow, concentrating the magic before launching it into Mahn. The emerald power erupted with such a blinding force that even he shielded his eyes from it. The demon twisted and convulsed; the magic incinerated his very essence. Mahn started to break apart, the particles spinning tightly in a narrow column that stretched toward the blue sky. It ruptured, sending bits and pieces of his evil magic near the forest to the north. Ramira collapsed, the resounding explosion tearing through her and out onto the plains. The blast leveled everyone and everything standing close by. Bodies and great chunks of sod were hurled backward. Loose sections of the city's outer walls slid to the ground, scattering those who had stood beneath them during the clash of powers. Silence ruled the land while those who had witnessed the ultimate battle nervously waited.

Zada saw Danyl standing as still as before; Ramira's lifeless body lay on the ground. Mahn was gone.

Danyl recalled the power, collecting it within him once more. Reality began to take hold of him. The essence of who he was, including his emotions and memories, returned to their proper places. It took several long seconds for the blank look to vacate his eyes and for the harsh truth of what he had done to sink in. Grief stuck in his throat as he gazed with sorrow upon the woman he loved. She lay in a heap upon the ground, hair and clothing covering her face.

Nothing happened for several moments; everyone was too stunned to move. The Vox/Allad absorbed the details around him, then he and the others disappeared from the land of light. Those gathered on the plains began to move and, although a few half-hearted skirmishes erupted, the warriors on both sides simply retreated from each other. Mahn's forces, now bereft of

417

his influence, wondered what they were doing here. Many ran away while others simply surrendered. After many days of fierce combat and countless losses on both sides, all felt drained and confused as to what to do. They ended up milling around each other, recognizing friends and foes alike. The resurgent cries of the wounded and dying filled their ears and prompted them into action. They were armed with a purpose and not a weapon, and tended to those in need regardless of which side of the battle they had fought on. The area around Ramira's crumpled form began to fill up quickly. Danyl raced toward her but even his swift horse was too slow. She was gone by the time he arrived. He scoured the area, the panic and loss in his eyes too painful to behold. Even the strong arms of his father and brother couldn't keep him still.

"Danyl...she's gone, son."

"No! She was just here!" he cried.

The prince knew she had shared in whatever he had done to Mahn. He had killed her. He had slain them both. He stared at the trampled earth, the memory of the tiny hand reaching out to him too much to bear.

Alyxandyr put his arms around his son, holding him tightly for he needed to feel Danyl as much as his son wanted his father's embrace. Styph placed one arm around them both and shared their grief. Then each of the other companions joined them.

Zada stood alone, watching the Vox that imprisoned Allad withdraw from the plains. The Vox had managed to acquire a formidable Herkah, one whose intelligence and supreme skills would make him a superior foe. It would, she knew, return to the foul depths from which it hailed and would torment Allad until he was released from its terrible grip. She swore she would fulfill that act. The nomad gazed at the knot of family and friends offering each other solace; her heart wanted desperately to join them. Her legs were unable to make the short journey to where they stood. She had crossed the Great White Desert, this land, and the vastness between worlds where shadows lived, yet did not have the strength to walk the short distance to them. She crossed her arms and hung her head, crying for Allad and all the others who had perished.

FOURTEEN

Those who survived finally sat down to eat long after the moon had risen. They had refused to abandon those in need on the plains, leaving only when everything was well under control. The physicians tended to the wounded, sewing up both man and elf, a duty that would take them well into the next day. It was impossible to bury all the men and horses that had fallen in battle. The bodies were burned on huge pyres along the eastern side of the city. The city walls had held but the damage they suffered would take weeks to repair, maybe longer considering so many able men had died. Cooper spent most of the afternoon trying to convince his confused and fearful men that they were no longer in danger, an odd task considering he usually instilled dread into them. Styph and Zada made sure enough food, blankets, and other essentials were available to everyone. They walked beside a wagonload of supplies, passing out items to friends and former foes. They replenished the cart several times before returning to the castle long after nightfall. The crown prince and the Herkah freshened up and joined their companions for dinner.

The night was balmy; the balcony doors were open to reveal a full moon. They ate out of need with few words being exchanged, their aching and exhausted limbs barely able to raise their forks to their mouths. Their empty hearts cried out as they stared at the vacant chairs around the table: Lance, Nyk, Allad, and the gentle Karolauren were among those that slept the eternal sleep...no, not quite. Allad yearned for that merciful rest. The demon inhabiting his body would surely give him anything but peace. And Ramira? What had befallen the woman with the red-gold hair? Did she inhabit that abominable lair or had Danyl somehow managed to release her from this world? Alyxandyr glanced around the table, noting the deep creases running along their foreheads, the dark circles under their eyes, and their pale faces. His fared no better. Although Seven had sustained severe injuries, he had insisted on dining with them. He nodded for Clare who poured them all glasses of his concoction after they had eaten. Zada filled a second set of glasses with Allad's liquid.

"We owe the dead a great debt," began Alyxandyr in somber tones, "may their souls rest in peace and may the spirits of those still living find solace in their sacrifices."

Strangely enough, not one person grimaced as the strong drinks burned their throats.

"I will, in the future, increase my vigilance and make sure we communicate more often," Cooper stated.

"We will all have to be more attentive," added Alyxandyr.

"What will you do now, Gard?" asked the First Advisor.

"I don't know, Mason. There is much to do here and I'm sure there is nothing left of our home. I will let my people decide."

"You are welcome to stay in the city or anywhere else within our lands," offered the elven king.

"Thank you, I'll let them know that."

"What about you, Zada? Will you go back to the desert?"

"It is our home," she replied.

"I doubt any of us will be leaving soon, at least not until our wounded are well enough to make the journey home," said Seven, the pain in his voice reflecting more than the wounds covering his body.

"You are all welcome to stay for as long as you need."

"Danyl?" Styph was concerned because his younger brother had not uttered a single word the entire time.

Danyl did not reply. He refilled his glass and went out onto the balcony. The Green Might had withdrawn back into his soul but it did not resume its slumber. Its time was not yet over. He drained the glass.

"Danyl?" Zada approached him and placed her hand on his as it rested on the balustrade.

"What?"

"The brown woman, Oma, loved Ramira as if she were her own child and thought the world of you. She wanted me to tell you that the bonds created during one's lifetime transcend even

420

death. She also wanted me to tell you what I saw when she took me back to Thebes."

And so Zada did. She revealed everything she had seen and experienced. Danyl listened intently. When she was finished, Danyl noticed that her story ended abruptly without explaining how the first king fit in or how Ramira ended up in the cave.

"Do you know what happened after the Broken Plain were created?"

"No, for some reason Oma did not show me."

The balcony door closed behind them; Zada's inner sight began to pulse. She sensed no danger but shivered nonetheless. A peculiar coolness washed over them both while they watched the shade materialize before them. Oma's eyes brimmed with understanding as she beheld the distraught pair. There was a great deal of compassion flowing from her shimmering form.

A small fountain of hope seemed to have erupted from within the dry wells housing their souls. Oma's heart ached for them just as it did for the young woman she had raised as her own child. The responsibility to destroy the demon had fallen upon this elf, even though he and his people had nothing to do with its resurrection a thousand years ago. That burden fell upon Ramira's shoulders. Although they had done everything in their power to avert such a catastrophe, she was still the reason for Mahn's existence. Oma placed her hands on theirs and took them through the rest of the journey…

But I will show you now.

Ramira trembled as she watched the total destruction of her home. The king held on tightly. He could feel her straining to free herself and run toward the destruction. Her eyes were wide and wild as she stared at the ruins of her home. Mahn, deprived of his prize, skulked away. The terrible sounds began to die down and soon only the flames feasting on Thebes' carcass moved.

"I have to go and see if anyone survived!"

"You will only find your own death within those ruins," he countered as he continued to hold onto her.

"I can't leave them…I have to help!"

"I will go with you."

"No, it isn't safe. Please, go to your people."

"Come with me…us," he corrected. "There is nothing left for you here."

"I cannot."

He nodded. "Be well then, and if you ever decide to leave, follow the sun as it rises in the east and you will find us there."

"Thank you," she replied and walked away from him. Her bracelet fell into his hand as she pulled her wrist away.

The first king doubted she would live to see another sunrise. He realized there was nothing he could do to help her people. The flames found another supply of fuel: they suddenly blasted up into the night sky, threatening to consume the very heavens. Alyxandyr left to meet up with his kin.

Ramira looked back once but the night hid him from her sight Every somber step back to Thebes reminded her that she was the reason for its destruction. She approached the boundary of the smoldering city and stood frozen within the silence hovering over the smoke and ashes. The demon had spared nothing.

Ramira trod amongst the crushed foundations and pockets of fire, jumping as the incredible heat caused stones to pop and fracture. She followed the perimeter until she was on the north side where she heard faint cries. There were indeed survivors. She called out to them and heard a distant reply. She spotted nearly a hundred or so huddled figures and approached them, their eyes wide with fright and confusion. She calmed them and asked if they had any provisions. They had nothing more than the clothes on their backs and a few personal items hastily thrown into packs. Ramira told them to head north along the mountains and wait for her there. She and a few others would scrounge for whatever staples they could find. Ramira assured them they would meet no later than the following morning.

The survivors moved out while Ramira and the others headed back into the city and, with any luck, find more survivors. Ramira picked through the debris, lifting small pieces of rubble to see if she could find anything underneath. She managed to find several blankets and a few broken vessels of wheat, which she scooped into one of the blankets. She carried her things toward a partially collapsed house, the back wall leaning precariously against a cracked sidewall. She dropped her bundle and carefully squeezed her way in. A fire in the house next door illuminated the kitchen area, one that looked familiar. A sob rose in her throat as spotted the broken rocking chair on the floor. She wiped away the tears and forced herself to gather up the food. She heard someone call out her name and crawled back out of Oma's house.

"Here!" she hailed the Theban. "Take these to the others. I'll follow along the perimeter of the city in case there are any more survivors. Hurry!"

Ramira watched the man disappear into the ruins and looked at the house one last time before moving on. She wiped away the sweat from her face, conscious of how hot it was getting. Then she detected the far off rumbling of thunder. No, not thunder. It originated in the ground beneath her. It grew in sound and frequency, toppling whatever still stood. She looked toward the palace, shocked as it began to sink into the sands. Ramira remained motionless as the massive building disappeared taking with it the avenues and surrounding structures. The ground buckled and shifted; great geysers of sand blew up into the night, blotting out the full moon. Ramira lost her footing and scrambled away from the eddy of sand pulling the royal residence under. She struggled to her feet and ran toward the dark mountains, looking back over her shoulder to watch the desert consume the city.

Ramira reached the base of the peaks and stopped, gasping for air and rubbing her cramped legs. She had to head north to catch up with her people but the spectacle before her would not release her from its hold. The churning sands revolved and dragged everything into the giant maw in the center. She shrank back into the shadows as Mahn soared over her, bellowing with rage at what was transpiring on the desert. He desperately tried to stop the city from disappearing, flinging great balls of power down into the void. The result was catastrophic. Huge chunks of debris and grains of sand gushed outward for miles around compelling Ramira to seek immediate shelter. She crawled up the side of the mountain and entered one of the crevasses, intending to wait out the destruction. It was not safe near the entrance, either. She went deeper and deeper into the fissure, urged on by the blasts pounding the passageway behind her. The rocky corridor began to collapse. She hesitated, wanting to get out the way she had come in but the mountain had other plans. If she waited any longer, she would be buried beneath tons of debris. She ran on, her mind never acknowledging her next step might send her toppling into an abyss or she might smash her head on an overhanging rock. It almost felt as if something or someone was guiding her as she sped through the black tunnel. She finally spotted a faint outline directly ahead and, as she lunged for the ill-defined opening, the last of the mountain crashed down behind her.

Ramira dropped to her knees, her chest rising and falling while the sweat poured from her body. She swayed unsteadily then dropped down onto all fours hoping the nausea would pass. She had to find a way to meet up with her people. Ramira finally began to breathe normally and attempted to rise but a gentle yet firm touch seemed to take hold of her.

Lie down and rest, child.

Ramira complied. She sensed a presence, one that collected every shred of memory and whisked them away where they would be safe. Ramira embraced the gauzy cocoon insulating her from the heartbreak…

~

"She went back," said Zada, realizing Ramira was the one who gave the Herkahs, once residents of Thebes, a second chance at life.

The Lady of the Sands knew if Ramira stayed, Mahn would have taken what he had so desperately wanted. The only way to avoid that was to compel her to escape. Ramira had no inclination to leave her people, which gave the Lady only one choice: cut off her return.

"Why didn't the first king wield his magic?" Danyl asked, the images he had seen while breaking the beads resurfacing in his mind.

He was not powerful enough.

Those words stunned Danyl for he had always believed the magic was most powerful in the first king, weakening or dispersing through the generations. In truth, it had strengthened, making him the most powerful bearer of the Green Might.

"Oma? Who is Ramira really?" Zada asked tentatively.

Zada saw Danyl stiffen, for Mahn had repeatedly told him that Ramira was just like him.

Danyl swallowed hard; he knew Oma had no reason to utter anything but the truth. What they heard, however, was something they were completely unprepared for and Danyl could do nothing but stare at the brown woman.

Ramira is a child of the darkness, birthed of the same evil that spawned Mahn.

A strangled cry of denial escaped the prince's throat. The mere thought of Mahn being right was a direct contradiction to the unconditional love he held for Ramira. It also began to reveal more truths that answered many questions. He forced himself to keep on listening, although Oma's words were like knives stabbing at his heart.

~

The Lady of the Sands had come to me with the news that this child housed the Source of Darkness. All three of us were nervous and frightened of the monumental task she handed to us. We were anxious when the time came for me to stand as midwife to the Ceraphine. My arms were the only contact she had when she was born. The Ceraphine had no desire to hold the infant she found pale and homely. Luckily, she chose to ignore the child, never realizing what rested within that tiny body. I held the most potent power in the land but instead of blanching with fear, I began to coo at the newborn. I saw a baby and not a tool of destruction. I cleaned her up and swaddled her in a blanket, grinning as if she were my own child but frowning at her dull hues.

I could not imagine her living her life wearing the dismal shades of her heritage. The Lady agreed and, while I held the newborn aloft upon the balcony, the Lady coaxed the setting sun to impart its beautiful hues into the new life. The Lady allowed me one more gift: a name. I chose 'Ramira', which means 'Child of the Light'. For some peculiar reason those acts instilled a sense of optimism into our dangerous task. It signified the first of many victories, both big and small, that we were able to win over the darkness. The Source of Darkness' unpredictability left us with quite the dilemma: kill her and set the dark magic free or try to offset its evil nature. Imhap taught her everything that his scrolls, tomes, and maps allowed while Horemb sharpened her skills with the knives. It fell to me to nurture her emotions. The day would come when she would find out that she housed the dark power but we clung to the belief that the good in her would temper it. We had enough faith in her that if she ever brandished the magic, it would be for a good, and not evil, purpose. Her life has given us joy while our deaths gave her life. The Source of Darkness, like your Green Might, will extend your lives beyond all others, but the day will come when you leave this land and go to a place the powers cannot follow.

"Ramira is a demon yet your influence changed the nature of what she was," breathed Zada.

"What will happen to you now, Oma?" Danyl was unsure of what to make of the answers. Mahn had not lied to him about her yet he was able to look beyond what she had been intended to be and what she had become. The intimacies they had shared did not collapse beneath the knowledge he had just acquired.

My task is complete and I will finally be able to rest.

"Does she know that she is a child of the darkness?" asked Zada.

No, Zada, she does not. Of the living, only the two of you know.

Danyl and Zada knew the truth they held was a tremendous burden they would carry their whole lives. The elf and the Herkah exchanged looks and vowed to keep secret what Oma had told them.

"Where is Ramira now, Oma?" he asked the shade, the

familiar longing strangling his voice.

She is where she is meant to be. Be well and do not forget us.

Oma faded away leaving Danyl and Zada alone on the balcony. Both hoped that Ramira she was not within that well of evil, but in a place that would grant her some measure of peace. For the first time since the onslaught began, the elf began to weep. Zada held him in her arms and added her own tears of sorrow to his.

~

The noxious morass to the north and east of where Thebes once stood began to bubble sending long, thin strands of yellowish mist into the night. The sickly fog began to spread outward carrying with it an awful stench and terrible wailing that echoed eerily across the desert. Ghostly lights flickered within the unhealthy haze pinpointing a cloaked figure walking the well-worn path leading into the heart of the swamp. The brawny form moved with a slightly unsteady motion as if unsure of its footing. Its bearing, however, never wavered. It halted briefly, turning around to stare back the way it had come, the cowl hiding its features. A pair of gloved hands reached up and pulled it back. The ghastly light revealed hawkish features and a pair of black eyes wild with anguish. The being desperately sought help but found only a glittering expanse of sand and a black, star encrusted sky. The Vox allowed its prisoner one final indulgence, the resounding roar of malice echoing across the frigid dunes. It rolled like thunder toward the heart of the desert, dislodging scorpions burrowed within the shifting dunes. The sound grew fainter the farther it traveled until the Great White Desert smothered it. The gloved hands reached up and tugged the hood back over the face before disappearing into the mist. A strangled cry marked the spot where it vanished.

~

The cold night air stirred and carried the scream to the place of the Horii. The vague silhouette of a woman placed her graceful hand across her breast and dropped her head in grief. She stood upon the dais marked by four columns, traces of earlier offerings, and an elegant fountain. Translucent curtains undulated in the twilight as they moved to the strains of the winds whispering over the dunes. Stars glittered brilliantly overhead vying with the bright face of the moon as it turned the desert into a sea of silver. The Lady turned her attention to the shape lying motionless in the middle of the platform. A sigh escaped her lips as she looked at the shrouded body. She knelt down beside it, placing her slim hand upon the forehead as a tear rolled down her cheek. She rued this task; it was the most unfair of them all and even with her formidable might was powerless to avoid it. She rose and walked onto the desert and away from what was about to transpire. She gazed at the form for another moment then raised her arms up to the heavens, invoking the Horii to mount the dais. She brought them down then waited.

The sands around the stone pavilion began to shift then roil. Steam rose from the sands, partially obscuring the platform as it sought to blur the night as well. The columns began to shake while the clay pots and bowls vibrated and danced across the stone platform. The fountain spewed water in every direction. The wind blew in gusts around the dais, stirring up the grains and flinging them everywhere, forcing even the Lady to shield her face. It reached its peak then began to abate until the desert was utterly still. The Lady took a deep breath and backed up a few more paces, staring at the subtle movements at the foot of the steps. First one then dozens of the Horii began to stream up onto the dais, converging around the motionless form without touching it. They began to circulate around it in unison, changing from white to silver to gray and then black. When all the Horii were completely dark, they surged as one through the wrapping and into the body. The sudden and vicious intrusion made the body lurch. The Lady could hardly breathe as she watched, her heart pounding loudly in her ears. She heard every disturbing sound the Horii were made from within the linen shroud. She watched with horror as bits and pieces of the covering shifted and stretched as the snake-like things burrowed into and out of the body. She knew all too well what the Horii were doing.

Forgive me, my child...

~

Alyxandyr surveyed the plains around the city, absently scratching the scab on his forearm. Two weeks had passed since the fighting had ended. Patches of grass sprang up from the torn up earth, the bright green clumps contrasting sharply with the black tents that once again filled the terrain. He glanced toward the walls, the new rocks and still drying mortar marking the damage done by the catapults. A group of elves and dwarves hoisted up a large slab, painstakingly trying to fit it in a gap on the rampart. Khadry hunters emerged from the orchard carrying deer, fowl, and rabbits back to the city. The elven king gathered his courage then looked at the blackened pits between the city and the orchard. He remembered every face cremated within those piles. The wrinkles on his forehead began to abate as he noticed bits of yellow and blue poking up through the scorched earth. The king sighed heavily and urged his horse back into the city. He rode up the main avenue, glancing from side to side. Shopkeepers waited on customers; blacksmiths hammered away on their anvils; children played near their homes and the old sat together on benches.

The elven king crossed the intersection and winked at Sophie as she chatted with a neighbor. Cricket and Anci giggled as they sat on the stoop. He approached the castle and relinquished the reins to one of the guards and walked tiredly up the stairs and into his home. Alyxandyr waved away an assistant trying to hand him a stack of reports and ascended the staircase to his rooms. He dismissed the guard at his door then closed it behind him. The king walked over to the balcony and gazed out across the city. He saw Danyl and Styph walk by, the crown prince's hand resting on his brother's stooped shoulders. The king's youngest son had yet to shed the guilt of Ramira's death.

Ramira was the magnet that had attracted Mahn, but she was also the reason they existed on this plain: if she had not warned the first king this land would surely be a different place. Her resiliency spanned the centuries and manifested itself in an entirely new world where peace actually had a chance to flourish. It was a shame she could not share in that victory or share her love with his son. Fate was not always fair or kind, a reality he learned from the moment he lost his queen up until now.

Alyxandyr gazed up at the clear blue sky, the warmth pulsing from the bright sun heating his tired face. It began to thaw the layers of cold dread and sorrow within his breast and chased away the shadow of despair hovering around him. He stirred the memories of his loved ones, offering to share the sunlight with them no matter where they were. The elven king spotted a small elven boy crying at the edge of the park, then watched as a Herkah crouched in front of him and wiped away his tears. The nomad picked him up; the boy buried his face on the Herkahs shoulder while he carried the boy to his mother. A Khadry helped a dwarf load his cart; an elf offered a Kepracarnian a basket of food. If someone had described such a scene to him a year ago, he would have thought him or her crazy. The road leading to such trust had been a long and bloody one all because of one woman's heroic courage and devotion.

"Thank you, Ramira."

FIFTEEN

Lanterns strung from brightly colored ribbons illuminated the center of the city. Lamps hung on poles beside tables of food and drink and glowed warmly from the windows of the homes fronting the square. Pots of simmering herbs and spices emitted delightful aromas throughout Bystyn. All shared the joyful atmosphere as they mingled with each other for the final time. They would be returning to their own homes the following day to pick up the pieces of their lives. Spring had not quite claimed the land but the balmy day and early evening brought everyone out to celebrate.

Alyxandyr escorted Zada through the throngs dressed in their finest clothing. They stopped and chatted now and then as they made their way to Sophie's house. Seven and Clare were already sitting on the steps next to Cooper, enjoying glasses of wine and plates of food. Anci and Cricket ran inside to get more goblets and another bottle.

"He looks so old, Alyx," said Zada watching Danyl approach. His hands were in his pockets and his gaze downcast unless someone spoke to him. He would nod politely and move on, his expression never changing.

"Something other than Ramira's death has devastated him."

"I think you're right, Clare, but I doubt he'll ever tell anyone," stated Seven.

Danyl greeted them and then sat down, accepting the goblet from Cricket. He offered her a slight smile as she leaned up against him. He put his arm around her and wondered when her crush on him would diminish. She still wore the little pouch holding the blue stone, a reminder, he guessed of the hard life she left behind. The musicians started to play a lively tune, goading even the most reluctant individual to tap their toes. Within moments elves, dwarves, and Herkahs clapped their hands and began to dance, integrating the dissimilar dancing styles into one chaotic movement.

"Look at all those fools! Must I teach them everything?"

They laughed as Seven limped over to the dancers, his hands gesturing into the air then toward his feet. He hopped and twirled then grabbed onto the nearest woman and proceeded to waltz unmethodically around in a circle. The dwarf king reeled to his own beat, the woman hanging on for dear life as the crowd clapped their approval.

A nebulous shape, barely discernible in the brilliant rays of the setting sun floated just outside the gate. It hesitated, wavering nervously back and forth. It drifted under the gate and up the avenue. The farther it traveled into the city the more pronounced its appearance became. What had started out as a thin wisp of mist began to congeal into a vague human shape.

~

Zada's hands froze. She turned her head toward the avenue and fixed her gaze on the people sauntering up to the square. Her inner sight clicked on. Bystyn and its bright colors transformed into various shades of gray; the lights appeared dingy yellow that matched the glow making its way up the avenue. Her face began to blanch; beads of perspiration formed on her brow. She did not see Sophie's hand covering her mouth or Clare slowly standing up. Zada did not hear the elven king speaking to her or notice Anci and Cricket holding on to each other. Cooper brushed his fingers against the back of his neck trying to shoo away the annoying insects crawling on his skin. Zada rose from the stoop and stared straight up the street as she woodenly made her way to the square. Danyl and the others were a step behind.

~

The indistinct figure continued on, heedless of the crowd parting to let it pass. People stopped talking and laughing, unsure of what to make of this person walking up the avenue. They retreated to the walkways, the music ceasing as the figure passed the halfway point. The revelers abandoned the square and were replaced by guards with drawn weapons. Silence reigned as the figure stopped at the edge of the plaza.

"Zada, is that what I think it is?" Alyxandyr could not look away from the shape.

Zada took a deep breath and glanced over at Danyl, the mystified look on his face shared with everyone else. Nothing happened for the longest time, and then the haze comprising the form dissipated leaving behind a slight shape clothed in a tattered and dirty cloak. A limp cowl hid its features; flashes of pale skin were visible between the rents in the garment. Bare feet encrusted with dust poked out from under the frayed hem. This poor wretch would have been tended to without a second thought had it not been for its peculiar entrance into Bystyn.

"Who are you and what do you want? Show yourself!" demanded the elven king.

Zada watched the creature flinch, its head dropping down to its chest while taking a step backward. Zada approached the bundle of rags; she ignored the protests erupting all around her. She halted a few paces away from the figure.

"Who are you?"

Zada held her breath as the being extended its arms from within the thin cloak and turned its trembling hands palm up. The Herkah noticed the tiny slash marks around her wrists. The scars continued up her arms then disappeared beneath the ragged edges of the sleeves. The nomad swallowed hard; her wrists and ankles burned in response. Zada inched forward and reached into the droopy hood with an unsteady hand.

"Zada! What's going on?" she heard Alyxandyr call from behind her.

Danyl stared at the poor creature trembling before Zada and wondered why the nomad was paying so much attention to it. It had cringed when he tried to go toward it and that had only increased his curiosity. He cautiously closed the distance between them, hesitating every time the creature took a step backward.

Zada lifted the wretch's chin just far enough for her to see inside the cowl. She bit her lip and fought back the tears as she looked upon the washed out features illuminated by the lanterns. Soft, silver eyes surrounded by skin so bleached they appeared nearly transparent beseeched the nomad. Guilt clouded them over and she tried to lower her head. Zada would not let her turn away.

"I had to come back, Zada," she said in a raspy voice.

"I know, child," she swallowed hard as Ramira's tears ran over her fingers.

"I'm...I'm one...of them."

"You were one of them, but that changed a long time ago."

"I cannot escape my heritage, Zada."

"You have risen above it and taken us with you."

"Maybe I shouldn't have come back."

"You are where you are meant to be."

The words left Zada's lips before she even realized it, the haunting echoes mingling with the truths before her. The Lady of the Sands had given Ramira another chance. She could not even begin to imagine what the Horii had done to her. The sacred spirits had determined she was worthy or the Lady would not have sent Ramira back into the world of the living. Zada glanced over her shoulder at Danyl. He scrutinized everything that was transpiring, his inquisitiveness transforming into suspicion. His ceased calculating what the creature might be and realized what it actually was. The Herkah looked to the west and held her breath. The setting sun was dazzling, painting the sky with brilliant shades of red, orange, lavender, and blue. Oma had held a newborn up to those colors centuries ago hoping they would camouflage her ancestry. The love and devotion of a long dead woman had altered Ramira from demon to human. Could Danyl's emotions repeat that transformation? Zada had precious little time to think about that. She gripped Ramira's hand and held out the other toward Danyl.

Danyl was afraid if he took a step forward the ghost would dissipate into thin air taking his fragile hope with it. Zada's tense nod for him to join them urged his rigid feet ahead. He walked through the tense silence on shaking legs, not daring to breathe fearing his exhalations would scatter the shade standing beside the nomad. He took Zada's hand. The nomad brought the two hands together and then moved away from them. The sunset neared its zenith.

Danyl slipped his hand into the hood and caressed her face, the feel of her skin a balm to his wounded soul. He began to relax as she tilted her head into his touch. The elf ignored the scarred arms snaking up his chest from within the tattered cloak. He inclined her head until he could see into the hood, the overjoyed look on his face chasing away the doubts clouding her features. He pulled her against his body then leaned forward and tenderly kissed her pale lips.

The elf's uncompromising passion flooded into her being, consuming the shadows of her forlorn spirit. It blazed more brightly than the Green Might and ignited her sense of self-worth. It illuminated the faces of all the people she had cherished, their looks of satisfaction and contentment fuel for the fire racing through her. She freely gave all of herself to him, allowing him access to even the darkest corners of her soul. He never faltered in his quest to revive her and that energized her even more. Her skin began to tingle and her eyes watered as his strength flowed into her.

Zada stared at Ramira's arms as they wrapped around the prince's neck. The scars shifted then receded; her skin's milky color was replaced by the faintest of bronze hues. The white wisp of hair poking out of the cowl deepened into a vibrant red-gold color. Ramira's hood started to slip off her head in slow motion. Zada watched the edge of the cowl delineate what had already been transformed. A cascade of red-gold hair spilled from the hood as it fell against her back. The nomad had been so mesmerized by the process she never noticed the others approach, watching as intently as she was. There was only one more alteration left.

Danyl reluctantly withdrew his lips and gazed into Ramira's face, oblivious of those who surrounded them. He, like the others, waited for her to open her eyes. She finally lifted her lids, blinking as if waking from a deep sleep. Danyl smiled broadly and Zada clapped her hands with joy as the twin amethysts twinkled brightly from their sockets. Danyl scooped her up in his arms, the Herkah adjusting the garment as he carried her to Sophie's house amid tumultuous cheers and clapping.

Seven clutched Clare's hand as they watched the pair disappear into the crowd, surfacing when Danyl climbed the front steps. Mason put his arms around Sophie, Anci, and Cricket. Gard stared at the couple for a few moments then shifted his gaze to the cobble-stoned street; his jaw set within his impassive face. Cooper crossed his arms and looked over at his family, the faint longing in his heart not yet strong enough to compel him toward them. Styph nodded with approval, grateful that his brother was able to find happiness. The crown prince looked over at his father and noted that the tiredness diminished from his features. The unmistakable touch of a slender and graceful hand rested upon Alyxandyr's arm yet he did not glance down to see who stood beside him. He inhaled deeply, the scent of roses bringing peace to his soul as he placed his hand over the spectral one.

~

The Lady of the Sands stood in front of the stone pavilion and gathered her garments close to her ethereal shape. The quest for the Source of Darkness had not quite turned out the way Mahn had anticipated. He had overlooked one very crucial truth: the ultimate evil had forgotten how truly powerful the spirit was. The danger was not past for the equally disturbing Vox had, for the most part, survived the battle and lurked along the edges of darkness. The present, however, would allow those who dwelled in the land to replenish their lives and hopefully stabilize and strengthen their futures. With her role completed, the Lady of the Sands burst into a cloud of sparkling brilliance that floated down upon the dunes, becoming indistinguishable from the millions of grains constituting the Great White Desert.

The End